PRAISE F
SMALL ANIMALS CAUGHT IN TRAPS

"[*Small Animals Caught in Traps*] gives you love
and heartache, disappointment and joy in equal
measure . . . A wonderful read to go along
with coffee or whiskey, or whiskey in coffee."
—PEDRO HOFFMEISTER,
author of *American Afterlife*

"Draws you in and holds you tight through
an emotional and educational journey across
the wilderness of the wild soul."
—TIM TIGNER,
bestselling author of *The Price of Time*

"With precision-tuned character strokes, pitch-perfect
dialogue, and devastating plot developments, Bernard
transforms these scruffy individuals into the flawed heroes
of their own lives. This is a novel of consequence."
—COAST WEEKEND

SMALL ANIMALS CAUGHT in TRAPS

BOOKS BY C. B. BERNARD

Small Animals Caught in Traps

Chasing Alaska: A Portrait of the Last Frontier Then and Now

SMALL ANIMALS CAUGHT in TRAPS

A Novel

C. B. BERNARD

BLACK STONE
PUBLISHING

The characters and events in this book are fictitious.
Any similarity to real persons, living or dead, is coincidental
and not intended by the author.

Printed in the United States of America
Originally published in hardcover by Blackstone Publishing in 2023

First paperback edition: 2024
ISBN 979-8-212-87679-7
Fiction / Literary

Version 1

Blackstone Publishing
31 Mistletoe Rd.
Ashland, OR 97520

www.BlackstonePublishing.com

For my parents.
And for their parents.

"Are you happy now?"
—Richard Shindell

"Hell no, I ain't happy."
—Drive-By Truckers

I

DISAPPOINTMENT, OREGON

1

Lewis remembered trying to hide his fear from his father as he approached the animal, though it bared its teeth and hissed, arching its back and scraping the ground with long claws. The trap had torn its leg half off and left its fur spattered with blood. He remembered, too, how it studied him with black eyes, frantic with thirst, with hunger, with the terror that had possessed it since the steel jaw bit down on its hindquarter.

When it lunged, he'd flinched, stumbling backward and falling in the dirt at The Old Man's feet. But the trap was chained to a stake. The animal could not reach him.

"What is it?" he asked.

His father spit on the ground beside him and lit a cigarette. "Mink."

Foam gathered around the animal's mouth as it thrashed the chain, trying to get at them. They'd set the trap near a trout stream last weekend and had returned to check it. Lewis wished he had not run ahead of his father on the trail. The mink had seen him first, which made him responsible for its suffering, or at least complicit.

"We have to help it," he said. In response, his father smacked him with the back of his hand hard enough to darken his vision.

"The hell we do. What the hell you think we set the trap for in the first place?" The Old Man spit again. He was forever spitting, wads of phlegm yellowed with nicotine and whatever it was inside him that so bittered his world.

The chain rattled as the mink threw itself at the brush, no longer trying to attack but trying to flee. Their arrival had worsened its fear. With each lunge, the steel teeth bit deeper into its leg, peeling back fur and exposing flesh and then bone. They watched it turn on itself in a fury, chewing at its trapped leg until blood covered its face and ears too.

"Look what it will do to itself." His father sounded amused. "That's how bad it wants to escape. Shit." He drew the word out into an appreciative sigh. "Even if it gets away there won't be nothing of it left."

As if it had understood, the mink stopped fighting and lay flat on its side. Matted with dirt and leaves, its filthy coat rose and fell with each diminished breath. Lewis knew the collective nouns for most animals—a muster of peacocks, a sleuth of bears; *terms of venery*, they were called—but he couldn't remember the name for a group of mink. There wasn't one. They're solitary animals.

"We have to let it go," he said again. He knew it might draw him another fist, but his father just looked at him.

"Don't be that guy." It was something The Old Man said all the time, pointing at a car that cut them off in traffic, a man holding his wife's purse in the grocery store, a street-corner beggar in tattered clothes. He took a drag from his cigarette, exhaling through narrowed lips and nostrils. Squinting through the smoke, he shook his head slowly and flicked the cigarette butt at the boy's chest. It exploded against the fabric of his shirt in a flurry of sparks.

Leaning his fly rod against a maple red with autumn, he took off his vest. The vest had more pockets than Lewis could count, a fleece patch where the heart should be decorated with brightly colored trout flies. The hooks flashed in the sun like the medals of an army general. He turned the vest inside out, wrapped it around his hand, and approached the mink. Its visible eye communicated something—fear, maybe, or recognition—but the mink had worn itself out, too tired to move. The chain stretched taut to the stake behind it, making a straight line, an arrow pointing deep into the woods. An arrow pointing to freedom. The Old Man squatted close and reached down slowly with the vest, grabbing the mink behind the head with one quick movement and lifting it in front of him, taking the tension from the chain.

"Coat's still decent." He turned the lithe body around to study it. "Even with the leg, it's worth something."

"Are you going to let it go?"

The Old Man looked at Lewis as if he were a trap closed around *his* leg. When he put his other hand on the mink, it was almost the length of the animal. Lewis hoped he would have hands that big someday. Tracing a line up the mink's belly to its small chest, his father felt around, dug two long fingers into the fur, and squeezed. The mink went limp in his hand.

"If you pinch the heart, you kill it without leaving any marks. My own father taught me that, just like his father taught him. Now I'm teaching you."

The chain rattled as he dropped the dead animal onto the ground.

"Maybe someday you'll teach your own son too," he said, though his expression made clear that he didn't see any more reason to hope for such a thing than he did to hope for anything at all.

Remembering that day and remembering The Old Man as he watches the obstetrician at the foot of his wife's hospital bed, Lewis wonders if there's anything crueler than hope. The doctor has thin wrists, slender fingers, hands you wouldn't trust to hold your drink, but he's delivered most of the babies born in the county over the last half century and claims to have only dropped a few.

"Strike one," he says, affecting an umpire's booming drawl as he catches the baby with hands cupped between Janey's legs. Lewis—now a fly-fishing guide and a long time gone from that day with his father—brushes aside the analogy with one of his own.

"A keeper." He smiles at his wife, who is still panting for breath, knees up on the bed in front of her, red hair fanned over the pillow like flames. "He came right to the boat."

"*She*," the doctor says.

"She?"

"Congratulations, Mr. and Mrs. Yaw. You have a beautiful baby girl."

"A girl?"

"I can show you how to tell the difference, if you like."

Janey laughs, but it's not effortless. Laid bare by the delivery, by the drugs they've administered, her voice betrays her worry.

"Is she healthy?"

Lewis peers down at the table where the nurse, a substantial woman with ankles thick as coffee cans, is swaddling their daughter, womb-slick and wide-eyed like a caught fish. He wanted a son. A son to teach everything he knows, to fish and to fight. A son to teach what it means to be a man. Not just a man, but the kind of man people count on. How did it never occur to him that he might get a daughter instead?

"Lewis? Is she healthy?"

He looks at the baby again. She's already stopped crying

and seems to grin brightly through the slime of vernix, as if enjoying herself very much. Lewis knows the smile is not real—a reflex, a wrinkle, a trick of the light. And yet . . .

"Yes," he tries to say, but nearly chokes on it. On the hope. Babies can't even support the weight of their own heads—how can he expect this one to bear the burden of so much hope? Fearing it will crush her if she discovers it, he tries to keep it to himself, to contain it, already working to protect this little girl, this plump, pale raisin pulled from between his wife's legs, utterly helpless, reliant upon the very world he hopes she might someday change.

"A girl," Janey says. Though her voice is still breathless, dazed, there's humor in it now. Relief. "Awww, Lewis, you're outnumbered."

He'd been reluctant to have a child at all. Why bring someone into a world so comfortable with its own heartlessness? Why risk passing on his own family's legacy of failure and disappointment? This baby might be the only thing Janey has ever wanted. It's the only thing she's ever asked of him. A child of her own, a family, a means to restore the balance, reparations for her own unforgivable childhood and for his too. He's less sure that it works that way, less sure either of them can ever make amends for the things their own parents did to them. All they can do is to try not to make the same mistakes. Or worse ones. That part, at least, ought to be a breeze.

Then a rumble of thunder reaches them, even there, deep inside the small hospital. He feels it as a low and sustained growl in his gut. The hair on his neck stands at attention. When the lights in the room flicker and dim, his confidence does too, a reminder that the darkness can find him anywhere.

"That's just the storm," the doctor says. "Not to worry. The emergency generators should kick on at any moment."

A fraction of a second later, they do, and just like that the light is restored.

"She's beautiful, isn't she?" the nurse asks, holding up his daughter.

Lewis looks at her closely. She's a constipation of wrinkles, a tumbleweed of hair. She's *not* beautiful, but he cannot deny the appeal of her gummy grin, as if she considers her own arrival the punch line to a joke nine months in the telling, the thunder a perfectly timed rim shot.

"I thought we were having a boy," he says. "There are so many things I wanted to teach him. I don't know what to do with a girl."

The nurse looks at him with something like annoyed impatience. "Teach her all the same things. She'll be even better at them."

Maybe he's had it wrong, he thinks, realizing for the first time how much a daughter can teach *him*. How much he can learn from *her*. This little girl can soften his edges, which Janey says are sharp enough to saw wood. This little girl will demand those parts of him that he keeps locked away. They'll teach each other everything he and his own father never learned together.

All he has to do is not screw her up. All he has to do is not let her down.

"What do you think, Lewis?" Janey asks as the nurse hands her their ungainly baby. "Does she look like either of us?"

Lewis had been a moderately successful heavyweight before he gave up boxing to be with Janey, trading his fists for fishing, the ring for the river. Though it's been a few years, he still knows how—and when—to pull a punch. He smiles upon his wife with love but does not answer the question.

———

The storm hovers over the state, a dark airship dropping anchor. Rain pours from the sky, unending, formless, an artillery of watery soldiers aiming at the earth below. Lightning cleaves trees and splinters rooftops, leaving scars where it torches the ground. The Terrebonne River floods. First it jumps its banks. Then it fills the canyons. Still the rain falls. When the wind blows, water threatens the town from all directions at once. Trees topple. Their char-black limbs and trunks block streets. Roads disappear beneath mud and water. Transformers explode in a synchronized string across the town. Sump pumps fail. Telephones die. Hillsides slump and collapse, shrugging under the weight of the mud and crushing cars, trees, houses.

Janey watches the baby while Lewis white-knuckles the steering wheel of the pickup.

"We should have stayed at the hospital another day. Half the county's lost power. What if it's out at home too?" She stares into the gloom.

"We've got a woodstove, J. Candles. We'll be fine," he says, with typically disproportionate calm.

"You know you can't beat the weather with brute force, right?"

"A warrior is worthless unless he rises above others and stands strong in the midst of a storm." It's a samurai maxim.

She turns her glare his way. "Don't fortune cookie me, Yaw. You're not a warrior anymore. You're someone's father. Slow down."

Lewis looks away from the road long enough to give her the kind of smile that used to make other boxers' knees knock in the ring. She returns it. He slows the truck.

When they reach town, they find the streets empty, puddles turned to ponds, asphalt to riverbed, the roads to streams that ripple in the falling rain. As they turn onto their street, a black cat appears in the road, frozen in their headlights. Saturated with rain, its hair sticks to its sides, ruffled around the head and ears, the look on its face one of misery and indignity. Lewis brakes to a stop. The cat stares at them, eyes a furious green in the high beams. They stare at the cat. It's a standoff. Then the cat runs the rest of the way across the road and stands at the shoulder, watching them.

"Turn around, Lewis. It's bad luck."

He's never known her to be superstitious. Maybe this is just the beginning—maybe having a baby can make someone turn on even their most deeply held beliefs, finding worry everywhere.

"There's no other way onto the street, J."

"Make a loop. Give it a couple of minutes."

"Luck's just something people pin their failures on."

"Do you really want to take that chance with a new baby?"

"That cat crossed *my* path, J. He's the one who's in for it. It's *his* luck that just turned." Lewis steps on the accelerator and the cat scurries into the shadows.

At the house, he parks beside the new minivan and unfolds a paint-stained tarp from behind the seat to hold over their heads while they run from driveway to door. They've barely made it five steps when the wind catches the tarp like a sail, nearly pulling him off his feet. For a moment he wants to hold on, to let it lift him, to see where it will take him, but he lets go and the storm lofts it high into the air where it hangs for a moment, a perfect rectangle silhouetted against the lightning like a patch on the sky. Then the wind sucks it away.

He ushers a wet Janey and the baby through the door and into the kitchen. With all the houses on their street dark, he doesn't even bother trying a light switch.

"Told you the lights would be out," Janey says, stripping wet blankets off the baby.

Lewis builds a fire in the woodstove and lights candles.

"Told you we'd be fine," he says. She shakes the water from her hair and smiles at the baby.

"That smug fool is your daddy," she says. "Lewis Yaw, King of the Jungle." In response, he grins and beats his chest.

When the stove begins to warm, he puts soup on, premade and covered in the dark fridge, and while it heats, he retrieves the mattress from their bedroom. Bucked by the humidity, the hallway floorboards creak beneath his feet like an old boat.

"Remind me to fix the floor," he yells into the other room. The floorboards creak again as he carries the mattress back down the hallway into the living room and lays it near the stove.

"Don't forget to fix the floor, Lewis."

"*That* smug fool," he tells the baby, "is your mother, Jane Elizabeth Yaw." She feigns a curtsy as he fetches their soup.

The three of them crowd the mattress together for their meal, huddled like a pack of dogs. Lewis and Janey eat noisily, slurping spoonfuls of salmon chowder. She feeds the baby, too, and afterward they feel the fatigue like the notes of a song drifting through the house, one played just for them. The baby drifts off first, tired from the excitement and lulled into oblivion by the warmth of the fire and the rain clawing at the shingles. Then Janey. Lewis closes his eyes, and soon he sleeps too. Though the nightmares still rob him of sleep most nights, he counters with frequent naps and has trained himself to nap anywhere and at any time. Something soldiers do. Dogs.

When he awakens later, Janey is still asleep, the three of them lying there as a family for the first time, a pocket of quiet amidst the chaos. Feeling a measure of peace the storm cannot take from him, he never wants to move from the pile of limbs—his wife's, his own, the baby's, their corporeal distinctions blurred. He stares with loving amazement at his little girl. Slowly, he leans toward her until their noses touch. She coos what he chooses to interpret as an acknowledgment.

"You sure know how to make an entrance," he tells her.

Outside, the unbalanced world rips itself apart. Oregon rips itself apart. Though the region takes more than its fair share of rainfall, this is too much and too fast to be absorbed, proof that too much of even a necessary part of your own nature can overwhelm you. Lightning flashes, and a chaser of thunder trembles the walls and windows.

A shudder of indigestion moves through the baby's body, as if she's swallowed the thunder. As if she's *made* the thunder. Lewis reaches over and picks her up. She kicks a stockinged foot, and he catches the scent of sour milk in the air. After a few minutes, her breathing begins to slow again. Soon she closes her eyes. They lie that way for a long time, father and daughter, a man in search of hope holding a bundle of hope.

Then hope farts in its sleep. Lewis gets up and pours himself a drink.

2

Fenwick pulls his enormous truck into the driveway and steps out into water deep as his shins. Wearing waders, he walks straight through the puddles like a stout bird in a bath. When Lewis meets him at the door with a handshake, free hands on each other's shoulders, water pours off the wide brim of his Australian bush hat. He unzips his boat coat and pulls out an underinflated foil balloon on a yellow ribbon that rises half-heartedly to hover at eye level a foot shy of the ceiling.

Lewis squints at it. "*Congratulations On the New Job?*"

"All they had. Lucky the store was open at all."

"It's perfect," Janey says. She gets to her feet with the bundle of blankets in her arms and leans toward him so he can see the baby.

"Look at that smile! Big as a hammock," Fenwick says. "I think he likes me."

Lewis laughs. "She's just mesmerized. You're the first Black person she's seen."

Fenwick's eyebrows rise like twin drawbridges.

"She? Oh shit, Confucius. You're outnumbered." He peers

into the shroud of blankets. "It's OK, sweetie," he says, his deep voice free of baby talk. "In this part of Oregon, I'm the first Black person *anyone* has seen."

Janey is almost his height, which is to say that neither of them is particularly tall. Her arms too full to hug, she sticks her neck out, lips puckered, and Fenwick leans in for a kiss on the cheek, a gesture both comic and intimate.

"Want to hold her?"

"Hell yes, I want to hold her." He removes his dripping coat and hat and gives them to Lewis. The enormous key chain he wears on his belt rattles as he steps out of his waders and hangs them over the woodstove like a sea lion pelt. They drip onto the cast iron, sizzling loudly, as rhythmic as a heartbeat. Wiping his hands on his wool shirt, he takes the baby with unpracticed awkwardness. "What do I do?"

"Don't drop her."

"That's it?"

"No bright lights, don't get her wet, and don't feed her after midnight."

"A fishing guide's daughter born in the rain. Gonna be hard not to get her wet. What are we calling her?"

"Grayling Yaw, meet your uncle, Fenwick Pope."

Right on cue, the baby reaches out and smacks his cheek with a little fist.

"A fighter like her father," Fenwick says. "She's a keeper."

Lewis smiles at his friend.

"Came right to the boat."

———

First coffee. Then coffee with whiskey. Then whiskey, rain painting the windows while they talk. Fenwick makes a toast, a ritual they've shared since Lewis apprenticed with him on the Deschutes River nearly a decade earlier.

"Confusion to the enemy."

He raises his glass, and Lewis taps it with his own.

"And to everyone else."

Fenwick tells them about the damage he's seen around town. How the storm has hit not just Disappointment but most of the region hard. A bear has been spotted in town, digging through dumpsters and scavenging for food in houses and stores abandoned during the flood.

"Probably lost habitat to the storm," he says. "Five or six sightings already. I saw it myself a couple of blocks from the diner, walking down the damn street like it had no care in the world. Soaking wet. Covered in mud. Carrying a grease-stained takeout bag in its mouth like it was going to work."

"Black bear?" Lewis asks.

"Roger that. They shot the last Oregon grizzly decades ago." Fenwick sips from the mason jar they gave him for a glass. "Every now and then some hunter or hiker or hippie will come haulin' ass acrosst town with a bullshit story about seeing one in the woods, but they're always black bears." He speaks with a syntax informed by his time in both the army and the rural Northwest: the bridge gets you *acrosst* the river; Oregon is south of *Warshington*; the boat *drug* its anchor in the wind, creating a situation that was *fubar*.

"All those people seeing them, you don't think it's possible there are still grizzlies?"

"A lot of people see Sasquatch in those woods too. That doesn't make *him* real."

"And yet I married him," Janey says. She blows on her tea. "What's going to happen to him? To the bear?"

"Depends. Some of the boys are looking for it." He means the other fishing guides.

"Who?"

"Littlejohn. Atcheson. Sipsey. The Adventures of Wheatfall and Fuckface. Good luck to the poor beast if *they* find it first."

"Wheatfall would probably train it to juggle and ride a unicycle."

"Littlejohn will make a rug out of it."

"God knows what Fuckface will do to it."

"Do you have to call him that?" Janey asks. They answer in unison. *Yes.*

"What about the sheriff?"

"He's got his deputies driving around, and the state is sending biologists." Fenwick spits the word, a fishing guide's Pavlovian response to state-sponsored scientists. "They'll try to dart it, tag it, and relocate it somewhere else."

"Where?"

"To Portland, if we're lucky," he says, invoking the city as shorthand for the hopelessly urban, for disproportionate progressivism. "Imagine it running through the streets? Let's see how all those tree huggers react when they actually come face-to-face with the wilderness they're always preaching about saving."

He laughs, and though his laughter is not unkind, it startles the baby awake. They all hold their breath to see if she will cry, but she just opens her eyes and looks around the room, as if to ask, *Hey, what did I miss?*

———

Running in the rain-sullied darkness after Fenwick leaves, Lewis watches for the bear, hoping to see it, some sign of it, but sees only the town shuttered against the storm. Windows boarded shut, lights out. A glimpse of what might have been after the mill shut down, the empty town emptied. Nearly every shop is closed, even the grocery, the storefronts dark, windows streaked like shower doors. The only place open is the convenience store, which must be on a generator, like the chronically nonsensical sign in front of the bank, currently announcing the time and the temperature: 17 PM, 200°F

In the eight years they've lived in Disappointment, the town—once on the verge of a death precipitated by the closing paper mill and the mass exodus it triggered—has begun to resuscitate itself, with new businesses opening and new families drawn by the temptations of affordable property and natural beauty. Still it remains the runt of central Oregon, little more than a couple hundred people on a good day. It harbors few pretensions about itself. If they're going to raise a daughter, this is as good a place as any.

The wind and the rain hide the sound of the approaching truck's clunking diesel until it's upon him, and the big Dodge passes with a deep-throated roar. Menacingly close, it swerves into a puddle to throw a muddy wave that crests without breaking to swallow him like a surfer riding the tube. When the truck honks a taunt, Lewis wipes his eyes on his sleeve and sees the bright yellow Gadsden flag painted across the rear window of the cab, the gun rack, the Cascadia bumper sticker.

Littlejohn.

He swears and flips the bird at the retreating truck, but it's already gone and the storm just steals his voice.

Littlejohn is another fishing guide on the Terrebonne, but they're not friends. Littlejohn does not have friends. He does not have family. As far as Lewis knows, he doesn't even have a first name. Rumor is he's got a cabin on land somewhere outside town where he's prepping for some imagined and encroaching apocalypse, but nobody knows where, exactly. There's skill involved in maintaining such mystery in a town this small—or at least effort. And it speaks to Littlejohn's character that he makes that effort. He drives a preposterously large truck with an extended cab and bed and a lifted chassis, rims like aboveground pools, cab-mounted light bars. The effect—like his tattoos, the KA-BAR knife and Sig Sauer in a black nylon holster he wears on his belt, and nearly everything else about him—is meant to be intimidating. To some people it is. But Lewis Yaw does not get intimidated. Immune to the effect, he sees only the effort. Littlejohn might be able to fish, but Lewis has already learned everything he is going to from men like him.

Don't be that guy.

Shadowboxing as he runs, he turns at the river and follows it through the park built on the old mill site. For half a century the mill propped the town on its shoulders, turning Oregon's forests to pulp and the sky above Disappointment to black smoke, only to be torn down in a week. It was already closed when Lewis arrived in Disappointment, just as the textile mills along the river he'd grown up on in Massachusetts had closed long before he was born. The storm's reach is visible everywhere he looks. He stays well above the flooded river as he runs, past the pay phone—the phone book on its coiled steel chain hanging into the puddle beneath it like an anchor—across the park, onto the footbridge. Built high enough to allow drift boats to pass beneath, the Terrebonne at flood now kisses the bottom rail. The river carries tree stumps and trash cans and other debris, and the bridge shakes each time something collides with it, disappears, and reemerges on the other side.

Jabbing left and swinging two hard rights at the rain as he runs, Lewis slips its watery punches. At the five-mile mark he turns around and runs back to the park, where he does fifty sit-ups and two hundred push-ups in the mud, the ground cold and wet but no wetter than his clothes and skin already are. The mud stinks. He works until his breath is thin, his arms and chest burn, works until he can't smell the mud anymore but is dizzy with the remembered stench of sweat and Albolene and disinfectant. Just like that he's back on the old mats at the boxing gym, pushing himself past his limits while Jimmy sits on a stool, clipping his nails, counting every second or third push-up aloud. "Another hunnert, Lou," Jimmy says, as casually as if he's asking for another ice cube in his drink. Then his arms give out and he's face down in the cold mud, the rain pouring down all around him, and he's laughing out loud.

Rolling over onto his back, Lewis closes his eyes. The wind howls at him. The rain falls in sheets. The river roars across the park. All white noise. In less than a minute he is asleep.

He awakens later with no sense of how much time has passed. Only that he is no longer alone. A waterlogged puppy the color of a bruise barks at him, tugging at his clothes with its teeth. No collar. No tags. Just a tiny wet nose and hairless tail.

As long as Lewis can remember, he's possessed some canine magnetism that borders on the preternatural. Dogs drawn to him on the street approach with tails and tongues wagging, breaking away from their owners to run to his side—unfriendly dogs, shy dogs, antisocial dogs. Looking around the park, he sees no signs of anyone else, no hint of where the puppy came from. He sits up and holds out his arms. It runs into his hands. Though it trembles beneath its matted fur, when he picks it up and holds it close to his face, it touches its forehead against his, seeking comfort. Or maybe bestowing it.

First the storm brought him a daughter, and now a dog.

"Is this a rescue?" he asks. "Are you rescuing me?"

The dog licks him with a tiny, dry tongue, the only dry thing left in the world.

———

An hour later he stands in the doorway, face and sneakers covered with mud, pants clinging to his body, long hair matted so tightly it looks painted on. A bear of a man holding a gallon of milk and a wet paper bag, he easily fills the door frame, as if to keep the storm at bay with his body alone. *The only body big enough to hold that heart*, Janey likes to tell him.

"You're back," she says, trying to hide the wave of relief that ripples across her face. "Is it bad out there?"

"Yes."

"You were gone a long time."

"Something came up."

"What's in the bag?"

"Dog food."

Janey screws her face up as if she's misheard him.

"Dog food?"

"Dog food," he says again, and reaches into his shirt for the puppy.

3

A few weeks later, Lewis rocks Gray's carrier with his foot while poring over old newspapers at a microfilm terminal at the library in Bend. The research librarian keeps dropping off more material for him, stopping each time to coo at the baby.

"Anything to do with bears," he'd told her when she asked what he was looking for. She's a cheerful woman with big eyes and delicate features, maybe five feet if she stands on the *Oxford English Dictionary*. Her hands aren't much bigger than Gray's. Lewis towers over her, even sitting at the station. He feels enormous and ungainly and woefully out of place.

"Bear research sounds interesting. What are you working on?"

"My family genealogy," he says, and she shakes her small head sadly.

He wants to believe Fenwick is mistaken about the disappearance of grizzlies from Oregon. Or maybe he just wants proof—reassurance that wildness is a natural and necessary state, that even when it is stripped away, the earth can heal like skin regenerating. But everything he reads supports the Pope's claims that hunters had all but eliminated them from the state by 1915.

A trickle of sightings in the ensuing years mean a few survived, or wandered in from Washington or Idaho, but in 1931, a federal trapper killed the last documented Oregon brown bear.

Bears once occupied the state in what must have felt like unassailable numbers. He finds stories about them roaming the countryside, mauling livestock, raiding chicken coops. Dozens of articles devoted to a single bear made it famous for slaughtering cattle across Oregon and Northern California and eluding capture for more than a decade, even when the federal government put a bounty on its head. At the site of each kill, bloody crime scenes of cattle limbs and entrails, the bear left its calling card: distinctive tracks caused by a clubfoot it had earned ripping its own leg from a spring-loaded trap. That particular bear weighed more than a ton. The bounty hunters who finally tracked and killed it in 1890 found "more than a quart of lead" buried in the yellowed fat beneath its skin, a decade of bullets fired by the ranchers upon whose cattle it had dined. The grizzly's exploits made national news—for newspaper readers on the East Coast, it represented the wild and untamed West—and, ultimately, so did its death. Ranchers had its hide stuffed and mounted and sent on tour around the country to reclaim some of their financial losses. The hide disappeared from the Chicago World's Fair in 1893, having presumably burned up in a fire.

"Hell of a way to go," Lewis says aloud, annoyed at his discovery.

The girl at the next table looks up from her work, eyebrows furrowed at his interruption, and shushes him.

"Sorry."

She glares a moment longer before returning to her book. She's wearing a Bush/Cheney T-shirt and a pink-rubber WWJD bracelet.

"What's your name?" he asks, and she slams the book closed.

"Stacey."

"What are you reading, Stacey?"

Taking great pains to show her own annoyance, she does not answer him but holds the book at arm's length like a model on *The Price Is Right* so that he can read the cover.

"*Anna Karenina*? I read that."

"Good for you."

"You know, she dies in the end."

"Are you serious right now?"

"Suicide. By train."

"You're an asshole, man."

Lewis nods gravely. "I can be."

Gray makes a sound like she wants attention. When he lifts her from her seat and tucks her into his neck, hugging her close, she burps a parachute of formula that unfolds onto his shirt. Stacey laughs.

"Girl power," she says, and returns to her book.

———

Nearly every day brings a new bear sighting around Disappointment. Sheriff's deputies, biologists, and hunters have so far failed to capture the ursine celebrity. It steals food from dog bowls, bird feeders, and henhouses. Cats disappear. Occasionally it lifts a small dog for its trouble, a schnauzer for a snack. All over town it leaves bear sign in cooling piles, taunts to its would-be captors, reminders of its continued and unchallenged freedom. Scat on the sidewalk in front of the donut shop, deep scratches in the door of the taco stand. Soon everyone in town has a bear story—a hulking shadow on a porch at sunset, an alley ambush while loading a dumpster, a dark blur at the diner window. Everyone except Lewis. He sees matted grass along the river where it has lain down to sleep, claw marks in tree bark, a bit of fur caught on a fence. While running, he steps in still-steaming mounds of berry-laden shit. But he never sees the bear itself.

Everywhere he goes, he watches for it. His eagerness borders on desperation.

He's seen bears before. When he was wandering west after graduation, a black bear crossed the road in front of his truck outside Banff. He saw another in Yellowstone, surrounded by tourists, paparazzi with priapic camera lenses. When they were still new to the Pacific Northwest, he and Janey were camping on the Olympic Peninsula when they watched something big and brown lumber across the beach. No more than fifty yards in front of their tent, it rose up on two legs when the wind shifted off the land, clumsy and impressive at once, and sniffed the air. When it turned in their direction, white teeth and white eyes, the black nose, Lewis knew that it saw them. *I see you too*, he whispered. Then the breeze shifted once more and the bear could no longer smell them. But they could smell *it*. Foul and savage. Salt and rancid meat. The brininess of the low tide. It dropped to all fours and continued along its path. They were just a distraction to the bear, but to them the bear was a glimpse of a world that existed in the same place as their own world but remained invisible to most people. A gift. He's seen bears before, but seeing one here, in Disappointment— in his own town—would mean something different entirely. The wildness he left Massachusetts to find, the kind of place he wanted to live in? Seeing the bear would be proof that he's succeeded. *Gone a decade and still looking to make a point*, he thinks, a little ashamed.

But more than that, he wants Gray to live in that kind of world, where bears don't just exist but roam free in spite of centuries of encroaching civilization, in spite of all the people who view them as intrusive and unwanted. He wants his daughter to live in the kind of world he dreamed of as a kid.

"They should name him," Janey says one night after a local radio story about the bear's lingering presence. "Make him a mascot for the town. They could put him on T-shirts or hats or something, raise a little money for the schools."

"Disappointment the Bear?"

"Well. They'd need to come up with a better name for it. Dipsy, maybe."

"That's not better. That's worse."

"Beary White?"

"No."

"Beary Manilow?"

"Jesus. No. Anyway, it doesn't need a name. It's an animal."

"You named Johnson."

"She's a dog."

"Dogs are animals."

"No," Lewis says, with unintended sharpness. "That's just anthropomorphizing it."

"Maybe you've heard of Yogi? Baloo? Paddington? Gentle Ben?"

"This isn't a cartoon, J. It's a wild animal. It deserves dignity. Respect."

Seeing something in his eyes, she lets it go with a nod.

"Fenwick says somebody's been dumping carcasses in the river."

"Deer," Lewis says. "On the fire road." He's seen them himself while out running. Bloody hides. Heads. Bones made bare. Lesser organs, muscle and tendon, hooves. Nature deconstructed. Nature made grotesque.

"Why?"

"Someone's taking them illegally. They're out of season, but even during the season you're only allowed one. Whoever it is, they're taking too many of them."

"A poacher?"

"I think it might be one of the guides."

Janey cocks her head, like she does, to show surprise.

"Why do you say that?"

"Hardly anyone else uses that fire road."

"Will they attract the bear? The carcasses?"

"I don't think so," Lewis says. "It's a dump site. Most of the food's gone. It's just scraps now. The birds had already found it when I was there. Crows and jays, a few turkey vultures. It's more likely to attract rats, possums, and skunks. That bear is looking elsewhere."

"Like McDonald's?"

It's a joke. But that night he spots more sign when he's out running with the dog, heaps of scat littered with something he can't identify. When he crouches down for a closer look and aims his flashlight at it, he sees shreds of a Big Mac wrapper.

Maybe Janey is right. Maybe the bear is becoming human.

The disillusionment winds him.

4

The baby grows, and so does the dog, one a pudgy little person with an enormous smile and ears, the other a Newfoundland the size of a compact car. Johnson is protective of Gray. She sleeps at the foot of her crib, follows her from room to room when she's in her parents' arms. Gray delights in dog kisses, the big tongue like a wet necktie falling from the gaping mouth. A weird and slobbery symbiosis, a joy to watch.

"Someday a long time from now," he tells Gray, slipping her out of a diaper so soiled as to feel malicious, "you'll have to do this for *me*. And I promise you, pal, my revenge will be sweet."

She smiles her gummy smile, a stalactite of spit growing in the open cave of her mouth.

"I grow old, I grow old," he says, recalling one of the poems Finneran made him memorize in high school English, fragments of which still come back to him like birds darting across the sky. "My adult diapers smell like mold."

It takes him by surprise how quickly and easily their lives absorb her, everything reforming itself like skin healing around a foreign object. After her first few weeks at home, Lewis returns

to the river. Summer passes in a blur of clients and boat work,
sleepless nights and bottle feedings.

Lying on the kitchen floor one evening with Johnson's heavy
head on his leg, he bench-presses a drooling Gray while Janey
plays her cello after dinner. Some nights she practices—formal
and repetitive bow exercises monkeying with overpressure,
ponticello and tasto, scratch tone and flautando—and some
nights she *plays*. When they first met, she occasionally sat in
with a string quartet of other musicians her cello teacher had
introduced her to, and Lewis would leave Jimmy's sore and exhausted, red-skinned from a hot shower, to attend the subdued
performances at cocktail hours and charity events. He still remembers how she'd looked in those black evening dresses, red
hair spilling like lava over her bare shoulders as she worked
the bow. She quit performing in public when they moved to
Oregon, instead using her evenings to take classes at the com-
munity college in Bend. But she continued to play for herself,
and now she plays for an audience of two: him and the baby.
Sitting on a pillow on a hard-backed chair with a beer on the
floor beside her, she straddles the big instrument like a saddle
and chooses a piece of music either to match her mood or to
alter it. Supriani's baroque fingerblisterer "Toccata Decima."
Dall'Abaco's "Capriccio Primo." Nirvana's "Smells Like Teen
Spirit." She does a mean Pink Floyd cover that can affect the
atmosphere in the house, as if the cello itself was somehow
transformative, not just a musical instrument but an instrument of change.

But Lewis knows that power does not belong to the cello
at all—it belongs to Janey. And he feels it as he lifts and lowers
his daughter in sync with the rising and falling notes. He can
still smell the Terrebonne on his clothes from his day in the
boat with clients, the sun on his skin, fish scales and sunscreen

on his fingers. *This is my family*, he thinks. The accompanying feeling takes him some time to identify as satisfaction.

A family. Satisfaction. He's never had either before.

Daughter fills father's heart like the storm filled the river, swelling it beyond capacity until it overflows, until it becomes something else entirely, something strong enough to reshape the landscape that contains it. When she smiles, Lewis feels the hope again. Hope so deep and fast he worries it will wear him away, eroding his cynicism and exposing his optimistic core to the world.

"Hope in one hand and shit in the other and see which makes your garden grow faster," The Old Man used to say.

Fuck The Old Man.

"Hope is the horse I ride," he tells Gray. She rewards him with an optimistic dribble of spit. He hands her over to her eager mother and takes the dog outside for a run.

———

The Old Man never wanted a child. He and Lewis's mother had an arrangement—one child, hers to raise and love, and in exchange, he would get to spend the rest of his life with her. He had a limited range, a deficit of empathy, but for her he could tolerate almost anything. Her intervals of moodiness. Her desperation for motherhood. Anything except the one thing she'd saddled him with: a life without her, the burden of raising that child alone, a burden she'd thrust upon him two weeks after giving birth when she slit her wrists and lay down in their bed to die with her new son in her arms.

How could The Old Man ever look at Lewis again without seeing that baby, stuck to her body by her own drying blood? The one thing he'd ever loved in this world, and the child who stole her from him. Even then, denied his end of the bargain and stuck with hers, he couldn't blame her. So he blamed Lewis instead.

Fighting had always been a part of The Old Man's nature, like the patches of dry skin on his elbows or the freckles on his hands. Determined to make it a part of his son's nature, too, he gave Lewis a pair of boxing gloves when he was ten. Maybe he thought it leveled the playing field to give him the pretense of fighting back. An asshole's alchemy, turning abuse into sport.

"Someone's got to make a man out of you," he said, like he was doing Lewis a favor. When he laced up the gloves, eighteen-ounce Everlasts the color of fresh blood, Lewis could barely lift them. Then his father pulled on his own gloves and knocked him into the dirt. The Old Man had hands like freight trains. Like fire engines.

That same year he gave Lewis a battered cane Horrocks-Ibbotson, a production fly rod made by cheap labor in overseas factories during the Allied occupation. He could barely bring himself to touch it, whether for its inferiority or its foreignness.

"It's *Japanese*," he said, spitting the word like rotten meat, "but it ought to catch fish."

Its provenance did not matter to Lewis. For the way it made the rest of his life disappear when he stood waist-deep in the cool water of the Shawsheen River, throwing inelegant casts with flies he'd tied with feathers scavenged from sidewalks, it might as well have been a magic wand.

As he got older, he got better at defending himself, better at punching back. They'd trade blows in the backyard, the base-ment, the living room, until one of them was spitting mad and one spitting blood. That's what passed for communication be-tween them. For intimacy. That and fishing, wordless weekends on some New Hampshire trout stream barely acknowledging each other's existence. That his father loved to fish might have been the bastard's single greatest quality. Maybe his only redeeming one. Put a fly rod in his hand and he became almost likable, if you allowed for some wide interpretation of *likable*. And *almost*. At least he couldn't take a swing at you if his hands were full.

By high school they'd stopped fishing together, but they still fought, their relationship reduced to a shared and uneasy coexistence in the small, yellow house, the persistent threat of violence like a lodger whose very presence moderated their behavior. Once Lewis began to study boxing, training kept him away from home most nights, and he saw less and less of his father as he spent more time out of the house. With money he earned working summer construction jobs, he bought an old pickup. Weekends he'd drive himself north out of Massachusetts with a map unfolded on the cracked vinyl bench seat, crisscrossing back roads in search of trout streams, camping in its bed or on the ground in its lee, waking beneath low-hanging skies to a thermos of lukewarm coffee, straight-backed and waist-deep in the water by the time the sun rose. The pull of the river centered him. The cold, firm pressure against his legs anchored him to the planet like augmented gravity. It gave him strength. Some mornings he struggled to tie flies to his tippet with his hands swollen from a fight at Jimmy's the night before, a few rounds against some bruiser with a forehead like a mailbox. Tucking the rod beneath his armpit, he'd sink his hands to the elbows and let the cold water soothe them as the rising sun revealed the world around him piecemeal, one stunning bit at a time. Moss on the river rock. Ferns along the bank. A spider web glistening with dew. It seemed a world away from the boxing gym, draped with serenity. A stillness. A peace.

There was no stillness in the boxing ring. Only motion. A fighter who stopped moving had already lost. But in nature Lewis sought and found stillness everywhere. He struggled to reconcile those disparate parts of himself, the one that fed on violence and the other on the natural world, and realized he was happiest in the overlap.

The natural world contained violence of its own. Fishing in Vermont, he'd seen northern pike as long as his leg drag ducklings below the surface of a pond, splaying a ring of feathers that floated like the petals of a wind-spent flower. Fisher cats killed for sport, toying with their prey and leaving the lifeless bodies on the trail for Lewis to step over. The first deer he'd shot had been a doe, a mistake of eagerness—when he'd opened her belly to peel out her guts, a pair of fawns appeared from the brush and shouldered past him to nurse at their mother's corpse.

Violence made no exception for beauty. Lewis saw beauty in the gym too. The human body sharpened like a sword, the metronome of sinew as a fighter jumped rope. Abstracts of blood on the canvas. Beauty made no exception for violence, either.

He needed both worlds. Without either he would be incomplete. So he mapped the borders of the two worlds whose parts comprised him and staked a flag where they met.

He wants more for Grayling. He wants her to know all the beauty but none of the disappointment. He wants her never to go a day without knowing her father loved her, that he was proud of her, that he did his best.

A pair of ungainly beasts, he and the dog wind their way through the park and back into town. Near the bank, they round a corner and almost collide with a couple standing listlessly in the shadows, blocking the sidewalk. She's smoking. He's fuming. As Lewis slows, he can see it in the man's body language—the clenched fists, how the strained muscles misshape his stance. He doesn't recognize them, the couple, which is unusual in a town so small, but he recognizes the anger. The intent. He slows as he approaches. Johnson does the same.

"Can I pet your dog?" the woman says. Though she's young, her voice is husky with smoke.

"Not friendly," Lewis says. The man steps into his path.

"It looks friendly." His voice is a challenge, laced with hostility.

"Not the dog," Lewis says, taking a step closer so he's inches from the man. "*Me.*"

At this range the man realizes his miscalculation. His posture changes. He straightens his back, arches his shoulders. When he moves into the dim light from the streetlamp, Lewis can see that he's not a man at all, but a boy. A teenager, maybe. Taking a step back, he puts a protective arm around the girl and ushers her away into the night.

A block later, across from the Salt Lick, Johnson stops to go on the sidewalk, leaving a vengeful pile. While Lewis cleans up behind her with one of the plastic grocery bags he carries for that purpose, he sees Littlejohn's truck in the bar's lot, parked at an angle across three spaces.

"Pinheads and assholes," The Old Man used to say. "If you don't know which one you are, you're probably both."

"Come on, girl," Lewis says. They cross the street to the parking lot and he can smell the sweat and the beer. Music leaks through the walls and windows, raised voices, the sound of pool cues making contact with billiard balls and Keno machines ringing and buzzing. The flag-plastered rear window of Littlejohn's truck is open. Lewis unknots the bag of dog shit and lobs it into the cab.

The Old Man parented with his fists and his fury. He led with his flaws. With no mother to counterpunch, Lewis looked elsewhere. To Finneran. To Jimmy and Ed. They taught him that any dumb bastard with fists can leave a mark on somebody, but it takes something more to leave one upon the entire world. In their words and in their actions he began to see possibility. He began to see that he did not have to be like his father. That he did not have to *become* his father. He could be whatever he wanted.

That's when he started thinking about college. It's when he started thinking about heading out West after he graduated, starting his own life in a place of his choosing. It's also when he began developing a code. In books Finneran had given him, he read about the samurai and Bushido, their code of honor. The idea made enough of an impression on him that he studied it until well-versed. He still quotes from it often enough that Fenwick calls him Confucius, conflating not just multiple philosophies but different cultures entirely.

It didn't take long to find that the limitations of applying a code written for a warrior class of feudal Japan left wide room for interpretation to modern life, so Lewis set out to formulate his own. He bought a cheap black notebook that fit in his pocket and carried it everywhere with him, recording these rules of engagement for life in its pages, rules of honor and respect to help him find his path through a complicated world. Those rules helped get him through.

Just like boxing. Just like fishing.

And now, he thinks, as he turns for home with six miles in his tired legs, he's going to teach those rules to Gray.

Remembering his own venomous father as he runs the last mile through the night, remembering the things done to him and the things they did to each other, remembering about the darkness that consumed The Old Man and how it's been chasing Lewis his whole life, he wonders if it will be enough. The code.

By welcoming the baby into his life, he's also welcomed hope itself, and he can't help but wonder which it will be that ruins him.

II

TERMS OF VENERY

5

Gray sits alone in the corner wearing a grim expression and a child-sized pair of Carhartt overalls the color of French mustard. The knees are worn nearly threadbare, the straps frayed. Her mother waged a brief and futile campaign to get her to change for the party, but she politely declined. Though she is not a tiny child and is, in fact, big for her age, she looks tiny on the otherwise empty couch, an effect heightened by the arrival of her uncle Fenwick, who sits heavily beside her, sinking far enough into the cushions to slide her toward him.

"Sorry to interrupt your solitude, Hoss. But you know that's your name on the cake in the other room, right?"

"It's quieter here."

"How old are you now? Sixteen? Seventeen?"

"I'm ten."

"Anyone ever tell you that you're a lot like your old man?"

"Really?" She sounds as if she finds this information interesting. Her uncle squints at her, at the flyaway ears, the ziggurat of hair.

"Sure. Looking for alone time in the middle of your own party? That's classic Lewis Yaw. Do you like to fish?"

"Yes."

"Do you like the Red Sox?"

"They're my favorite team."

"Are you stubborn and ill-tempered? Do you talk like Confucius? Do your farts smell like salmon and elk jerky?"

"Pay no attention to your uncle, whatever he's telling you," Lewis says from the kitchen as he puts down the platter of elk burgers he's just pulled from the grill. Janey has already laid out the rolls and toppings alongside the food brought by their guests, and there's little space left on the table. That's the way it is in Disappointment—invite someone to your house and they show up with food, as surely as if it's written into the residency bylaws. There are more people crammed into the tiny house than he thought possible, like a fraternity stunt or a Guinness World Record attempt.

Grabbing a half-empty bottle of Old Crow he opened an hour earlier, he bookends his daughter on the couch, leveling out the cushions.

"I was just telling Gray that when I first met you, you looked as young as she does," Fenwick says.

"That's a lie. I just looked young next to *you*. You won't believe this, Gray, but your uncle used to be a hell of a fisherman, and as thin and good-looking as me. Now he's fat as a Model T."

"What's a Model T?"

"It was your uncle's first car."

Fenwick gets to his feet. "You won't believe *this*, Hoss, but your father and I used to be friends," he says over his shoulder as he heads into the kitchen for food. "Now I just tolerate his company so I can spend time with you."

Johnson emerges from the crowd, almost a magic trick,

hiding an animal that size in such a small place. She burrows her heavy head in Lewis's lap and slobbers on his pants. Scratching behind a big ear, he leans in and puts his forehead against hers, a behavior they've shared since the day they found each other.

"Why do you do that, Pop?"

"We're reading each other's minds."

Gray looks skeptical. "What's she thinking?"

"She's thinking that it's her birthday too, but no one threw *her* a party."

"She's seventy in dog years."

"You too, pal."

"I'm just ten."

"What do you mean *just*? Ten is old. You're practically a grown-up now."

"I'm just a kid."

"But you're a Yaw, and Yaws mature early. When I was your age, I already had my beard."

"You did?"

"Sure. You've got some catching up to do, pal."

"Pay no attention to your father, Gray," Janey says, materializing to scoop dirty plates off the coffee table. "Whatever he's telling you." All afternoon he's watched her move among their guests like a bee in clover, and she looks tired, though he's smart enough not to tell her so. Or maybe she's annoyed, the children hopped up on sugar and frosting, the tipsy neighbors, the endless dish-clearing and resetting.

"What do I do?" Gray asks, her expression earnest.

"Do?"

"To catch up, Pop? What do I do?"

Janey gives Lewis a pointed look. He takes another sip of bourbon, takes Gray's face in his hands, and stares at her intently, turning her head to different angles for inspection.

"I think I see the problem," he says. "You need to stop shaving immediately."

———

That morning he'd made her favorite breakfast, pancakes with kernels of sweet corn in the batter and strawberry milk. Remembering his own birthdays, and how the memories still prick him like thorns, he wanted to make hers better. They ate together in front of the TV, the three of them, and then Lewis gave her the first present of the day: a new book of trivia, a more sentimental gift than she might realize.

When he was younger—younger, even, than she is now—he'd found a book of trivia deep in the back of a scuffed cabinet, mixed in among his father's Chilton manuals and Sears catalogs. It had belonged to his mother, making it a rare find; along with Lewis himself and The Old Man's resentment, one of the few artifacts that proved she'd ever even existed. She'd dog-eared pages and left a codebook of marginalia throughout in a cramped but unrushed script. Where she'd written her name on the inside cover in looping penmanship, he traced it with his finger. Each night, waiting for his father to stumble home from the bar, or listening for malice in his footsteps as he ascended the stairs, Lewis lay in bed with a flashlight searching the passages she'd underlined for clues about her, sniffing the pages for her lingering scent. Though he'd never met her, he loved her. Eventually he read the book enough times to memorize whole pieces of it. He forced himself to recall them as a survival mechanism during moments of pain or tests of endurance, plucking trivia from his mind like fireflies from the night. Lemons float, but limes sink. Crocodiles are more closely related to birds than to lizards. Cans were invented fifty years before can openers. That's how he made it through those nights, through the beatings, through the long, lonely hours that followed after finding The Old Man passed out on the floor soaked in whiskey, piss, and tears.

When he produced the gift at the table that morning, wrapped and ribboned, Janey's expression could have levitated him. They bought Gray other things, too, he and Janey, but the book is a gift from him alone, a practice he started last year when he gave her a kite they could build and fly together. One more year and it's a tradition.

Gray's been carrying the book around all day, paging through it. Taking her by the hand, Lewis leads her into the other room, and whistles for quiet—loud and piercing, buoyant with whiskey—and when he has everyone's attention, says, "For her birthday, Grayling is going to entertain us."

She looks up, first at him, and then around the circle of adults with the aloof suspicion of a cop who's just pulled over a speeding driver. "I am?"

"A reading from the Book of Trivia."

She smiles and flips through the book, looking for an interesting bit. It's her mother's smile on her father's face, a topiary of hair that came from neither of them. Janey grew up in foster homes; maybe one of her biological parents was a shrub.

"A typical cloud weighs more than a million pounds," she reads.

"Holy shit," Fenwick says, and Gray giggles.

"Well that's fascinating," says John Harrison, a lawyer of some sort who just moved to Disappointment from California. "Please, enlighten us further, Ms. Yaw." He and his wife built a cookie-cutter house that's big and bland-looking, yet still ostentatious, somehow. It sits on what had been a wooded lot across the street. Just seeing it every morning makes Lewis angry.

"An octopus has three hearts," Gray reads.

"That's three more than a lawyer. Right, Harrison?" Lewis gets to his feet before his neighbor can respond. "Who needs another drink?"

Harrison takes a deep breath. Though he hasn't been drinking, he looks ready to start. "Vodka tonic, please," he says. Frail and lanky, like a spaghetti strand in Brooks Brothers clothing, he seems to be pondering not just how he came to find himself in this conversation, but how he ended up at a ten-year old's birthday party in the first place. He's overdressed in suit pants and a crewneck sweater with the crisp points of his collar peering out like a confused compass rose. His wife, Carole, wears a cocktail dress with enough jewelry to summon pirates. They're an anomaly among working-class neighbors in a working-class town, and both dress the part.

Lewis gives him a hard look. "I'm the first guy to admit that my old man was an asshole, but he used to say that men should drink brown liquor and leave the clear stuff for women."

Harrison stares back with unbridled confidence. Maybe he's a trial lawyer.

"What would your father have said to the millions of Russian men who drink vodka every day?"

"He would have called them communists and then tried to kill them."

Fenwick laughs from across the room, an involuntary snort that he tries to swallow. Janey throws Lewis an amused look with a warning buried in it. He's been drinking for a few hours now, and she knows it. He can feel it, how it softens the edges. They've gone a little mushy, like mud on the shoulders of the road. *Keep it in the tracks*, she's telling him. Looking around the room, he sees all of their friends and neighbors staring at him. Gray too, standing in the center holding her book. On her birthday last year they built the kite he gave her on his fly-tying bench in the garage and then took it to the park. There's a moment when you're trying to launch a kite when you're running as fast as you can, dragging it behind you, and you can see the wings start to find the wind but can't yet tell whether it's going to catch it and lift it high or wrench it around and crash it into the ground. The expression on his daughter's face tells him they've reached that moment.

Don't be that guy.

"Keep the troops entertained while I fill glasses, pal," he says, and moves to the kitchen.

"Saudi Arabia imports camels from Australia."

"Is that true?" Iris Boothman asks, wiping her nose with a tissue she pulls from the sleeve of her sweater. A notorious window-watcher who keeps a scientifically close eye on the street's comings and goings, she's a neighborhood overwatch with cotton-swab hair. Thirty years older than any other neighbor, and an Evangelical Christian, she likes to make it clear not only that she knows your business but that she doesn't approve of it.

"Sure," Fenwick says. "That's why there are so many kangaroos there. Camels are their natural predators."

Gray gives her uncle a look that says *stop being silly. There's definitely some of her mother in there*, Lewis thinks, watching from the kitchen.

"Fin whales urinate two hundred fifty gallons per day."

"Sweet Jesus," says Iris's husband, Roy. She scolds him immediately. He rolls his eyes and grips his aluminum walker more tightly. The walker itself is battered, ancient, with tennis balls for feet, the side rails scraped raw, as if he can't fit through doorways or was dragged behind a truck.

"It's illegal to lock your car in Churchill, Manitoba," Gray reads, "in case someone needs shelter from a marauding polar bear."

"We've got bear problems too," Lucy DeLong says. "They should make that a law here."

"Our bear never hurt anybody," Lewis says, delivering a tray full of cocktails. A decade after it first appeared, the town bear continues to haunt Disappointment, stealing food and pets and leaving scat in the streets, but he still has not seen it.

"Not yet."

"A grizzly bear has enough bite strength to crush a bowling ball," Gray reads.

"Our Realtor told us about the town's bear problem," Carole Harrison says. "I think it's deplorable that a wild animal like that is allowed to continue roaming around so freely, threatening our safety, when it's clearly dangerous."

"Bears were here before people were," Lewis says. "I would think that gives them some rights. And like I said, in ten years it hasn't hurt a single person."

"Anyway, ours ain't a grizzly," Fenwick says. "It's black."

"How can you tell?" Carole asks.

"I'm an expert."

"On bears?"

"On being Black."

The discomfort in her smile is worth the price of admission, Lewis thinks.

"Speaking of biting," Gray reads, "New Yorkers bite ten times more people each year than sharks."

"You're a very intelligent child," Carole says. "What do you want to be when you grow up?"

"A fishing guide. Like my dad."

The look on Carole Harrison's face is clear. If she's trying to hide it, she's not very good at it.

Janey sees it too. "Thank you, Gray," she says. "Why don't you go play with your friends?"

"OK, Mom."

Realizing the entertainment is over, Iris begins to clap, the look on her face sincere to the point of comic effect—almost rapturous. The others follow her lead, and there's a round of awkward applause. Gray smiles at the adults oddly and skips out of the room.

6

"Your daughter has a very bright future," Carole Harrison says. Over six feet tall, she towers over everyone except Lewis. Her own husband is slight in a way that suggests either a sickly childhood or a diet of nuts and leaves. "Surely you want something more for her than to be a fishing guide?"

"Something more?" Lewis asks. Janey shoots him a glance, this one a warning shot across his bow, a reminder that her amusement has a shelf life. "She's just a kid, Carole. She's got her whole life to decide who she is and what she wants to do."

"But don't you want to encourage her to have other opportunities? There's a whole world beyond Disappointment."

She's not wrong—when Lewis was a kid he wanted desperately for someone to show him how much he was missing, to give him permission to reach for it, and the first time the cage door opened, he fled. But on the other hand, fuck Carole Harrison.

"That doesn't mean it's better. We didn't settle, Carole. We're not stuck here. This is where we want to be."

"We chose it here too," her husband says with pointed

conciliation. Then he tries to change the subject. "These burgers are quite good. Everything is good."

Lewis has spent enough time on the water to recognize what he's doing: throwing his wife a life preserver.

"You can thank Lewis," Janey says. "He shot the elk in the Wallowas."

As Harrison stares at the half eaten burger on his plate with morbid interest, maybe realizing for the first time that it had been a living animal with watery eyes and a heart, Lewis takes a moment to admire his wife's deftness.

"If you want to grill it, you gotta kill it," Fenwick says.

Iris glares at him. "The Good Lord has blessed us with his bounty."

"I know we're new to town, but we *adore* it here," Carole says. Lewis finds her brittle enough to break. "It's a wonderful place to retire. I just can't imagine starting out here. In California we were exposed to so many wonderful things and people from so many different backgrounds. It's so *diverse* there."

Her husband takes an audible breath, recognizing, perhaps, that a life preserver won't help someone who doesn't know she is drowning.

"We have diversity here, too," Lewis says. "We have Fenwick."

"He means 'cause I'm Black," Fenwick says, amiably. "But I'm also a Baptist, which makes me a twofer."

"What about college?" Carole asks. "Surely you want Gray to go to college?"

"She's ten."

"Not now, of course. When it's time. That way, at least, she would be exposed to other things. To other ways of life."

Watching the way his neighbor waves her mostly empty wine glass, Lewis wonders how drunk she is, wonders if it is more or less than him.

"You know what I want for my daughter?" he asks, his tone no longer a dog whistle you need to be married to him to hear. There's an edge to his voice, but this time he's put it there, honed it with a deliberateness that's not lost on his wife, who glares his way. But the whiskey has loosened his tongue and he just runs through the stop sign. "Whatever *she* wants for *herself*. Not everyone wants the same things out of life."

The atmosphere in the room has changed, as if the cabin has depressurized. He can almost see the other guests' eyes starting to bulge, their skin stretching.

"I didn't mean to disparage your work," Carole says, her conviction dwindling. "I was just questioning whether it was appropriate or not. For her."

Lewis has seen clients fall out of boats and thrash in the current, arms and legs flailing without actually moving anywhere. All they're doing is tiring themselves out. After that, all that's left is to sink. Before he can respond, Janey tags in.

"You mean appropriate for a girl?"

Carole says nothing, having finally realized she's lost at sea. She looks at her husband, too far away to rescue her. The rest of the room has gone silent. Fenwick looks like he wishes he'd worn his waders.

"Lewis went to college," Janey says. "A good school too. He chose to be a guide because he loved the work and loved being outdoors. I wanted to play cello for the Boston Symphony Orchestra. When that didn't happen, I cleaned toilets to pay for night school so that I could earn a degree. Is that *appropriate* enough for you? I did it—I got my degree. But you know what I wanted even more than that? A family. I wanted to be a mother. More than I wanted to be a cellist or a lawyer or anything else."

"Especially a lawyer," Lewis says. God help the Harrisons now that his wife has joined this conversation.

"Shut up, Lewis," Janey says lightly. "I chose to be a mother. I chose to be a wife. We chose to live here and to do what we do with our lives. These are our friends and neighbors. We love them dearly. These are *your* neighbors now, too, Carole. This is the town I've called home for a long time, and this is my house. I guess I'm not sure why you think it's OK to come to our party and insult us. Because when you question our choices and our lifestyle, that's exactly what you're doing."

Though Janey's voice remains calm and her tone friendly, her bluntness catches Carole Harrison off guard. A deep blush colors her well-structured face, surprising Lewis. Staring into the dregs of her white wine, she takes a moment to gather herself. She looks as if she's considering escape by diving into the glass. The silence does not last long, but it feels long enough for civilizations to rise and fall.

Then Fenwick brings it to an abrupt end. "Well, I didn't choose any of this," he says, clearing his throat with the sound of a muffler backfiring. "I wanted to be tall and thin and play basketball like Michael Jordan."

Everyone laughs, happy for an excuse to change the subject. Carole Harrison takes advantage of the opportunity.

"I think I misspoke," she says. "I'm sorry. I think I've had too much wine."

Her husband pats her leg.

"I wanted to be a nun," Iris says. "Roy wanted to be a rodeo clown."

"It's true," Roy says. "My dad took us to the Pendleton Round-Up every year. All my brothers wanted to be bull riders. Cowboys. But I thought the clowns were braver."

"I wanted to be an actress," Lucy says. "I wanted to live in New York. Or Hollywood. I wanted to be anything but a small-town mom. I grew up in a town smaller than this one, in

Idaho, and couldn't imagine spending my life this way. Then I moved to Seattle with some friends. I was so excited to be in a city, so excited to have so many things to see and do. I only lasted two weeks. It was so loud, so fast-paced. It smelled like car exhaust and pee. Everyone was so . . . aggressive. I like it here. We like living here, even though Will has to go away to work. It's worth it. The people are really nice."

When she looks pointedly at the new neighbors, Lewis searches her expression for a trace of meanness but finds none, just a genuine and welcoming warmth.

"This is fun," he says. "Who wants another drink?"

———

After the guests leave they tackle the mess in a bucket brigade, like they're fighting a barn fire. Lewis washes the dishes and platters Fenwick gathers and stacks on the counter; Janey dries them while Gray collects wrapping paper and ribbons that she stuffs into trash bags. When they've made sufficient progress, Janey waves them off, and Lewis and Fenwick adjourn to the driveway for another round of whiskey. They stand on opposite sides of the trailered boat, arms draped over the gunwales, their glasses and a new bottle of Old Crow on the bench seat between them.

"Your new neighbors are interesting people," Fenwick says, nodding across the street at the Harrisons' uninspired house. A recently planted cordon of decidedly non-native palm trees lines the front, as if it's not so much a house as a wormhole through which they can see California.

"People like them come up here and try to turn Oregon into California. They think they're conquerors, but they're not—they're immigrants."

"We were immigrants too, once."

"No. We were refugees."

Fenwick nods in acknowledgment of their shitty childhoods, a shared bond they worked out between them while emptying bottles and filling boats.

"Harrison's such a tight-ass, he folds his dirty laundry before he puts it in the hamper," Lewis says.

His friend lights a Tareyton and pockets the dead match. "I used to have a client like him. A judge from San Francisco or some such. Real rigid asshole, always taking out clean handkerchiefs and wiping everything down, like a magician how he could pull so many handkerchiefs out of his pockets. Showed up every year for his trip in brand-new jeans with creases ironed acrosst the legs."

"Could he fish?"

"Could he fish. That old bastard couldn't catch a cold in a kindergarten."

"I'd be surprised if Harrison owned jeans. They're too provincial."

"What's 'provincial'?" Gray asks, surprising them both. She's standing behind the boat's transom, quietly listening to their conversation.

Fenwick takes a drag from his cigarette, almost dainty in his meaty hands, his swollen lips.

"Honestly, Hoss, I don't know. Must be one of those words your old man learned in college."

"That didn't take you long," Lewis says, and his friend smiles.

"No, it didn't. And I don't imagine I'm done yet, either." Finishing his drink, he puts the empty mason jar upside down on the boat seat. "Better get home before the dead houseplants miss me."

They walk him down the driveway to his truck, Lewis and Gray and the big dog lumbering at their feet.

"Say goodbye to your uncle," Lewis says.

Gray and Fenwick respond in unison like a vaudeville act. "Goodbye to your uncle." She giggles and Fenwick high-fives her.

"Thank you for the birthday gift."

"You show your old man what I got you?"

She fishes the charm out of her pocket, a rabbit's foot dyed pink on a metal chain.

"It's good luck."

"Tell that to the rabbit," Lewis says.

"Pay no attention to your father, Hoss."

"I know."

"You tell your uncle what your mom and dad got you?"

"Oh yeah! We're going to the coast this summer. On a vacation. We're going to see whales and lighthouses."

"Vacation, huh? Sounds good to me. Maybe someday I'll get a day off." He opens the door to his truck and starts to climb in, but then stops and turns around. "Better give your uncle a hug."

Gray leans in and squeezes him, eliciting a trumpeting fart that causes her to step back with a look of shock on her face. Maybe it's awe.

"Now that you're practically an adult, I think you're old enough to know this secret," Fenwick tells her. "If you fart when people hug you, it makes them feel strong."

"Do *not* do that, Gray."

"Give me a hug, Lewis."

"Hell no," Lewis says, but hugs his old friend anyway. Remembering The Old Man, his body tenses involuntarily at the contact. It's muscle memory, even after all these years. The muscles contract. The limbs stiffen. His breath comes up short as his heart shifts gear. The body does not forget. It saddens him, and he hopes his friend does not notice.

When Fenwick starts his truck, the big diesel chugs like a locomotive and a cloud of smoke shoots out the exhaust. The window opens, and he sticks his thick head out.

"Hey Confucius. You really go to college?"

"I did."

"What'd you study?"

"Literature."

"No shit? You ever feel like you're wasting your degree, fishing for a living?"

"No."

Fenwick chews his lip, considering. "Then, tell me this, Confucius. How many fish has your fancy college literature degree helped you catch?"

"Just one," Lewis says, and holds up his middle finger. Fenwick is still laughing as he drives away.

———

When they walk into the kitchen, Janey is leaning against the counter with a glass of zinfandel and a fatigued look on her face. She's made as much progress as she intends to for the night.

"Careful, Lewis," she says. "Someone might see you smiling."

"I'm smiling because they're all gone. Every last one of them." He takes the glass from her hand and wraps her in his arms.

"Eww," Gray says, but when Lewis extends his arms she joins the hug too. His wingspan is long enough to encircle both of them with room to spare. Sensing a display of affection and feeling left out, Johnson lurches into the room and presses against them with force enough to almost knock the three of them over.

"Hell of a thing, isn't it?" Janey says. Her breath warms his neck.

"What's that, J?"

"Family."

———

Despite the fatigue, the food, the whiskey, Lewis's mind is on fire when he climbs into bed that night. Janey puts her head on his shoulder, and he tries to time his breathing to hers but can't. The dog's snoring fills the hallway, and with each wheezy breath the walls seem to expand and contract, as if the house itself is snoring.

Soon Janey's breathing deepens. Her chest rises with each breath. When he's sure she's asleep, he gets up, pulls on his fatigues, and laces up his sneakers for a run. As he tiptoes down the hall, the floorboards creak, waking the dog, who wags her tail and gets up to join him. She's too old for it. Her giant joints will bother her for days. But she loves it and misses it, and he wants to give her this. A fair trade: a little pain for a little joy. He'd take all the pain in the world for a little joy, he thinks. Maybe he already has.

They run through the spring darkness into town. As they pass the Salt Lick, Littlejohn's truck cuts in front of them and pulls into the lot. Lewis stops running as Littlejohn steps out of the cab, but Johnson walks over to the other guide and sits at his feet. A blatant act of betrayal if ever there was one.

"Your dog has good taste."

"My dog eats trash and licks her own asshole."

Littlejohn laughs. "You have a good night, Yaw," he says, and heads into the bar.

The air grows cooler as they near the river. Soon Lewis feels its breath on his cheeks, condensation that lasts just a fraction of a second before evaporating. A fleeting kiss. When the dog stops in a copse of lodgepole pine at the water's edge, the hair along her back bristles. Where she puts her nose, Lewis sees the pile, solid nuggets peppered with berries and leaves. Bear scat. He has to admire the damn bear, leaving berry-strewn piles like cairns to its own memory even as it eludes capture. A goddamned legend.

"That bear ought to be embarrassed," he tells Johnson. "You leave piles bigger than that."

They resume their pace until they cross the footbridge and reach the forest road. There he slows a bit, his footing uneven in the dark, his stride whiskey-loose, his breath short.

Growing up, the best he could hope for on his birthday was to be ignored. The Old Man did not feel it a day worth celebrating. The birth of the son fate burdened him with coincided with the anniversary of his mother's death, a near-Catholic collision of heaven and hell he never learned to reconcile. His birthday was a prism that split his father's resentment into a spectrum of abuse. Some years his only gift was a belt, lashes instead of candles, stripes across his back. One year he locked Lewis in the basement until it passed. He kept a trunk in the basement from his Navy days, his name and rank stenciled on it—Lewis spent an entire day and night sitting on it among the spiderwebs and boxes and reloading equipment, the smell of must and mold. That was his fifth birthday. For his sixth, The Old Man locked him *in* the trunk.

As the memories overtake him, he lengthens his strides and quickens his pace in a ridiculous effort to outrun them. His lungs burn. Something beats against his skull from the inside out, something trapped. The memory itself, maybe. Or the whiskey souring in his stomach, the meatballs and sausages and hamburgers, the pound of potato salad and its curdling mayo, the vanilla frosted cake. Still he runs. The aging dog struggles to keep pace. Lewis can see the pain in her mismatched eyes, the stutter in her gait. Though she's been nothing but loyal and affectionate, he cannot bring himself to slow for her, and it shames him.

In a burst of speed born of urgency, he sprints ahead, leaving her behind. His lungs explode, turning to cinder and disintegrating in his chest. The fire spreads to his legs, each muscle a conflagration. Still he runs, pushing through the pain until he can push through it no more. Finally he stops, drops to all fours in the dirt and crawls down the bank as the past wells up inside him, choking him worse than hope ever could. With a gruesome sound, he vomits into the Terrebonne. The heaves are violent. Noisy. Explosive. They come not just from his stomach but from his childhood, one for every year.

Johnson arrives, panting, and circles him with concern, nudging him with a wet nose. Then she lies down beside him, happy for the break, huffing and puffing like a furry bellows. Lewis vomits again and watches his past hit the surface of the river.

The water dilutes it. The current carries it away.

If only it was that easy, he thinks, and pukes again.

7

It's already ninety degrees when he wakes with a headache like a clothes dryer filled with quarters. The heat feels malicious. He's mistrustful of it—it makes him stupid and angry. The air is full of smoke from wildfires burning for the past few weeks, not just in Oregon but in Washington, Idaho, Montana, and British Columbia, and the right wind can carry smoke for hundreds of miles. The eye-watering haze hurts to breathe. The flames are devastating hundreds of thousands of acres of forest and meadowland, eating trees and cabins and lodges and entire communities in their path, burning animals alive. Some days ash falls from the sky like snow, filling the boat, covering the roof and the yard. The ash is tiny bits of all of that, specks of houses and trees and people and animals. All because some careless driver tossed a cigarette out his window. *Nature is an asshole*, he thinks, *but humans will always be worse.*

The smoke and heat and a sulking mood conspire with his hangover to poison him as he pulls to the curb to pick up his client.

"It's a beautiful morning to be alive," the man says, opening the door. Lewis winces at the sheer audacity of conversation in his current state.

"I wish I was." His own voice echoes in his woodpeckered brain.

The client studies him for a moment, the bloodshot eyes, the sunken expression.

"Robert Benchley said the only cure for a real hangover is death."

Lewis nods, slowly. "Where do I sign up?"

The client lifts up the pink box of donuts he's holding. He brought them from Portland, a simple, thoughtful act that hits Lewis like a shot of adrenaline. When he climbs into the truck smiling and friendly without being obsequious or aggressive, it gives Lewis a renewed hope.

"I drove in from Portland last night. Four hours of beauty. I love Oregon."

"Where are you from?"

"Oregon."

"Lived here your whole life?"

"Not yet," he says, and laughs a genuine laugh that steals all the corniness from the joke and dissipates it into the humid air. "I worked for the county in Portland for most of my career, since right after college. This fishing trip was a retirement gift from my coworkers."

"Let's make it count," Lewis says.

"It's already great."

At the put-in he wanders off to take pictures while Lewis readies the boat. Distracted by the storm in his head, he forgets to hold the painter line when he skids the boat down the launch and has to chase after it, sliding through the dirt and rocks and diving into the river as it floats away from the bank.

Even in the heat, the cold water makes his headache ring like a tuning fork.

When he grabs the painter and turns around to swim back toward the bank, he hears a familiar voice over his shoulder, coming from the river channel.

"Lewis Fucking Yaw."

"King of the Jungle," Lewis says reflexively as a boat materializes out of the smoke with two ghostly fishermen in the bow. He recognizes the boat even before he sees Littlejohn at the oars, a grin on his face, disgust in his eyes. Littlejohn says something else as he passes, not to Lewis but to his clients. They laugh as the boat disappears downstream.

Clambering ashore, Lewis ties his own boat off to a tree and empties the water out of his boots as his client watches with rapt amusement.

When the shuttle van arrives, Fenwick spills out and spots his wet clothes right away.

"You go for a swim?"

"I let go of the painter."

"Lewis Yaw screwed up? Aww, shit. I guess there really is a first time for everything."

"Even monkeys fall from trees."

"Fucking Confucius."

Lewis nods at the van. "Speaking of monkeys, where are yours? The Pope's driving himself today?"

Fenwick looks at him hard and spits in the dirt.

"One of my drivers has mono."

He provides the shuttle service through the Vatican—the fly shop he owns—picking up clients at hotels or bed-and-breakfasts in and around town and dropping them at their guides' favored put-ins. The guides call the drivers his Flying Monkeys—high school students, hired because they're affordable and easy to replace. They bring a bike with them to drop the trailers and then ride the bikes back, racing along the fire road in a horde that earned their nickname.

"Mono?"

"The kissing disease. I'm not sure how that little turd got it. The only thing he ever kisses is my ass."

"Your ass is too big for mono. Your ass is stereo."

Fenwick laughs, a hearty laugh that nonetheless fails to improve Lewis's mood.

"Hey," the client yells good-naturedly from the boat. "Are we going to fish, or are you two going to make out?"

Fenwick grabs Lewis's head on either side and cradles it in both hands like a watermelon. "We're going to make out," he says, and plants a wet, loud kiss on his forehead.

"Damn it, Pope," Lewis says. "You better not give me mono."

———

Once they're on the water, the day begins to turn around. A light breeze dissipates the smoke and mitigates the heat a bit. Though a mediocre fisherman, he's an ideal client. Some fish he misses because he's staring so intently at the scenery. Those he catches he holds like marvels, speaking softly to them as he studies their noble lines.

"That's one scrawny bastard," Lewis says when he boats an undersized steelhead, but the client looks no less joyous cradling it in his wet hands.

"Celebrate every win, no matter how small."

Even the coffee seems to please him. Standing in the bow with the river behind him like a stage curtain, he plants his nose in the mug and sniffs deeply before each sip.

Halfway through the day Lewis beaches the boat on a

sandbar and they sit on damp stones, enjoying the break and sandwiches left over from Gray's party.

"Are you always this relaxed?"

"Not at all. I spent the last three decades under work-induced stress. Long hours, angry people, high blood pressure. My jaw clenched so tight I could eat coal and spit diamonds."

"What happened?"

"I retired."

"So, that's it? You retire and you're suddenly happy?"

"No. I made a choice."

"To do what?"

"To be happy."

"Just like that? You just flip a switch?"

"Just like that. I've been working toward retirement my entire life, and I'll be darned if I'm not going to soak up every minute of it. My own father died before he could retire. He had a heart attack behind the wheel of his Oldsmobile commuting to his sixty-hour-a-week job. Imagine that? Dying in traffic?"

"Or an Oldsmobile," Lewis says, and the man laughs. "I can't picture retiring from guiding. Someday a client will turn around in the bow to find me dead in the stern, hands gripping the oars, and row me to shore."

"Life is not a permanent condition, my friend."

"Kafka said that the meaning of life is that it ends."

"Well, he's not wrong. My time will come eventually, and that day is a lot closer than it used to be. I don't want to die on my way to work; I want to die doing something fun. I want to die *fulfilled*. Every minute I have left on this planet is a gift, and I plan to enjoy each one of them. You're darn right I flipped a switch. From here on out, the world can call me Mr. Happy."

Lewis doesn't often drink on the boat, and never in front of clients. But his retreating hangover has scraped the fields bare, and irrigating them might help.

"Do you like bourbon, Mr. Happy?" He offers his flask to the client, who shakes it off.

"Sure," he says, producing a flask of his own from somewhere within his waders. "But I like scotch even better."

"You are truly living your best life."

"We only get one."

They touch flasks, and Lewis toasts.

"Here's to staying positive and testing negative." Something The Old Man used to say.

"To our wives and girlfriends," Mr. Happy says. "May they never meet."

———

After lunch they have better luck, as if settling his stomach somehow settles the empathic river too. When Lewis spots a big steelhead lurking in a clear pool, he alerts Mr. Happy.

"Fish at two o'clock," he says, calm and soft, a drill sergeant in a library. "Put the Kaufmann into the current twenty feet upstream of him and let it sink."

The client leaps to his feet and grabs the Sage rod tied with the Kaufmann stone fly and launches a messy cast in his haste to follow orders. The heavy fly hits the surface like the Apollo landing capsule.

"Let it sink."

The high-vis yellow line connects the boat to the river where it disappears into the water about twenty feet off the starboard bow. They watch intently as the current pulls it downstream toward the fish.

"Mend the line."

Mr. Happy mends, flicking the tip of the rod to send a loosely coiled loop upstream, creating slack so the fly can drift at its own pace instead of getting dragged by the current. The fish hovers six feet beneath the surface like a chrome zeppelin. The big black-and-brown fly drifts two feet shy of its mouth.

"Again," Lewis says, admonishing him when he begins to strip line in a frantic retrieve. "Calmly. Like you're stroking a scared dog."

Steelhead are rainbow trout that run to sea, like salmon. Trout that grow salmon-sized. They're wary and athletic, fierce fighters on a hook called "the fish of a thousand casts" because of the challenge in catching them. The line gathers in yellow coils at Mr. Happy's feet, filling the boat like Rapunzel's hair. When he recovers enough of it, he roll-casts the line out over the water, his expression so serious it borders on grim. The cast creates a rooster tail of spray as it passes the boat. He reclaims more line, false-casts once, and shoots the fly with a mechanically sound cast, extending his arms and pointing the tip of the rod at the surface like a nine-foot-long magic wand. A coil of line rolls past the boat like an optical illusion or a swarm of acrobatic birds. Lewis has been watching fly-casts his whole life and never grows tired of the beauty in the physics.

"If there is magic on this planet, it is contained in water."

"That's beautiful."

"Something I read once."

"Do you read a lot?"

"Pay attention to the fish."

Mr. Happy shoots the line. It unfurls gently and lands with hardly a splash.

"Good," Lewis says, and sees the client's pleased smile. "Now let it sink. Mend it."

Obedient, he mends the line once, twice, adding slack and

removing tension. The fly approaches the fish. The fish studies it with what looks like nonchalance.

"Give him time."

The fish considers the fly for a long draw. Then he rejects it, and the Kaufmann drifts an inch farther.

"Wait." As they watch, the fish moves almost imperceptibly and sips the big fly into its mouth. Thirty feet of distance and six feet of rushing water separate them, but he swears he hears it slurp.

"Set the hook," he says.

Mr. Happy raises the rod and the line goes tight. He whoops with joy.

"Imagine surviving for years in the vastness of the ocean, avoiding apex predators and commercial salmon fleets, only to fall for a fake bug tied with feathers and yarn in the safety of a quiet river?"

"Just goes to show you," Lewis says. "Never let your guard down."

———

They round the bend at Dancer's Elbow and find Littlejohn's boat beached on a sandbar, the polished aluminum bright as a second sun. His clients sit on opposite sides of a small table tucking into a lavish feast, white napkins and bottles of wine served by a caterer in a black tie. The men wear waders and vests, the sandbar around them littered with river rock and scrub brush. Cigar smoke hovers above the island like black tornadoes. Littlejohn pays the caterer to meet the boat, serving the food hot from the back of a van. For the pleasure, he charges more than Lewis or the other guides, and attracts clientele with deep pockets.

It's a gimmick. Lewis would rather just feed clients egg salad sandwiches and put them on more fish.

When Littlejohn sees them coming, he struts to the sandbar's edge, unbuttons the fly of his jeans, and pisses into the river at his feet, staring boldly as they pass. Lewis laughs and points an oar.

"I'm not surprised you're fishing with worms, but that one's awfully small."

The other guide shakes his dick and raises a middle finger. "Fuck you, Yaw."

"Don't be that guy," Lewis tells Mr. Happy.

"Who is he?"

"That's Littlejohn."

Mr. Happy laughs aloud, a laugh so unselfconscious it's practically a giggle.

"More like Little*johnson*," he says, and laughs again.

8

Still towing the boat, and still reeking of fish, Lewis picks Gray up from her friend's house. Her friend's mother greets him at the door, a slight woman in a Coldplay T-shirt. As a thank-you, Lewis presents her with a thick steelhead fillet wrapped in newspaper. She eyes it suspiciously. Fish are currency in his world—sporting guides can't sell to market, but there's nothing to stop them from using the meat to barter. Not only does he bring fish to nearly every dinner or party to which he and Janey are invited, but he also gives dozens of pounds of it away to grateful friends and neighbors and to the homeless shelter in Bend. He's traded it for products and services on the informal underground economy that runs towns like Disappointment.

"If it were any fresher it would still be swimming," he says.

"What do I do with it?" She has a mole on one cheek the color of a well-done hamburger, a peace symbol tattooed just below her left ear. The mole is the shape of the state of Ohio.

"If you plant it in your garden, more fish will grow."

"Seriously?"

"Can't hurt to try."

From somewhere within the house behind her Lewis can hear a television. The smell of cats is strong. She scratches her neck where she's tattooed, as if reconsidering peace as a concept, but does not laugh.

"Wait here." She takes the fish by the tail end of the fillet and carries it like a dead rat. She does not return. A few minutes later Gray comes to the door, clutching her raincoat, buoyant with joy. She's had a good day. Do kids make a choice to be happy, too, or is it their default? When, exactly, does it become a choice?

"We played Monkey in the Middle with Brittany's brother. I was the monkey."

"Of course you were. You've got the ears of a first-class chimpanzee."

"Chimpanzees are not monkeys."

"If it looks like a duck and smells like a duck, it's a duck."

"What does that mean?"

"It means close enough."

"You always say that close only counts in horseshoes and handkerchiefs."

"Hand grenades. Horseshoes and hand grenades."

"So either you were wrong then or you're wrong now."

"I see law school is going well."

"What does *that* mean?"

"It means you're getting too smart. We might have to let you watch more television to rot your brain a little."

Lewis hoists her into the truck. Her hair is cut short, boyish. Her teeth are crooked, just a bit, but endearingly so. Like her mother's.

"How come I don't have any brothers or sisters?"

"Because we're going for quality. Not quantity."

"Be serious."

"Be serious?" He rolls his head on his neck, first starboard, then port, until it cracks. "I guess because if we had other kids, I wouldn't get to spend so much time with you."

"Brittany's brother was gross. He picks his nose and smells like dog turds."

"All boys do."

Lewis closes her door and circles around to his side. When he climbs in and starts the engine, it sounds like a room full of old men clearing their throats.

"Who are my grandparents?" she asks without warning or preamble. Those were the punches Jimmy used to warn him about—the ones you couldn't see coming.

"Your grandparents?"

"Brittany's grandparents ate lunch with us. We had veggie burgers and salad. It was kind of gross."

"Her grandparents too, huh? Was this a play date or a family reunion?"

"They live in the basement."

"Like rats and spiders."

"Where do my grandparents live?"

Get your hands up, Lou, Jimmy yells from the corner. *Protect yourself.*

"They're all gone, pal," he says.

"Gone where?" she asks, first forcing him into the corner and then continuing to hit him. A natural fighter.

"Just gone, Gray. They're dead."

Her eyes darken as she furrows her brow. A different person might try to soften the blow, use different words. *They've passed. They've gone to heaven.* But death is a natural state. She's grown up killing fish, eating venison and elk. To call it by name is to be respectful.

"All of them?"

Stay off the ropes, Lou.

Is it normal to grieve people you've never met? He grieved his mother. Gray is grieving grandparents she never seemed aware of before. Maybe grief is like cancer, how it can live undetected inside you for years until a doctor finds it and then once you know it's there, you're dying and your entire outlook on the world changes. Maybe Gray feels the emptiness now that he's made her aware of it now that he's drawn her a map. He wants to tell her the truth about The Old Man, just like he did when she was a baby. He wants to tell her the truth about everything, lay the world bare and shine the lights brightly. But he also wants to protect her. A father's instinct, a father's dilemma. Honesty is his rule, but she's just a kid. He doesn't see the point of illuminating all of the world's darkest corners.

"All of them, pal." It's not a lie. Three out of four is a majority—he's just rounding up. The Old Man is dead to *him*, and that's as good as dead. At least as far as Gray needs to know.

"What happened to them?"

Lewis takes another breath and puts the truck in gear. Though he's got his boot on the brake, they lurch forward a couple of feet, the transmission worn, the fluid fouled, the entire truck on the verge of surrender. He wonders what the right move is, wonders what to tell her, wonders what will make her feel better and what won't make her feel any worse.

"Everybody dies, Gray. That's just the way of the world."

He doesn't need to see the expression on her face to know he's made a mistake.

9

They drive wordlessly, listening to the old Ford's complaints. The odometer shows sixty-five thousand miles and change, but it rolls over every hundred thousand and Lewis has lost count of how many times it has reset. It's the same truck he's had since high school; he bought it used.

They stop for gas and coffee. From the register he watches Gray climb out of the truck and start emptying trash from its bed into the garbage bin, unsolicited. Empty sandwich bags, a handful of blackened banana peels, a dozen Styrofoam coffee cups. Rusted cans older than she is. There are flies with broken hooks and torn feathers, busted fly rod sections, flashlights with dead batteries. Candy bar wrappers, lengths of tangled monofilament, battered coffee thermoses. It's an archaeological dig. Everything she can toss, she does. By the time Lewis has paid, she's emptied it of anything expendable, though it's still cluttered with anchor chains and coolers and more substantial junk. When he returns to the truck, she's holding an old golf club and a greasy paper bag full of golf balls. The driver is covered in rust.

"Are these yours?"

Lewis shrugs. "Maybe."

She looks at him suspiciously but does not pursue her interrogation. She puts the club and bag of balls back in the bed and climbs into the cab.

"This isn't the way home," she says, a few minutes later.

"Nope."

"Where are we going?"

"Does it matter?"

"Not really."

He watches her taking in their surroundings, trying to figure out their destination. The mystery seems to have distracted her from her earlier line of questioning, as was his plan.

"Did you know that sharks sleep with their eyes open?" Gray asks.

"Sure. Do you know what you call a group of sharks?"

"No."

"A shiver. Or a shoal."

"Did you know that you're more likely to be elected president than to be bitten by a shark?"

"I did not. Did you learn that in school, or in your trivia book?"

"Shark Week," she says.

The world outside the windows is expansive and beautiful. Outside Disappointment, the forest begins to give way to the high desert, and the colors change from greens to browns. They listen to the wind whipping through the cab, the sounds of other traffic. Most kids might have reached for the truck's radio by now, but Gray enjoys the silence as much as he does.

When the road slopes left, Lewis turns down a long, unpaved road that winds into the woods. The trees cluster more tightly as it narrows, blocking out the sunlight so it feels as though they are driving deeper into the heart of the forest. The air feels cooler in the shade, less dry, as if they can feel the moist breath of the trees. When the road begins to climb, the truck's engine strains as they follow it until the trees clear and they emerge without notice into blinding sunlight.

They've reached a high bluff overlooking the canyon below and the hills that rim it, the mountainous horizon. The Terrebonne runs like a vein pulsing with blue blood through the high desert far beneath them, the earth stretched around it like sun-dried and cracked skin. Disappointment occupies a part of the state where the Coast Range and Cascade Mountains yield to the volcanically formed Columbia Plateau, one of several dramatic landscape shifts across the state. It feels like they can see the line where the land changes from the forest to the dry rocks of the high desert—the contrasting beauty of the evergreen forest, the sunbaked rock and clay, the scrub of western juniper and ponderosa pine, the otherworldly hue of the river.

Lewis pulls the golf club from the truck's bed and points it at the Terrebonne beneath them. He takes a tee from the bag, pierces the dry earth, and centers a ball on it. Then he winds up and swings. His swing is awkward, all strength and no style, but he connects.

"I love that sound," he says. Together they watch the ball rise high off the lip of the canyon and slice wide, arcing in two directions at once before falling like a star. Gray steps a little closer to the edge, her eyes following the ball as it hits the rock far below with a different sound entirely, a satisfying knock, bouncing high into the air before disappearing into the river.

"Whoa."

"*Whoa* is right, pal."

"I didn't know you golfed."

"I don't. Sometimes I come up here and hit balls as a kind

of . . . I don't know. Stress relief. I only own the one club. Fished it out of the river one day when a client wrapped his line around it. God knows how long it sat on the bottom, or what the hell it was even doing there. That's why it's so rusty." He holds it at arm's length, studying it. "But this is not golfing. Not really."

"What are you stressed about?"

"What?"

"You said you came here to hit balls for stress relief. What are you stressed about?"

Lewis looks at his daughter and considers his answer carefully for the second time that day. He carries things around and hopes they make him stronger, hopes he doesn't buckle under the weight. Instead of answering, he reaches down and musses her hair.

"Don't worry about that stuff, pal."

"Can I try golfing?"

"First, a little business. I need you to keep this a secret."

"From who?"

"Everyone."

"How come?"

"When you have something that's yours and yours alone, sometimes you can lose some of the magic by telling other people about it."

"But you're telling me."

"I am." Lewis sees that she understands. "Also, we're probably not supposed to hit golf balls into the river."

"We're not?"

"No. But it's a victimless crime."

"What's 'victimless'?"

"It means it doesn't hurt anybody."

"What about the fish?"

"The fish don't care."

"Promise?"

"Promise."

"So you want me to lie to Mom?"

Lewis smiles. "Some lies are victimless crimes too," he says.

"Like what?"

"Like that river down there. 'Terrebonne' means *good earth*, but it's all water."

Teeing up another ball, he swings again and drives it high over the river. When it hooks to the right, they crane their necks to follow it.

"You don't ever want to tell a lie that will hurt someone, but sometimes it's OK to keep things to yourself."

"Do you keep other things to yourself? Besides this?"

"Kiddo, I am a safe nobody can crack."

He sees she's troubled by what he is telling her and decides to meet her halfway.

"I'll make you a deal. If anyone asks if your old man hits golf balls off cliffs, you have my blessing to tell them I do. But unless they ask, you don't bring it up. Deal?"

He fake-spits into his palm and reaches out. Gray stares at him for a long few moments, considering it. Then she copies him, spitting a dry wheeze of dust. They shake.

"Deal," she says. He hands her the club.

———

After an hour or so, when only a dozen balls remain, he calls the day done.

"Let's get dinner and head home," he says. "Your mother's probably noticed we're not around by now."

Gray lays the club in the bed of the truck but brings the bag into the cab with her, and while he drives, fishes the balls out one at a time to study them. He buys them used, in bulk, for a couple of bucks a pound from a kid who collects them from local courses. Each brand has its own markings, a logo or slogan, some marketing distinction, but otherwise they all look the same—dimpled little moons fallen from the night sky. They bear scuff marks left by club faces, collisions with trees or fence posts, long bounces in the grass. It's comforting that their imperfections do not limit them.

"Did my grandfather golf?"

To his surprise, the trepidation he felt discussing her grandparents earlier in the day is gone, replaced by the good mood spending the afternoon with his daughter has bestowed upon him. He answers without hesitation.

"I don't know about your mom's father. She never knew her parents. But my father? No he did not. He had a pretty clear opinion about the type of man who would pull on knickers and chase a ball around for leisure."

"But he chased fish?"

"Fishing wasn't leisure to him."

"What was it?"

"It was church. It was how he remained part of the food chain. It was how he kept close to nature. Putting a fly rod in his hand was almost transformative."

"What's 'transformative'?"

"It means it could change him. Your grandfather was not a particularly sympathetic character."

"What's 'sympathetic'?"

"What exactly do they teach you in school? It's not vocabulary." He smiles to show he is joking.

"Be serious, Pop."

"It means your grandfather wasn't very likable. I only saw him happy once or twice in all the years I knew him, both times on a trout stream. He only loved two things in this world. Fishing was one of them."

"Were *you* the other?"

"No. I wasn't."

Lewis keeps his eyes on the road as they drive. He can hear the rustle of paper as she opens the bag again, the golf balls clicking like ice cubes.

"How come you never talk about him?"

"I thought we *were* talking about him."

"But you don't usually."

He takes a deep breath, buying time. It's like licking a finger and holding it to the wind, trying to get a sense for which direction his mood might turn. Spending the afternoon with his daughter was good for him. He thinks the weather will hold.

"OK, pal. What do you want to know?"

Before she can respond, a silver Prius launches out of a side street like a silent, clumsy turtle, cutting them off. Lewis swears loudly and locks the brakes. The truck skids sidelong, lurching them forward in their seats. They strain against their seat belts—not hard enough to hurt, but abruptly enough to startle them—and the paper bag in Gray's lap tips, spilling golf balls that cascade onto the floor of the cab.

"You OK?"

"Yes."

"You sure?"

"Yes."

Lewis checks his mirrors and pulls forward. The golf balls roll across the floor like bilge water in a skiff, bumping against the doors and the supports beneath the seats. The sound surrounds them, coming from everywhere and nowhere at once. He pulls into a parking lot, and together they retrieve them, piling them back into the bag. But when they pull out of the lot a few minutes later, they can still hear one rolling around, a stray that somehow found its way beneath the floor panel and into the frame.

When they get home, he spends a fruitless hour with a flashlight looking around the truck. He looks under the seats, everywhere he can. Though he knows it's there, he never sees it. A reminder, he supposes, that some things are impossible to find even though you're sure they exist.

10

That night they lie in bed in a quiet house, Gray and the dog asleep in her room.

"I can feel your heartbeat," Janey says, her head on his chest.

"How's it feel?"

"Slow."

She used to joke about it, how his resting heartbeat hovered somewhere between comatose and dead. But this time there's no joking, and they lie there in the silence until it feels like there's something else there. Something that won't leave on its own.

"What are you thinking, J?"

"Oh. I don't know. I had a conversation with Gray tonight, while I was cooking dinner. She asked why she doesn't have brothers or sisters."

"She asked me the same thing earlier."

Janey takes a deep breath in the dark beside him. He feels her body tense against his. She's so much smaller than he is, but somehow so much bigger too. Half a minute passes before she lets the air out again in a long, lingering breath. Then she lifts her head from his chest.

"I want another baby, Lewis."

It is not what he expected. It is not at all what he expected, and she knows it. She puts her head back on his chest, puts her hand beside it, and measures his heartbeat.

"Not so calm anymore," she says.

The Old Man taught him to hunt by taking him up for long walks in the New Hampshire woods to show him how to walk quietly, how to look before every step. You have to know where you are putting your foot to know what impact it will have—a rustle of leaves or a twig snapping is enough to scare deer away. He taught him, too, how to look for the deer.

"You can't just scour the woods for 'em," he said, "because those fuckers are designed to hide. They got antlers that look like tree branches. Coats the color of dirt and bark. You could trip over one and think it's a fuckin' log. The trick is, you got to widen your focus. Make it bigger instead of smaller. Try to see the entire forest."

It's no different hunting for the truth. Sometimes you have to tread softly and quietly and figure out a way to see it. As he often does in such moments, he waits for the right answer to reveal itself.

Does Gray want a brother or sister? She has no family beyond him and Janey. Fenwick. No siblings, no grandparents, no aunts or uncles, no cousins. Lewis himself grew up the same way, with one fewer parent and a lot less love. He would have given anything for any one of those things, any family at all. But he's also thinking about Mr. Happy, and Janey, and their belief that happiness is a choice. All day he's been questioning his own choices, every one that he's made over the years. Because the fact is, he's not happy and he's never been happy. Not a day in his life. At times he's found a kind of contentment. And certainly he's experienced joy. But happiness? *No.* He's sure of it. And he wonders if maybe he's made the choice to be unhappy without knowing it. If maybe he's fucked up somewhere along the way.

Would another child make him happy? If it will make Janey and Gray happy, maybe that's reason enough to say yes.

Isn't it?

But he remembers, too, the darkness that follows him. How he's afraid of passing it on. How much work it is, all of it, every day. And he knows he's found the answer, knows that he does not want another child—not the way a child should be wanted.

Taking a deep breath of his own, he holds it and lets another half-minute pass.

Janey will wait until he answers her. She will wait forever. And when he does speak she will listen to his words carefully, scrutinizing his tone. If he is going to speak at all, he knows he'd better do it with conviction. He does not want to speak any other way.

A minute passes. Then another. And another.

After a while, he gets up and goes for a run.

11

A rare day: no clients booked, no place to be. A morning without obligation, the unfamiliar luxury of time. Still he's up and dressed before first light. Staring at feathers at the fly-tying bench in the garage, he sips his coffee slowly, trying to savor it in a way he rarely bothers. But the coffee is bitter and unpleasant, and the bitterness frustrates him. It's the same coffee he makes every day. The same water. The taste is an illusion, he knows. An artifact. A proxy. His body's way of reminding him how badly he mishandled his conversation with Janey last night.

Tying flies to distract himself, he loses track of time until he hears her minivan start outside. He lifts open the garage door, hoping to catch her and make amends, but she's already halfway down the driveway, backing into the street and leaving for work without even a wave.

In the house he finds a note. It buoys him until he sees it's just a laundry list of tasks she's left him for his day off. That sinks him a little deeper—he's getting off easy and he knows it.

Emptying the dregs from his mug, he pours a second cup, which tastes even worse. Like the motor oil he drains from the truck, thick as mud and filled with tiny metal shavings. Lewis sweetens it with a little Old Crow. Just a finger or two. He takes a sip of the coffee and it's just as bad. It's still his mind fucking with him, he knows, but he throws it in the sink anyway, a dark cloud against the white porcelain sky. Then he refills the mug with the bourbon, sweetens it with a little coffee, and takes a sip.

That, at last, tastes better. He drains half the mug and tops it again with coffee.

Gray strolls into the kitchen wearing the Red Sox sweatshirt and shorts she sleeps in, her hair matted on one side and standing upright on the other. Johnson follows her in and lies down at her feet, big head on big paws, rattling the dishes in the cupboards. When the dog exhales, he can feel her breath from across the room.

"Morning," he says.

"Do you have any pictures?"

"Pictures?"

"Of my grandparents."

Resurrecting a conversation he thought dead is like resurrecting the dead themselves, summoning ghosts. They pass through him with a chill that raises the hairs on his neck, the bumps on his skin. He takes a sip and swears the coffee's gone cold again.

"No. I don't have any pictures."

"Why not?"

"Your grandfather—my father—was neither sentimental nor nostalgic."

"What's 'nostalgic'?"

"It means he didn't care about things like feelings. He didn't bother with things like memories. And he sure as hell didn't take any pictures."

Lewis stares at his daughter staring at him until he realizes she's waiting for him to elaborate.

"He had pictures of my mother. Your grandmother. From their wedding. I saw them once, but I wasn't supposed to." When Lewis tugs at the memory, waking for school and going downstairs to find The Old Man passed out at the kitchen table, it feels like it was only yesterday, the image of his father face down on a tear-stained wedding album, surrounded by empty bottles, strong and clear. "He kept them to himself. He kept them hidden."

Hearing something in his tone, maybe, Gray cocks her head and looks at him, just like Janey does. So much of him in his daughter and so much of his wife. How those influences choose which moment to express themselves will always be a mystery to him. He can only hope that there's a method to it, and that the right ones pick the right times to reveal themselves.

Their eyes meet. They stare at each other, neither looking away, each of them trying to read the other's expression. And then it turns into a staring contest. Lewis Yaw does not lose staring contests.

"Can you look?"

"What's that?"

"Can you look and see if you have any pictures?"

"I don't think I do, Gray, but I'll look."

"Promise?"

"I promise."

"Now, Pop? Will you look *now*?"

"I'll *look*," he says, his voice several degrees too sharp. He follows it with a sigh. Though he's endlessly patient as a fisherman and guide, in most other aspects of his life, his natural instinct is toward shortness, as if he's spent all his capital on the water, all his patience, and every other transaction is a deficit.

The Old Man was the same way; Lewis knows what it feels to be on the receiving end, knows what it feels to be a constant thorn in someone's foot, and does not want his daughter to know that feeling.

"I'll look," he says, more gently, pouring more coffee into the mug.

"Thanks." Then she gives him another funny look and glares at the bottle of bourbon he's holding. It's not even eight a.m.

Lewis takes a sip. The coffee has gone cold again.

———

Janey pulls into the driveway while he's rifling through boxes in the garage. She stands in the doorway and looks at him expectantly.

"What are you looking for?"

"Pictures for Gray."

"Pictures of what?"

"I don't really know." When Janey continues to stare, he stops what he's doing and gives her his full attention. "She's been asking about her grandparents lately. She asked for pictures."

Janey nods. She's keeping her distance, he notices. Normally she'd jump in and find a solution, offer to help. But she's letting him deal with it. Still punishing him.

"Do you know what a sacrificial zinc is?" he asks her.

"No."

"Saltwater corrodes metal, right? It's ruthless. To prevent the electrochemical reaction that causes it, you fit the metal parts of seagoing boats with disposable pieces of a metal alloy with a more negative reduction potential to draw away the corrosion."

She says nothing but lifts a single eyebrow.

"The saltwater consumes the inexpensive fittings instead of the engine, propeller, or on a metal boat, the hull itself. Technically, it's called a galvanic or cathodic protection system, but fishermen call them sacrificial zincs."

"Lewis," she says.

"I'm just looking for some picture I can give her that will get her off my back about this. A sacrificial zinc."

"There's just the one."

"That's what I told her. My father."

"Not one *grandparent*, Lewis. One *picture*."

"I didn't keep any."

"No," she says. "*You* didn't." Janey stares at him until he understands.

"Where is it?"

"There's a box marked Old Medical Bills. Get it down."

He scans the labels on the wall of boxes, the winter clothing, the Christmas decorations, Gray's old schoolwork, until he finds the one she wants and opens it.

"Flat on the bottom," she says, still in the doorway.

From underneath all the other files, Lewis fishes out an unmarked manila envelope. Inside are two prints. One is a black-and-white of him and The Old Man in the driveway holding trophy-sized trout, just back from a weekend in the woods. A neighbor took it with his new twin-lens Yashica and left it in their mailbox after he developed and printed it. The other is an old Kodachrome eight-by-ten of the house Lewis grew up in back in Massachusetts. *Photography is capturing light, but some moments are without light at all*, he thinks, looking again at the picture of him and his father. Without a word, he puts it back in the envelope and closes the box. The house in the other photo is small, yellow, and unexceptional, but his stomach churns just looking at it. Gray has none of his associations.

For her it's a thread to a past that's only hypothetical. Maybe it will be enough to satisfy her newfound curiosity.

"This will do," he says. "Thanks."

But when he looks up, she's already gone.

———

Gray is still in her pajamas when he calls her into the kitchen. She looks first at him and then at her mother.

"You got your hair done, Mom," she says. "I like it."

Lewis looks at Janey. "You did?"

"Jeez, Pop. It's a lot shorter. It's different on both sides. It looks so good, Mom."

He studies his wife, trying to spot the difference, but cannot see it.

"I like it," he says. Janey narrows her eyes.

"I found this for you, Gray." He holds up the photo. "It's not much, but it's something."

She and Janey come around to stand beside him and the three of them study the photo together, the overgrown front lawn, the weathered and chipped paint, the old truck in the driveway. The print is scratched and faded, showing nearly as much neglect as the house itself.

"Did I live there?"

"No, honey. You were born *here*, in this house."

"Did you live there, Mom?"

"No. That's the house where your father grew up. Where he lived with your grandfather. That's where he lived when I met him."

"That was my bedroom," Lewis says, leaning over Gray's shoulder to point at the upstairs window to the right of the front door.

"The two windows and the front door make it look like it's smiling," Gray says.

Lewis tenses involuntarily. Janey puts a reassuring hand on his back, surprising him. He welcomes it.

"I don't think that house is smiling, pal."

"Can I hang this? In my bedroom?"

"Why?"

"I don't know," she says. "I like it."

"Are you sure, honey?"

"I'm sure, Mom."

"Lewis? Is that OK?"

"If that's what she wants."

He takes the photo back out to the garage and staples together a simple frame from unfinished scrap wood and a pane from an old window. He mats it with cardboard, mounts the print, and hangs it on a single nail over her bed. Then they all stand together staring at it some more.

"Who lives there now, Pop?"

He hesitates before answering, not long enough for her to notice but long enough for Janey to. Again she puts her hand on his back, a firm, gentle pressure.

"I don't know, pal."

It's not a lie. Maybe The Old Man still lives there, the walls hardened with smoke, the windows brittle with bitterness, the scratched linoleum buried beneath a field of empty beer cans. Maybe he's long gone, dead, moved on someplace, back to Vermont. Maybe the house itself is long gone, too, razed and carted away like the shuttered mill, the lot graded and rezoned and filled with some thin-walled cookie-cutter McMansion with walk-in closets and a TV the size of Delaware. Or maybe he passed out with a Lucky Strike in his mouth and burned it— and himself—to the ground.

"That must be why it's sad."

"Sad?"

"The house looks sad."

"I thought you said it was smiling."

"It is. It's even yellow, like a happy face. But it's not a happy smile." She reaches up and traces a curved line across the house, like a frown. "I think the house is sad."

"I can see that," Janey says. "I could *always* see that."

"How about you, Pop?"

He says nothing, not for a long minute, long enough for the silence to become conspicuous. They both turn to look at him.

"Lewis?" Janey says.

"It's just a house."

12

Jimmy used to make fighters run in weighted vests, twenty-five pounds of lead ballast strapped to their chests like bombs. When Lewis runs that night, it feels like he's built his own vest, the weight he carries heavier than anything Jimmy ever asked of him. With each stride it pulls him down to the earth, heavy as history itself. There's no moon. The night is fiercely dark. Shadows cling to him like cobwebs as he runs.

The forest road is treacherous, the river path even worse. Worried about turning an ankle or twisting a knee, he crosses back across the footbridge toward town. When he hears the river beneath him through the slats of the bridge, it sounds like it's laughing at him.

At the park he runs on grass already damp with dew. When he reaches the street, the ground beneath him is steadier, but the streetlights create shadows that change shape and direction as he runs. It's disorienting how the shadows twist and move, sidling past in his peripheral vision, spinning and bobbing. Several times, as he nears the narrow end of the anaerobic funnel, he thinks he sees something following him. Each time he stops to look and finds nothing but shadow. By the time he turns for home, he's exhausted.

At Greer Lane, he rounds the corner onto his street and stops short. There's something lying in the road. Something big. Much bigger than him, sprawled in an ungainly pile as if it fell from a great height.

Moving closer tentatively, he can see splayed limbs but the shapes do not make sense to him. They don't conform to any pattern that makes the creature recognizable. *Maybe it's not recognizable*, he thinks, still gasping for breath. Maybe his confusion is not a trick of the light or an artifact of his own inability to process his vision but the reality of this monster lying in the street by his house.

He takes out the small flashlight he carries in his fatigues and steps closer still, tracing the light across the bulk until he finds the eye. Large and unblinking, it reflects the light back at him. From there he finds the ears, the antlers, the beard, and knows that it's an elk. But the shape of it confuses him. It's got the head of an elk, but what beast makes up its body?

Stepping around it, he follows the shadows that surround the animal with the light, but the shadows don't disappear. They're not shadows at all but a growing, amorphous tide of blood that stains the pavement as it spills out of the elk's devastated body. When he puts a finger in the spreading pool, the blood is still warm. He sees, too, why the shape confuses him. The animal has been split open and pulled apart, its insides exposed in a grotesque display. The way it is twisted, he thinks its spine might be broken.

Only two creatures are capable of such an act: man, and bear. Shining the light into the shadows around him, he's unsure which is responsible, and equally unsure which possibility unsettles him more.

13

They load the Previa until it's stuffed like a toy box and drive west across the state to Astoria, where the broad mouth of the Columbia River—and fog thick as gruel—separates Oregon from Washington. From there they make their way south along the Pacific Coast Highway, four nights, four towns, eleven light-houses, and dozens of beaches. Some are vast and rocky, others sandy, windswept expanses, each of them ragged-edged and unrefined, as if the forces of nature that shaped the contours of North America—the forests, the prairies, the mountains, the plains—lost motivation before reaching the edge of the continent, leaving a coast that's beautiful but unfinished, raw, an eternal argument between water and earth.

In Newport, they walk through the commercial fishing harbor and stop to watch a lazy orgy of sea lions. Piled atop one another on the docks, scores of them flop and bark and bare their teeth, their donkey cries carrying throughout the bayside town.

"What about them?" Gray asks her father, always testing him. "What do you call them?"

"A colony. A crash. A hurdle. A bob."

"What about eagles?" she wants to know, pointing at one high over the city hillside.

"A convocation."

"Starfish?"

"A constellation," he says. Janey looks at him skeptically. "I think."

They play Frisbee on Nye Beach, throwing every third or fourth time for the aging dog, who chases it into the water and emerges from the surf like Godzilla on the shores of Tokyo. When she's too tired, she buries it in the sand. Lewis and Gray put on baseball gloves and matching Red Sox caps and play catch while Janey reads, swaddled in a blanket in a beach chair. They watch surfers in black wet suits sign the foamy pages of the breaking waves. A hot day at the Oregon coast means luke-warm and windy, while a cold day means cold and windy, the difference between summer and winter sometimes just twenty degrees and a measurable wind speed.

The ocean is the temperature of a melting Popsicle. Un-daunted, Gray splashes around in it while Lewis fishes in thick neoprene waders, casting flies into the froth for surf perch, sea-run cutthroat trout, rockfish.

"You don't like to swim, Pop?"

"It's too cold."

"If I can handle it, you can handle it."

"She's right, Lewis," Janey says without looking up from her book.

"What do you call a bunch of chickens?"

"Or just one?"

"Don't you know who I am?" he says, stripping off his waders and shirt. "I'm Lewis Yaw, King of the Ocean. Let's see how tough you really are, pal. First one out of the water loses."

"Deal," Gray says, and they race into the surf side by side. They laugh and shriek as the cold strikes from below, gripping from the inside out. Lewis dives under immediately, but Gray wades in with a sustained sound that's half laugh, half moan. He surfaces near her, pops under again, and surfaces behind her, splashing her with an armful of the icy Pacific. The sheer joy distracts her from the cold.

But within minutes he can see her shivering, her skin tone notably bluer. His own frigid limbs have become abstract ideas he can no longer feel or control.

"Are you getting out, Pop?" He hears the hope in her voice. Despite her gangliness, evident in her green swimsuit, his daughter is tough. Stubborn. Watching her fight the pain, he recognizes something in her.

"Why would I get out? This water is beautiful. It's like taking a bath."

She sticks it out, shivering visibly. Her laughter has stopped, her mood changed. This is not fun for her anymore.

"Maybe when we get out and dry off, we should go for ice cream," he says. She says nothing, shaking uncontrollably, staring him down. Still he shows no sign of getting out.

"I give up!" she yells and wades to shore, where Janey greets her with a waiting towel and the embrace of her warm blanket.

Lewis turns his back to them and stares out at the ocean, the horizon broken only by a handful of sails and the boxy silhouette of a tanker. The Old Man used to sing a drunken nursery rhyme about a sailor who went to sea to see what he could see, but all that he could see was sea, sea, sea. He used to take Lewis camping. They fished together around New England. They hunted deer and birds in New Hampshire and Maine. But none of these trips was a vacation—they never had one of those. He'd seen his father pass out, almost too drunk, even, to breathe, but he'd never seen him relax. He kept his boots on until the moment he got into bed.

Lewis has spent his whole life trying to not be like his father. But every day he finds his fingerprints someplace new. As he wills himself not to feel the cold of the ocean, he knows that it's something The Old Man would do: refuse to show weakness, refuse to admit pain. The realization makes the water too cold for him to bear. He's made his point.

But it's against his nature to surrender. Though his insides are like shattered ice that has refrozen and shattered again, he ignores the pain as long as he can and wades calmly back to his family, revealing no sign of struggle. Gray is huddled under the blanket, pouting and shivering at the same time.

"Congratulations," Janey says as she hands him a towel. "You beat a ten-year-old. You must be very proud."

———

The darkness both repels and beckons him. The only way he knows to fight it off is to keep running, so he runs the streets while his wife and daughter sleep, long miles along dark beaches where the tide licks the shore. He explores the harbors, where fishermen ready gear beneath sodium lights, breathing in diesel and the smell of fish and paint.

When he's done, he wakes Gray for breakfast so Janey can sleep in, taking her out for coffee and donuts.

"Cup of joe and a side of dough. Breakfast of champions."

Looking skeptical, she watches him empty his flask into his mug when the waitress turns her back.

"Then what's that?"

"Breakfast of the gods."

After they eat, they walk on the beach. Seagulls on patrol

strut and rise into the air, dropping again in a flurry of wings and a chorus of squawks, looking for food, maybe, or fulfilling some genetic purpose. Maybe they're just bored.

"What do you call a group of seagulls, pal?"

"A murder."

"That's crows."

"A flock?"

"A flock. A colony. A flotilla. A swoop. A scavenging. A screech. A squabble."

"A squabble is my favorite."

"It's the sound they make. An onomatopoeia of birds."

"What's bears?"

"A sleuth."

"Ducks?"

"A badling, a paddling, a raft, a plump."

She thinks hard, trying to stump him.

"What about flies?"

"A business of flies," he says, one of his favorites. He likes how it recognizes the somber, corporate gathering around rotting flesh, their capitalistic relationship with death, their supervisory relationship with maggots.

The sand yields beneath them as they walk, the shifting ground undecided. Gray falls behind, walking with her head down and trying to match his strides. She jumps from boot-print to bootprint, able to fit both feet in one of his. When he curves toward the water, just above the tide line, his footsteps disappear moments after he leaves them, a palimpsest of wet sand. No longer able to follow his, she creates her own path, running tight circles around him.

The tide is out. They peer into tide pools looking for starfish, beach glass, crabs. The diffraction bends the light, distorts the perspective, giving the pools the look of another world. He's always known there to be a world beneath the water.

"What do you say, kiddo? Get home to your mother?"

"OK."

When they turn back, the wind is in their faces and the going notably harder. The breeze lifts sand and water and swirls it around them, sucking them in. Gray is quiet, her expression serious, as if her mood has turned with the wind. After a while, she stops and looks him in the eyes.

"What are those marks?"

"What marks?"

"When we went swimming yesterday. You took your shirt off. All the marks on you, on your front and your back. Are those from boxing?"

Behind her, the Pacific stretches as far as he can see, vast and deep, all the way to the horizon. The largest ocean in the world. It hides untold things—shipwrecks, creatures, fault lines—but it won't hide him. Billions and billions of gallons of water and still not enough to wash away the past. Every time he thinks he's thrown it far enough to sink it, the tide washes it ashore again.

"No. Those are from when I was a kid. About your age."

"You had an accident?"

"It wasn't an accident."

"Did you hurt yourself on purpose?"

"No. Someone else did."

Her eyes widen like the sea as her features sink like the sand. For a moment he both loves her for her empathy and resents her for her pity, an impulse he forces himself to reject. In her unblinking eyes, he sees himself, six years old, seven, too young, not young enough, waking to an unfamiliar sound. A sound that frightened him. He sees himself climbing out of bed and tiptoeing down the dark hallway to his father's bedroom door.

He sees himself opening it, despite his fear, and entering to the smell of foul air, whiskey, sweat. He remembers his father curled on the floor, clutching some silky piece of clothing, sobbing into it. How he stood there, paralyzed, as The Old Man looked up at him, his face wet, and said, "I miss her." Lewis was too young to understand what he was witnessing, too inexperienced in the ways of the world and all its disappointments. But even then he knew that nothing good would come of it. Even then he knew that seeing his father helpless and exposed would cost him. The Old Man would make him pay for seeing his weakness.

Gray takes her father's hand, big enough to swallow her own, and her cold skin snaps him back to the present.

"Whoever did that to you? I hope you hurt them back."

Then she lets go of his hand and resumes walking.

Lewis follows her after a minute. He has to hurry to catch up.

III

NATURE IS AN ASSHOLE

14

Morning finds them on the river. Lewis broods in the stern, his mood uncertain, a riotous weather vane pointing everywhere and nowhere at all, while Gray chats with the client near the bow. She's been apprenticing with him as a guide for a few years now, weekends and summers, and she's a natural. Today's client—a graceful widow from Boise using her husband's life insurance settlement to travel to all the rivers he fished in his lifetime, as if hoping to pluck not just steelhead and trout from their waters but memories of him too—takes to Gray immediately. She handles the gear expertly, finds fish and directs the woman's casts with a gentle and instructive confidence. She even takes the time to point out moments of natural beauty: a dragonfly resting on the shell of a basking turtle, a shaft of sunlight on a copse of shore willow. Lewis oars quietly, content to let his daughter lead. She gets the guiding experience; he gets to sink uninterrupted into his own thoughts.

At least until another boat rounds the upstream bend. Lewis steels himself for Littlejohn, whose presence, he knows, will strip all the uncertainty from his mood. But it's just The Adventures of Wheatfall and Fuckface with a pair of hapless-looking clients sandwiched between them.

God help anyone who manages to look hapless around Fuckface.

The boat approaches. Wheatfall maintains a respectful distance so as to not tangle lines or interfere with casting and ships his oars.

"It's Iditarod day," he says.

The excitement in his voice carries easily across the water. Lewis perks up.

"Today?"

"You know it."

"Where's the start?"

"The Taco Truck. You in?"

"Of course we're in," he says.

Wheatfall executes a crisp salute. Lewis returns it. Gray shoots him an inquisitive look, but he shakes his head.

Not in front of the client.

A few other boats pass that morning. Each of the guides shares the same message, and with it, a thrum of energy and anticipation that builds throughout the day until it's almost audible, like a chorus of cicadas in the trees along the banks. If their client is curious, she does not show it—she's focused on fishing for any signs of her dead husband's presence in the Terrebonne—but Gray is. Lewis sees it in the way she keeps looking back at him, trying to read his mood.

They limit out around two. It takes another half hour to reach the Taco Truck, the local name for the takeout on the river bend where a blowdown folded a boat perfectly in half when the guide failed to outrow a storm current.

Most of the other guides are already there, trucks and trailers parked in an orderly line and dripping onto the dirt and gravel of the forest road. The remainder arrive while he and

Gray trailer their own boat and join the formation. It has taken a heroic effort by Fenwick's Flying Monkeys to shuttle all the trucks and empty trailers to the same takeout and the clients back to town, and Lewis knows Wheatfall will reward them by waiting until they return to start the festivities.

"You going to tell me what the Iditarod is?" Gray asks him once they are in line.

"It's a famous sled dog race in Alaska."

"I know that. And?"

"Wait and see, Gray."

With so many guides and their rigs at a single takeout, a minor chaos feels inevitable, but they're all in good spirits, talking, laughing, comparing notes on the day's clients and sharing fishing reports. Several of the trucks have coolers in the beds. Beers are passed around, and Fuckface offers one to Gray.

"Vitamin R," he says, handing her a can of Rainier so cold it hurts to hold.

She looks at her father and he nods.

"It's OK." Watching her take a tentative sip, he wonders if she's ever tasted beer before. He remembers his own first time, finishing one of The Old Man's after he'd passed out in the kitchen to see what the cans that held such sway on his father's life contained. But Gray seems more curious about the activity around her than the can in her hand.

When the shuttle van arrives and all the Flying Monkeys spill out, Wheatfall climbs onto the roof of the truck at the front of the line and whistles for attention. He's the ringmaster. The emcee. The guides mill forward to stand around him and he greets them from his perch.

"Welcome to the Iditarod," he yells.

The crowd cheers.

"You know the rules," he yells, and most of the guides answer in unison, a call and response.

"There are no rules!"

"That's right! But let me go over them just the same."

Another cheer.

"They're very simple. Racers compete in the order in which they're parked. Drivers keep a straight line, no matter what. The audience votes with its voices."

Another cheer.

"And how is the winner determined?" Wheatfall asks, playing to the crowd.

The crowd plays along. "There is no winner!"

"That's right! And why is there no winner?"

"Because we're all a bunch of losers!"

Wheatfall is obviously enjoying himself, and so is Gray— whatever is about to happen, Lewis knows, she's ready for it.

"Since my nephew and I got here first, we go first," Wheatfall says. The guides shout again as he leaps down into the bed of the truck and clambers across the trailer tongue into the boat. A Flying Monkey throws him a football helmet in the regional school colors, and Wheatfall takes off his baseball hat, folds it into his pocket, and straps the helmet on.

"Let's get closer," Lewis says as Fuckface climbs into the driver's seat.

The forest road runs straight for about a half mile, paralleling the river, and they walk ahead with some of the other guides, lining both shoulders for a few hundred yards. Fenwick joins them, a beer in each hand. When Lewis takes one, he replaces it with another from his back pocket.

"First dog sled race, Hoss?"

"I guess so."

"You're going to love it."

Fuckface starts the truck. He revs the engine. Wheatfall unties the painter line from the bow of the boat and walks it back to stand near the stern, facing forward. Pulling the line tight, he wraps it around his fist a couple of times and braces himself.

"Ready," he yells. The guides cheer.

Fuckface hits the gas and the big truck accelerates, pulling the boat down the forest road. With minimal shocks, the trailer reacts to every heave and rut, rocking and swaying to its own momentum. Wheatfall leans back against the force of gravity, whooping like a rodeo rider and gripping the painter tightly as he fights to keep his balance. The rush of guides shout and clap and raise their bottles as he passes. When Fuckface hits a pothole deep enough to crater a compact car, the truck lists hard to port and the trailer bucks starboard, throwing Wheatfall into the air. For a moment he floats weightless above the boat—it's almost beautiful, Lewis thinks, or a kind of beauty, at least—before crashing ass-first, hard, into the deck of the boat. Which, if he's being honest, is another kind of beauty altogether. Fuckface brakes the truck. Wheatfall climbs slowly to his feet in a cloud of road dust, raises his skinny arms overhead in victory, and the guides shout and rush to meet him.

Each guide who wants one gets a turn. The rides grow more daring as they progress, bolstered by confidence, by peer pressure, by beer. The mystery gone, Gray laughs and shouts with the others.

"How long has this been going on?" she asks.

"Wheatfall went to Alaska a few years ago and came back with the idea."

"How come I'm just learning about it now?"

He smiles at her. "Because you weren't a guide until now, Gray."

When it's their turn, someone hands him a helmet.

"I'd let you go, but your mother would kill me," he tells her. "She'd kill us both."

"That doesn't mean you can't drive," he says, buckling the strap beneath his chin.

"Me?"

"Nothing to it. You heard Wheatfall. Go a little faster than you're comfortable with, and keep it in a straight line."

"Come on, Hoss," her uncle says. "I'll ride shotgun."

The crowd cheers as they climb into the truck. Lewis pulls himself up into the boat, takes hold of the painter, and yells to Gray.

Through the back window, he can see her watching him in the rearview mirror. She drives slowly at first and the crowd boos. When she finds her confidence, she floors it. He grips the line around his fist tightly as the boat bucks beneath him. Lewis sways with it, his years of footwork in the boxing ring a boon to his balance.

The trees and guides pass in a blur. The push of air against his face, the adrenaline, the beer, the speed, all of it a dizzying rush he takes deep inside him like a breath. He closes his eyes, which intensifies the experience, exaggerating each pitch and yaw of the boat, creating a kind of gravitational hyperbole. The speed increases, or seems to, until it feels like time itself is passing, as if he is moving not along a forest road but across the years to an earlier point in his life when mortality has not yet occurred to him and life remains more possibility than reminiscence. The boat bobs beneath him, an alive and wild beast he rides to the past, further and further, to his thirties, his twenties, to high school, childhood, until he begins to wonder if he can ride it until he erases himself completely.

And then, just for a moment, he stops thinking.

For just a moment, his mind is at rest.

For a moment, he just *is*. The feeling is like nothing he's ever felt before. Undiluted. Uncomplicated. Pure.

And then Gray locks up the brakes. The truck jitters to a stop, spewing a rooster tail of gravel dust as Lewis opens his eyes to find himself sailing over the prow and down onto the road itself. He lands hard, rolls, and skids to the shoulder.

He's firmly back in the present and everything hurts. The guides have gone quiet, waiting. Gray and Fenwick open the doors and leap out of the truck.

"Pop?" she says, looking anxious.

He gives her a thumbs-up and the guides cheer.

"Who's next?" Wheatfall shouts with glee.

15

Having learned to see the world from between raised fists at an early age, it was inevitable that Lewis would fight at school. He despised bullies—an impulse he didn't need the school psychologist to explain—and the school itself seemed, to him, an industrial plant designed to manufacture them. Among them was Patrick McGonaghy, a dim-witted asshole with an overbite and sharp elbows Lewis had known since first grade. An early puberty gave him muscled arms, a longer reach, and the mystique of dark hairs on his upper lip. Next to Tommy Lambert, who had a stutter and skin thin enough to reveal the green lines of his veins, McGonaghy looked like a professional wrestler in his forties. Lambert looked like he'd been born too early to be fully formed. When McGonaghy tripped him in the hallway between classes, Lewis—who had also begun to grow at an earlier age than his peers and showed no sign of stopping—hit him square in the face.

Mr. Finneran, the English teacher, pulled them apart, dragging Lewis into his classroom and pinning him against the blackboard. Lewis had thirty pounds and six inches on him, but the teacher lifted him like a linen bathrobe and hung him in the chalk dust. Finneran had been a Golden Gloves champion at Rutgers. He had a forehead like the Giza pyramid, hair-darkened arms thick as undersea cables. When Lewis spit out his defense, a confusion of adrenaline and injustice, he looked disappointed.

"Mr. McGonaghy is an asshole with a bright future in floor mopping. But it's not your job to police him, Mr. Yaw."

"So I'm supposed to just let him get away with being an asshole?"

"You could spend your whole life fighting assholes, Mr. Yaw, and achieve nothing."

"But—"

"There are courses of intervention or remedial action you might choose other than violence."

"Some people only understand violence."

"On that we agree, Mr. Yaw. Don't be that guy."

Hearing the familiar phrase had a strangely calming effect on Lewis. The Old Man said it with spite, singling out people he felt were too pathetic or despicable to deserve to exist. But when Finneran said it, it felt like an opportunity. It felt like a challenge.

Letting go of Lewis's shirt, he smoothed out the fabric and brushed chalk from his shoulders. Then he leaned over his desk and wrote a name and address on a piece of note paper.

"There are two men in your future, Mr. Yaw. It's up to you to decide which you become. You've just demonstrated one of them. It's my belief that that's the wrong one. It takes more strength to pull yourself out of the ditch than to walk around it in the first place."

"Who is this?"

"I want you to go see him."

"What is he? A therapist or something?"

"Something like that. Promise me you'll go."

"I don't—"

"Promise me, Mr. Yaw. Can you do that?"

Lewis shrugged. Finneran nodded. A kind of receipt, the promise made and noted.

That afternoon he walked two miles across the river to a graffitied door in a crumbling mill building shrugging like a shoulder over the muddy bank. Brick dust hung in the air, and passing traffic shook the sidewalk. Inside, he walked down a long hallway that opened into a cavernous room and blinked until his eyes adjusted to the light. When they did, he saw not a therapist's office but a boxing gym. The onslaught of sweat and restrained chaos felt peculiarly familiar. Guys working heavy bags and mitts, chinning themselves on hanging bars, skipping rope. The squeak of rubber soles, the dull slap of gloves on flesh. He could hear fighters panting like the sweaty breath of the gym itself, the rhythm of the speed bags its thrumming heartbeat.

In the center were two raised canvas rings elevated above the training floor. Lewis watched, transfixed by the two lean boys in headgear ducking, bobbing, and swinging.

"I help you, kid?" Lewis turned to find a man with a body like a beer keg and a face like a cheese grater.

"I'm looking for Jimmy Bruce. My English teacher sent me."

"Finneran?"

"You know him?"

"I trained him. Had a left like a dump truck in a slingshot. Footwork like Sammy Davis Jr."

"Was he good?"

"Nah. Poor bastard had Sammy Davis Jr.'s eyesight too."

Jimmy showed him around and introduced him to the other trainers, career boxers with iron arms and soft guts, noses like melting candles.

"Finneran sent him," he said each time, and each time Lewis saw how the other men took note. An insight, that an English teacher could command respect from such men.

"Finneran and I have a deal, kid. You keep an A in his class, you train here for free. We got a deal?"

"I already know how to fight."

"Any asshole can fight, kid. We're going to teach you to box."

"What's the difference?"

Jimmy spit onto the floor without looking away from him.

"Learn how to box and you'll never have to fight again."

"OK," Lewis said. "We have a deal."

———

A big teenager with hard fists, Lewis could hit, but he had no defense to speak of. The Old Man hadn't taught him to block punches, just how to cause pain—and, by extension, how to take it. Never how to avoid it.

"Do as much damage as you can as fast as you can," he'd always said, knocking Lewis to the grass, his voice like a skinned knee. "Break his fuckin' nose, or his jaw, or ribs. He can't hurt you if he's in the dirt." He'd taught by example, kicking Lewis where he lay, leaving bootprints on his back. That wasn't boxing. That wasn't even fighting. That was something else entirely. Something predatory. Something feral. Something Lewis struggled to unlearn in the ring.

"Maybe you just like to hit things," Jimmy yelled after pulling Lewis off a bigger fighter with the help of another trainer. It came as a surprise to Lewis that there were lines you did not cross.

But the other side of it was that he knew how to get hit and how to not let it ruin him when he did. Some fighters crumpled like marionettes with their strings cut when they caught a punch wrong. Not Lewis. He took it like medicine. He took it like a deep breath.

He felt like he'd found something he'd been looking his entire miserable life for without even knowing he'd been looking. Boxing felt right to him. Not good, exactly. But he felt like a puzzle piece that had been pressed into the only spot it fit. The punches made sense, the ones he delivered and the ones he received.

Jimmy's face had the texture of a leaf of cabbage. He bore the same expression whether he was yelling at one of his fighters or pondering a ham sandwich for lunch, which made him inscrutable. He liked Lewis's hunger, his strength and instinct, he said, but he went too far sometimes, not trying to beat the other guy so much as break him.

Some things Jimmy would not ask directly, but Lewis knew he wondered them just the same. Who had taught him to fight. Who gave him the bruises he showed up with, the archipelago of scars, a chain of wrinkled islands, the patches of discolored flesh on his chest and back. When Lewis slipped his leash while sparring and went after the other guy with fury, he could see it in Jimmy's eyes later, wondering who it was that he'd been trying to kill. If Lewis started tearing another fighter to pieces, he'd shake the ropes like a toddler in his crib.

"You're a goddamned bucket when you're supposed to be a spigot. Don't drain all that rage at once. Trickle it out."

Leaning in the corner with the water bottle while another trainer peeled Lewis's opponent off the mat, Jimmy would sigh.

"Where the hell you learned to do that? You training somewhere else?"

"No, sir," he said, spitting his mouthguard into Jimmy's hand.

"Next time you call me *sir* you do push-ups."

"Yes, sir."

Jimmy stared until Lewis dropped to the canvas. The gloves forced him to do knuckle push-ups that burned his chest and arms.

"How angry you was, back in the ring?" Jimmy said. "Don't be that guy."

"Finneran says that too."

"Where you think *he* learned it, genius? Teachers start out as students."

The canvas reeked of sweat and blood, of Albolene and bleach. Still, Lewis liked it better than the smell of his own house, the whiskey and burnt meat. The foulness of The Old Man, the stink of disappointment. Resentment like charred wood.

"I'm gonna call you Lou, OK? Takes too much work to say Lewis."

"Sure thing, James," Lewis said between breaths. The trainer laughed.

"I like you, kid."

Another insight, how a nod from a stranger felt better than anything his own father had ever said to him.

———

Jimmy's own claim to fame had been a less-than-illustrious record as a light heavyweight, Eddie told him. Eddie was a trainer who served as the gym's cut man. He was Irish like The Old Man, but Boston Irish, with breath like a furnace, ears that someone turned inside out, hands like blocks of ice. But he was an artist as he wrapped Lewis's hands before a bout, gentle as butterfly wings, twisting the cotton straps like they were gold threads.

"Jimmy was a smart fighter, but a shitty one. Some smart-ass writer started calling him 'Jimmy the Bruise' in the papers 'cause he got hit so much. A nickname like that, even a good fighter can't slip that punch." He mispronounced nearly every word, his Irish brogue and Southie slur in conflict with one another. *Smaht fightah. Paypahs.*

"What happened?"

"Retired five-and-thirty and bought the gym. Been paying it off ever since."

"His Elba."

"His what?"

Lewis spoke differently too. Most of the other boxers had been raised amidst the urban decay of the gym's old mill town. He carried stacks of books from Finneran's class in his duffel with his sweatsuit and gloves and read them during rubdowns or between bouts. The other fighters eyed the books as suspiciously as if they were bombs or filthy diapers. They slid down locker-room benches to avoid them. Lewis knew they tainted him, the simple fact of their presence and his interest in them. But the books gave him hope, something in short demand in his life. He loved boxing, but boxing was not about hope. Boxing was about something different. "How about you, Eddie? Did you have a nickname?"

The trainer swallowed deeply as he wound the wraps around the knuckles, across the palms, snug at the wrist. Do it wrong and the bones would shatter. Do it wrong and you ruin a fighter's career.

"Special Ed."

"How come?"

"'Cause I got hit so much it made me retarded." *Retahded.* Lewis worked to not crack a smile.

"But Jimmy? Man, he has a beautiful mind for boxing.

He can see things in the ring no one else can. He's got a knack for ahticulatin' those things to other fighters, though he could never get his own body to do them. A champion stuck inside a loser's body."

"Like Stephen Hawking."

"Who?"

"The physicist in the wheelchair."

Eddie stared blank-eyed.

"Lou Gehrig's disease," Lewis said.

"Oh, sure. But Lou Gehrig. He was a ballplayer, not a psychiatrlst." The trainer's expression turned grim. "You don't talk like a fighter, Lou," he said, a reminder that no matter how much timc Lewis spent at the gym, he would never belong *there*, either. The first place Lewis truly loved did not love him back. He hoped that someday he would find a place that did, yet to learn that you don't find such places—you make them.

———

He waited until Gray turned thirteen before he gave her boxing gloves. He chose a pair light enough to suit her, and asked her if she wanted to learn. If she said no, he would return them.

"Yes," she said.

"Then follow me into the garage."

While he wrapped her hands, he laid down the law.

"See that heavy bag over there? That bag is the only thing you will hit. You will not punch anything else, and you will not punch *anyone* else. Got it?"

"Got it."

"You will never hit the bag without these gloves, because you'll break your hands. Got it?"

"Got it, Pop."

That summer, he taught her how to punch, focusing on form over power to minimize injury and maximize efficiency. He taught her different punches and made her practice each until they became muscle memory. He taught her to use them together in combinations, calling them out. *Jab, jab, hook. Jab, cross, uppercut.* He taught her footwork to keep her balance, to stay fast and light on her feet, and showed her how the footwork fed the punches and the power. He taught her to work the speed bag, how it rewards rhythm and timing and punishes a lack of concentration. They did it together. He made it fun for her. She enjoyed it, and that made it fun for him too.

Fuck The Old Man.

The more she learned, the more she wanted to learn. He taught her how to block punches, how to slip them, how to use footwork to dance out of their way. When she wanted to start sparring, they cleared it with Janey, who agreed on terms. Light contact only. Gray wears headgear. Lewis pulls his punches. Still, it hurts—he can see it in her eyes when he's rung her bell. He sees, too, how she shakes it off, how she comes back after him. Just like he used to do at Jimmy's. Except at her age he was all temper; she's all calm. All cool. It's a puzzle to solve, a mental exercise. How to get past his defenses. How to clock him. She doesn't connect often, but when she does, she hits him hard. She's fast and agile, with a strong hook and a blinding jab. They've been training a few days a week for three years. It's shaped her shoulders and arms, giving her definition rather than bulk. It's given her confidence.

As he wraps her hands, he tells stories about Finneran, Jimmy, and Special Ed, tells her how if you're lucky, sometimes, something can happen that changes the course of your life. Or someone. The stories make him miss them in a way they wouldn't approve of. They'd like Gray, he knows, even if they wouldn't know what to make of her, of a girl like her. A girl with fists.

Boxing. Fishing. Guiding. She's so good at so many of the same things as him, and better at others. When she brings friends to the house, Lewis sees how easy it is for her, the frictionless ease with which she moves through the world. There's so much of him in her, but so much, too, that astonishes him. He sees Janey in her, too, in her empathy and her kindness, in the lack of cynicism with which she views the world—and for that he is endlessly grateful—but watching her hose out the bilge or clean a fish, or watching the strength she puts behind each cross she throws at the bag, he sees a younger version of himself, female, happy, well-adjusted. Wherever he's going, at forty-three he's more than halfway there, but in Gray he sees a second chance, maybe. Or a legacy.

Don't fuck it up, he tells himself.

Don't be that guy.

She wakes up early every morning before school and goes for a run. He's seen her out there, shadowboxing as she goes. She's got a long stride and good speed. Though she follows a similar path to the one he takes each night, into town and along the river, they never run together. She's never asked, and he's never offered. He doesn't know why *she* doesn't ask, but his own reasons are simple, and nonnegotiable. If there's as much of him in her as he thinks, she might someday need to run to escape the darkness just like him. If that day comes, he doesn't want to slow her down.

16

The day after the Iditarod, Gray has school, leaving Lewis alone
with a boat full of clients from Toronto sufficiently obnoxious
to make him question American foreign relations. On the first
cast, one of them manages to hook himself in the face. Worse, he
spends the rest of the day complaining about it, so Lewis works
twice as hard to keep them happy. By the time they limit out,
they've drunk enough single malt to pickle all the fish they've
caught, drinking from a thirty-two-year-old bottle that cost
more than he'll earn for the day. Scotch old enough to order itself
at a bar. Though he might live his entire life and never understand how the world works, the inequities of it, when they offer
him a cup he declines. Having never tasted anything that old or
expensive, he's afraid a little perspective will ruin cheap whiskey
for him. At the takeout he beaches the boat and watches them
stumble ashore, opening their flies and writing their names in
the sand. It might be the most expensive bathroom break he's
ever witnessed, city boys engaged in one of life's great pleasures,
for a man to piss outside.

That night he drives into town, antsy and unsettled again,

all the joy he'd felt during the Iditarod already gone. Mayflies—a critical insect in the world of fly-fishing—have a lifespan of a single day, but in his experience, the life expectancy of joy is even shorter.

He taps the steering wheel in an uncharacteristic show of nervous energy. "Your motor's running," Janey would tell him. At the Salt Lick, he parks beside Fenwick's truck. A number of the guides' trucks are there, too, including Littlejohn's, so large it's almost an obscenity.

Inside he finds them huddled around a handful of tables dragged together and littered with pitchers, glasses, and ashtrays. Engaged in some kind of serious conversation, their voices are a few measurable decibels louder than any others in the room, louder than the tinny music, even, that pours from the jukebox's shitty speakers. Lewis goes straight to the bar and orders a whiskey that he downs immediately.

"That shot didn't stand a chance." The voice comes from behind him, deep and unpleasant.

"Littlejohn," he says.

"Little late for a married man to be out hitting the bars, ain't it, Yaw? If I had your wife, I'd be home with her."

"If Janey were your wife, she'd be here drinking."

Littlejohn laughs, and even his laugh is unpleasant. He signals Rooster, the bartender, for another round. Rooster has center-parted gray hair feathered over his ears. He carries an oversize plastic comb in the back pocket of his jeans and is constantly peering at his reflection in the big mirror behind the bar, running the bright-red comb across his head. He refills Lewis's bourbon and a second glass beside it for Littlejohn.

"What's with the parley?"

"Deciding what to do about the bear."

"Why now?"

"The Adventures of Wheatfall and Fuckface had a coupla' ladies from Portland in their boat. The bear chased them off a sandbar and into the river. Stole their fish and everything." Littlejohn is built like a chest freezer. Like a brick shithouse. He smells like cheap aftershave and athlete's foot. The tattoos on his arms are buried beneath a thick mat of hair, poorly done, prison-ink style, or maybe Navy like The Old Man's, wavering lines lacking any artistic depth fading with age. By *ladies* he means men of insufficient masculinity.

"Where?"

"Dancer's Elbow." It's a good steelhead run with a graceful bend.

"Anyone hurt?"

"Their fish cooler didn't survive the raid."

Lewis raises his glass.

"To our fallen comrade, Coleman, who gave his life so that others may live."

Littlejohn glares at him without raising his glass.

"That fucking bear is a menace. That's why we're all here tonight. To make plans to get rid of it once and for all."

Lewis signals Rooster, who fills their glasses and then slips his comb from his jeans. Loose flakes of dandruff fall like snow onto the dark wood of the bar.

"So it's not a parley. It's a posse."

"Goddamned right."

"How do you know it's the same bear?"

"Who gives a shit if it's the same bear? This ain't a fucking animal welfare state."

Eventually, most people give you an excuse to like them. Not Littlejohn. He gives only reasons not to, and he seems to seek out lines to cross, as if guiding is what he does for fun but his real job—maybe even his calling—is pissing people off.

Though they've fished the same river for more than a decade, Lewis knows almost nothing about him. He wears fatigues and enough camo to hide a school bus. He believes in black helicopters, vaccination conspiracies, and chemtrails. He loves his country but hates his government. Fenwick says he played in the NFL, or tried to. Made a team but got cut early. Maybe that's the chip he carries around. Or maybe he's just an asshole and always has been—hell, maybe that's why he was cut in the first place. Everything else is speculation. Except that he's a bully, and the worst kind of bully: the kind who never grows out of it. Shorter than Lewis, but bigger, he's big enough to look malformed, as if all the muscles are contracting his body into a semipermanent flex. Arms thick as cordwood. Chest and shoulders trying to tear their way out of his shirt. He works hard to intimidate people, leaning in close and using his size and appearance to violate personal space as a way of reminding them of the threat he poses.

"The only good bear," he says, "is a dead bear."

That need to be menacing is psychological. Pathological, maybe. It's also pathetic. Lewis sips his bourbon.

"They were here first. The bears."

"Well, I'll be here last. It's no different than a rancher defending his cattle from wolves. I'm well within my rights to kill that motherfucker."

"The law disagrees. Fish aren't livestock, they're a natural resource. We have to share them with the birds and the bears, just like we have to share them with each other."

"Natural resource?" He nearly spits the words. "You sound like a fucking biologist."

Lewis entered the bar annoyed. Littlejohn has done nothing to alleviate that, and neither has the bourbon.

"Would it help if I use smaller words?"

Littlejohn slams his glass on the bar and turns so that he's in Lewis's face, chest to chest. His chest is enormous, pectorals bulging like a pair of frozen turkeys beneath his shirt. With a purposeful slowness, Lewis gets to his feet and takes a step closer. At six five, he looks down on him by half a foot. Somewhere inside him, his fight instinct has kicked in, a switch flipped. The bad mood that's been bearing down on him, the claustrophobia, all of it—his body seems to recognize that it can fight them away, like it used to do so long ago. It's something he has not felt in years. Something familiar. It's almost reassuring, in a way that he knows will trouble him later.

"How 'bout I fix it so you can't talk at all," Littlejohn says, his red face practically glowing. The pores on his veined nose give it the texture of concrete.

Lewis sees that he's already moved his hand to the grip of the pistol at his waist. Which means that, for all his bluster, Littlejohn is actually afraid. He closes his fists and relaxes his muscles.

But before either of them can act, Fenwick steps between them like he's cutting in on the dance floor and sweeps Littlejohn aside. It's like moving furniture. A refrigerator. A gun safe.

"Gentlemen, if you're going to measure your dicks, can you do it someplace private so as not to embarrass the rest of us?"

"Fuck you, Pope," Littlejohn says. "You here to protect your boyfriend?"

"He ain't the one I'm protecting."

Fenwick pushes back with more force as Littlejohn lunges. Some of the other guides leap to their feet, knocking over chairs. Atcheson and Sipsey grab him by the arms and help the Pope pull him away. Lewis sits back down on his stool with his back to the bar, as if he's completely unbothered and uninterested, and picks up his drink. Fuming and straining at his restraints, Littlejohn points at him over Fenwick's shoulder.

"You and me, Yaw. Maybe not tonight. But someday. I promise you. I fucking promise you."

Lewis stares back and drains his glass with a leisurely grace, as if he's got all the time in the world.

"You," Fenwick tells him, "are not helping."

———

Though he's only been at the Salt Lick for twenty minutes, he's had four or five drinks. Despite his outward calm, his heart is a fist-sized volcano. It's not fear; it's adrenaline, muscle memory, his heart shooting hot lava through his arteries.

"Don't worry about Littlejohn," Fenwick says, following him outside. "He's always had a stick up his ass."

"Did I look worried?"

"Actually, you looked like you were having fun."

"I don't do fun."

"No, you don't, do you?" The Pope lights a cigarette. "That guy is a first-ballot candidate for the asshole Hall of Fame." When they reach Lewis's truck, he leans with his back against the bed and pushes smoke out through his nostrils and mouth. It looks blue under the parking lot lights.

"He says they're going Charles Bronson on the bear."

"I think your buddy Littlejohn is gonna have it mounted on the wall of his bedroom by the time this all ends. Right next to his Nazi flag and autographed collectible J. Edgar Hoover girdle."

"How about The Adventures of Wheatfall and Fuckface?"

"You know Wheatfall. You could shit in his shorts and he'd thank you politely. But Fuckface was fit to be tied, and so were their clients. The bear spooked 'em good."

They're quiet for a minute. Lewis looks up at the starless sky. The air is warm but autumn is knocking politely.

"They've got a point, you know," Fenwick says. "If that bear ain't afraid of people anymore, it's a problem. It's conditioned. Just a matter of time."

Lewis leans against his truck, arms over the sides of the bed, but says nothing.

"You don't agree," Fenwick says.

"No."

"What if it was your family instead of some of Wheatfall's clients? What if it was Gray?"

"It wasn't."

"Didn't realize you'd joined the Local Bears Union."

"It's a symbol. The bear."

"Of what?"

Lewis shrugs. "Wildness, I guess. Freedom. The fucking majesty of nature."

"You know it eats out of dumpsters, right?"

"I just like the idea that it exists. That we share this world with it."

Fenwick smokes thoughtfully. Then he throws the butt onto the ground at his feet and grinds it into the dirt. "By the way, when I said earlier that I would be embarrassed during a dick-measuring contest, I misspoke."

"We'd both lose. Littlejohn's the biggest prick I know."

Lewis climbs into his truck and shuts the door. Fenwick leans in the open window. "Wheatfall swears it was a griz. Fuck-face thinks so too."

"What do you think?"

"What do I think? I think all bears look like grizzlies when they're close enough to lick you. But I also think Wheatfall smokes shit he shouldn't smoke. And you know Fuckface. The kid's got a big heart, but he's a mouth breather."

When Lewis starts the truck, a chorus of belts squeal like

he's murdering seals. "The first time my father took me camping," he says, "he told me the best way to tell a brown bear from
a black bear was to get it to chase you."

"How's that?"

"You climb a tree. If it's a black bear, it will climb up after
you. If it's a grizzly, it will knock the tree down."

"I guided a coupla seasons in Alaska when I was first out
of the army," Fenwick says. "My first day out on the Naknek, I
ran into a bear, and brother, it scared the hell out of me. When
I got back to town, I went straight to the outfitter and picked
out a sweet little Colt .45. I asked the guy behind the counter if
it would work as a bear gun. 'Well, that's good enough for black
bear,' he said. 'For brown bear, you'd need some Vaseline too.'"

"Vaseline?"

"He leaned over the counter, looked me in the eyes, and
said, 'The Vaseline's so's it won't hurt so much when the bear
shoves that gun up your ass.'"

Lewis laughs.

"Maybe that's what happened to Littlejohn," he says, and
pulls away into the night.

———

Home is just a couple of miles away. Outside town, the road
narrows and climbs. There's a view on clear days, but it's too
dark to see the mountains, almost too dark to see the trees that
line the shoulder, even. The world reduced to what fits within
the cones of his lights.

The adrenaline from his encounter with Littlejohn has worn
off, diluted by fatigue and alcohol. He's bone-tired. Existentially
tired. As his eyes grow heavy with exhaustion and whiskey, he rolls
down his window to let in air. Maybe he'll actually sleep tonight.

Probably not.

As he rounds the last corner before his street, his lights settle on a man standing in the middle of the road. Before his foot even presses the brake pedal—before his brain even files the command to do so—Lewis plows into him.

The collision is violent, stopping the truck's momentum and smashing Lewis's head against the steering wheel, or maybe the dash, as the body obliterates the windshield and rolls over the roof of the cab. There's a second impact from behind as all the tools and trash and anchor chain in the truck's bed shatter the cab's rear window, raining glass on his head and neck. The stalled truck rolls to a stop. The sudden silence is terrifying.

His reaction time slowed by the bourbon, by exhaustion, maybe by his head injury, Lewis sits stunned. The steering wheel itself is bent on both sides of the steering column, ten and two. The splintered windshield is covered in blood, bowed inward over the dash. The silence becomes a ringing in his head, rising and falling on itself like a Shepard tone.

It takes him a moment to gather himself. Once he does, he tries to open the door, but it's stuck. He throws himself against it until it opens and steps onto the tar. A single golf ball rolls out of the wreckage, curving with the slope of the road and stopping when it reaches the dirt shoulder.

There's blood on his shirt and hands. There's blood on the truck's hood and grille. There's blood spilled on the road in puddles and splatters. The grille is crushed, the hood crumpled, the engine shoved back against the firewall. Fluids pour out and mix with the blood, turning the road slick.

Both headlights are gone, there are no streetlights, and the night is too dark to see much of anything. Lewis pats his wet vest until he finds his flashlight. Gripped by a kind of fear he's never experienced, the kind of fear that recognizes that life as he knows it is about to change forever, he walks around behind the truck to find the man he has hit.

Best case, he finds him alive. The worst case he can't fathom.

His heart kicks at his chest, sounding out the bruised ribs he'll discover later as the gathering pain begins to marshal forces. Taking a deep breath, he turns on the flashlight and aims it into the night.

17

Fenwick climbs out of his truck and takes in the scene. Using the big military flashlight he keeps in his glovebox, he inspects the truck's crumpled prow, the shattered windshield doused with blood, the dented roof, the crumpled quarter panel and accordioned door. Lewis sits on the open tailgate as his friend circles the wreckage. He's dropped two flares in the road. They burn an unnatural red, comets stalled in their arc by some supernatural force, sparking languidly.

"You bring the shovel, axe, and coolers?"

"And the bone saw. Where's the body?"

Without getting up, Lewis points into the darkness. Fenwick aims his flashlight at the shoulder of the road where it lies sprawled at unnatural angles, broken limbs splayed. He points the light at his feet and sees the pool of blood he's standing in. When he lifts one foot, the sticky, drying blood drips from it like jelly from a sandwich. He tucks the flashlight under his arm and lights a cigarette against the stench. The jackrabbit flame of the match reveals his face.

"Yaw one," he says. "Bear zero."

Lewis nods in the darkness. "I'd say it's more of a tie."

"On the bright side, you finally got to see it. The bear."

Fenwick sits beside him and puts his cigarette in his mouth, where it glows like another road flare, and takes Lewis's face with both hands. The gesture is almost intimate. He turns it from side to side, looking at the bruises and blood.

"You OK?"

"I'm gonna be sore in the morning."

"Not as sore as him."

The bear is close to a thousand pounds, fat with salmon and donuts and all the other scavenged spoils of civilization. Lewis hops down with a lightness his fatigue can't diminish and crouches beside it, putting a hand against a paw. The paw dwarfs it, the thick pads marred with scratches, rough like sandpaper, the nails sharp and dense and impossibly long.

"Wheatfall and Fuckface were right," Fenwick says. "That's no black bear."

He pulls his truck closer so that his headlights and fog lamps illuminate the scene, and they get to work skinning and gutting the bear and loading the meat into the coolers. The hide is ruined. Lewis wants to keep it anyway. Beneath it is a winter's worth of meat they'll distribute throughout town, giving roasts and sausage to anyone who lost chickens or dogs or bird feeders. In death, the bear will feed the same people it stole from while it was alive. The labor is messy. A few minutes after they start, they're slathered with a slime of blood and other fluids from the animal's burst innards. It's going to be hours before they finish.

Working silently and efficiently, they slit the hide from breastbone to groin and peel it away and sever the connecting tissue from organs that hang like rotten fruit inside the body cavity. While Fenwick holds the legs spread, Lewis splits the pelvic bone with the axe. Then he cuts out the bladder and lower intestines, slices through the diaphragm, and removes the lungs, which he throws on the gut pile. He cuts the heart free and holds it in one hand. Intact. Heavy. This bear has been in Disappointment almost as long as he has.

"Look at this," Fenwick says, lifting a piece of meat. With his knife, he pries something out of the flesh and wipes it on his shirt until it gleams in the headlights. It's a bullet, a big one, squashed flat by the impact. "How long has this tough old bastard been carrying this thing around?"

"We all have something buried inside us," Lewis says. He wipes blood from his forehead onto the back of his hand and throws the heart into one of the coolers with the rest of the meat.

———

The bear haunts his dreams for the next few weeks. It's always there—at least when he's able to sleep—a hint of a ghost that prickles his skin. The feeling follows him when he's awake, too, a lurking presence that keeps him on edge. For so long he wanted only to see the bear; now it won't leave him alone.

Worse, maybe, is the bureaucracy and paperwork. Even an accidental killing has consequences. Fenwick drives him to the ODFW offices in Bend, where he's interviewed in a brightly lit room by a brown-shirted officer and a field biologist who "good cop, bad cop" him before handing him a pen and a ream of forms to complete.

"I wasn't hunting," Lewis says. "I wasn't poaching. I hit the bear with my truck. Maybe I should talk to a traffic cop instead?"

"You killed the first brown bear spotted in Oregon since the 1930s," the biologist tells him, with a look of disgust Lewis hasn't seen since he left Massachusetts.

The officer just looks bored. "Sir," he says, tapping his pen against the paperwork. "I need a formal justification for the termination of life."

Lewis chews it over. "Put down jaywalking," he says.

There's the insurance claim for the truck too. More paperwork. With his injuries still fresh, he takes the check to the dealership and limps around the lot looking at the rows of brand-new rigs. All the unmarred finishes and the gleaming metal and tires make him uncomfortable. He had his last truck for twenty years. The idea of a new one feels like a reward or a trophy he does not deserve. Finally he settles on one that's a few years old, a few thousand miles, and they load all his stuff out of the bed of Fenwick's truck into it. It all looks foreign, out of place. Driving it home, he feels like he's molted and grown a new shell.

A week passes, and then another. The cuts on his face scab over. His bruises fade. The new tires get dirty, the paint covered with dust. Soon he's able to start running again. When he sleeps, the bear is still there, but it feels less aggressive and less angry. As if they've come to an understanding. As if they've agreed to coexist.

Then one night he dreams not of the bear but of The Old Man and wakes in the middle of the night wondering if he had ever dreamed of the bear at all. Maybe it was his father the entire time.

He listens for the noise that woke him to repeat itself. It's the dog. She's taken to sleeping on Gray's floor, too tired and sore to jump onto her bed, but now she's made her way down the hall to his bedside. When she nuzzles his face, her nose is dry. A series of wheezy breaths out, the undercurrent of whining, a cry made weak by her failing lungs. He leans over so he's forehead to forehead with her and scratches behind her ears. Her mismatched eyes are milky. His hands find the fist-sized tumors that have arisen all over her body, as if she's swallowed every tennis ball she ever played with and now they are working their way back from the inside out.

She's come to tell him she's suffering. She's come to tell him she's afraid.

He puts his pillow on the floor for her, and she lies down upon it all at once, as if she's collapsing.

Lewis wakes Janey.

"It's Johnson," he says.

"Does she want to go out?"

"She wants to say goodbye."

He can't see Janey's eyes, but he knows what she's thinking. He's thinking the same thing. This dog. Their daughter. They've known each other their entire lives, brought to this place on the same day by the same storm. How will the world continue for any of them without all of them?

What will it look like if it does?

Janey scoots across the sheets to take his place, and despite her pain and discomfort, Johnson wags her tail with pleasure.

"Stay with her," Lewis says. As he barefoots down the hall to wake Gray, the floorboards creak.

"What's wrong, Pop?"

"It's the dog."

"What happened?"

"Get dressed," he says. "Meet me outside."

18

It's an effort to lift Johnson into the bed of the truck. She's heavy, but she does not fight, compliant even racked with pain. A good dog. Lewis scratches her chin and steps aside for Janey, who kisses her on the nose and whispers in her ear. Lewis can't hear her, but he knows what she is saying just the same. *Thank you for taking care of our girl. Thank you for finding us.* She kisses the dog one last time, and kisses Gray. When she turns to him and leans in close, she raises her eyebrows over her wet eyes. It's a question—but she's not going to like the answer. He shuts the tailgate, and Gray hops over it, settling lightly in the truck's bed.

"I'm riding back here."

Lewis nods. He's already cleared a space and spread out a sheaf of blankets. When she sits down the dog lays beside her, heavy head in her lap.

"Give her some of these painkillers at night," the vet told them when Johnson first started to limp. Standing next to Johnson, the tiny, pigeon-toed woman looked as if she had not been built to scale. "They're the strongest we have. We call them Gorilla Slayers, because they'd knock even King Kong for a loop."

"How long does she have?"

She looked Gray in the eyes and answered with kindness in her voice and an honesty Lewis appreciated.

"Not long."

That was four years ago. Before they left the house, Lewis coaxed two of the pills into Johnson with a spoonful of peanut butter, and they've calmed her considerably. Gray seems calm too. He's grateful for that. She'll need it where they're going.

Beyond the edges of town, he turns away from the river and into the woods at the old forest road. Trees pass like fence posts. He drives slowly, trying not to bounce Gray and the dog from the bed. When he figures they've gone far enough, he pulls to the shoulder and kills the engine.

The day's first light has just begun to show itself, even there in the woods, filtered through the canopy of trees. Soon it will lend a soft, golden cast to everything it touches, rounding all the world's edges. As it rises it will sharpen those same edges once again as the day gathers itself.

Around back, in the light, he sees Gray more closely. She's not relaxed at all, but stoic. Red-eyed. Johnson rests with her head in her lap, meaty tongue hanging, chest rising and falling with the effort of breathing, as if each breath takes something from her, something finite, a little bit of her evaporating into the ether. He lifts her out and puts her down gently. She's too blind to see where they are, he knows, but she can smell the leaves and the dirt. She knows.

She gets unsteadily to her own feet and shakes herself off, bolstered by the pills, bolstered by their sudden arrival in the forest. Bolstered by her own dignity, which will outlast her. This is his final gift to her.

"Good girl," he says. She looks his way, following his voice. "Good girl."

Lewis takes the Winchester from the cab and works the bolt, checking the breech. Gray flinches at the sound. The dawn is reflected in her wet eyes as she stares at him. He hands her the shovel.

"Ready?"

"I don't know," she says. "No."

Lewis nods. "Me neither," he says.

They walk slowly, speaking Johnson's name aloud to keep her on trail. The dog moves cautiously, as if the ground itself has become temporal, as if it might turn to mist at any moment. Numbed by the pills, she acts drunk. Pleasantly so.

They stop often to let her rest. She sniffs the air with her grizzled snout, squatting to water roots and plants.

"Good girl," Gray says often. "Good girl."

Each time, Johnson wags her tail.

Lewis has brought salmon jerky and a brick of cheddar. As they walk, he slices off pieces and feeds them to her. They never allowed her people food, but over the years she found her way to some of it anyway. Cheese is her favorite. Even so, she sips it from his hand delicately, never hungrily. If there's an afterlife for dogs, let it be filled with tennis balls and cheese.

"Where are we going, Pop?"

"Nowhere, really. Just letting her walk one more time."

"She can barely see."

"She doesn't have to. Imagine the woods from her perspective. All the scents. The sounds. It's got layers for her that we don't get to experience. Let's give them to her one last time so she has something to remember."

Gray doesn't respond. Lewis turns, and when she sees him looking, she wipes her eyes.

"Sorry," she says.

"Don't be."

"Aren't you sad?"

"I've known this dog as long as I've known you, Gray. I can't imagine this family without her."

"How do you make it hurt less?"

"You don't."

Watching his daughter, he knows that what he has said is not enough.

"She's got more pain than joy, now, Gray. That's not fair to her. You have to know when it's time to let someone go."

"OK," she says, her voice heavy.

"No, Gray. I know it's not OK. But that's the way of the world, and we're not going to be the ones to stop it."

He steps away to give her privacy, looking instead at the forest canopy overhead, dense and green, the mottled light reaching through the leaves in intricate patterns that lend it a sense of motion. Dust rises from the floor, pollen from the plants. Carried on the light breeze, it rises and drifts through the thin shafts of sun. A moth floats through the air in an unsteady arc, a slow and erratic white comet, but he sees no other signs of life. No squirrels chattering. No birds calling. It's as if the forest itself has granted them a few moments alone with the old dog.

Johnson sits just a foot away, relaxed, the pills keeping her pain momentarily at bay. She sniffs contentedly.

"How do we know when it's time?"

"It's time."

"What do I do?"

"Say goodbye."

"Then what?"

"Just say goodbye to her, Gray."

She takes a knee in front of the dog and leans in so Johnson can lick her face. She scratches behind the heavy ears. She reaches back and rubs the brittle haunches. Reflexively, the dog thrums a leg. Gray whispers something Lewis cannot hear.

After a minute, he kneels too. He strokes the dog's back, and some of her fur comes off in his hand. There are bare spots of skin along her spine. The skin is calloused and leathery. She licks his wrist, and her tongue hangs. A waterfall of saliva drips to the ground. He searches her tired face for the puppy he found sixteen years ago, the puppy who found him. When he puts his head to hers, she presses against him. In the milky eyes, the powdered snout, the brown teeth, Lewis sees the unconditional love she extended to them. He feels, too, the weight of the rifle on his shoulder and it shames him.

He stands and grabs Gray's wrist gently, turning it over and putting the bag of treats in her palm.

"Give them to her now," he says.

"How many?"

"All of them, Gray. Let her have them all."

She looks at him. Looks at the dog. Looks down at her hand, the hunks of dried salmon, the slices of cheese.

"Lie down, girl," she says. Johnson obeys, haltingly, her joints stiff enough to need oil. If only he could hit all her Zerk fittings with a grease gun and give her another sixteen years, give them all another sixteen years.

Gray stares at him, her features fierce. She puts the treats in a pile in front of the dog's nose. "Here you go, girl." Her voice falters. "Here you go."

Johnson sniffs the pile. When she begins to eat, she does so almost reluctantly, as if she's afraid of getting caught. *We've not spoiled you*, Lewis thinks. *You're a dog and we loved you but you're still a dog. A good dog. But just a dog.*

Gray looks at him again. When he motions her to the side, her eyes fill again, like some dam has broken, but she climbs to her feet and steps away from Johnson. Her hands are shaking. He looks at his own hands, thinking of all that they've proven

capable of, all the violence, all the tenderness. He knows which
surprised him more and that shames him too. He thinks of all
the tools they've wielded, all the fish they've caught. He built a
boat with them, milled the lumber, straked the ribs, planed the
rails until they were smooth as eddy water. He held his baby
daughter with these same hands. He beat his father with these
hands. Before that, when they were smaller, he used these to
wipe his own tears from his face when his father beat *him*. Now
they are big hands, long-fingered, rough-knuckled, thick with
calluses and scars. The *volar interossei* and *lumbricals* stand out
like rivers on a topographical map, names he remembers from
school, cords beneath the skin. The skin is as leathery as the
patches on the old dog's back. No matter what he has ever asked
of them, these hands have never failed him. They do not shake
in the face of what he is about to ask, and that saddens him.

Walking around behind the dog, he unshoulders the .30-30
from its sling, a caliber big enough for bear. The steel barrel is
still cool from the truck, the wood damp with condensation.
He raises the Winchester to his shoulder and shuts his eyes.

For a long time he holds them closed, listening to the forest,
to the wheezing dog. He can hear her licking her lips, happy
for the moment, free of pain, in the woods and fresh air with
people she loves. He can hear Gray, too, her stuttered breathing. When he opens them again, it's not Johnson he sees, but
another dog, a Lab black as a shadow, black as a bruise. Black
as a stain on the street. A vision, maybe. Or a ghost. He blinks
her away and sees Johnson lying contentedly on the trail with
her big paws crossed in front of her, a mound of fur and heart.

He closes one eye, which moves her a lateral foot. A trick—
parallax. The Old Man taught him that, taught him about
cross-dominant vision, how his dominant eye is the opposite
of his dominant hand, which makes it more difficult to shoot.

Lewis suffers from it, thirty percent of the world suffers from it, but his father saw it as just another flaw, another shortcoming, another failure of character. Remembering that, he remembers, too, the sheen of The Old Man's hair, the blood in the corners of his eyes, his sharp yellow teeth, the whiskey and onions on his breath, and squeezes the trigger.

The sound startles the quiet birds from the trees, an intrusion in the forest and in their lives. It startles Gray, too, the sound rising from the ground beneath them and past their eyes and ears and noses and over their heads and into the air above them, into the forest canopy, and then beyond it into the sky itself. An echo of the sound returns, half as loud, hollow, diminishing. Lewis listens to it and wonders what has been lost.

19

Their seat belts strain to hold them as the truck slides and bounces on the uneven road, rattling the shovel in the bed. At the house, Gray gets out without a word and runs inside. Lewis follows her after a minute. Janey sits at the table with a mug of coffee. She nods down the hall toward Gray's bedroom, her expression a warning.

"I'll talk to her," he says.

As he approaches her room, the floorboard creaks, alerting her.

"Leave me alone," she says before he can even knock.

"Remind me to fix that goddamned floor," he says to Janey as he passes through the kitchen on his way back out to the truck. She gets up and follows him outside.

When he takes the rifle from behind the seat and opens the breech to make sure it's empty, she eyes the Winchester with an expression he's sure is meant for him.

"You didn't have to bring her along."

"She can handle it."

"Lewis. You didn't have to bring her." There's something

in her voice that he does not recognize. It crawls inside of him.

"You shouldn't own a dog if you can't do right by it when the time comes, J. She needs to learn that. She needs to learn that kind of responsibility."

"Did your father teach you that?"

Lewis glares at her. She stares back, hard, as if she doesn't recognize him. He looks down at the empty rifle and smells the burnt powder on it, the memories triggered by that smell.

"We can't protect her forever, J."

"We can try. We're *supposed* to try."

He takes a deep breath and smells the dog on his clothes, the dirt on his hands, smells the spent cartridge in his vest pocket. The hard lump of brass presses against his chest. The Old Man used to reload his own cartridges and made Lewis collect empty shells at the range to bring home for reuse. "Police your brass," he'd say. Lewis still collects them. A muscle memory, loyalty to routine. When he exhales, it comes out as a sigh.

"Everything dies, J. Someday she'll bury worse things than a dog."

"Not with a shovel, Lewis."

Janey's voice has changed. He looks at her again and sees that she is crying.

"Where did you think we were going? What did you think we were going to do?"

"I thought you'd wait."

"For what?"

"For Johnson."

"To do what?"

"To die," she says. "I thought you'd wait for her to die and then bury her in the woods. Not kill her yourself."

"She was in pain," he says, his own voice calm, his words deliberate. "Putting her down was doing right by the dog."

Janey hits him in the chest, open-palmed, tentative, as if trying it out to see how it feels. Lewis doesn't budge. He doesn't block her; he just takes the blow. She hits him again, harder, her fist closed, and still he does not react. She looks at him, horrified. For a moment they are both still.

And then she is chaos and motion, she is fury, she's a terror of punches raining against him. She wails as she pummels him, wails when he grabs her tiny wrists and pulls her against him, wails as he hugs her, smothering her until she stops fighting. Still she wails, her cries muffled against his chest.

He holds her until they slow.

He holds her until they stop.

It's a long time.

"What about what's right by your daughter, Lewis?"

"I'm trying, J."

Finally, she hugs him back. With her anger spent, the flames out, she feels insubstantial in his arms. So light. It frightens him that she is the only thing holding him to this earth. He puts a hand on the back of her head and holds her tight. He sees the dirt on his hands, the calluses from the shovel, the scarred and twisted knuckles. They're his father's hands.

"I'm doing my best," he says, and hopes like hell it's enough.

———

When he runs that night, fleet-footed memories of the youthful dog nip at his heels. Let the sweat be a proxy, or the pain in his legs and lungs and heart, and let it release itself, he thinks, sprinting through the trees along the dark river. Not a prayer so much as a plea, and not to God but to something else.

Afterward he knows he cannot sleep, so he drags a kitchen chair and a bottle of Old Crow into the front yard. The inconsequential ambient light leaves a sky filled with stars. When he was a kid, the Massachusetts sky seemed endless, the stars infinite, but here there are so many more. What else does the world contain that he has so far failed to see for all his desperate looking?

Though he's tried to learn, he's never been good at recognizing constellations. Just like life, they're a series of dots he fails to connect. But somewhere overhead are Canis Major and Canis Minor, the Greater and Lesser Dogs. He's had two dogs in his own life and loved them both. Somewhere, too, is Orion the Hunter. Major and Minor belonged to him, hunting at his side through the great forests of mythology. Lewis wonders how they came to their own fates and what role Orion himself played in them.

Dizzied by stars and by whiskey, his mind loses focus and his anchor begins to drag. When the door to the house opens, he half expects the dog to emerge, but there is no dog. Not anymore. Just Gray shuffling outside in her pajamas. She leans against the house and peers into the same sky as him. Then she looks around, as if she's heard something, and sees him on the lawn. She stares for a moment, wondering if he's really there, or why, and on her stare he feels a charge of emotion somehow bridging the distance between them. It flips his stomach. When she turns around and goes back into the house, he exhales, deflated.

But the door opens again and she reappears with another chair. She carries it across the lawn, sets it beside his, and flops down upon it. Lewis takes off his jacket and hands it to her. She accepts it but does not say anything, and neither does he. Not for a long while. He's afraid to speak, afraid even to move to lift the bottle to his lips, though he perseveres. Her presence feels like a victory, or at least a truce.

Overhead the moon rolls slowly along its arc.

Minutes pass. Hours pass.

Eventually light begins to appear in the sky, a subtle shift rather than a dramatic announcement. The light begins to take color, a palette of spilled ink. Then the rising sun chases the stars, and the hunter and his dogs flee into the retreating darkness. It's a new day with all the dogs in the past.

Momentarily buoyed by the sunrise and the whiskey, Lewis clears his throat.

"I have the day off," he says.

"Congratulations." Though dripping with sarcasm, Gray's voice gives him hope.

Horse is the hope I ride.

"Let's go fishing. Just you and me."

"You're drunk."

"So what?"

She doesn't respond for a long time, doesn't move, just sits back with her face pointed at the sky. If he could not see that her eyes were open, he might believe she was asleep.

They shoot horses, don't they?

A long time passes. Five minutes. Ten.

More.

His bottle is empty. As the colors of the sunrise sort themselves out, the fire fades and the blue of the day smothers it. There are no clouds. A lone goose, honking morosely, crosses the sky with its long neck extended.

When Gray finally answers him, her voice is tired. Sad. Resigned.

"OK," she says. "Let's go fishing. But I'm driving."

20

They leave a note for Janey and head to the river, maintaining a sustained silence that feels like a cold, dog-shaped giant wedged between them. Eager but respectful, Lewis circles Gray warily at the put-in, still a little drunk. She executes her duties by rote, freeing lines and unhinging the trailer, and the boat skids down the ramp and hits the water like it's made of bricks.

She rides in the bow, leaning over the gunwale with her head on her strong arms. Now and then she lifts it to watch something—a blue heron wading among the reeds, a pair of turtles with graffitied shell markings, river otters splashing like city kids in a public pool.

"A romp," Lewis says. "A bevy. A lodge. A family."

Gray says nothing, her features set, unyielding. Not a challenge, but something else. He nods to say he won't talk again until she does.

The day grows far too hot far too quickly. No one predicted it, not the TV news or the radio or his gut. It hadn't seemed possible just an hour or two earlier, sitting on the lawn, his feet wet with dew. The sun bears down like it's getting closer and closer to the earth, like it might never stop. Maybe today's the day it crashes into the planet. Maybe today's the day humanity ends, he thinks, splashing the wooden seats with water when they grow uncomfortably warm. A metal boat would be unbearable. If Littlejohn's on the Terrebonne today, Lewis hopes his expensive boat is searing his ass like a steak.

A wooden boat is more work to maintain, but it's part of the natural world rather than an intrusion into it. The rails are Doug fir he steamed and bent to follow the hull's gentle curves. He planed the wood and sanded it to perfection, stained it against water and sun. It looks like honey in the sunlight, walnut in the shade, the grain almost brindle. The boat is so efficient, it responds to the slightest request from his oars. It's easy to steer too far, easy to overcorrect. A metaphor, he thinks. Despite the heat, the river is fast and cold, and he has to stop himself from dipping an oar and splashing Gray playfully, an old habit.

They round a bend and see a boy about Gray's age fishing from the bank, or trying to. He wears ill-fitting neoprene waders that bunch out on either side of his belt, making him look like a hastily tied balloon animal. His fly line is tangled in a knot so complex, so elegant, that it might be fatal—he'll have to cut it. Lewis is not unfamiliar with such knots; the more you work them, the worse they get.

"You know him?"

Gray looks where he nods and studies the boy, who sees them looking and sheepishly raises a hand.

"No."

His line is not just knotted but tangled in the willows behind him, too, victim of a sagging backcast.

"Poor bastard," he says. "Someone should teach him to fish." He considers it a victory that she does not argue with him.

After an hour they still have not wet a line. If she wants to fish, she'll say something. Lewis contents himself with oaring the boat dutifully.

Gray swivels to watch a sedge of sandhill cranes pass over-head, tracing their route through the sky like an artillery gunner. Their dull brown-and-gray bodies stretch behind red crowns like aircraft nose lights, impressive birds whose flight defies physics and whose cries defy brass instruments.

After a while he finds himself wanting to fish in a way he has not in a long time. Fishing has become so tied up in work, in client headaches and technique refinement. He wants to feel what he felt when he was a kid. The freedom. The simplicity. A line in the water connecting him to another life fighting for itself. Without a word, he beaches the boat on a sandbar and ties it off to a downed ash. Grabbing one of the rigged rods from its bungeed holder, he sets off on foot, leaving his daughter alone.

At the far shore of the small island, he strips line from his reel into bright yellow coils at his feet. When it's loose, he takes a breath—it feels like the first he's taken all day—and begins false casting. He's done it countless times and his body knows the physics instinctually, the straight wrist, the tipping point when the line is balanced and level in the air behind him. He knows trick casts to beat the wind if it's over one shoulder or the other or blowing in his face. He knows how to load the line vertically when his back is up against a rock or trees, leaving no room to backcast. He can dance the fly over the surface of the water like a skittish bug looking for a place to land. After a lifetime of devotion, he's become adept, a samurai with a fly rod for a sword. He can shoot the tapered line a hundred feet with pinpoint accuracy and drop a fly into a shot glass without a splash. It's science, but it still feels like magic.

The island is shaped like a fist. Lewis stands at the end of a knuckle protruding into the current. The river whispers on three sides like an old friend, seductive and familiar but still filled with mystery after so many years—like the best things in life, ultimately unknowable. Absorbed in the act of fishing, he pushes Gray from his mind. He's not catching anything, but he's not trying, either, not really. He's content to cast and retrieve, to watch the river, to step into the cold water until it reaches the tops of his boots, and then deeper, so it darkens the thighs of his Carhartts. Still the current tugs at him, urging him in further.

After an hour, he reels in his line and walks around to look for Gray. As he approaches, he watches her cast, her tanned arm directing a funnel of brightly colored fly line that surrounds her like a swarm of birds. He watches the mesmerizing loop that forms in the line, watches how she controls it, how it rolls forward as she shoots the line into the river and lays it down exactly where she wants it.

It's the cast of an artist. His daughter.

She strips in line and shouts as a fish takes the fly. The single war whoop of surprise and excitement is too primal for any cynicism or anger. Her line goes tight as she sets the hook, and the rod bends like a car antenna, butt to tip.

When the fish starts to run, his instinct is to guide her, to offer counsel about keeping the tip high and letting the rod do the work. But she knows. She can fish. She doesn't need him.

"Pop," she yells.

Lewis doesn't need to be asked twice. Crossing the sandbar at a run, he retrieves the net from the boat. By the time he reaches her, she's laughing, as excited as the first time she caught a fish. The sound is unfiltered and beautiful and infectious. The fish flashes just beneath the surface.

"I can see him."

She laughs some more, and in her laughter he hears unmistakable joy.

"He's going to walk." As if on cue, the fish leaps clear of the water, remaining vertical even as it sweeps horizontally across the surface, dancing on its tail.

"Bow before your queen," he says, and she drops the tip of the rod to keep the line from snapping.

A few minutes later she lands the fish, easing it into the shallow water where Lewis sweeps it into the net. It's a lithe and beautiful thing, with bright eyes and skin, golden-colored, with a dark back and a flush of red in its flanks. A fish to be proud of, nearly perfect in every way.

Every way except one. There's a lump in its belly, halfway between the pectoral and pelvic fins, distended, hard, perfectly round. Gray holds the dripping salmon and shows it to her father.

"What is it? What's wrong with it?"

"I don't know," he says. "I've never seen anything like it."

She hands it to him, deferential. He clubs it with the stock of the net, lays it on a flat rock, and drags his knife the length of the belly, gills to tail like he's unzipping it. He opens the salmon with both hands like a fortune cookie and empties its insides onto the gravel. A warm mess of organs and innards and blood spills out. He finds the stomach, the tumorous growth pushing at the lining, and slits it gently open.

A golf ball rolls out at their feet. It gleams wet and bright in the sun.

He looks up at his daughter, but she's already walking away.

21

Lewis stays drunk all day, a perpetual motion machine that pours bourbon and pisses on the grass and repeats. He eats in town without his family, tacos and beer, and then goes for a run in the dark. His sweat reeks of whiskey. He feels like he's running through his own mind, the way everything he passes bears the weight of his past, every inch of Disappointment laden with history, as if he'd scattered his memories from above. They chose this place. They chose this life. They drew the borders. He does what he wants to do for work, and against all odds, he found someone to share it all with. So what else is there? The answer, of course, is the reason he's running, the thorn that has worked its way under his skin, irritating him into fever.

Littlejohn's truck is outside the Salt Lick, double-parked as usual, a tarp lashed tight over the bed. Breathing heavily as he runs past it, Lewis catches a scent of rotting meat, a scent of game. He circles back to the truck, unhooks a bungee, and lifts the corner of the tarp. The smell rushes at him.

He fishes the little Maglite from his fatigues and shines it into the dark bed. A pair of lifeless eyes stare back at him.

Lifting the tarp higher, he sees a handful of severed deer heads laying on a pile of body parts, bones and muscles and tendon hanging from bloody folds of skin. In all, he counts at least four carcasses, maybe five.

Littlejohn's the poacher.

Of course he is.

The truck's windows are closed, but the doors are unlocked, the keys in the ignition. Who would steal from Littlejohn?

Lewis Fucking Yaw, King of the Jungle. That's who.

He pockets the keys on their carabiner chain and rehooks the bungee before resuming his run.

At the park, he starts gathering speed, sprinting alongside the river. Thinking about the last few days, the dog, the fish, Janey, Gray, he runs faster and faster. At the edge of the park, the last of the streetlights shines through the trees, casting leafy shadows that look low-resolution, eight-bit graphics that confuse his depth of field. He crosses the footbridge onto the forest road. There are no lights to see by, but still he runs, faster and faster and faster still, gaining speed as he goes, gaining momentum, gaining resolve. When he finally stumbles, he crashes forward in a spiral of limbs, lurching out of control toward the riverbank, but catches himself before he falls and slumps, bent at the waist, gasping for breath.

After a few minutes he backtracks to the footbridge at a walk. From the bridge he can hear the salmon-choked river beneath him, though he can't see it in the dark.

When Gray was just a kid, he brought her here to see the salmon in the creek that feeds the river. They stood in the shallow water, wading among the tens of thousands of fish that return to the Terrebonne each year, spawned out and sparse at the end of their life's journey as they built their spawning redds in the gravel. Their deteriorating bodies clogged the narrow creek like a flood barrier of sandbags as a squadron of scavenger birds hovered above.

She looked mystified by the scene, all the fish, the rotted flesh, the exposed bones. The current moved the carcasses of the dead fish hypnotically back and forth, swishing their tails and animating them like ghosts. Other fish held on to the last fleeting hours of their existence, stubborn with biological imperative. They'd built their redds. They'd deposited their eggs. All that remained was to guard them with their final dying moments, as they'd been programmed to do. Gray splashed among them in bilge boots he'd spray-painted brown. They were yellow when Janey bought them, covered with cartoon characters, the only ones they could find in her size, but she wanted them to look like his. The paint had faded and checked like the fish, which had already lost their silver sheen, their scales dull as bruises. Scabs of flesh flaked off in the current, enough in total to stitch together another hundred fish. Opportunistic gulls walked among them, pecking without discrimination between the living and the dead. Occasionally a fresh fish would move through, bright and strong, its clock ticking as it muscled its way to spawning grounds farther upstream.

"Gross," she said.

"It's not gross, Gray. It's life."

"It looks like death."

"It's that too. It's both. You can't have one without the other."

"Why are they like that?"

"After they were born, these fish swam all the way downstream to the Columbia River, and then all the way to the Pacific Ocean. They stayed at sea for years, getting bigger and stronger. Then they all swam back to the Columbia and all the way upstream to the Terrebonne, and then all the way here, to this creek. Thousands of miles of ocean and river, swimming over waterfalls and around rocks, all so they could return home to where they were born."

"Over waterfalls?"

"That's right."

"Why?"

"They're tenacious and intractable."

"What's 'intractable'?"

"It means that once they decide they want to come home, nothing can stop them."

"How do they find their way home?"

"Nobody really knows. Home's a powerful thing. No matter how far away you get, it always pulls at you, for better or worse."

"Why do they come back?"

"To spawn."

"What's 'spawn'?"

"Spawning is having babies. After they mate, the females build nests in the gravel and sand on the river bottom. They lay their eggs in the nests just before they die. Then the males protect the eggs until they die too."

"Why do the parents die?"

"Because having children is exhausting."

Gray cocked her head, considering what he'd said before ruling it out.

"No, really. Why do they have to die?"

"So their bodies can become food for all the things that live in the river. Those things then become food for the baby fish. The parents give their lives so their kids have a better chance at survival."

"Wait," she said, starting to understand. "The baby fish eat their dead parents?"

Lewis nodded.

"Gross," she said again, drawing out the word. "Are these the salmon you catch? The same ones?"

"They are."

"They look different."

"That's because they've been in the fresh water too long. Their bodies start to change when they leave the salt water and enter the river. The closer they get to where they were born, the more they change. Some grow humps. Some change colors. The males' jaws turn into what they call a *kype*—sort of a sharp hook that they use to attack other males."

"What are the humps for?"

"It's nature's way of making sure they won't spawn in water that's too shallow. The males get even bigger humps to make them more visible to the bears and other predators, which gives their mates a better chance at living long enough to build the nest and lay the eggs."

"Where are the bears?"

"What?"

"You said there were bears that eat the salmon. Where are the bears?"

"Right here," he said, raising his arms at his side and roaring as he chased her, shrieking and laughing, through the shallows. There were so many salmon it was difficult to stomp his feet without stepping on them. Still playing bear, he plucked a squirming fish from the water with his hands and lifted it high. It was nearly as long as a baseball bat, soft and mealy to the touch. When he bit into it, roaring, he expected more laughter, but his daughter's expression went cold, her eyes grew wide, and she began to cry. He dropped the salmon, spit a mouthful of scales into the river, and reached to console her with hands thick with slime, but it was already too late.

Standing in the dark so many years later, he leans over the railing, wrecked. Beneath him, the river and its shoal of desperate salmon murmur their dissent. And he'd thought it was a good memory. He drops Littlejohn's key chain into the river and turns for home.

22

Just home from the tavern, and still sharp around the edges, The Old Man shakes Lewis awake. His breath a hurricane of smoke and whiskey, he's lean like wire, cast iron beneath calloused skin. Years of labor have hardened his muscles. His hands are steel traps; when he grabs you, you have to chew off your leg to escape him.

Rising to the surface of the dream, Lewis is slow to grasp what's happening, and even slower to act. Muscle memory kicks in. He's no longer a weak-limbed boy, enfeebled by sleep, but a grown man. A brute in his own right. A beast made dangerous by years of training, enabled by instinct, possessed with muscle and anger and something that burns inside him. His own hands are as big as shovels, and when he puts them around The Old Man's neck, it is with the intention of choking the life out of him. It's self-defense. It's instinct. It's retribution for the years of abuse, the beatings, the lovelessness. With a breaking wave of strength, he throws his father off the bed.

"Lewis!"

His effort is violent, his rage explosive, but the feeling it gives him is not one of victory. There is no satisfaction. Instead, something feels wrong. How light his father is. The slenderness of his arms, the weight of his bones.

"Lewis!"

The voice reaches him through the fog, and it is not his father's.

He wakes already on his feet, advancing with his fists up, to find Janey coiled on the floor where he has thrown her. Red welts mottle her neck. They'll turn to bruises, one for each finger, ten black olives on her napkin-white skin.

"Lewis, please!" Her eyes are wild with fear, rimmed with tears. His own eyes burn. His mouth is dry. Everything hurts, his head, the palms of his hands, his shoulders, his legs.

"J," he says, reaching for her, but she bats his hand away and folds her arms in front of her like origami. Like a bat's wings.

"You hurt me." She speaks the words tenuously at first, as if she's just realizing them to be true or is afraid to speak them aloud. But then she speaks them more emphatically. "You hurt me. You *hurt* me. You were choking me!" She's frantic now, furious and afraid.

He tries to mount a defense, tries to explain, but cannot. "I didn't . . . It wasn't . . ." He isn't even sure what happened, not entirely. She rubs her neck and throat but does not get up, does not get to her feet.

"What the hell, Lewis?" She's screaming now, her voice a fire that will immolate him if it lasts. "You were choking me! You hurt me!" But it doesn't last—it falters. That's when her tears come, tears of anger and fear, tears of pain, and he knows her tears can kill him even faster.

He tries to think of something to say, some word that will explain what he thought was happening, some word to justify it, but knows no such word. No such word exists.

"I would never—" he starts, but Janey cuts him off.

"You did! You just did!"

Keeping one hand on her neck, she puts the other on the chair behind her and pushes herself unsteadily to her feet. It's the chair where she sits to play her cello. There's a stack of books on it, his books. When she sees them, she picks one up—a hardcover—and hurls it at him. Instinctively, he raises his hands to protect his face. The corner of the book connects with his forearm, stinging. She chucks another book at him and it opens midflight like wings, turning into a diving bird of prey. He lowers his face and it connects with his head.

When he looks up again, she's got the last book in her hand, wound up to throw, but she stops. "You're bleeding," she says.

Not without concern. But not without anger, either.

Lewis looks down and sees the blood on his hands, his forearms, the blood on the pillow and sheets. But the blood is dried.

"Why are you bleeding, Lewis?"

"I . . ." he starts, but he can't remember, can't think straight. When he tries, his dreams run roughshod through his memories, turning them to chaos. He's confused.

"Lewis. Why are you bleeding?" It's not a question. It's a demand.

Slowly he pieces together the night, disassembling it from the past, reassembling it. He remembers the river, clotted with fish. He remembers running home, faster and faster, sprinting until his lungs felt like stretched balloons. He remembers the noise behind him, approaching, gaining on him. Finally, he remembers the fear, remembers turning to look over his shoulder, remembers how there was nothing behind him but darkness. Remembers falling, the gravel tearing his pants, his skin, the palms of his hands.

It's clear now. The pain. The whiskey before, the whiskey after. So much of both.

Janey studies him. Her expression is not kind, and not sympathetic. He reaches for her, to hug her, but she flinches. Raises her hand. Steps back. Shakes her head, no.

He sits back down on the bed, defeated. Deflated.

"It's not a big deal," he says, and sees that she does not believe him. "I'm fine," he says, and she doesn't believe that either. "It's just a cut."

She glares at him with all the heat of an inferno. "It's not your cut I'm worried about, Lewis." She approaches the bed, but before she reaches him, she stops and looks down at the floor. Then back up at him. Then back down at the floor. She bends and reaches down. When she straightens up, she's holding two empty bottles of Old Crow.

"Two," she says.

"Two," Lewis says, answering a question she had not asked and realizing he's still drunk.

Janey stares, not amused.

"J."

"Don't."

"J," he says again.

"*Don't.*"

"I'm sorry," he says.

"I know you were asleep, Lewis. But if you ever lay your hands on me like that again . . ." She does not finish and does not have to. Before he can say anything else, she is already gone, the bottles rocking on the floor where she dropped them, the floorboard creaking beneath her feet as she storms down the hallway and leaves him behind.

Lewis lies back down on the bed. A passing cloud blocks the sun streaming in through the window, and darkness moves across the room, covering first the dresser and then the rug. Then it reaches the bed. Then his feet. He lies still as it moves toward him, lies still as it covers him, and when it covers him completely, he feels a chill, the room a few degrees colder without the sun.

Without Janey.

"It's fine," he says. To no one. To himself.

"I'm fine," he says. Quietly at first, but then louder.

"I'm fine," he says.

He even wants to believe it.

Eventually the bottles stop rocking.

23

Both Janey and Gray keep their distance from him all through the next week. It's an emotional no-fly zone more than a physical one, but obvious nonetheless. Gray does not show up to the garage on the night they usually train together. Lewis works the bag alone, pretending not to watch the door, rather than standing around looking like the spurned asshole he feels like. At dinner she stays quiet. Reserved. She doesn't blatantly ignore him, but it's clear that the thing between them is growing. As it expands, it pushes them further apart. Janey does not try to coax her out. He made the mess, and it's his to clean. There's something bad between them, too—something fetid. An infection. He can smell it on her. Disapproval. Disappointment. Disgust. She wears scarves so Gray won't see the marks on her neck, but they're still there, and both of them know it.

After a week, the unease begins to define him. The weight on his chest interferes with his client interactions, turning him short-tempered and limiting his tips. At the Vatican, he feels it on his skin. A discomfort.

"You look like shit warmed over," Fenwick tells him.

"Warmed shit seems aspirational."

"That good, huh?"

"I'm fine."

"Course you are."

But is he? He feels it when he's alone too. Like he's sprung a leak and his confidence is pouring out, leaving only doubt and insecurity. It spills over into a second week, and a third. Each night he runs, the darkness on his heels. Each night he drinks, pacing in circles as if the whiskey bottle is a stake to which his mood has chained him. Each night he does not sleep. When he closes his eyes, the waiting darkness swallows him.

The sleeplessness compounds, each night a log he stacks until the pile is high enough to burn himself on. He's been here before, or someplace like it. The fire will consume everything around him if he doesn't get away. It's what he's always done when he can't run fast enough or far enough or often enough to keep the darkness at bay: he leaves. A few days alone, a week in the woods, some time in the mountains far from home. A chance to let himself breathe, a few feral days without anyone watching. Time to break himself down and rebuild without clients or family or anyone to perform for. Isn't that what life lived among other people and their expectations and desires *is*? A performance?

After dinner that night, he paces the bedroom.

"Your motor's running," Janey says, hugging her cello while she practices scales, occasionally bowing notes like the song of a mournful and confused bird. He can't tell if the coolness between them is distraction or lingering resentment.

"I'm taking off for a few days. Just to figure things out."

She nods but doesn't look up from the sheet music on the floor.

I need to go before this gets any worse, he thinks. Janey lifts her head to look at him. Her eyes have lost none of their color or brightness, as if they don't reflect light from outside so much as broadcast it from within, but they're more clouded than usual. There's something behind them.

"Before what gets any worse?"

Lewis recoils, unsure whether she read his mind or he spoke out loud. "Fighting with Gray."

"Running from her won't help."

"I'm not running. I don't run."

He sounds defensive and knows it. Janey looks at him hard. With her bow hand, she reaches behind her chair, picks up one of his muddy running shoes, and dangles it from a lace like a rat by its tail.

"I don't run *from fights*," he says.

"I'm not sure what scares me more," she says with a patience that feels like pity. "That you think what you're running from every night is not a fight, or that you think what's going on between you and your daughter *is*."

———

Half an hour later he's sprinting alongside the river, the air foul with rotting salmon. The season is almost over. The fish are spawned out from their merciless, fatal need to breed. The air is September crisp, but with a hint of unseasonable warmth turned sour off the water. As he runs through the darkness, and from the darkness, he's both thinking about what Janey said and trying to trick himself into not thinking about it when the solution comes to him. He turns immediately for home.

Without showering or changing, he approaches Gray's door.

"Come in," she says.

"How'd you know I was here?"

"Squeaky floorboard."

He opens the door; she wrinkles her face.

"Also, the smell."

"I was running. It's sweat."

"Smells worse than that."

"Spawned-out salmon."

"Did you roll in them?"

A moment passes in which he knows they're both thinking of the dog, how she would splash among the fetid fish in the river shallows, drag them ashore, slide around on them until slime covered her coat.

So this is how it's going to go, he thinks.

There's a notebook open on her lap, a textbook on the bed beside her. For a second Lewis sees himself in his childhood bedroom, studying in a quiet race to finish before The Old Man stumbled home from the tavern full of whiskey and menace. The picture of his old childhood home hangs over her bed, slightly askew, as if to thumb its nose at him. He hopes the chill he feels is the sweat cooling on his skin.

"I'm heading into the Wallowas for a few days, Gray. Hike up to tree line. Sleep outside. Maybe shoot an elk."

"OK."

"Come with me."

"What?"

"Come with me. Will you come with me?"

"Why?"

The word rings out in the quiet room like a gunshot. Lewis doesn't lean against the doorframe so much as fall against it, wounded.

"Why?" he asks, repeating it dumbly, returning weak fire.

"School just started. I can't fall behind this early in the year."

"Skip a day. Today's what, Wednesday? We'll leave early

Friday morning. You can skip that day and Monday too. Nothing good ever happens on a Monday anyway. We'll make it a quick trip. Just a long weekend."

His daughter looks at him, tapping a pen against her leg. Lewis finds himself frustratingly unable to read her mind or her expression. Beneath him is unfamiliar ground.

"It will be good for you."

Still she says nothing.

"It will be good for *us*."

Tap. Tap. Tap.

"Please," he says, and that feels unfamiliar too.

"Fine." Without ceremony or flourish, she turns back to her homework.

Foolishly, Lewis smiles, but Gray does not see it. He's been dismissed.

24

On Thursday he helps Fenwick move into an old RV he bought at auction and parked on land fronting the river. They load boxes from the shop, where he's been living, and caravan them to the new place, where they park beside each other in the mud.

"Helping friends move is the price I pay for having a pickup," Lewis says.

"My truck's bigger than yours, asshole."

"It's always about size with you."

The property is pretty enough. The meadow stretches from the road back to the Terrebonne, three or four acres of deep grass and flowers. But the motor home damn near ruins the view. The moss-covered vinyl is stained from years of sun and rain, the tires are cracked, the wheels rusted, and the whole thing lists alarmingly to starboard.

"I think she's a fixer-upper."

"I guess I've got a thing for those." His last wife worked at the DMV and had a fondness for all-night Keno. When she left after two long years of marriage, he sold the house to pay off her debts and has been sleeping on a cot in the back room of the Vatican ever since.

"How old is this thing?"

"This *thing* is a Pace Arrow, and it's what state of the art looked like in 1972."

"It's almost as old as I am. What is it, twenty feet?"

"Twenty-two."

"Well, then."

"It's bigger than where I've been sleeping, and it's got a kitchen. Anyway, it's only temporary."

"Sure," Lewis says. "Everything's temporary."

The work is quick and the day warm. They earn their sweat. When they've finished, Lewis retrieves one last box from his truck. It's big and heavy, wrapped in shiny foil wrapping paper and tied with a ribbon.

"Housewarming gift. Janey wrapped it."

"I figured."

Inside the box is the skin of the bear, tanned and preserved. The hair is soft and thick, lustrous, brindle.

"Is this . . . ?"

Lewis nods.

"Man oh man. Why are you giving it to me?"

"I don't imagine this tin can you've decided to live in has much in the way of insulation. This'll give you something warm to sleep under until you find wife number three."

"Four."

"Four?"

"Some men date. Others marry."

"Keep trying, pal. There's a chair for every ass—even you."

Fenwick laughs, a loud and genuine bark.

"This place is a little claustrophobic," Lewis says, taking in the faded upholstery and dark wood paneling and breathing in the musty smell. When he stretches his arms, he can touch both walls.

"Hell, it's just me living here. How much space do I need?"

"Feels like a coffin."

"You're mistaken. It's a cocoon. I'll emerge when I'm good and ready, and I'll be goddamned beautiful."

He digs through the boxes they've hauled until he finds an expensive bottle of single malt a client gave him. When they exit the Arrow, it bows on its rusted springs and groans beneath their weight.

There's a stone wall at the edge of the property, along the river. They sit side by side, the sun hitting the flowing water. It reflects back at them like a kaleidoscope, the light broken into shards.

"This stone wall reminds me of New England," Lewis says. "You're living in a Robert Frost poem."

"You ever miss it? New England?"

Lewis looks out at the river and the field. In just a few weeks, the rain will return, the river will run high, and the meadow will turn to mud, but for now, at least, the grass is still green and September feels like summer. "Do you miss your ex-wives?"

"No. And yes. Our relationships work better as memories."

"It's the same for me and New England."

Fenwick uncaps the bottle and raises it in front of him.

"A drink before the war," he says, and takes a long pull.

"If fortune torments me, let hope content me," Lewis says.

Fenwick raises an eyebrow.

"Frost?"

"Shakespeare."

They drink in silence for a few minutes, the stones of the wall beneath them sun-warm, the current steady and loud.

"We put Johnson down."

"Shit." Fenwick draws out the word. Lewis looks at him,

then looks away. Taking the bottle, he tells him about Gray. Though he sticks to the facts and skirts the issues, they're plain to see if you're looking, and he knows his friend is.

"Sooner or later she was going to learn that all dogs bite. My old man thought his belt was a reasonable parenting tool. Maybe that's why I never had kids of my own, 'cause I was too afraid I'd be like him."

"I worry about the same thing."

"How bad was yours?"

"How bad? He wouldn't have pissed on me if I was on fire, but he might have if I was not." It's a joke, but only sort of, and Fenwick doesn't laugh. He stares at the river and takes a long sip.

"Mine had fists like frozen chickens. Broke three knuckles on my forehead the day I turned sixteen. He didn't like my mother giving me any attention, even on my birthday."

"Mine used to walk into a room when I was doing homework or watching TV, or even sleeping, and just haul off and punch me. Hard. He used to box in the Navy, and he knew how to hit."

"You ever ask him why?"

"'Just so you know who's boss.'"

Fenwick lifts up his shirt. The dark skin is striated with lighter scars, ribbons of tissue, horizontal stripes like pained equators. "Belt marks," he says.

Lewis peels his down over his shoulder from the collar to show the pink skin where the burns healed. "Boiling water."

Fenwick rolls up a sleeve to expose a constellation of stars against the night sky of his skin. "Mine used to smoke Dutch Treats. When he was done, he'd put them out on me."

Lewis pulls up his shirt to reveal his own galaxy of scars. "Lucky Strikes," he says. "I can still smell it, the cigarettes and the skin."

Fenwick chuckles, but it's a sad chuckle. He takes a sip. "We don't have to become them."

"Don't we?"

"We don't. It helps to remember that."

"I'm not sure anything helps."

"I've got a lot of my mother in me too. My mother was a good woman. She didn't deserve that mean fucker she married."

"I never met my mother," Lewis says. "But I know she loved my old man. It kind of scares the shit out of me, that anyone could love someone like him."

"There's a chair for every ass," Fenwick says. "Maybe even me." Lewis smiles and they touch glasses. After that, neither of them says anything for a long while. They sip scotch and watch the river and the clouds, the silence as comfortable as a blanket or an old bear skin.

"You got a good family, Lewis. You've done right by them. Made all the right choices. You're not like him."

"Maybe."

"I made all the wrong choices. That's why I'm living alone in a jacked RV in the middle of fucking nowhere." He studies the bottle and the whiskey in it. "But even so, I know I ain't like my father, either. We're better than them. We broke the cycle."

"There are worse things in this world than being alone," Lewis says.

A fusillade of birds explodes overhead, darkening the sky. They both watch, the motion reckless and beautiful. Just like that the birds disappear over the river and the sky is quiet again.

"Gray and I are heading up to the Wallowas tomorrow morning for a few days in the woods. You going to be OK out here on your own?"

He nods. "How 'bout you?"

"I'll be fine."

"Keep your pecker up," Fenwick says, the Black Pope offering his benediction.

25

After dinner he loads the truck for their trip. Restless, and needing something to ground him, he fetches the rifles and sits down to clean and oil them at the kitchen table. The solvent, Hoppes No. 9, smells both acrid and sweet. The olfactory contradiction triggers a complex nostalgia for when The Old Man taught him to wet the patches, to push them through the barrel with the rod, to oil the wood and steel. He remembers, too, his watchful eyes, the voice heavy with spite.

"You're doing it wrong."

"I'm doing it like you taught me."

"Not the guns, asshole. Raising your daughter. Being a man. You're doing it all wrong."

The voice is clear and close and mean, and the words startle Lewis. He looks up to see The Old Man in his kitchen, vapor turned to sinew, a spiteful ghost occupying the opposite chair. Recognizing the smell of whiskey and onions on his breath, the wolf-sharp teeth, yellow as piss, Lewis lifts the disassembled rifle and points it at his father.

"Fuck you," he says.

"I was fucked the day you were born, boy."

When The Old Man looks longingly at the bottle of bourbon, Lewis lays the Winchester on the table and pours himself another glass.

"What do you know about parenting? What do you know about being a man?"

"I know you're doing everything wrong, boy, just like I said you would. I know you're a goddamned disappointment. Just like I said you'd be."

Lewis sips slowly and loudly, and when he empties the glass, he sighs contentedly and fills it once more. The Old Man eyes it with visible envy.

"Woulda broke your mother's heart to see who you become. You're lucky she ain't here to see it."

"I never got to meet my own mother. That's some kind of lucky."

"You're the reason she's dead, boy."

Lewis stands quickly with his fists raised, sending his chair clattering across the floor behind him, but his father is gone, sinew returned to vapor. He looks at his shaking hands. They are recognizably his, still those of a middle-aged man. He only *feels* like a child again.

"Lewis?"

He looks up to see Janey standing in the doorway, looking frightened.

"How long have you been standing there?"

"Longer than you've been standing *there*."

He nods. Wipes his hands on his shirt. Bends over to retrieve the fallen chair.

"Lewis."

"What?"

"Put the guns away."

———

He locks the rifles in the truck with the camping gear and returns to find Janey leaning against the counter. Only the pot lights above the sink are lit, and the light makes bold shadows of her features, giving her angles she doesn't have and sharpening her features. She holds a beer with both hands, and stares into the bottle as if it contains not just a magical blend of hops and grains and water but actual magic. As if it contains all the answers to all the questions. Lewis knows the feeling, and knows, too, the inevitable disappointment that follows. Still, he fetches the Old Crow from the table, pours himself a glass, and leans beside her. When their bodies touch, Janey doesn't flinch or pull away. A minor victory.

"You need to get your head out of your ass, Lewis."

He says nothing. What is there to say? She's right.

"It feels different this time," she says, with a bit more kindness. "Your mood."

"It's not."

"I'm telling you that it *feels* different, Lewis."

The whiskey burns pleasantly as it goes down. So much of the pleasure comes from the smell. It smells like the Hoppes No. 9. Maybe bourbon is just cleaning solvent for the human soul.

Wet the patches. Ram them through.

"Different how?"

Janey swirls the beer around in her bottle. "I know how hard you fight it. I know how hard you've always fought it. But this time . . . I don't know." She takes a deep breath. He can feel it in her body, how it expands her. She's so slender that even a breath can make her bigger. "This time it feels like maybe you're losing the fight."

So that's what this is.

"I'm not, J."

"Maybe it's time, Lewis."

"Time for what?"

"To see someone. Talk to someone."

"We *are* talking."

"Not me, Lewis. Someone else. A doctor. There's medicine. Therapy. You don't have to fight this alone."

He takes another sip, choosing his words.

"I didn't think I *was* alone."

"That's not what I mean, Lewis. It's just that . . . This time feels different."

"You said that," he tells her, though he knows it won't help. Not that tone. Not that volume.

And it doesn't. But he can still feel her hip against his thigh. That she does not recoil means that she's sticking with him, or maybe just not backing down.

"What's it like this time, Lewis? Can you tell me what it's like?"

They've had this conversation before. A hundred times. A thousand. But how can he explain it? How can he articulate it? It's darkness. It's the absence of light. Describing it falls somewhere between science and poetry, stuck in the cracks where he can't reach.

"It's like I've only got one oar. I can still row, but only in circles. And my instinct is to row harder, which only makes bigger circles."

"Can't you stop rowing?" It's not a question, and he doesn't answer it.

"It's like driving the truck. But the steering wheel is loose, so the truck doesn't go where I steer it."

Janey looks at the floor. She looks at her beer. She has not looked at him since they began this conversation.

"This time it feels like Gray and I are in the truck with you."

He raises his glass to his mouth and sees that his hands are shaking, just a little, trembling the surface of the whiskey like a wind across a lake, and it worries him.

What are you afraid of?

Even as he asks the question, he knows the answer—he's afraid she's right, that it *is* different this time. He's afraid The Old Man was right too. That he's never been anything but a disappointment, and never will be. Not to him. Not to his mother, who took her own life rather than be a part of his. Not even to his wife and daughter, the only people in this world he really wants to please.

"Say something, Lewis."

"I'm just an angler in the lake of darkness."

"What's that?"

"Shakespeare."

"Lewis," she says, but he cuts her off.

"I'm fine." He makes his voice sound determined. Final. He does not want to talk anymore. They reached the edge of what he's comfortable talking about. There's a wall around the border and she has him pressed against it, a fighter against the ropes. "Really. I'm fine. Or I will be. This trip. I need it. I just need to get away for a bit."

It's worked before, a trip to the mountains with no expectations for his behavior, no restraint. It always helps. Sleeping beneath open skies, stars as far as he can see, brutal climbs on scree slopes. Fire-burnt coffee, no clients, no responsibilities.

No need to pretend.

"No need to pretend what?" she asks, and he knows he's done it again.

"No need to pretend I'm human."

She finally looks at him, and he wishes she hadn't.

"Why are you bringing Gray?"

"Why?"

"Why are you bringing Gray? You always go alone. Whatever it is you do out there, in the mountains, you can't do that if she's there. You can't just go feral on her. That's not fair. You can't do that to her."

"Things haven't been right between us, J. I need to make them right."

There's a moment without talking when he hears the hum of the refrigerator, the tick of the clock on the stove, the drip of water from the faucet. Steady. Rhythmic. Where their bodies press together, it's a finite point, but it's enough—he can feel her heart beating. He can hear it, too, or imagines he can. Why can't he hear his own heartbeat?

"You think this will help?"

His glass is almost empty and he has no answer for his wife, not to this question and not to any of them. For the first time in a long time, he feels lost—something he has not felt since he was a kid. Since then he's always known where he was going, or at least where he wanted to go, a magnetic north to which he was inexorably drawn. Now he's there and doesn't know how to stay. He has a foot and a half on his wife, more than a hundred pounds, but she makes him feel tiny. Insignificant. He's a planet, an ice giant, uninhabitable rocks and darkness and cold. She's the sun he orbits, all life-giving warmth and light.

"Things will be better when we get back, J. *I'll* be better."

Is there anything he won't do to please her? Even lie?

He drains his glass and turns for the whiskey. She has not taken even a sip of her beer, the bottle still full to the mouth, a jacket of condensation beading the glass. When he nods at it, she lifts it at arm's length, as if surprised to find it in her hands. As if it's something dangerous she's afraid to bring too close. Then she turns to the sink and pours the beer down the drain.

She does not turn back around. Her shoulders begin to tremble, and her breathing changes as she starts to cry.

Reach for her, he thinks.

But he does not reach for her. He does not move.

"You promise this will work?" she asks, the strength gone from her voice. She sounds afraid. "You promise you'll get better?"

"I always do."

"It's different this time."

"It's not."

"Yes," she says. "It is."

"Why?"

"Because. I'm pregnant, Lewis."

———

He's still leaning against the counter long after she goes to bed. Rooted to his spot, he feels heavy as the earth itself, lashed to an anchor as the tide rises. Maybe he'll never be able to move again. Maybe he'll stand leaning against the counter while the world spins, those he loves living on around him, aging and maturing until their last days, when some new family moves into the house and the years pass, the walls changing color, the windows growing darker and lighter over and over and over again as time reels past, still unable to move.

Or afraid to.

Go to her, he thinks. But he doesn't.

When the bottle is empty, he separates himself from the counter with an effort that shatters something within him. He rinses his glass in the sink and wipes it dry, rinses Janey's beer bottle and puts it in the bin. As he walks down the hallway toward their bedroom, the oak floor squeaks beneath his weight.

It's an original floor, the boards fit beautifully, each snugged into place by the others around it and nailed down, but still the wood warps and swells. Sometimes the head of a nail will rise from the surface. They make it treacherous for socks or bare feet.

From the garage he fetches his toolbox, his carpenter's hammer, the ash handle worn smooth, and the punch, a bullet-shaped cylinder of cold metal. Down on his knees, he drives the unseated nails back into place one at a time, three strikes with the hammer for each, three strikes that ring out like gunshots, again and again and again.

The noise is undeniably loud. Offensively loud. The bedroom doors open. Gray looks confused, standing in her sweatpants and Red Sox jersey, her hair a tangle as she yawns. Janey watches him with an expression that does something to him, an expression that cuts through the darkness like a searchlight. For a moment he feels its warmth wash over him and the weight of the hammer disappears, the blur of the whiskey sharpens into focus, and the uncertainty of the future no longer worries him. They look at each other, the three of them, his family, together in the hallway of the home they share, and Lewis feels something deep inside him where he long ago stopped looking.

————

It's almost midnight. A half-moon hangs in the sky as he runs through town, the whiskey like sparks in his throat. The stars shine and the streetlights all seem to be working, but he's never seen Disappointment so dark. The darkness feels liquid, thick as ink. It fills his lungs, pinning his legs and arms like an oil-slick seabird's wings. When he runs faster, it only hurts more, and by the time he makes it back to the house he can barely stand.

It's just a few hours until sunrise. He waits for it, all but holding his breath. He and Gray are on their way to the mountains before it arrives, gone before Janey even wakes up.

IV

THIS IS WHAT WE DO

26

Gray naps for the first few hours, waking only when a bump in the road bounces her head against the window. She swallows the pool of spit that's formed in her lower lip and sneaks a glance at her father. He's restless, drumming his hands on the wheel and shaking his leg like he's working a floor loom. "Your engine's running," her mother would say. Gray almost says it herself, but she doesn't want to play that role with him and doesn't want him to know she's awake yet. His nervous energy fills the cab. She can't remember ever feeling it from him before. Maybe it's her—maybe he's nervous that she's come along on a trip he usually makes alone. Maybe it's more than that. Ever since they went into the woods with Johnson, he's been annoyed with her and edgy as hell. She knows she disappointed him by not being as strong as he wanted her to. Even though she tried, she still cried. Like a baby.

Like a girl.

She couldn't help it. He has to know that, doesn't he?

"He loved that dog too," her mother said, trying to reassure her.

"So why didn't *he* cry?"

"Everybody deals with things differently. That's just not your father's way."

"I don't want it to be my way, either."

"Don't be ashamed of crying, Gray. There's no shame in that, and there's no shame in being sad when you lose someone you love."

Maybe it's something else entirely that's bugging him. Who knows? As long as she can remember, he's had moods, but they're not usually this bad and they don't always last this long. She sneaks another glance at him and he catches her looking and smiles, but the smile looks forced. She says nothing. She doesn't mean for it to be a choice, but it feels like one.

After a few minutes, the silence starts to feel uncomfortable. A few minutes after that, it becomes unbearable. Her father opens his window. Oregon rushes in at seventy miles an hour, whipping a whirlwind of heat and noise and highway dust around the cab with a noise far worse than the silence. He closes the window again almost immediately.

Gray watches the Wallowas loom on the horizon, beautiful ridges of rock and shadow, patches of snow high against the sun. They're beautiful, but they never seem to grow any closer, and she wonders how much longer the drive is going to take.

When a time-worn gas station appears, her father pulls into the lot alongside rusty hand pumps and an antique bottled-Coke machine filled with spiderwebs.

"I'll get coffee while you hit the bathroom," he says.

"I'm good."

"Go while we're stopped so we don't have to stop to go." It's what he tells clients on the boat, trying to get them to consolidate bathroom breaks and limit their time without hooks in the water. She's annoyed but gets out of the truck anyway.

The bathroom is around back, and suitably gross. She's peed in worse places. Splotches of mold grow on chipped tiles discolored and stained with God knows what. While she goes, she reads the graffiti on the wall to entertain herself, a mix of foul language, phone numbers, and bad jokes. A lot of it is misspelled. *No illeagles! Fuck shcool.* Anything worth doing is worth doing right, her father always tells her. Except vandalism, apparently.

She emerges into the sunlight, blinking, and watches a dog approach the truck, a goitered coonhound as old as the station itself. Maybe older. Seeing a dog causes something to rise inside her, something involuntary and sad.

"Hey buddy," her father says, squatting to greet it, but it stops and bares its teeth, the hair on its back bristling. "It's OK, boy." He takes a step closer and offers his hand. The dog growls a warning. Then it begins to bark, a raspy and hoarse baying, like an asthmatic wolf, and he backs away until it stops.

"Careful," he says when he sees her. "This one's mean."

The dog sees her too. Wagging its bent tail like an arthritic metronome, it limps over, presses its head against her thigh, and licks her hand.

———

At the trailhead, the truck kicks up a cloud of dust that is still settling when her father opens his door. It overtakes him, covering his clothes and skin, and Gray laughs inside the truck. He's still coughing and brushing himself off when she gets out. When he sees her watching, he laughs too, and she takes it as a good sign.

"Cell phone." He holds out a hand. All her life the size of his hands have surprised her. Her own hands are big too, the fingers long and slender, but his look like they could crush a toaster.

"Seriously?"

"That's the whole point of being here."

She turns off her phone and he tucks it into the glove box. "Grab the rifles."

She fetches them from the truck and hands him one, which he takes from its case. It's the Ruger 270 with the stainless barrel and synthetic stock. He opens the bolt and checks to make sure it isn't loaded. He knows it's not—he zipped it into its case himself—but he checks anyway, a routine she's seen him perform a thousand times. The sliding bolt rings loud and out of place in the wide-open space of the trailhead, far from the ambient noise of civilization.

The cartridges are in their packs, in separate boxes, different colors to distinguish the different calibers. He made her watch a TV show about gun safety when she was younger, which she thought was going to be boring but she liked anyway. It showed cartridges being made at the factory. They begin as disks stamped from sheets of a single metal, copper nickel or brass, and are rammed through a die over and over to stretch them into shape. Then a machine trims and grooves them so the rifle can extract them when they're spent. Another machine punches a pocket for the primer. Even after all that, they're still just dumb metal cylinders. It's not until they're fitted with slugs and primer that they become something else.

"Some might argue that the true power of a firearm is not measured by its caliber, but by its ability to divide and polarize entire societies," the narrator said. "But it's difficult to argue the critical role they've played in America's history, making them a tool both useful and dangerous."

"That guy talking?" she said. "*He* sounds like a tool both useful and dangerous."

Remembering their laughter and how easily it came to them then, Gray almost smiles but catches herself.

They trade rifles. When she opens the Ruger's bolt and checks the chamber, even though she just watched him check it, he nods. This time she smiles—she can't help it.

Her father opens the other case and takes out the old Winchester .30-30. It's the rifle he brought into the woods that day with Johnson.

"Do you want this one instead?" he asks when he sees her staring at it.

"No."

"I don't mind, Gray."

"I said no." He looks at her, trying to understand, but she can tell he doesn't. He nods and checks the Winchester's breech.

"OK then. Ready?"

Gray nods, and without another word, they shoulder their packs and set off into the mountains.

27

The Wallowas range diagonally across the northeast corner of Oregon, almost entirely within the bounds of the federally designated Eagle Cap Wilderness. The serrated edges of the mountains shred the clouds into ribbons that wave like banners over deep glacial valleys and ponds. The more popular trails bear heavy traffic during the summer, recreational hikers in zip-off pants and bandannas, backpackers shuffling like nylon-shelled crabs, climbers with coiled ropes like snake handlers, but September is the shoulder season, and they've avoided the busy areas. It will mean some bushwhacking along game paths, but it feels good to unfold the kinks the long drive has left in her legs. Each step takes them further from home. Each step, too, brings them toward something else.

The woods and mountains have always had a powerful effect on her father. In the past he's returned different from when he left, all pretense and civility stripped away, leaving him simpler and happier, like a caged bear released into the wild. Already she can see that his nervous energy is gone and he's more at ease. Though she's reluctant to admit it, she feels better, too, and as the trail rises in earnest, straining her legs and lungs, she likes it. It feels earned.

After a couple of hours the canopy opens up to reveal sky, and Gray blinks in the suddenness of light. They've reached the tree line. Just ahead, the ground levels out into a small clearing in the lee of a high granite ridge. Nightfall is just a few hours away.

"This is as far as we go."

He points out the sights while they set up camp: a hanging glacier high on a nearby peak; a subalpine lake shimmering in the distance; scree slopes overhead.

"There are bighorn sheep up here. Black bear, cougars, lynx. A few years ago, a trail camera set up by the state picked up a wolverine, but it's the only time anybody's seen one in the Wallowas."

"Have you seen any of those?"

"No, but a few years ago I saw a wolf." He points just beyond their campsite. "It walked into this clearing, all alone, a big gray male with white feet and black bristles along his back. I couldn't believe how big he was. How beautiful. The state tracks them, but there was no collar on this one. No tag. Just a lone wolf free to wander the wild."

Gray hears something in his voice. Longing, maybe. Envy.

"When I was your age, I didn't even know wolves still existed in the wild. The wildest thing I knew lived in my house. The wildest thing I knew raised me."

The revelation surprises her. As long as she can remember, he's changed the subject every time she's asked about her grandfather, as if even a mention is an infection all the antibodies in his system have to band together to fight off, but now he's volunteering information. Is this why he brought her along? She meets his eyes, but his face darkens and he looks away. After that, he doesn't say anything for so long that she begins to wonder if the conversation is over.

"The wildest things aren't in the forests or jungles, or even in the shadows," he says, finally. "They're inside *us*. We spend our lives building cages—work, marriage, friendships, families—to contain them."

"Does Mom know you feel that way about marriage?" She means it as a joke but he looks at her with disappointment.

"Everybody's got wildness in them, Gray. Some people are just better at caging it."

Unsure how to respond, she follows his lead and turns back to the work at hand. As she uncoils a skein of parachute cord and drapes it over a fallen lodgepole pine, she tries to picture her father here, alone, as the wolf crossed his path. What that must have felt like. What it must have meant to him. She pulls the line taut.

"Aren't wolves pack animals?" she asks, thinking out loud as she loops the cord over itself and ties a trucker's hitch to cinch it.

"They are."

"Why was that one alone?"

"Some wolves just do better that way. They do better being alone."

"That doesn't make any sense. There aren't that many left out here, not anymore. You'd think they'd stick together. I wonder why that one left its pack?"

"I don't know, Gray."

"I mean, don't you think it's weird that it just left its mate or cubs behind and set out on its own?"

Her father looks up from the knot he's tying long enough to make eye contact with her. Then he looks away, high up at the sharp outlines of a ridge gone to silhouette against the setting sun, as if he's hiding his face. As if he's afraid to let her see his expression. It's a reminder that they're not there yet, not back to where they were. That there's still a space between them, and if they're not careful, one of them might fall into it.

———

A simple camp, two tarps strung between anemic firs growing at the edge of the tree line. That's how he likes to sleep—no tent, exposed to the open air. They arrange their sleeping bags beneath one of the tarps, head to foot, and spread their gear beneath the other. With the hatchet, he digs a perimeter of shallow trenches for rain, and then gathers wood while Gray builds the fire. When he returns with an armful of downfall and kindling and sees the flames leaping high above the circle of stones she arranged, he nods approvingly.

Working by headlamp as darkness begins to fall, he cooks some of last year's elk, brought frozen from home and thawed as they hiked. There are glass onions, too, one of her favorite camp meals, giant Walla Walla sweets hollowed out and stuffed with spiced beef and rice and cooked over the embers in tinfoil. There are canned beans and thick wedges of bread to mop up the sauce. It's a lot of food. After hiking for so long, they don't eat their dinners so much as brutalize them. When they're done, he stuffs the paper plates into the fire. Gray watches them curl and crisp, turning to ash and rising on the thermals like tiny birds.

It's early still, but they're tired, and when the fire begins to burn low, they climb into their sleeping bags. Gray's feels like a cocoon, a pleasant blend of confinement and comfort that smells of camp smoke, sweat and fish, pine and hemlock and pollen. It smells like the world itself.

As the fire burns itself out, the light retreats, replaced by darkness. First the clearing around them disappears. Then the trees they've staked their tarps to. Soon she can see only right in front of her, her father's sleeping bag, her own. She holds her hands in front of her face and as the fire goes out, those disappear too. She and her father have vanished so completely and convincingly that she says his name aloud to make sure he's still there, and to make sure that she is too.

"Good night, Gray."

There's no alarm, no place to be, and she does not wake until her body is ready. When she does, the world she watched vanish has reappeared. She lies still, taking stock of herself—a systems check. Her muscles have recovered from the hike, and each breath of fresh mountain air brings a minor and subtle joy. There's a clarity to her thoughts. She has to pee. She slips out of her bag and into a sweatshirt and makes her way behind a rock to the designated restroom. Already she can feel her rhythms changing, syncing with the natural beats of the world around her. Birdsong, wind through high grass, the rattle of branches. There's no passing traffic to drown them out, no doors slamming, no ringing phones or TV news. So much of her life belongs to this world already, to nature, to wild places, to cold rivers, open skies, and leaping fish. Surrendering the rest of it seems easy. In that moment she knows that she loves it here, and she's glad she came.

Her father is sitting on a rock at the edge of their camp, staring into the distance with a cup of coffee in his hands. The percolator hangs over the fire. Gray pours herself a cup and joins him, and he nods but says nothing. While she feels rejuvenated, he looks spent, depleted, even in the forgiving light of morning. The lines in his face are as deep and sharp as the crags above their camp, his eyes dark. But he seems content, so she says nothing, either, and they sit on the big rock staring across the valley at the ridges and slopes, the flowers and meadow grass swaying in the gentle breeze.

If time were to stop just then, all the clocks to freeze, Gray isn't sure she'd notice. She isn't sure she'd mind.

Eventually he gets up and makes breakfast, bacon and beans, slabs of bread toasted in the grease. They eat wordlessly. Afterward Gray pushes the paper plates into the fire.

"What do we do now, Pop?"

"This, Gray. This is what we do."

28

That afternoon they find an elk. Hiking above a grass-choked valley beyond camp with lunch still warm in their bellies, they see the scat, pellet groups the size of house cats, and follow it up a ridge. At the crest, her father points down into the valley, and Gray sees the bull nibbling at the tender leaves of a young aspen. The meadow is a blur of colors, like fingers through wet paint, red and purple and yellow. The color of coffee with milk, the bull stands out as if in bas relief, black at the neck and mane, white in the rump, antlers like defoliated trees growing atop his enormous head. A breeze ripples through the field as if it's the animal's breath.

"He's beautiful."

"But where's his harem?"

"You got one wrong." She punches her father in the arm.

"What do you mean?"

"The term of venery. It's a *herd* of elks."

"A harem is something else. The males stick together most of the year until the rut, when the dominant bulls find groups of cows to follow. Once they do, they sort of take charge of them, and the group becomes their harem. Once a bull has a harem, he'll defend it by fighting any other bulls that challenge."

"How do you know this one's dominant?"

"Just look at him."

The bull is bigger than most elk she's seen, feeding with alert confidence, raising his head now and then to scan for threats. Even from the distant ridge she can feel its strength.

"Pretty good life," she says.

"What's that?"

"Being a bull. He lives with a bunch of ladies who let him fight and eat and do whatever he wants."

Her father smiles sidelong at her. "Don't kid yourself. Taking care of women is *work*."

She punches him in the arm again, and this time he grins.

They glass the elk for more than an hour, watching for signs of his harem or other bulls. Whatever it is that's been between them feels like it has melted some, closing the distance a bit. Her father talks more. Jokes more. Gray welcomes it, lets it warm her like the sun.

When they hike back to camp, she gets the fire going and he cooks. Beans. Jerky. Hardtack. Potatoes. They talk more while they eat, laughing easily, telling stories, talking about baseball, fishing, nonsense, all in one fell swoop, as if making up for the past few tight-lipped weeks. The ease of conversation makes her realize just how bad things had gotten. But there's still something between them, she knows, and will be until she addresses it.

"I've been meaning to say I'm sorry."

He looks at her quizzically, head cocked. "For what?"

"For letting you down."

"What are you talking about, Gray?"

"I know you were disappointed in me that day. With Johnson. For not being tougher."

"No," he says.

"For crying."

"No, Gray. I wasn't disappointed."

"I tried to be stronger. I wanted to be. I tried not to cry. But . . ."

"Gray—"

"I know you wanted me to be tougher, and I wasn't. I'm sorry I disappointed you."

"I wasn't disappointed, Gray. Not in *you*."

The fire crackles, and for a few moments there's only silence to compete with it. Gray counts the length of the silence, assigning the duration some meaning she doesn't understand yet.

One, two, three, four . . .

"I had a dog when I was a kid. A black Lab named Quarry. I loved that dog like you would not believe, Gray. She was the first thing I ever loved, and I've never loved anything the same way since."

"Thanks a lot."

"No, Gray. Listen. Quarry? She died. She died, and that was the first time I realized that could happen. That the things I love might not always be there. My mother died, too, and of course I loved her, but she died before I knew her, so I really only loved the idea of her. When I say I've never loved anything the same way, I don't mean that I love you or your mother less than I loved that dog. I just mean that Quarry was the first thing I ever loved. I loved Quarry without caution. I loved her with abandon. It's harder now, because . . ."

He does not finish. He doesn't have to.

"How did she die?"

"My father came home drunk one night and hit her with the truck. She was in terrible pain. Couldn't walk. I could see the fear in her eyes, could see how much she wanted me to do something to make the pain stop."

"What did you do?"

"My dad got the shovel out of the garage and handed it to me. 'Hit her,' he said. 'Hit her hard.' I could hear the whiskey in his voice. Could feel the spit on my face with each word. 'She needs help,' I said. I wanted to take her to a vet. I wanted to save her. But we couldn't save her. She was too far gone."

The shifting wind blows smoke into Gray's eyes so they water and sting. She waits but he does not finish the story, not on his own. It feels important to her to know how it ends.

"What did you . . . do?"

Five, six, seven.

"My father yelled at me for crying. 'Look at you,' he said, 'crying at your age like a goddamned girl. Over what? A fuckin' dog?' I didn't know what to do. Either way I was going to let one of them down. I didn't know what to do."

He goes quiet as the memory overtakes him. Gray watches him, unsure what to say.

"Sometimes, when something you love is in pain," he says, "the best thing you can do for them is to end it for them. The pain."

Gray stares at the fire, allowing him his silence, letting the night embrace them, listening to the fire. She pokes at it with a stick, rearranging the wood and giving a little life to the flames.

"Quarry is a good name," she says, finally. "Was she a hunting dog?"

"She was. But that's not why I called her that. I named her after a boxer, Jerry Quarry. He was pretty good for a while. Came from a boxing family, started young, and went on to win the Golden Gloves by knocking out every other fighter he faced, all five of them."

"Was he your favorite boxer?"

"He was on a TV show I loved. My father loved him too. At least until he fought Ali a couple of times and lost. Jerry Quarry was a bleeder, and The Old Man always held that against him."

"How about Johnson? Why did you name her that?"

Her father smiles.

"Because even as a puppy, she snored like an outboard motor," he says, pursing his lips and blowing a long, wet raspberry, a reasonable impression of both the dog and a speedboat. Gray laughs, and the laugh comes so easily and from so deep inside her that the sadness comes with it, for Johnson, for her father, and she is crying and laughing at the same time. She wipes the tears from her eyes and cheeks, and when she's done she looks at her father and sees that he is looking at her.

"That day in the woods? I handled that wrong, Gray. I know I did. And I'm sorry. I wasn't disappointed in *you*. I was disappointed in *myself*."

She sees the look on his face, the discomfort. It's like ripping a fishhook out of his skin, how it hurts him to apologize, even to think it. How it takes a piece of him with it when he does. Why is it so hard?

"I'm not sure I've ever heard you say that before."

"What?"

"I'm sorry."

"The plow doesn't apologize to the field."

"What does that mean?"

"It means you can't expect more out of something than its own nature."

"What does *that* mean?"

"*That*," he says, "means that I'm an asshole."

The dwindling firelight consumes his face, half his body

in light, half in shadows. She gets up, walks over to her father, and, without a word, hugs him.

His body tenses at the touch, his muscles contracting, his limbs going tight. It's a rejection.

She feels it immediately and lets go.

"Gray," he says, but she stands up and backs away until the darkness swallows him completely.

29

The next morning they track the elk and find the harem grazing in a subalpine meadow, a fringe of trees for shelter. Gray counts eight cows and a dozen yearlings. Most are bedded down. A few skittish cows hover near their calves, which dart through the deep grass in frantic, finite bursts of energy. The bull stands apart, fresh mud drying on his coat from a recent wallow. His antlers are tall and complicated, already fully hardened to bone, and he's shed the velvet and rubbed them brown.

"It's a sign of his confidence," her father says, "how he lets the females linger in the open. Isn't he impressive?"

Through the field glasses, Gray sees fire in the bull's eyes, in the way he exhales and stamps his legs.

"They're *all* beautiful."

"Packing him out is going to mean work. We'll have to quarter him, but even so, we're looking at three trips to the truck. Maybe four. And don't forget, we can't tell anyone about this."

"What do you mean?"

"When we get back to town. We can tell your mother and

Uncle Fenwick, but that's it. Elk season doesn't open for rifles until October. Right now it's only open for bow hunting."

"We're poaching?"

"We're feeding our family. We've taken fish out of season before. We take fish after we limit out all the time. How is this any different?"

"How is this any different from what Littlejohn is doing? You said he was a prick for shooting all those deer out of season."

"Littlejohn *is* a prick. The deer have nothing to do with it."

"So?"

"He's shooting dozens of deer, year after year, decimating the population. The state *allows* us to take an elk. We're just taking it a few weeks early."

"That's still breaking the law."

"It's a victimless crime, Gray."

She remembers the last time he told her that, the memory a lump in her stomach, perfectly round, the size of a golf ball. She can tell, too, that he doesn't remember saying it.

"If we shoot that bull, we take him away from his family? From all those other elk? What happens to them? What happens to all those calves if we kill their father?"

"That's not his family, it's his harem. And those aren't his kids, Gray. They're just strays he gathered."

"Like Mom."

"What?"

"Mom was a foster kid."

"What that elk did was more like kidnapping than adoption."

"They seem happy enough."

"You ever hear of Stockholm syndrome?"

"No."

He looks at her for a moment, his frustration evident. When

he rolls his head, first left, hard, and then right, she hears his neck crack. It sounds like something breaking.

"How about anthropomorphism? You ever hear of that?"

"Yes."

"That's what you're doing. You're anthropomorphizing the elk. It's a mistake."

Lying on their stomachs side by side on a granite slab the size of their bathroom, Gray can feel bruises forming where her hip and elbow bones touch the rock.

"What will happen to them when he dies?"

"Another bull will find them and add them to his harem."

"Just like that?"

"Nature's not sentimental."

"It just seems . . . cold."

"It's survival, Gray. Not romance. Nature's an asshole."

"If you shoot him, doesn't that make *you* the asshole?" Though she means to sound lighthearted, that's not how it comes out. There's a weight to her words that drags them into the dirt.

"I don't get it, Gray. I've seen you club and gut a thousand fish. More. You think elk have feelings but fish don't? You don't seem to mind when you're eating the meat."

Rebuked, she says nothing, but he attacks again while she's on the ropes. It's his instinct, his training, something he does without thought.

"What did you think we came here to do? We're part of the food chain. The top of it. We're not going to shoot that bull out of spite, and we're not going to shoot him for fun. We're going to shoot him because he'll feed us for a whole year."

"I know that."

"So what's the problem?"

Despite the weak late-season sun, she can feel the heat of

a mild sunburn on her neck and ears, on her nose. Maybe it's the elevation. The air is thinner, the sun closer. She takes a deep breath, hoping the fresh air will help her thoughts, but her breath is toxic after two nights in camp, no showers, no tooth-brush, and her teeth feel like they need a shave.

Why can't she just tell him the truth? That she's lost her taste for this, for hunting, for killing, ever since that day in the woods with the dog. Maybe it's only temporary. Maybe it's not. She doesn't know how to tell him without disappointing him. She doesn't know how to tell him without making it sound like blame.

"This is why we're here, Gray. This is why we came."

"I thought we came for time alone. For time together. I thought we came here to be surrounded by nature."

"This *is* nature."

She can hear the annoyance in his voice, but something else too: finality. The conversation is over. He grabs his rifle, brings it into shooting position, and leans into it with his eye against the scope.

"Get the Ruger and sight him in. Aim just above and behind the forelegs. That's where the lungs are, hanging like large pink fruit. If my shot doesn't drop him, you hit him again."

She knows he's regulating his breathing, relaxing his mus-cles, just like he taught her to do.

"Let me know when you're ready, Gray."

She picks up her rifle. Instead of aiming at the bull, she gets to her feet, slings it over her shoulder, and starts walking back to camp. She's fifty feet away before her father notices. Though she can hear him swearing, she keeps walking, faster and faster, the rifle banging against the back of her thigh, her heart beat-ing louder and more quickly until it fills her head like a war drum. The gunshot behind her is loud enough to drown it out.

Impossibly loud. It echoes off the rock around them, creating what sounds like other gunshots that all echo together, joined by the memory of the gunshot that ended Johnson's life. Gray holds her hands over her ears, but it's too late to block them out, any of them, and as she runs back to camp, she knows she will hear them echoing for a long time to come.

30

Gray stokes the fire needlessly high and hangs the percolator over the flames. When it starts to boil she pours herself a cup. Then she sits down with the book she brought with her—her English teacher assigned it over the summer, and it's due next week—and reads it to pass the time while she waits for her father to return from the hunt.

He does so noisily, stomping around the camp, his anger as evident as that of a kid in the throes of a tantrum. She does not ask about the elk. He pours himself coffee and joins her. Right away she sees his hands are shaking. Coffee splashes over the rim of his mug in fracture waves, spilling onto his boots. His legs are shaking too.

It's not anger; it's something else.

"Are you OK, Pop?"

"I'm fine."

"You're shaking."

"I'm fine," he says again, sharply, but backpedals when he sees the concern on her face. "I think I'm coming down with something. A fever, maybe. It came out of nowhere."

She puts down her book.

"It's just a chill, Gray. That's all." He takes a sharp breath, and it seems to hurt him.

"The coffee will help," she says. But it doesn't. After a few minutes he gets up and roots around in his pack for his flask. Gray returns to her book half-heartedly, lifting her eyes to study him between paragraphs as he pulls out the rest of his clothes and puts them on piece by piece: a lined flannel shirt over his vest, a wool halibut jacket, his raincoat. She's wearing only a light fleece over a T-shirt. He's bundled in layers, hugging himself for warmth.

By nightfall he's shaking too violently to open the cans for dinner without dropping them. When Gray takes them, it frightens her that he does not protest.

"Dinner's good." It's an effort toward normalcy, a baited hook to see if he will respond. He does.

"Fresh elk would be better."

Gray gets to her feet and tosses the empty cans into the flames. "I'm going to bed," she says, and he waves her off.

Later she hears him scraping around in the darkness. Then she smells his breath on her face, the whiskey, the beans, and knows he's just inches away, checking if she's asleep. She pretends she's asleep because something tells her it would be worse not to.

His bag rustles from his shivering. What if he's really sick? What if he gets worse? It's a long hike out, and she's not confident she could find the way. How would she even get him down the mountain? She wishes she had her phone, wishes she could call her mother or her uncle. As she listens to his shaking, she's slow to recognize that it's not all that she's hearing. His breath comes in short, stuttered gasps, muffled by his sleeping bag. He's not just shivering—he's crying.

Gray slips out of her bag and crouches over him. He recoils

from the light of her headlamp, the muscles around his mouth and eyes puckered and tense. She's never seen her father cry before. There's fear in his eyes, and she's never seen that before, either. She hadn't even thought him capable of it. It shocks her that he doesn't roll away, doesn't cover himself. It's as if he's defenseless—something else she's never seen before. As if he believes it too late to hide from whatever is causing his fear. Or too late to hide it from her.

"Pop, what's wrong?"

He says nothing and rolls on his side, crying loudly. When she tries to touch him, to comfort him, he jerks away.

She does not sleep the rest of the night, sitting wrapped in her sleeping bag with her back against one of the small trees they've lashed their tarps to, watching over her father. His crying does not stop. It doesn't even slow.

"It's OK," she says occasionally, though she is not sure that it is. "It's OK, Pop. It's OK."

———

The morning sunlight fails to warm or console him. In the light of day he looks smaller, his bulk shrunken, as if he's cried away water weight and trembled away pounds. Maybe it's just in Gray's mind, her image of him diminished.

She tries to engage him with coffee, food, conversation. He ignores it all. The coffee grows cold and the food sits uneaten until a brigade of ants discovers it, little black soldiers marching up and into the can.

"An army," she says. "A colony. A nest. A swarm."

His wet eyes show no understanding, and he does not respond. Something in him has broken. Snapped.

Did I do this to him?

By nightfall the crying stops and her father falls asleep. Relieved and exhausted, she eats dinner straight out of a can warmed over the fire. She's wound up with fear, from her mind wandering like an unleashed animal, but the fatigue weighs her down, so she pulls herself into her sleeping bag beside him. His breathing is steady. Regular. *He's better*, she thinks. Within a few minutes, she falls asleep too.

During the night she wakes to find the stars gone, the sky not just dark but smothering. Airless. For a moment she does not remember where she is and does not understand. Then it comes back to her, and she holds her breath and listens for her father.

She can hear insects, the retreating wingbeats of a night bird, branches rattling like bones. She can hear her heartbeat. And then she can hear her father too. He's moving around on the other side of camp, the sound muffled by distance.

Gray gets up and follows the sound. As she gets closer, she can hear that he's begun to cry again. She turns on her headlamp and sees him sitting in the dirt, his back against the big rock, holding the Winchester in his shaking hands. The rifle's stock is in the dirt between his boots and the barrel rests beneath his chin. Without hesitating, she takes it from him, slides open the bolt, and ejects the lone shell from the chamber. It falls to the dewy grass with a thud. She picks it up and throws it as far as she can, and does not hear it land.

"Pop?" she says.

"Gray," he says.

And then it begins to rain.

31

The first time he took her hunting she was too young to carry a gun. They spent the day walking through deep grass on a client's ranch in Eastern Washington. His dogs, a symmetrical pair of English setters, nosed ahead of them like bird-flushing bookends. When they got into birds around lunchtime, the hunters fired, the pheasants fell, and the dogs retrieved them. Instead of returning it to the shooter, one of them brought one of the birds to Gray. Unsure what to do, she looked at her father.

"Hold your hands out," he said. The dog dropped the still-warm pheasant into them. The golden feathers shimmered in the sun, the deep green of the neck, a pinprick of blood the color of the bird's wattle. But the bird was still alive and began to thrash in her hands.

"It's OK," her father said, either to her or to the bird. He closed her hands in one of his own, holding the bird still, and with the other, twisted its beautiful neck until it popped. The bundle of feathers went limp in her hands.

Her tears arrived without warning.

"Don't cry." Her father repositioned himself between her

and the other hunters so they could not see her. "It's OK to be sad. Just keep it to yourself."

"Why?"

"As a girl, you're always going to have to work twice as hard to prove yourself. It's not fair, but that's the way it is. Don't ever let anyone see your weakness. Better to let them think you're heartless than weak. Men like this respect heartless, but they'll never forgive weak."

Now his own tears are as ceaseless as the rain soaking them until the ground beneath them feels unstable, shifting, fragile. Time blurs as days pass and neither stops.

Gray is covered in mud and chilled to the bone. She gathers firewood she cannot keep dry and huddles beneath the tarp, watching her father with growing dread as the rain gathers volume and strength. They're almost out of food. Their campsite, which once felt like the pinnacle of freedom, has become a watery prison. The rain feels like a sign. The rain feels like punishment.

This is her fault, she thinks. She wasn't strong enough when he needed her to be. She's *still* not strong enough. The rain does not stop and neither does her father, and she does not know what to do about any of it.

They're days overdue. Gray imagines her mother growing frantic, calling Uncle Fenwick, calling hospitals, calling the police. She wishes they'd brought phones, wishes they'd brought more food, wishes they'd brought a tent. She wishes she knew what to do.

The rain soaks through her jacket, soaks through the flannel and wool she wears beneath it, soaks through her Carhartts and long johns, soaks through her skin until even her heart and soul are wet. She can't get any more wet. *There's no such thing*, she thinks. As if to prove her wrong, the wind rises up, the sky ignites, and thunder cracks open the night. She feels the lightning lifting the wet hair from her neck, feels the wet ground tremble beneath her.

"Please," she says. To her father, maybe. Or to herself. "Please."

She says it again.

"Please."

And then again and again and again, begging, pleading, repeating it over and over until it becomes a mantra, a way of breathing, an incantation, and still the rain does not stop. Still the wind does not stop. Still her father's tears do not stop.

"Please. Please. Please." She says it until her voice is hoarse, until her throat hurts, says it until she can't hear herself anymore.

"Please. Please. Please. Please."

She does not know how long she says it for and does not know how much longer she can continue—she knows only the word. *Please.*

"Please," she says. "Please. Please. Please." She can barely form the word before the rain washes it away.

Her father opens his eyes. He looks around like he's seeing the rain for the first time. The tarp stretched over them is shredded by the wind like the wings of an ancient dragon, and water pours off the corners in waves, pours through the holes and weaknesses in the nylon and runs all around them, too much of it to be confined to the shallow trenches he dug around their camp. It runs beneath their sleeping bags and the thin foam pads, it soaks the foam and the down, soaking them. Another flash of lightning, another shatter of thunder.

Her father looks lost. Helpless. But he's awake. The incantation has worked.

"Please," she says. "I need you. I don't know what to do."

The rain and tears streak the dirt on his face like the makeup of some dark clown. Gray is crying too. She's desperate. Frightened.

"Please," she says again. "Please."

The beating rain steals her voice and gives it to the wind. The wind hurls it into the sky for the lightning to pierce and the thunder to swallow.

She reaches for her father, for what's left of him, and hugs him tightly. She feels like a little girl again, small despite her own size and strength. She puts her head to his like he used to do with the dog, hands on either side of it so their foreheads touch.

"Please."

"It's OK, Gray. I'm here."

———

Wind hurls the rain like stones. It whips the tarps, the battered flags of a nation whose borders have been breached. Trees bend. Branches snap. The mountains are under siege.

"Do we hike out?" She yells to be heard over the storm.

"No."

"But we're almost out of food. The storm. And you're . . ." she says, but cannot finish her sentence.

"It's too far to the truck. We might find worse trouble. Better to wait it out."

"What do you think I've been doing?" Frayed by exhaustion and fear and panic, her voice cuts him.

"I'm sorry, Gray." He nods, a quick tilt of the head. She returns it.

Lightning cleaves the sky, illuminating his face as the thunder hammers at them, and he does not even flinch. *This* is her father, she thinks, recognizing him for the first time in days. She called him and he came. Everything's going to be OK.

He gets up and aims his headlamp into the night. It has no chance against the rain, caught and refracted by millions of droplets, so he shines it at the ground, which looks like it is moving, the dirt turned to mud, the mud turned to water, the water rushing down the mountain toward the rivers. If it keeps raining, the water will carry them with it. Water will always find its way.

"Wait here," he says.

"Pop."

"Wait here, Gray. It's OK."

She watches him turn and stumble, unused to his own feet, upright for the first time in days. He looks weak. Atrophied. He's not eaten, not washed, barely slept. He's inhuman, a rag doll. Something broken.

But he's still her father. Lewis Yaw, King of the Jungle.

He disappears into the storm and reemerges with their packs, which he lashes together over a branch and hoists off the flooding ground.

"Where are the rifles?"

Gray does not answer.

"The rifles, Gray. Where are they?"

She retrieves them from the moss-covered downfall where she has hidden them and hands him one. He gives her a curious look. When he tries to work the bolts to make sure it's not loaded, he finds the bolts missing. She's removed them both and hidden them in the foot of her sleeping bag. He looks at her again but says nothing as he tucks the rifles into the carry straps on their hanging packs.

"Get back in your sleeping bag, Gray."

"It's soaked."

"It'll keep you warm enough to avoid hypothermia. Get back in."

They duck beneath the remains of the tarp, a useless gesture, the tarp itself no longer a form of shelter but a visual measurement of the velocity of the wind, and slide into their bags. The wet down feels like a heavy, sopping grave. He rolls against her, pressing himself against her shaking body, spooning front to back as the night splinters into glass around them.

"We'll be warmer this way."

She grabs his arms and hugs him. There's panic in her grip, but love too. Relief. This time he does not tense, he does not withdraw. This time, her father hugs her back.

"How long have I . . . What day is it?"

They left Friday. They were supposed to be home Monday.

"It's Thursday."

"Thursday? We've been here six days?"

Gray nods, afraid to speak.

"I'm back now, Gray. It's OK. I'm back."

"I'm sorry if I panicked. I was scared. You scared me."

"Six days is not panicking, Gray."

"It came out of nowhere." She means the storm.

"That's how it happens," he says, and holds her tight.

32

The storm passes sometime before morning. It's too dark to see anything, but Gray can sense a loosening in the ground and air, the world itself a fist opening.

"Are you awake?" her father asks.

"How could I sleep through that?"

"Have you slept at all this week?"

Gray does not answer, which is enough.

"Now's your chance," he says, and she closes her eyes.

———

When she opens them again, it's daylight. The fire is burning. Her father is up. He's not resurrected so much as reanimated, more zombie than messiah. He looks withered. Spent. The storm has stripped leaves from trees and scattered fallen branches. Shimmering puddles reflect a muddy sky.

"I see you gathered some wood." She can hear his amusement at the woodpile, a staggering tower of branches and limbs. It's a monument to her fear, to how scared she was, to how long she thought they might be stuck there. The wet fire sends billowing clouds of smoke into the morning sky to drift across the valley. Smoke signals, though she can't tell what message he's sending, or to whom.

They drink their coffee on their feet, close to the fire. Their wet clothes steam in the heat. The coffee is like drinking hope, but the hope runs out and her father dumps the grounds into the flames.

"What now?"

"Now we go home."

They break camp, cutting down what remains of the tarps and packing their gear. As she gathers her things, Gray decides that her book is too wet to salvage, the pages clumped, the cover wrinkled. When she throws it into the flames, her father joins her to watch the pages curl and sizzle.

"Did you ever finish it?"

"Almost."

"What was it?"

"Ray Bradbury. *Fahrenheit 451.*"

"Good book."

"I guess. How does it end?"

Her father looks at the fire. "Ironically," he says.

When they've packed everything, he shovels dirt onto the fire until it is only smoke. Gray watches, wondering if there are things in this world that can't be unseen, wondering if you can ever see flesh again once someone shows you the blood and bone beneath their skin. He shoulders his pack and picks up his rifle. Out of habit, he reaches to check the missing bolt.

"I'm assuming you have these?"

Gray nods.

"Then let's go home," he says, and sets off on the trail so that all she can do is follow him.

33

Emptied of food, their packs are lighter, but they're carrying home something they did not bring with them. The hike is long and slow. When they reach the truck, Gray digs out their phones to call home, but they've been gone too long. The batteries are dead.

"Mom's going to have to wait a little longer."

Her father nods and starts the engine.

They don't talk the entire ride home. Though Gray has questions, she's tired, wet, cold, and just *being* takes effort. She has questions she's not yet ready to know the answers to, so she tucks them away for later.

It's late afternoon when they reach Disappointment. The town looks the same, but something feels different. Not unfamiliar, but *changed*, as if they've been away not for a week but for years. As they cross the Terrebonne and get closer to home, the feeling grows stronger. She wonders if her father feels it too but doesn't know how to ask.

"Home again, home again, jiggety jig," he says, in a lackluster singsong. "To market, to market, to buy a fat pig."

"What does that mean?"

"I have no idea. It's something your uncle says."

Left onto Main. Right onto Alder. Past the bank, the big electric sign out front declaring the time and temperature, reliably wrong.

"Look at that." Gray matter-of-factly reads the display. "It's thirty-two after seventeen, and already nine hundred degrees."

"It feels cooler. Must be the humidity."

"Uncle Fenwick says *that* too. 'It's not the heat—it's the stupidity.'"

"Your uncle says lots of things." Her father musters a weak smile. "Your uncle is a corny bastard."

It's not much, but it feels good to make lighthearted small talk. It feels *normal*.

"Mom's going to kill you, you know."

He nods, hands on the wheel, eyes back on the road. "I know."

"Are you OK? I mean, really?"

Her father nods again, considering it. "We'll see," he says. It's not exactly reassuring.

Gray wants a hot shower. She wants dry clothes and a warm bed. She wants a hamburger and a burrito and a few hours in front of the TV with her feet up on the couch and a soft pillow beneath her head. She wants her mother to know they're OK, or at least alive. But she also wants to tell her what happened, to tell her about her father, about the tears, and to ask if it's happened before. If it has, is that better or worse?

They turn onto Greer Lane and stop. Uncle Fenwick's hulking pickup is parked at the end of their long driveway, blocking their way. Her father taps the horn twice, a gentle call, and when that goes without notice for more than a few seconds, he leans on it.

"Mr. Harrison's going to love that," she says and sees the faintest flicker of a smile on his face before he hits it again.

The door to their house opens and her uncle steps outside. He peers down the driveway, nearsighted with age, and even from a distance Gray can see that he looks exhausted, looks like he just woke up. Or maybe she's projecting, the week's fatigue spreading like contagion. Her father pumps the horn again and Uncle Fenwick holds up a finger, telling them to wait, and disappears back inside the house.

"What an asshole," her father says, without malice.

A minute later her uncle reappears and trots down the gravel toward them and approaches her side of the truck. She rolls down the window.

"I've been trying to reach you."

"Phones are dead."

"You were due back days ago."

"Yeah. There was a storm."

He leans in to look at them more closely, taking in the wet and bedraggled clothes, the mud, the filth and exhaustion on their faces. "Are you two OK?"

"We're fine," Gray says. Her father leans across the cab.

"Move your goddamned truck, Pope." She can smell his breath, can smell the smoke and the forest and the sweat. "I'm ready to be home."

"Maybe let's talk first."

"What?"

"Can we talk first?"

Gray has known her uncle her entire life, has seen him go through divorces and fishless years, has seen him drunk. She's seen worry work his features like gravity. But she's never seen what she sees in his face now. It's something more than the fatigue she thought she recognized. Something more dangerous. Something worse.

"What the fuck is going on, Pope?"

"Can we just get out and talk?"

Her father grips the steering wheel with both hands and sighs. She hears his exasperation, sees the muscles in his hands tighten like cords as he clenches the wheel. Then he lets go, turns off the ignition, opens his door, gets out.

Uncle Fenwick takes a step back from Gray's door and opens it for her, but before she can get out, he sees her father walking up the driveway and rushes to give chase. "Lewis," he says, firmly, but her father does not slow. Her uncle runs after him, moving at a pace Gray does not associate with him. Moving quickly is something he undertakes neither easily nor often. "Lewis," he says again, this time with an urgency that he cannot—or does not bother to—hide.

When he catches up, he puts his hand on her father's shoulder. Her father spins, knocking his hand away, and shoves him unceremoniously onto his ass.

"Pop," Gray says. A gentle rebuff. But when she sees her father's face, she knows that he has heard the urgency in her uncle's voice, too, that he recognized it before she did, and that he's afraid.

Seeing his fear gives rise to her own, a spark catching fire, and just like that, it consumes her. How long have they been gone? Simple math seems out of reach. For days she's been afraid, more afraid than she's ever been, and just as she began to beat it back, just as she gained some ground, it overtakes her once again.

Uncle Fenwick sits in the gravel, elbows on the ground behind him, looking up at them forlornly. Her father steps closer to stand over him, putting him in his shadow.

"Where is she, Pope?"

Gray hears the fear but hears anger, too, now. She catches up with them and takes her father by the arm. To restrain him. To comfort him.

"Where is who? Mom?"

Her father shakes her off his arm and points at her uncle. "Where is she? Just fucking say it."

Uncle Fenwick has not moved. Gray reaches out her other hand, and when he takes it, she helps him to his feet. He dusts himself off, takes a deep breath, and steps closer to her father. He wears a black work shirt, a long-sleeved button-down with a simple fly rod embroidered on the chest. The line curls back to spell out the name of his shop. Her father puts a hand on the logo and shoves him again. Despite her uncle's weight and strength, the shove moves him more than a foot, but this time he does not fall. Instead he closes the distance again without hesitation, standing his ground. Much shorter than her father, he cranes his neck to meet his eyes. Her father looks furious, on the verge of chaos, but on her uncle's face Gray sees desperation. Resolve. For a moment she thinks they're arguing, thinks they might fight, misunderstanding what is happening between them. Then something changes in her uncle's expression, something yields, and she sees that he's not fighting, he's crying, and that he suddenly looks less like a man in charge than a man forced to do something unfathomable. What does it mean that the last few days have reduced the two strongest men in her life to tears?

"Where the fuck is she, Pope?"

"I'm sorry, Lewis."

"Say it."

"She's gone. She's gone."

"What are you talking about?" Gray asks. "Who's gone?"

"Your mother . . . There's been an accident."

"What do you mean gone? What kind of accident?" She's confused, not thinking straight, the week in the mountains a fog clouding her thoughts. She looks at her father. "Pop?"

"Say it, Pope. Say it."

"She called me when you didn't come home. Said she couldn't get ahold of you. She was sick. Fever. Pain. She felt dizzy. Probably the flu, she said. I told her not to worry about you, you two could take care of yourselves. Told her to get some rest and said I'd come by to check in on her." He looks down at the ground. He moves the gravel around with the toe of his boot. "I called the house that night but she didn't answer. I figured she'd gone to bed."

Her uncle stops, unsure how to continue. Or maybe he knows how and he's just gathering strength. Before he can, her father shoves him again, one handed, and points at him. Uncle Fenwick takes a step back.

"When she didn't answer the next day, either, I kept calling, and that afternoon I came by to check on her . . ."

His words trail off but he continues to work his mouth, as if he's trying to speak but can't. Can't find the words. Can't find the breath. Then he stops, mouth open, spit pooling until it drips down his bottom lip, and shakes his head.

"I found her bleeding on the floor. The kitchen. By the table. She . . . wasn't breathing."

He looks down at the ground, looks up at the sky. He bites his lip. He looks at her. Finally, he looks at her father. Gray looks at her father too. She needs him to tell her how to make sense of what's happening, of what it all means. But her father does not say anything, and he does not move. Not for a long time. When he does, he swings a straight right that meets her uncle's jaw and drops him like a paper fan closing.

Uncle Fenwick looks up at him with a broken expression, blood on his chin, his cheek and upper lip already swelling.

"You fucking say it, Pope. You fucking say it."

"Say what?" Gray still does not understand, not entirely. "Say what?"

"She's dead, Lewis. I'm so sorry, Hoss. Your mother's gone. She's gone. She's gone."

———

Gray makes an involuntary noise, less like words than some frightened animal escaping from her mouth, and all her air goes with it. The news has knocked the breath from her lungs. She's been hit in the chest before, off guard, knows how it feels to lose your wind, how the lungs expel it all at once. She knows, too, how to stay calm until they refill themselves. But this feels different. This feels like she lost breath she might never recover.

There's a fraction of a second, the beat of a bird's wings, a blink, when she is no longer a part of the world but above it. Behind it. As if the world is no longer flesh and bone and asphalt and steel but an image, an idea, a memory. A disappointment. In that moment she ceases to be herself. In that moment she becomes only the struggle for air, the struggle to understand what's happening, the struggle to know what to do. How can she move forward into this next clock-tick of time, this next fraction of a second, never mind the hundreds of millions of seconds that stretch ahead of her like a frigid and wave-torn sea she must cross?

Seeing it on her face, her uncle leaps to his feet and reaches for her. She swats his hand away, focused on breathing, focused on not disappearing from this earth, from this driveway, from this moment.

"Lewis, help her sit down," he says, but her father is not there anymore. He's already running up the driveway toward the house.

Her uncle looks at her but is already stepping away to follow.

"Go," she says, or tries to, her voice a wheeze, a ghost, an effort. "Go." He takes off toward the house after her father.

She grabs at her chest. She pounds it with her fists. She tries to inhale but cannot find air. Then she tries to scream, but no sound escapes her. Not at first. She tries again and again and again until a feral, pitched cry rises from within her, a cry that shocks her in its volume, its timbre, its sustained length. The scream opens her lungs again.

She gasps as air rushes in once more. With her second breath, she's already chasing after her uncle and father.

At the top of the driveway, she sees Uncle Fenwick reach the house and throw open the door. Her father is already inside. She's in the present, in the moment, focused only on catching up to them, but a tiny, distant part of her mind is already worrying about what she'll find when she does. As she nears the house, she imagines her mother sprawled across the kitchen floor, reaching for something, someone, who is not there, reaching for *them*, for her and her father, a butterfly of blood pooled on the linoleum around her.

But then she's through the door into the kitchen and there's nothing there, no body, no blood, just the horror of its emptiness, no one in the doorway, no one at the table, no one to welcome them home. The house looks just like they left it nearly a week ago. The air reeks of bleach.

She hears her father moving through the rooms, searching for her mother, searching for a sign that her uncle is wrong, searching for some explanation or clue that will explain it if he is not.

Uncle Fenwick appears in the kitchen, out of breath, pale, and sees her. Then her father joins them. He looked wild after their week in the mountains, and now he looks wilder still.

"Pop?" she says, but her father says nothing.

Gray reaches for him, reaches to hug him. She wants comfort, to find it and to give it. But his expression is not comforting.

His expression is not one of a man in control. It's not even one of a man in pain.

It's the expression of a man who's drowning.

He drops to the clean floor and retches, a violent sound that echoes through the small house. She and her uncle watch as the heaves turn to deep sobs that shake his entire body. Gray can feel the vibrations through the floor, as if the sadness is a kind of energy spreading among them across the spot where her mother's body had lain.

She has a moment of clarity. This is her family now. Her uncle. Her father. This is what's left. Watching her father, she remembers the mountains, remembers the sound of his sobbing filling their camp. She looks at her uncle, her father on the floor between them. They're the only people left in this world who love him, but neither of them can save him. Not anymore.

And then he's on his feet and stumbling out the door, crashing through the screen without bothering to open it. They follow him outside into the yard, where he stands with his back to them, staring into the woods behind the house.

"Pop?" It's not just a question—it's a thousand questions, as if all that remains of her life is questions. What happened to her father in the mountains? What happened to her mother while they were gone? What happens now?

Her father looks at her. For a long moment he holds her gaze. If she's seeking answers in his eyes, she does not find them. She finds only darkness.

Then he turns and runs. He runs across the yard, runs to the tree line, runs into the woods and scrambles up the slope behind the house faster than she would have thought possible. As they watch, her father disappears into the trees and shadows, and though they stand at the edge of the yard and call his name for hours, he does not come back.

34

When her father does not return, Gray and her uncle sleep at the Arrow, where she can shower and eat her first real meal in days. He asks if she wants to stay at Greer Lane but she says no before he even finishes the question. Her situation is too new, the news too recent. The smell of the freshly cleaned floor. She's not ready to be back inside the house and does not know if she ever will be. At the Arrow, her uncle makes a meal she does not—*can* not—eat. A part of her hovers on the brink of panic, but the exhaustion gets to her faster and she all but collapses, no longer trusting her legs to hold her upright.

She sleeps only in troubled fits and spurts, wrapped like a casserole in the scratchy bedding. She dreams of darkness and wakes often, covered in sweat.

Though she listens for her father, he does not come.

Uncle Fenwick does not let her out of his sight. He keeps an all-night vigil at the galley table with a bottle for company, and is still there when she wakes to sunlight through the scratched plastic windows. A grizzled sentry. A gargoyle with morning breath.

"How'd you sleep, Hoss? Bad dreams?"

"They weren't dreams."

"No."

Gray sees the pain on his face. He loved her mother. He's worried about her father. But she knows that it's *her* pain he's seeing, *her* pain he's feeling, which gives her the urge to console *him*. She holds up the cushion she's been using as a pillow. Upholstered in offensively gaudy fabric, it's both cheap and rough, a strenuously outdated brown-and-yellow plaid.

"Anyway, how could I *not* have bad dreams with my head on something this ugly all night?"

Her uncle smiles, and it feels familiar. She'd almost forgotten what familiar felt like.

"Would you believe patterns like that were the height of fashion in the seventies?" he says.

"Really? How did anyone sleep?"

"Well, we smoked a lot of grass and had a lot of sex." He pours her a cup of coffee and Gray sits up to drink it. "You want to tell me what happened in the mountains?"

It's a good question. She barely remembers, it seems so long ago. It's as if she's stockpiling grief like firewood and the pile is already alarmingly high. High enough for an inferno. Eventually she's going to have to put out that fire, she knows. But not right now—not around her uncle. Her tears have caused enough problems already. There's something wrong with her father, something worse, maybe, than her father being missing, worse than his grief, and she doesn't know how he can deal with what's happened starting from such a broken place. Not without her.

"We should get back to the house in case he's there." She pulls back the sheets and climbs out of bed. Only then does she remember that she's wearing one of her uncle's T-shirts and a pair of his boxer shorts. All the clothes she brought to the

Wallowas were soaked through and filthy. Everything else she owned is inside the house she's unwilling, or afraid, to enter. "I don't have any clothes, do I?"

"Don't worry, Hoss. One of the Flying Monkeys brought them to the laundromat. He'll be here after breakfast." Most of the Flying Monkeys are Gray's classmates, high school boys wrecked by puberty.

"Those pimple-faced goons are probably texting each other pictures of my underwear."

Her uncle shrugs. "Probably."

She tries to laugh but it comes out wrong, and then she starts to cry. Embarrassed, she wipes her eyes with the palm of her hand, wipes her nose with the hem of the T-shirt she's wearing.

"You know what, Hoss? Why don't you keep that shirt."

Gray half-laughs again and tears up some more.

"You probably have a million questions," he says.

She nods. Sniffs. Nods again.

"OK. We'll talk. But first let's try to find your old man."

———

She feels physically sick as they pull onto Greer Lane. Her father's truck is where he left it, at the end of the driveway, but he's not there and there's no sign of him. Confronted with her mother's death, her missing father, she feels powerless. Adrift. Wherever he is, he needs her. But she needs *him*, too, and in that moment of weakness, wishes he was there to help her. "Wish in one hand and shit in the other and see which makes your garden grow faster," he used to tell her. Something her grandfather used to say. Like that was supposed to console her.

"Where is he?" She's overcome with anger. "Why isn't he here?"

Uncle Fenwick puts a hand on her shoulder, but she shakes it off and clenches her fists, her jaw, every muscle in her body, trying to contain the rage. One moment she wants to put her fist through a wall. The next she wants to curl up in a ball and succumb to the grief and sadness. The conflicting emotions roil her, leaving her unsteady and off balance.

But she can't surrender to grief for her mother—not yet—because she has to worry about her father. How could he leave her alone like this?

Sensing her mood, her uncle lowers his head. "Whatever you're thinking about your old man, go easy on him. You gotta give people room to deal with things like this in their own way. Give him time." His words are reasonable, but Gray hears the undercurrent of anger in them, too, just as she can hear him trying to hide it.

"He should be here."

"He should." Swallowing hard, he sniffs deeply and clears his throat, as if physically moving the right words from his brain to his mouth. "But listen to me, and listen good, 'cause I need for you to hear this. Not everyone can survive something like this. I'm being honest as I know how to be, now, so I want you to hear what I'm saying. Not everyone bounces back from this kind of thing."

Gray looks into his eyes, hard, challenging him. When he does not look away, she realizes he means her father, not her. And that's a possibility she had not considered—that her father might come back, but he won't be himself and maybe never will again.

"Is this your pep talk?"

"I'm afraid it's the best I've got."

"Well, it sucks."

She stands at the front door for a few long minutes but cannot bring herself to open it. Instead, she crosses the driveway to the garage and lifts open the big bay door, retrieves two lawn chairs from inside, and sets them in the doorway.

"I want to wait for him." She sinks into one of them. "If he comes back, I want to be here."

Her uncle takes the empty seat beside her. "Then let's wait."

"You don't have to wait with me, you know."

"Try and stop me, Hoss. If you're on watch, I'm on watch. We'll be tireless," he says.

Within minutes, he is asleep.

———

Gray wishes she could sleep too. Better that than sitting in silence, letting the grief and the fear and the rage well up like a chorus of voices in her head. Besides, she has the feeling they're going to need their strength. Rather than stare at the house, taunting her with its secrets, she stares across the street at the Harrisons' charmless house. She sees the door open and her neighbors step outside. When Mrs. Harrison waves nervously as they begin walking across the street and up the long driveway, she elbows her uncle awake.

"Make them go away."

There's a solicitousness to their voices that annoys her, an exaggeration of respect that comes across as condescension. They don't stay long. Her uncle walks them to the end of the driveway and chats with them for a few minutes before sending them home.

"I don't want them tiptoeing around me," Gray tells him when he returns to his chair.

"They're just being polite."

"I don't like it. It's creepy."

"Well, get used to it. What happened to your mother? It

will change everything. Everyone who knew you before is gonna treat you different now. So will everyone else you meet, too, once they find out what happened."

What happened. It's still too new and unthinkable to even name yet.

"Even you? Are *you* going to treat me different too?"

Her uncle lights a cigarette. A long, thin cloud of smoke hangs in the air, heavy and vaguely translucent, a half-hearted ghost. "'Fraid so."

The air is still as brick. When the cloud of smoke fails to dissipate, he drops the cigarette in the driveway and crushes it beneath his boot.

"You know they're still watching, right?" Gray nods across the street. Her uncle follows her gaze. The Harrisons' faces are crowded together in a downstairs window, pale streaks behind the glass.

"Yeah, well. I asked them to keep an eye on you while I'm gone."

"Gone where?"

"To look for him."

"I don't need babysitters." She kicks a stone across the driveway. It skids under the boat trailer and rattles against the steel frame. "Where are you going to look?"

"The river. The Salt Lick. The streets. He's on foot; he can't be *that* far."

They stand side by side, unsure what comes next. It's a new world. Their compasses are still spinning, looking for magnetic north. New maps will have to be drawn.

"You gonna be OK?" Seeing something in her expression, he hurries to clarify. "I mean, while I'm gone?"

"I'll be fine."

But as soon as he leaves, she wonders if that's true. She

wonders if she's made a mistake. Left alone, she's wide open, with no choice but to think about what happened. Her mother is dead. Her father is missing. When she remembers him sobbing in the dark, rifle in his hands, she feels the sickness rising inside her again, the wave of voices fleeing her head for her stomach, and runs for the grass as her stomach lurches. The darkness begins at the edges of her vision and races toward the center. She sees the Harrisons' door flashing in the sun as it opens. It's the last thing she remembers.

———

Her uncle bends over her with an expression of amused concern, his eyes red, his breath horrific.

"How you doin', Hoss?"

She breathes in deeply, squinting into the sun. "Just fine, thanks. Why do you ask?"

"'Cause you look like you've been shot at and missed, but shit on and hit."

"Ouch?"

"If you're feeling up to sarcasm, you must feel better than you look."

A little embarrassed, and a little confused, Gray sits up. Slowly. Her gut feels hollowed. Her head aches resoundingly.

"I thought you said you were going to treat me differently now."

"I didn't say it was going to be better."

She smiles. It's as close as she can come to a laugh. Her uncle punches her on the arm.

"Good for you. It's good to act human even when you don't feel it. Your old man has never really learned that lesson."

"Maybe he's not human."

"That would explain a lot of things."

"You didn't find him?"

"No sign, even."

He looks around the yard, as if her father might be there. As if they've simply overlooked him. "Harrison says you went down like a ton of bricks, but that you aimed for the grass and stuck the landing. Gave 'em a hell of a scare. I don't think he and the missus are used to much excitement beyond a fluctuating stock market or a new brand of toilet paper." He nods over his shoulder, a little surreptitiously, and Gray looks past him to see the neighbors standing nervously at the driveway's edge. When they wave, tentatively, she waves back. "In other news, I brought you lunch."

He drops a greasy paper bag into her hands. Triggered by the smell of food, Gray tears it open to find a stack of burgers on a bed of fries. She devours the first of the burgers at an alarming rate, without any pleasure, as if someone has removed the taste from the food in a lab. Her hunger surprises her. Her uncle withdraws a burger for himself and a second for her, which she takes without hesitation. It's the first real food she's eaten in days. No wonder she fainted.

"I put the word out around town," he says between bites. "The guides are watching for him. Disappointment's a small town. He'll turn up."

"What about the police?"

"It's too soon, officially, but I put a word in with a friend and the sheriff's department is keeping their eyes open." He stares at her long enough to make her uncomfortable. "So what do you want to do, Hoss? You want to stay here tonight? You want to stay at the Arrow?"

Wherever her father is, she does not want to let him down. She does not want to disappoint him.

"What would he do?"

"I've been wondering that myself." Her uncle wipes his face with a greasy hand. "This is out of character for him. It's not like him to run from something. It's not like him to leave you. And if I'm being honest, it's pissing me off."

She's angry too. The anger has to compete with the grief that pushes at her skin from within, like an infection, so that everything pulses and throbs and hurts to the touch. When she remembers the Wallowas, how he couldn't get out of his sleeping bag, couldn't stop crying, she knows that he came into this grief already disadvantaged, and the worry hits her like a fever.

"I think he's really sad." She's unsure how much to tell her uncle.

"The saddest. We all are."

"I mean, I think he was sad before. In the mountains."

He looks at her for a long few seconds, as if trying to gauge something, but she can't tell what. "Your old man was sad long before that, even. It goes way back with him. Long as I've known him."

"What do you mean?"

"There was a time, years ago. You were just little, I think. Maybe you weren't even born yet. I can't remember. Your mother called me up, asked if I could take care of his clients for a couple days. Said he couldn't work."

"Was he sick?"

"Well. It's a kind of sickness."

It's the first time she's heard the story. She never knew her father to miss a day of work. He's too stubborn to get sick.

"Some people," her uncle says. "They live in a shadow and they just can't get out of it, no matter what they try. It's not their fault. And it don't matter how strong they are, or how tough, 'cause it ain't the kind of thing you can fight off."

Gray hears what he's saying. She knows what it's called. She's never heard anyone call it that at home—not about her father. Her mother never talked about it, and now it's too late to ask her.

Just thinking about her mother makes her heart quicken and stall. It must show on her face, because her uncle looks away respectfully to give her a minute to steady herself.

"I'm worried about him," she says, remembering the rifle bolts still in her pack.

"Me too, Hoss."

"No. I'm worried he's . . . I'm worried he's going to . . . to hurt himself."

He looks at her closely, weighing her words. "Don't worry. We'll find him and we'll help get him right. We can be mad at him later. Deal?" He reaches out a hand that's still greasy from the burger.

Gray takes it and rises to her feet, grateful for the assist.

35

Still not ready to step back inside the house and unwilling to leave Greer Lane in case her father comes back, they spend the night in the garage with the bay doors open to the world. Gray sleeps curled on a camp mat, woken by every wind-dropped twig and every yard noise real or imagined, her uncle upright in a lawn chair. He snores until the daylight reaches him and then wakes complaining that he didn't sleep a wink.

Morning brings overcast skies and the scent of rain, but no sign of her father. Her outlook sinks. Until now she's been able to convince herself that he needed time to react, time to grieve alone, but he's been gone long enough that she's worried something truly bad has happened. Though her uncle's eyes tell her that he suspects the same, neither gives voice to their fear.

She boils hose water for coffee on the camp stove she fetches from her father's truck. Through the trees they see lights go on at the DeLongs' house, at Roy and Iris Boothman's, the world and the people who inhabit it rising to face another day and its myriad challenges. The coffee is bitter going down. It scalds her throat and roils her stomach.

"I could murder some bacon and eggs," her uncle says. "What do you say we go inside and I'll whip something up?"

She shakes her head. *No.*

"Well, we shouldn't be drinking this rocket fuel on an empty stomach, Hoss. How 'bout we go into town? We could eat at the diner and then drive around looking for him."

"What if he comes while we're gone?"

"You should take a break. We both should. If you won't go inside here, let's at least go back to the Arrow and shower. We can change clothes and eat something, then we'll come back and wait together some more."

"I'm fine."

Her uncle looks ready to argue. Before they can reach an impasse, Mrs. Harrison renders their debate moot, appearing in the driveway with a basketful of muffins and a carafe of coffee. She greets them with a forced brightness as her husband follows dolefully with a tray of mugs, cream and sugar, ramekins of butter and jellies.

"Any sign of your father?"

The spread they've prepared, like the gesture itself, is at once simple and elegant, and it moves Gray almost to tears. But that makes her feel foolish, and she changes tack, overcorrecting.

"Does it look like he's here?" Hearing the abruptness in her own voice, she's unsure which is worse, the initial show of emotion or the fact that it embarrassed her. Uncle Fenwick turns her way and she sees the worry in his expression.

"I'm sorry," she says. "I think I'm just hungry." She smiles sadly at her neighbors, a proxy apology Mr. Harrison returns with a nod.

"Is there anything I can do? Perhaps I could lend my energies to the search party." His wife puts a hand on his back, lending support to his bravery. Though it's just 6 a.m., he's already in a crisp collared shirt and starched jeans, shoes shined like they were enameled.

"Appreciate that," Uncle Fenwick says. "I reckon we'll let you know if we get a posse together."

Mrs. Harrison looks at Gray. "You poor girl."

"I'm fine," she says, the edge returned to her voice.

"Thank you for breakfast," her uncle says, both releasing and protecting the neighbors. Happy to be excused, they walk briskly down the driveway, his arm over her shoulder, her head bowed dramatically beneath the weight of the moment.

The muffins are a chore, pumpkin with seeds, a dry lightness that tastes like dairy substitute—a distinct lack of sweetness—but the coffee is good, and Uncle Fenwick pours them each a second cup. The bottle of Old Crow on her father's fly-tying bench has two hands' worth of fingers remaining in it. Though it's still early morning, he retrieves it and waves it around like a priest's thurible.

"Your old man loves this stuff. If anything will bring him home, it's this." Realizing the implication of his words—that maybe she's not reason enough for her father to return—he looks embarrassed.

"It can't hurt," she says. He nods and sweetens both their cups from the bottle.

"He ever tell you Mark Twain used to drink this stuff? Old Crow?"

"No."

"And Ulysses S. Grant."

"Must be good."

"It ain't."

"Why does he like it so much?"

"One of life's great mysteries, Hoss, why a guy as tall as your old man spends so much time crawling around the bottom shelf."

The bourbon adds a bite to the coffee, a strength but also a sweetness like toffee or caramel. There's a warmth in her belly and that gives her hope. Maybe that's what her father sees in it. Or wants to.

Hope.

———

Left alone again when her uncle runs to town, Gray summons the strength to venture back inside the house. There's a moment in the doorway when she pauses half in, half out, paralyzed at the border between worlds. And then momentum catches up to her and she's in the kitchen, clenching her fists nervously. She walks from room to room, marveling at the foreignness of it all. How could something so familiar, so comfortable for so long feel suddenly so malicious? How could the only home she's ever known reject her with such insistence? The couch in the family room where they sat together watching television. The kitchen table where they ate meals together, did homework together, laughed and talked and argued. In her bedroom, she packs a few things into a backpack—clean underwear, jeans and sneakers, a baseball hat—and, on a whim, takes the photograph from the wall over her bed. It's the yellow house in Massachusetts where her father grew up. She's been staring at it for so many years, imagining what it's like inside, that it almost feels like her own home—maybe even more like home, now, than this building where her mother died.

In her parents' room she finds her mother's cello on its stand, the gorgeous, honeyed wood catching the sunlight through the window. When she closes her eyes, she hears it clearly, the deep, mournful notes, and something in her stomach leaps into her throat. She tries to swallow it down but it tastes like burnt flesh, and she barely makes it to the bathroom in time to vomit it into the toilet, dropping the framed picture as she flings open the seat.

Afterward, when her stomach is hollowed out and her throat burns with stomach acids, she retrieves it from the floor and shakes the glass shards from the frame. They fall to the ground like the pieces of her life.

After that she returns to the relative safety of the garage. Still seeking distraction, she reads the labels on the boxes stacked against the back wall. They've been there as long as she can remember, stored relics and artifacts of their lives, but they never interested her before. They're labeled in her mother's handwriting, which gives her momentary pause, a trail on a map that will lead her no place good if she follows it. WINTER CLOTHES. GRAY CHILDHOOD. CHRISTMAS DECORATIONS. An old toaster box labeled MEMORIES. The very idea strikes Gray as odd, that memories are something that can be contained in cardboard and stored alongside Christmas ornaments and ski gloves. Other boxes bear her father's handwriting, scattered among the rest with no logic that she can see. That's just like her parents, to be organized enough to save and label things but not so organized as to have a system or a method to the madness. A utilitarian approach; good enough is great. His blocky script is messy enough almost to require its own Rosetta Stone. EASTERN FLIES. ODFW PAPERWORK. TB RESEARCH, which she assumes means "Terrebonne" and not "tuberculosis."

One box, smaller and narrower than the others, says SUMMER 1993 over the logo for the Saucony running shoes it once held. Gray slips it free like a mason extracting a single brick from a wall. Inside are dozens of postcards. She shuffles them like playing cards. Like she's practicing a new card trick. They're from all across the northern United States, each addressed to her mother in Somerville, Massachusetts, and filled with her father's hurried handwriting, as if he was too busy to deal with individual letters, each letter losing something of itself in sacrifice to the words, each word constructed of lines that some letters share while other lines are missing entirely. Even written in pen, it looks like he carved the words into the paper, the pen a tiny tool in a strong hand. Gray puts her finger to the words and traces them, feeling the grooves of each line and each letter like Braille. It feels weird to read them, like she's intruding, or eavesdropping, but she doesn't stop. They *sound* like her father, and she can all but hear his voice, the downplayed excitement at the beauty of the glacial lakes in Banff, the herd of grazing elk in Jasper, the Snake River in Wyoming, a butte full of coyotes in Montana. On one, which bears a picture of the Corn Palace in Mitchell, South Dakota, he wrote only one cryptic sentence:

"HISTORY WILL BEGIN WITH US."

She's still staring at it, trying to understand what it means, when she hears her uncle's clunking diesel in the driveway. She slips the postcard in her pocket and puts the box away.

———

All day the temperature drops. Uncle Fenwick suggests, again, that they move inside the house. "There's beds, couches, a fridge," he argues. "There's even a shitter."

But she's not ready, the image of her mother sprawled across the linoleum so strong she needs to remind herself she only imagined it.

"What about the Arrow?"

Again she declines. "I want to wait for him," she says. Her uncle looks unhappy but nods his assent.

"You ready to tell me what happened in the Wallowas?"

She feels her uncle's stare. The longer she holds it, the heavier it gets.

"We were kind of fighting about something. He . . . He got sick. He couldn't get out of his sleeping bag, couldn't stop crying." She remembers hiding the rifle bolts as the wind lashed her with rain, remembers pleading with him for help, but when she tries to tell him about it, the words get stuck.

"He's going to be OK, Hoss. So are you."

She looks to him for reassurance, but he looks away into the woods.

It's been three days since her father vanished. Three days since they learned about her mother. For three days she's prolonged her mourning. Her hope is wavering, and she's beginning to fear that she will have more than just her mother to mourn. It will be the coldest night yet, the first hint of an overdue autumn.

At sundown a truck pulls into the driveway and they jump to their feet. The headlights light up the collection of vehicles parked there: her father's truck and Fenwick's, the trailered boat, her mother's minivan. Her uncle walks out to meet it, shielding his eyes against the headlights. The driver gets out, a long-limbed silhouette against the lights, and they talk for a minute before walking together into the garage.

"This is Dr. Childs," Uncle Fenwick says. "He, uh. He was your mother's doctor. Doc, this is Gray Yaw, Janey and Lewis's girl."

"Actually, we met when you were younger."

"We did? When?"

"I delivered you."

She's heard the story, how she came into this world carried on the shoulders of a storm, accompanied by thunder and lightning. How the rains flooded the land. How after that it was never the same again, and nobody knew if it was because of the storm or because of her. Her father used to tell it to her when she was a kid, and it strikes her as strange that this man who she does not know at all could have played such an important role in her origin story.

"Well, nice to see you again." She shakes his hand. It's startlingly thin, with long fingers and soft skin. "You're an obstetrician?"

"Yes."

"Named Childs?"

The doctor nods, not in agreement so much as with tired recognition, or a kind of resolve. "It's called an *aptronym*. A name suited to its owner. A college professor told me that one time after I delivered her twins. Chefs named Cook. A poet named Wordsworth. Some German psychiatrist named Angst. This professor—she had a long and protracted labor, during which she cited an entire litany of examples."

Gray looks at her uncle, who shrugs and clears his throat.

"I just came to offer my condolences," the doctor says. "I'm sorry about your mother."

Neither of them says anything after that, and in the awkward silence, Gray wonders why he's there, wonders why he's come to the house at night after all these years. And then she knows she's missing the obvious question.

"Why did my mother need an obstetrician?"

The doctor looks at her uncle with uncertainty, but Uncle Fenwick nods. Dr. Childs takes his hat from his head, a wool cowboy hat with a crisp brim, and clutches it to his chest. Without the hat, the light from the garage reaches his face and she sees that he's a lot older than she thought, with kind, worried eyes in a corduroy of creased skin.

"Do you know what an ectopic pregnancy is?"

"No."

"Nature is an example of complex and wonderful design work. The systems and processes of life are beautiful, and often mysterious. But like any system, sometimes they misfire. In an ectopic pregnancy, the fertilized egg implants and grows outside the cavity of the uterus, where it is intended to be. The likelihood of such an event increases in parallel with certain risk factors, such as advanced age, but once it happens, nothing can be done."

As he shifts from the awkwardness of offering condolences to the more familiar area of medical procedural talk, his voice grows more confident. More eager. He tucks his hat under his arm and gestures with his hands as he speaks, as if molding some of the words from clay, summoning others from the air around them. Gray has never seen such thin wrists.

"Ectopic pregnancies cannot proceed normally—a fertilized egg cannot survive outside of the uterus—but there's also significant risk for the mother. In the majority of ectopic pregnancies, the fertilized egg implants in the fallopian tube itself. If it is allowed to continue to grow, the tube begins to distend. Surgery is necessary to remove the fertilized egg and associated tissue. But in some cases, if the mother is not aware that the pregnancy is ectopic . . ."

He pauses, not for dramatic insistence but because of where his sentence is headed. Gray braces instinctively.

"When the fallopian tube is distended as far as it can possibly be, it ruptures. A rupture can hemorrhage—it can bleed quite heavily. As blood pools in the abdominal cavity, the body suffers from the sudden and extreme blood loss. Essentially, it goes into shock. As the blood pressure drops, the patient becomes lightheaded, dizzy, confused."

"She thought it was the flu," Uncle Fenwick says, to the doctor, or to Gray, or just to himself. The doctor nods again, always nodding, a rhetorical tic.

"This is a critical time. Shock is a medical emergency that demands immediate attention, and the tube itself, once ruptured, needs to be surgically removed. It's uncommon for patients to hemorrhage. But the likelihood increases severely without treatment."

Dr. Childs looks at her. "Do you understand what I'm telling you, Gray?"

She looks from him to her uncle and back again, the harsh, uneven light of the bare overhead bulb casting shadows that highlight their concerned expressions.

"My mother was pregnant."

He knits his eyebrows together, as if that particular fact had been presupposed before the start of the conversation. "That's right," he says.

An unborn sibling to mourn, now, too, the grief piling up like unread mail.

"Did my father know?"

The doctor looks from her to her uncle and back again, confused. This is not a question he knows the answer to, not one he is prepared to answer.

"My mother. If she'd gotten to the hospital faster, would it have mattered?"

"Well, yes, speed can be a determining factor in the effectiveness of treatment. It's difficult to say with any precision whether we would have been able to do anything for her, or whether that would have made any difference in the outcome. But generally speaking, yes."

"So if we'd been here when we were supposed to, my mother might still be alive?"

A long moment passes during which none of them speaks. What is there to say? The doctor looks into the crown of his hat, as if he's forgotten something there—an excuse to leave, a pack of cigarettes, a rabbit from an old magic trick—and then back up at Gray.

"Thank you, doctor," she says, dismissing him.

———

Her uncle walks Dr. Childs to his truck and then returns to the garage, shielding his eyes from the bare bulb with a hand as he steps into the light. Something has changed but she's not yet sure what. Maybe everything. She can feel it in the air, as if even the pressure is different, now, how it pushes at her skin, how it's heavier in her lungs.

"Hoss?"

"What."

"You can't blame yourself for not being here. You can't blame yourself for what happened."

Gray looks away, unable to face him when she answers.

"I don't."

———

Late that night, Gray wakes to Johnson's heavy breathing, her breaths rising and falling in the darkness. She smells woodsmoke and fir and sweat, but the night is cold and she finds the dog's presence reassuring. Comforting. She lies perfectly still, listening. It's too dark to see. Slowly she becomes aware of the hard floor beneath her, the discomfort of the thin camp mat. The smells are coming not from the air itself but from her sleeping bag, which still bears the memory of her week in the mountains. As her unquiet mind centers itself, she remembers where she is, and why, remembers that the heavy breaths filling the garage are not the dog's but those of her uncle, whose bulk is

C. B. BERNARD

stressing a lawn chair's heroic webbing across the empty bay. Cold air pours in through the open door.

How long will the rain hold off? What will it mean for her father if he is not yet home when it comes? Her mother is gone. The dog is gone. What's left? She knows she's longing for a return to a normal that no longer exists, and that it does not makes her both angry and sad.

Dreaming of Johnson makes Gray miss her, the warmth of her giant body, the rough tongue, even the venomous dog farts. But to think such things is to lower her chin in a fight, to expose herself to a beating. Though she tries to push the thoughts from her mind, they rush in like water, overtaking her until she feels panic.

How will she learn to get by without her?

How will anything ever be the same without her?

And even as she knows she's no longer thinking of the dog at all, Gray knows, too, that the world has been fractured by her absence, as if her parting had severed the strings tying them all together.

When her uncle begins to snore, she focuses on the sound to distract herself. It sounds like a rusted truck exhaust. Like an asthmatic sandhill crane. But between riffs, in the silence of his lungs at rest, she still hears the dog's heavy breathing. In the confusion of darkness and grief, her overtired mind is trying to trick her into believing that the dog has come back to her— whether to help or to haunt, she does not know.

She reaches for the Coleman lantern and turns it on to dispel any illusions or delusions. It's her only chance at sleep. The lantern throws a weak, pale light across the garage, creating shadows that flicker unsteadily. In the light Gray sees her father, face down on the cold, oil-stained floor just a few feet from her sleeping bag. He's asleep, or passed out, limbs spread like he's drowned. His clothes are filthy. Torn. Soaking wet. Water stains the cement around him like a shadow.

But Gray doesn't notice any of that. Only that he's there.

Only that he's come home.

Only that his long hair and beard have turned white as chalk.

36

They lay her mother to rest later that week. There is nothing
to bury but ashes, a tidy sum in an inornate container of bur-
nished metal. Gray can see her own reflection and her father's
in the domed lid as she carries it to the cemetery. They will bury
a portion there, and the rest they will scatter in the river with
which her mother shared her family so Gray and her father can
continue to be with her every day. To be indistinguishable from
the land and the water—her own wishes, spoken aloud long
ago, when it seemed impossible they would ever become necessary. No church. No priest. Just a simple ceremony, a wind like
a sigh, a phalanx of raised hands opening. Just like that, what's
left of her mother floats away on the breeze.

There's no eulogy. What could be said? Vast as language may
be, near-infinite possibilities to arrange letters in combination
to make any number of words, those words are insufficient. Her
father looks like he wants into the ground with her remnants.
Gray doesn't blame him. She feels a form of it. That they are
expected to go on living without her is a cruelty.

The fishing guides make an honor guard, lined up in their

ill-fitting suits and cleanest jeans, solemnly holding their hats over their chests. Neighbors bend under the weight of their grief. School friends are there, too, but Gray isn't even sure what friendship means now. She isn't sure what *anything* means now. They hug her nervously, looking rushed and uncomfortable and woefully out of place, as if sitting through an obligatory sales pitch long enough to claim the free meal that comes with it. They're afraid to get too close to her, afraid the death of a loved one might be contagious.

People from town have come too. Some because they knew her mother, maybe even loved her, some to show their support for Gray or her father, others because it's a small town and there's nothing else to do on a Thursday afternoon. There are people Gray does not recognize, people her mother worked with, maybe, as if she had a secret life—at work, in town, away from the house. She wonders how it is possible she knows so little about her parents and their friends, each of whom tries to console her, to pay respects, all wearing expressions of such pity that she wants to scream, wants to hit them, wants to punch something, anything, everything, wants to turn her insides out so the world can see what she's feeling, so they can feel it too. Show them the emptiness, the hole where her heart should be, and let them suffer through it alongside her.

There's a headstone, a round-shouldered slab, polished marble gleaming in the September sun. Gray leans in close to read it.

JANE ELIZABETH YAW

OCTOBER 17, 1971—SEPTEMBER 21, 2016

LEWIS YAW

JANUARY 17, 1970—

"It's you," she says to her father, surprised.

Slouched beside her, barely present, he hangs his head low, still looking for a way into the earth, and nods.

"What does that mean? Why is that there?"

"It doesn't mean anything."

"Why is your name on it?"

"Your mother bought the plot when she got pregnant with you. Part of the nesting instinct, I guess. The headstone came with it, pre-engraved." He sees the look on her face. "It's just a piece of rock, Gray."

"But—"

"Now's not the time, Hoss." Her uncle's been shadowing them like a Secret Service agent, black sport coat, black jeans, black shoes, and now he puts a heavy hand on her shoulder from behind. She can't help but feel that, by postponing so much of her emotional reckoning, she's shoveling a hole too deep to fill, but she nods her acquiescence.

That morning she found three dresses lain side by side on her small bed in the Arrow. Mrs. Harrison bought them for her, and together they exceeded the number of dresses she'd previously owned by three. Each was a different style, tasteful, dark, and as foreign to her as a burqa or chador. Mystified by their simple beauty, by the thin, soft fabric, she chose the one she thought she might be most comfortable in. All day she's been self-consciously aware of it, of how flimsy it is, and how sparse. When she arrived at the cemetery, Mrs. Harrison greeted her with tears, wrapping her bare shoulders and arms in a black sweater.

"You look so beautiful," she said. "Your mother would be so proud." But her eyes wandered first to Gray's hair, untamed and ruthless, and then to the shin-high bilge boots cuffed with her uncle's sweat socks visible beneath the hem of the knee-length dress. It had not occurred to anyone to consider footwear. All of Gray's shoes were chosen for water resistance and durability on the water or in the woods, not for fashion. At least her feet are comfortable; from her shins up, she's a twist, itchy and unfamiliar. Accustomed to the canvas duck of Carhartts, to sweatshirts and flannels, she tugs at her dress and wonders how women wear such things without feeling utterly vulnerable. That's the last thing she wants to feel today.

Uncle Fenwick moves to take his hand from her shoulder. Gray stops him, pinning it with her own. With her other hand, she reaches for her father's, which is as lifeless and cold as if it's *he* who has died. They stand like that, the three of them—all that remains of her family—staring at the headstone of the woman they each loved and lost, staring at her father's name, staring at the blank space beneath it that renders his eventual death inevitable. That inevitability feels like a knee to the gut. But the blank space means the unknown, and there's no point in worrying about the unknown—not when there's so much that's already known to worry about.

At least he's back. At least they're together. She squeezes her father's hand, both giving and seeking comfort, and turns to look at him. He manages a weak smile for her. The effort seems to exhaust him.

He pulls his flask from his pocket with his free hand and tilts it to his lips, and Gray has to squint when it glints in the sun.

———

Afterward they gather at the DeLongs'. The caravan from the cemetery is a sad parade of battered pickup trucks, most still towing drift boats on trailers. Riding in the back seat of their neighbors' BMW with her father, Gray sees Mrs. Harrison's expression reflected in the glass, sees the look she gives her husband.

"It's disrespectful. At least leave the boats at home."

Her father is sitting back in his seat with his head turned, watching the world outside. He says nothing.

"I think it's perfect," Gray says. "It's like a military parade, except with boats instead of tanks."

"Of course you're right, dear. I just hadn't thought of it that way."

"My mother would have loved it. She wouldn't want anyone to go out of their way or make too much of a fuss."

"They loved her too," her father says to the window, as if his comment is not in response to their conversation but to one happening in his head. "Everybody loved her."

Gray reaches for his hand and squeezes it to console him, the kind of gesture she wishes he would make, or *could* make, for her.

The house is a catastrophe of unfinished rooms, drywall pried from the ceiling for some incomplete repair, exposed beams and joists and wiring. The bathroom floor is just plywood subfloor, the pipe fittings for the sink and toilet visible.

"Will is remodeling the house when he's home," Mrs. DeLong says, by way of an explanation. "He's never home." Her husband is a tugboat pilot on the Columbia River and works in two-week shifts, during which Lucy slowly sinks beneath the surface of their lives until he returns and pulls her up again for air. The house is a cluttered mess, too many kids, the act of cleaning a war of attrition, signs of a life being lived. Gray finds it reassuring.

There are casseroles and cold cuts and what seems like a significant amount of drinking. There is laughter, too, as if the change in locations also signaled a change to a lighter mood.

But when people look at Gray, or dare to approach her, their expressions turn grim. That's what she'll remember from this day, she knows. The pale smiles. The dark clothes. Her father, unrecognizable in his grief. She watches people greet him and offer their consolation, both awkward and sincere, each couching it in something different: a nod, a handshake, a stiff hug. Old friends, neighbors, other guides. People he loves and who love him. One by one he considers them blankly, as if he cannot find the focus to place them. As if he's never seen them before. He looks lost, washed ashore by an unsteady tide onto a distant continent where the natives speak a language he does not.

When they found him on the floor of the garage, one eye was puffy and black, his lips split, blood crusted on his cheeks and chin, green bruises on his bloodied knuckles. His face remains discolored and swollen from whatever happened while he was missing. "Jesus," her uncle said, rolling him over, "he looks like ten pounds of shit in five pounds of flannel." Unable to wake him, they covered him in blankets and left him on the cold floor to sleep it off, watching over him with the concern of new parents. He did not wake for another whole day. Then he sat up with a gasp, a cadaver come back to life.

"Gray," he said when he saw her, his voice like stones in the river current. She ran to him, hugged him, and he did not flinch or pull away.

When she finally let go, he got to his feet, limped over to the fly-tying bench, and reached for the bottle of Old Crow.

He'd been unable to account for the days he'd been gone, unaware of how he earned his injuries. They took him to the Arrow to clean him up and feed him. When he went into the tiny bathroom to shower, he brought the whiskey bottle with him, an oxygen tank to help him breathe in this new and unfamiliar atmosphere. He emerged nearly unrecognizable, beard gone, white hair buzzed tight against his scalp. It was the first time she'd ever seen his chin.

A new man starting a new life, she'd thought.

But now she knows he is neither of those things, not a new man at all but some shadow of her father, not starting a new life but dropped unwillingly back into his old one. He even looks like a stranger in the ill-fitting jacket and tie. She's never known him without long hair, the samurai knot, the beard, never known him to look defeated, and only knows him as he has been, not as he is becoming. Where is the father she waited for? That's the father she wants back. But remembering the Wallowas, his tears, the rifle, she thinks that maybe he has not been that man for a while. Remembering how he put Johnson down without flinching, she thinks that maybe he's *never* been the man she thought. Sitting limply on the DeLongs' tattered sofa, he looks broken and shorn, leaning on the whiskey like a blind man with a cane. He's lost more weight. From the glances and double takes, she knows she's not the only one who finds his appearance jarring. Maybe the gravity of grief can pull at you, remold your body, reshape your features. Maybe it will happen to her too.

Most people are polite enough to not say anything. And then there's Littlejohn, in his black sweatshirt and black jeans, the color his only concession to the gravity of the event. Why did he even come? Standing by the buffet table, he's cornered that weasel-faced runt Sipsey, and The Adventures of Wheatfall and Fuckface, who look miserable. Wheatfall wears a collared shirt and tie and the woeful expression of a trapped animal, and his nephew has the same open-mouthed stare that earned him his nickname.

"Yaw looks like a fucking carp." Littlejohn puckers his cheeks and purses his lips like a fish sucking food. Sipsey laughs, a kind of snigger that makes Gray want to grab him by the anemic rat tail at the back of his acned head and stuff his face in the punch bowl. She glares their way and Littlejohn winks at her, all burst blood vessels and pockmarked cheeks.

"Sorry about your mother."

"Fuck you, Littlejohn."

"Yaw's girl's got a mouth on her," he says to the others.

Sipsey laughs again but stops short when Gray puts down her coffee and begins to march in their direction. As soon as she does—as soon as she takes her first step—she feels the air change. The ambient noise shifts as the crowd turns her way. It's a surprise to her, that she can generate such sparks and affect the dynamics of a room. And not an entirely unpleasant one, either. She's a tuning fork, struck, hearing her own music for the first time. Grief confuses her. But anger? Anger makes sense. Anger she can channel. Anger she can use. She wants to punch poor Wheatfall for not saying anything, wants to punch his dim-witted nephew for looking like such a fuckface all the goddamned time. She wants to punch Sipsey for consistently and reliably being such a bitch. But most of all she wants to punch Littlejohn, because she can tell with every ounce of skin and blood and bone in her body that it will make her feel better to do so.

What a sight she must make, tightening her fists and rushing toward them, wishing like hell she'd worn anything other than a stupid dress. Her uncle intercepts her, turning her away with strong hands.

"What's wrong with you, Littlejohn?"

"Sorry, Pope," Wheatfall says. "He's drunk."

"He's an asshole," Gray says.

"You're both right." As her uncle walks her away, she flips Littlejohn the bird over his shoulder and he smiles again. It's the kind of psychotic smile you have to practice. It gives Gray solace to picture him in front of a mirror, working on it.

Uncle Fenwick walks her into one of the kids' bedrooms and sits her down on a twin bed covered in *Transformers* bedding. "Maybe ease off on the spinach a bit, Popeye? You shouldn't let Bluto get to you so easily."

"What the hell is his problem?"

"Littlejohn is an unwiped ass of a human being and always has been. He and your old man have had bad blood as long as your folks have been in town."

"Why?"

"Why is the sky blue? He's a wall-to-wall asshole."

"Fuck him." The anger inside her is still alive, still beating at the bars of its cage. The speed and ease with which it awakened surprised her. She's filled with it, filled with anger—at Littlejohn, for being such a dick, but also because she knows he's right about her father. At the world, for what it's done to him—and for taking her mother away. At everyone who came that day because they're not her. Because she's not there and never will be.

"Fuck him is right, Hoss. Ignore him. Go keep your father company. You guys are going to need to lean on each other from now on. You might as well start getting used to it."

"That man on the couch in there? That's not my father. My father would have hit that puffed-up asshole until he couldn't lift his arm anymore."

"Then he would have used his other arm." Her uncle puts a hand on her shoulder. "You got to give him some time, Hoss."

Gray has always known her father to be the strongest man she will ever meet. But now she considers that strength has limits. "Control the ring," he used to tell her when they sparred. "Do whatever it takes to force the other guy to fight on your terms. Dictate the pace. Force him to the corners or fight him in the center—whatever you're more comfortable with—but make *him* fight on *your* terms. Once you let him force *his* fight on *you*, you've already lost." Maybe he only allowed into his life things he knew he could beat, and now, for the first time, he's found himself in a fight he does not understand.

How much of him was lost in the white hair piled like ashes on the bathroom floor? How much of him was lost in the Wallowas? Before then—before she was even born—how much of him was already lost? Only part of her father has returned, and until the rest of him does, all she can do is wait.

37

Already diminished, her father sinks deeper in the days that follow, becoming a malignant presence, a drunk and sulking silence, a ghost of a life haunting itself. Drawn and quartered by grief, he looks incapable of living. It's a mystery of physics that he's able to stand and breathe—a trick of the light, a dispensation of gravity. His mood is foul, his edges sharp. Gray is afraid of what he's becoming, afraid of what it will make him do. Most of all, she's afraid that this is the new normal and that they'll never return to how things were.

Of course, they can't. The math will never add up, the one will never carry over.

Is this what life will be like now? Her heart shattered, every emotion a painful imposition? Every memory laden with menace, emissaries of a world stolen from her? She wonders how long they will have to endure this, how long grief will insinuate itself into their lives. She does not want to feel pity for her father. She does not want it to last. So she gives him wide allowances—she knows what he's been through better than anyone—but where's the reciprocity? Watching him move through the days with such visible friction, she feels guilty for expecting him to comfort her when he's in such pain himself. But even her guilt has boundaries, and her father tests them with the selfishness of his own grief. They've not talked about her mother and they've not talked about what happened in the mountains, and with each day that passes her anger grows.

After his return, he refused to set foot inside their house. That was one point, at least, where their grief intersected. Her uncle—the only one among them who could breathe the air in that atmosphere—gathered some of her father's clothes, emptied the fridge of anything perishable, and turned off all the lights, readying the house to be vacant for an extended period of time. Then he welcomed them both into the Arrow.

"Are you sure?" Gray asked, loading the food into the tiny fridge. "It's going to be pretty tight for you in here." Her uncle looked around the RV a little mournfully and took a deep breath.

"You're my family, Hoss."

Each night he sets blankets out on the fold-a-bed for her father. Each night her father ignores them, wrapping himself in the bear skin and heading outside with a bottle of Old Crow clutched in his big paw.

"Should we bring him in?" she asks, looking out the window at the pile of bourbon and bear skin passed out in the meadow.

"Do you want to carry him?"

Concern for her father forestalls bereavement for her mother. Gray is afraid to give it space to breathe, because she knows it will expand, catch, consume her. She knows it will inhabit her. The loss expands inside her. Sometimes it's a hollowness, sometimes a sharp pain. Sometimes it makes her dizzy, giving her a queasy vertigo. Sometimes it makes her furious. She wants to go back to the house and pummel the heavy bag hanging in the garage until either it breaks or she does, but she doesn't dare leave her father. She lost her mother and she's afraid to lose him too.

So she scoops her sleeping bag from her own bed and follows him outside, sleeping within earshot on the hard, uneven ground, her growing resentment keeping pace with her fear and grief. Each night it gets darker and cooler. Each night the autumn rains draw inexorably close.

38

A week after the funeral, her uncle joins her at the galley table and sets a cup of coffee in front of her. "When are you planning on going back to school, Hoss?" he asks, recognizing, perhaps, that she needs a nudge.

Gray knows it too. But she isn't ready and tells him so.

"This is your senior year, Hoss. You gotta graduate."

"I can't leave him alone."

"He's *not* alone."

"You can't watch him all the time."

Her uncle waves her off. "It's fine. I'll bring him to work with me like a shop dog. Lots of fly shops have dogs."

She's running out of arguments, running out of strength to resist. "I'm not sure I *can* go back. I'm not sure I'm ready."

"You should go anyway."

"Why?"

"Because sitting around this goddamned trailer all day for the rest of your life isn't going to make you happy, Hoss. That ain't going to make *any* of us happy."

Gray can picture a map of the known world with all its

landmasses and oceans, the millions of miles of roads criss-crossing the continents and the millions more that aren't even marked, but she doesn't believe any of them can lead her back to happiness.

"Happy?" she asks. "What the hell is that?"

———

The first few days back test her endurance. She sits through class, eats her lunch, and barely interacts with anyone. She sees her friends, but they pass by as if they're in a different orbit, and she feels them drifting further away—there are few things less relatable among high school students than a dead mother.

But after that, the days stack up, playing out with a growing familiarity that quickly becomes routine, and like always, she finds comfort in the routine. Each morning she and her uncle eat breakfast together, eggs and toast and meat cooked on the two-burner propane stove. Before driving herself to school in her mother's minivan, she rouses her father—an act of noise and bravery, a lion tamer peering into the animal's mouth—and her uncle brings him to the Vatican and leaves him to sulk. After school Gray works a few hours at the shop tying flies and leaders and mapping Terrebonne fishing holes for visiting fishermen. The river is open to trout fishing year-round, and the winter steelhead run draws some out-of-town anglers, but business is slow; she's mostly there to keep an eye on her father.

The fall rains begin. Weeks pass without a break. The days are liquid, formless, the nights violent and wind-battered. The rain bears the appearance of intent, as if now that it has returned it plans never to leave again. Some days it rains so hard Gray fears the Arrow will float, carrying them away in their sleep like an ark. Except in the story of the ark, the flood was punishment for the world's sins and the passengers were saved; in their case, the survivors are the ones being punished.

In an RV, as on a sailboat, objects need to justify the space they occupy. The bench seats lift on hinges to serve as storage, the cutting board rests atop the low fridge. Flipped and folded, the couch becomes a table, and from her own bed, Gray can see her father asleep there. Like most nights, he was too drunk or lazy to make the conversion and sprawled instead on the hard tabletop in a swaddle of bear skin. The table is no bigger than a settee. His legs and arms spill off the edges like spare parts in a mannequin factory. She can see her uncle at the galley table, too, and his empty bed at the aft of the cabin, the driver and passenger seats in the cockpit beyond him. That's the entirety of their little world, encased in a thin metal shell with plastic windows and skylights pounded ceaselessly by the rain.

Even now, more than a month since they returned from the mountains, her sleeping bag still carries the scents of the woods, the sweat, the campfire smoke. Sometimes she smells the smoke in her sleep and dreams about fire, a weak and terrifying counterargument to all the water.

She gets up and fishes a sweatshirt from the drawers beneath her bed, where she keeps her clothes and schoolbooks along with the RV's jack, flares, and emergency pylons. Then she squeezes past her father, careful not to spill the dregs of the mostly empty bottle of bourbon balanced at his side. Each day it becomes more difficult to justify the space *he* occupies.

"It's progress," Uncle Fenwick says, as if reading her thoughts. "At least he's not sleeping outside anymore. Hell, at least he's sleeping."

Gray takes the coffee he offers. "He's not asleep. He's passed out."

"Progress doesn't always look like you want it to." The

sentiment is her father's, something he says often, or used to, as if the Arrow is so small, so cramped, the world the three of them share so finite that they're forced to share not just space and air but thoughts and words too.

They've learned an elaborate choreography of coexistence, stepping around and over each other, brushing body parts in narrow hallways, deferentially ignoring the unavoidable sounds and smells of humanity. Despite their physical proximity, she and her uncle continue to give her father emotional space, though increasingly it feels less like a show of respect than self-defense. With each week that passes he grows more surly, meaner, his sinking mood turning, somehow, more sour still.

Gray wants to see him fight the grief, the sadness, all of it, but instead sees surrender. Acquiescence. Fighting's always been his nature—maybe when her mother died, he lost the only thing he was fighting for. But what about *her*? Why won't he fight for *her*? Why isn't *she* enough? So she tells herself it's temporary, because that's what she needs to hear to maintain hope, says it over and over and over: this is temporary; this too shall pass.

But her father's condition wears on and on with no sign of ending. Watching him withdraw into grief and the bottle, Gray worries that all the good parts of him have evaporated until all that remains is concentrated misery.

"Is he ever going to get better?"

"Hard to say, Hoss." Her uncle's expression belies the calm patience urged by his words. He's worried. That makes her worry too.

"What if he doesn't?"

He reaches over her father's body to retrieve last night's mostly empty bottle, sniffs it, and pours the last remaining finger of bourbon into his own coffee. "People will let you get away with almost anything when you're grieving," he says. "But that sympathy has a shelf life. There's a contract. A social contract. You're supposed to try to get better."

"What if you don't?"

"What if you don't get better?"

"What if you don't try."

Her uncle rolls his head, cracking his neck. "After a while it makes people uncomfortable. You don't have to heal completely. You just have to make progress."

"What about me? Am I making progress?"

"Come on, Hoss. You know the answer to that."

When she left her father's side to go back to school for the first time and he did not vanish or burst into flames in her absence, she felt a kind of liberation. It gave her the confidence to spend a little more time away from him, a little more time on her own. And then one morning she woke up and went for a run before school, tracing a long, winding route along the river and into town. Pushing herself, punishing herself, she gathered strength as she ran, listening to the current, smelling the water and the forest, ignoring the pain in her legs and her lungs and her heart. The wind brought tears to her eyes. Or maybe they were tears for her mother, for her father, for all she'd lost and all she still had left to lose. Outside town she found herself at the cemetery, breezed through the iron gates without stopping, without slowing, her breath coming in heaves, and did not stop until she reached her mother's headstone, where she collapsed in the new grass in front of it, no longer unsure about her tears. It had felt good to let herself cry. Or a kind of good. It had felt good to let herself mourn, to openly miss her mother without fear of what it might do to her father. It felt good to allow a few minutes of self-pity without fear of disappointing him. It felt good to run, to breathe again, to stretch her legs outside the confines of the Arrow and the limited proximity of her father and Uncle Fenwick.

It felt so good that she did it again the next day and the day after that until it, too, became a routine, another way to seek comfort, waking in the dark RV, dressing in the confined space, and stepping outside into a world she'd almost forgotten existed.

"I don't miss her any less," she tells her uncle. "It doesn't hurt any less."

"No."

"So what am I supposed to do?"

"Look, Hoss. If an asteroid hits your yard and leaves a giant fuckin' hole, you ain't ever gonna stop noticing the hole."

"But?"

"Maybe you stop falling into it after awhile."

All her father knows right now is the hole. Gray wants him to climb out of it. She wants him to *want* to climb out of it. And with each day that he does not try, she feels herself growing away from him in small, controlled ways. Watching him retreat into his misery and surrender to his grief makes her more aware of her own, and of how she's coping with it. His weakness is a lever using the fulcrum of her mother's death to lift her own strength.

When he took her on as an apprentice guide, one of the first safety skills he taught her was how to rescue someone from drowning. How you don't get too close or they'll take you down with them. Her father is drowning; her instinct is to save him, but she knows she needs to swim for shore.

"He still hasn't been to visit her. When I ask him to go with me, he says, 'That's not her. It's just a rock.'"

"Give him time, Hoss."

"Why is he like this?"

It pains her to talk about her father this way. Especially with him in the room. It's like he's a corpse, an inhuman pile emanating fumes of alcohol from his pores, sweat, something sulfuric.

"Grief makes some people mean. Just like there are mean drunks, there are mean widows and widowers too. They think their lives are ruined and they never get past it, so they try to ruin other people's lives too. Some people are just so unhappy that they can't stand to see anybody else happy, either."

"What about him?" She stares at the collection of arms and legs and flannel and bear skin that her father has become. "What do you think?"

He looks almost peaceful. Most nights his sleep is troubled, not even sleep so much as whiskey hammering him into blackness. When he tosses and turns, the Arrow rocks on its springs. Some nights he yells out. Others, he cries like he did in the mountains. She knows her uncle has heard it—the space they share is too small for him to not have—but they do not acknowledge it, do not talk about it. Instead, they talk about her father's body odor, about his breath, about his constant flatulence, which rises in the night from his sleeping form and hovers like a cloud, whiskey atomized by his gastrointestinal system, each roar a resounding thunder strike that echoes throughout the tiny RV. Now, even as they watch, he erupts again, and her uncle winces.

"What do I think? I'll tell you what I think, Hoss. I think that bastard is trying to poison us."

39

Her uncle asks her to watch the shop while he runs errands. Gray jumps at the chance. The claustrophobia of the Arrow has begun to grate on them all, three restless animals pacing their cage, and she's grateful for a little time alone. Her father, too, is off on his own somewhere. She doesn't know where, and she is uneasy not knowing—the unfamiliarity of worrying about a parent discomforts her—but in the queue of her emotions awaiting a reckoning, that one is nowhere near the front of the line.

She's often found joy in fly-tying since her father taught her the basics when she was younger. Left alone, she sits at the shop's tying bench hoping to summon it now.

The bench itself is just a simple desk her uncle rescued from a yard sale. There's a tray for the tools—bobbin, bodkin, whip finisher, hackle pliers, and scissors—spools of thread on pegs, and a bookshelf stocked with feathers of all kinds, skeins of hackle and fur, and plastic bags filled with beads, weights, and wire. The cork blotter on the desk reeks of his cigarettes and spilled coffee. Gray doesn't mind the smell.

Each fly pattern has its own recipe and ingredients. Her

uncle has pinned handwritten instructions for the most common flies to the wall, but she knows most of them by heart. Each has its own name too. The naming conventions seem to follow certain patterns. Those that sound like fraternity brother nick- names: Stinker, Chaser, Egg Sucker, Leech. Those named for people: Adams, Kaufmann, Clouser, Wulff. Those named for the bugs or baitfish they are meant to mimic: Caddis, Stone- fly, Hopper, Midge. And those that read like a taxonomy of sex toys: Muddler, Stimulator, Articulated Magnum, Green-Butted Skunk. Like most guides, her father has personalized a number of patterns over the years, variants on common flies he adapted for the Terrebonne and named for their predominant character- istics: the Tycho Brahe, with its weighted lead nose; the Liberace, a glittery streamer laced with ice dub; and the Ringo Starr, with its generous mane of black feathers.

The act of tying is a kind of moving meditation, a simple, repetitive act that helps her focus when she's amped up or un- settled. For the past few weeks she's been nothing but. So she bends to the task, focused, intense, losing herself in the work to distract from her sadness and grief. She wraps thread around the hook shank in tight loops, working it like the beads of a rosary; ties in wings or marabou tail feathers; glues on eyes. When she finishes a fly, she takes it from the vice and embeds the hook in one of the foam panels tacked to the wall over the desk until it looks like a swarm of brightly colored insects has descended upon the workstation.

She's so intent on her work that she does not hear the door open, even with the bells lashed to the handle, does not notice that someone has entered the shop. She does not even notice as he stands behind her, watching over her shoulder as she puts wings on a Stoat's Tail and knots off the thread.

"You're really good at that," he says.

Gray jumps to her feet, tipping the chair over. It crashes to the floor.

"What the hell?" Since her mother died, her anger has lurked just beneath the surface, like a submarine mine waiting for something to float across it. Being startled is all it takes to detonate. "What's wrong with you?" Her voice is the force of the blast. Her sudden and unexpected rage startles him in turn, and he retreats so fast that he trips over a bench and falls to the floor.

She stands over him with her hands clenched at her sides. When he tries to stutter out an apology, he looks so forlorn, so pathetic, that it dissipates her anger, and just like that she's laughing at his clumsiness.

"I'm sorry." He sounds confused.

"Who are you?"

"Exley. I'm Exley."

"Exley? What kind of name is that?"

"It's a family name."

"You scared the shit out of me, Exley."

She reaches out a hand and lifts him to his feet. He's about her age, or a little older, and a little taller, with hair the color of a paper bag. He looks familiar, somehow, but she can't place him. Maybe he's one of her uncle's Flying Monkeys.

"I just came in to buy some flies," he says. "I didn't mean to scare you." Her grip is stronger than his. He looks at his hand when she lets it go. "You tie good flies."

"They're OK. I'm inconsistent. Sometimes they come out just how I wanted them to, but a lot of them look pretty beat up." Some tiers are artists, their flies exceptional, but Gray's are asymmetrical, with ragged lines and rough profiles. She's gotten better with practice, but true mastery seems to require a patience of which she is incapable.

"My uncle always says that perfect flies don't catch more fish," Exley says. "They just catch more fishermen."

"*My* uncle says the same thing." Customers don't like to buy the ugly flies, but the fish don't care. Flawed flies mimic injured bait, which makes them more attractive. Predators always target the weak because it takes less effort and there's less chance of failure. Nature rewards efficiency. "But I think he'd rather I tie the ones that sell better."

"Your uncle is the Pope?"

Gray studies him, trying to remember if she's seen him in the shop before, or at school. He's friendly in a way that most guys she knows are not. A lot of guys want you to know how tough they are, or at least how tough they think they are. Gray is tougher than most of them, but they're always trying to prove themselves, like that's what girls really want.

"My dad's a guide too," she says. "How about *your* uncle? Is he?"

"No. But he fishes a lot. He's been teaching me since I moved in with him and my aunt. I'm not very good yet, but I'm trying to learn."

And then she knows where she's seen him—hopelessly tangled in his own fly line, leashed to the willows on the banks of the Terrebonne.

Poor bastard.

"Why did you move in with them?"

His smile vanishes. "My mom died last year in a car accident." He looks down at his feet. "It wasn't her fault or anything. She was driving home from work at night and some drunk driver hit her head-on." He lifts his head again but can't seem to hold eye contact, and he looks past her, into the distance. "I never knew my dad, but I was always close to my uncle. I used to spend a lot of time here, visiting every summer. He got me a job doing landscaping, so I'm living with him and my aunt for a year. Then next fall I'm going to Oregon State."

When he looks at her again, she's crying, her tears as consistently accessible as her anger, always there, always looking for some weakness to breach. The fear returns to his face and another apology stutters its way to his lips.

"It's OK," she says. "It's not you." She takes a deep breath. "My mom died too. Last month."

"I'm really sorry."

"No, *I'm* sorry. I hate this. It feels like all I ever do anymore is cry. It's stupid. I can't even eat a sandwich without remembering how she used to make them for me, and then I'm crying again like an idiot. And when I'm not crying—"

"You're pissed off. All the time. Mad at everything and everyone."

Gray nods. "I feel like a freaking psycho."

"Yeah."

"When does it start to get easier?"

Exley bites his bottom lip.

"I'll let you know," he says. "At least you still have your dad."

———

The next day she goes for a run to burn off emotional energy. When she returns to the Arrow, her uncle's truck is gone, a dry rectangle of dirt in the muddy driveway where he'd been parked. Gray steps inside just as the sky opens up again. Hail pelts the metal roof like gunfire, filling the RV with a relentless, echoing din. But her father—sitting at the galley table, drinking—does not seem to notice, nor does he notice her arrival.

"This is what it must be like inside one of those stovetop

popcorn things." She watches for his reaction to judge his mood, like licking her finger to measure the wind.

He looks up from his glass, surprised to see her there. "Jiffy Pop."

"Jiffy Pop?"

"The magical treat. As fun to make as it is to eat." He sees her confusion. "Forty years later and that goddamned TV commercial is still stuck in my head."

A favorable wind, she thinks. *For a change.*

"Where's Uncle Fenwick?"

"He left you a note."

Gray finds the yellow sticky with his boxy print stuck to the fridge. *Home soon. Don't poke the bear.* She grabs a carton of juice, pulls out the chair opposite her father, and sits down with the bottle of Old Crow between them. He looks upon her intrusion with a benign expression she takes as encouragement.

"How are you doing, Pop?"

"Fine," he says. It's a muscle memory, she knows, an automatic response. She stares until he meets her eyes.

"No. Seriously. How are you doing?"

"Doing the best I can."

She holds his eyes until he looks away, something she could not have done before.

"Why, Gray? How do you *think* I'm doing?"

"I don't think you're doing well."

Her father drains the glass and refills it. More muscle memory. "No," he says. "I suppose not."

"Are you going to ask me how *I'm* doing?" She wants to sound gentle, wants to prompt him, but she can hear the need in her own voice and it irritates her. "Because I don't think I'm doing very well either." The seed of irritation blooms into an anger she lets flower, raising her voice and sharpening her tone.

"How come you don't think to ask your daughter how she's coping with her mother's death? Or with her father's . . . whatever this is? Do you just not care?"

"I'm sorry," he says.

"You're sorry?"

"I *am* sorry." He swirls the whiskey around his glass. "I wish I were more there for you. I wish . . . I'm doing the best I can, Gray."

"It's not enough." Her words surprise her—not that she feels that way, but that she says it aloud. That she doesn't choke on it.

After a moment, her father nods. "No. I know it's not."

"So what are you going to do about it?"

"I'll try harder." He doesn't look up from his drink, as if the whiskey is the most interesting thing in the world. "OK?"

"You'll try harder?"

"Isn't that what you want?"

"I want my mother back. *That's* what I want." The words are like a barbed hook, how they hurt coming out. "I want my father back too," she says, more gently.

Eyes still on his drink, he nods noncommittally. "I'm doing the best I can," he says again, as if he believes it. "None of this is easy for me, Gray."

She wants to hit him. Does he think it's easy for her? Why should she carry on with her life as if her own world has not just been rent apart when he won't even try? Why should she mollify her own anger and claw past her grief if he's just going to surrender to it? It's like he's just rolling over and playing dead. Another subsurface mine explodes, splashing shockwaves of anger throughout her, and she wants to hit her father for being so selfish. So thoughtless. So stupid.

"Did you know she was pregnant?" she asks instead. The question has the same effect as if she *did* hit him. He looks up, eyes suddenly focused, filled with light, and Gray sees that he knew. She watches the pain flood them, and then they go dark again, the light extinguished, the focus gone. He drains his glass, gets to his feet, and without another word, walks outside into the rain.

Deflated, she has neither the energy nor the interest to follow him. The sound of the rain grows louder and faster. The windows darken, and she knows she mistook for a favorable wind the first stirrings of a coming storm. Wherever her father has gone, she hopes he's getting soaked to the bone. After a while, she takes the bottle and pours some of the whiskey from it into his glass and holds it up to the light and looks into it to see what *he* sees in there. She's looking for answers—looking for hope—but all she sees is everything reflected in the glass upside down and without dimension, the round world made flat again.

40

Littlejohn struts into the Vatican, bowlegged as a pit bull. The collar of reindeer bells lashed to the door rings like it's Christmas, but Christmas is weeks away and his presence is no gift. Gray looks up from the tying rack, where she's whipping up Caddis flies for the spring hatch, as he lets himself behind the counter and fills a Styrofoam cup with coffee.

"Coffee is for staff and paying customers," her uncle says, popping out of the back room. "You gonna buy something, or just crop-dust us with Aqua Velva fumes?"

"Buy something? I can get all this shit online for half the cost."

"When you buy in person, you're supporting a local business. The free coffee is just a perk."

Littlejohn takes a sip and winces. "How old is this?"

"What day is it?"

"Jesus Christ, Pope."

"Feel free to leave a tip in the jar." Littlejohn gives him the finger. "If you ain't careful," her uncle says, "Gray might pluck the feathers off that bird and tie them into salmon flies."

Her father sits on a ratty sofa at the back of the shop across from a TV playing an infinite loop of fishing videos. Telegenic hosts in fast boats chase exotic species beneath blue skies. The footage bears no relation to actual fishing in Gray's experience, but who would watch fat guys in muddy waders and battered boats? Though her father stares at the screen, she's not convinced he's watching. There's a coffee mug in his hand, but she's not convinced it's coffee, either, based on the half-empty bottle of Old Crow on the table in front of him. He doesn't acknowledge Littlejohn's presence—not when he walks between him and the TV, blocking his view, and not when he takes the bottle of bourbon and pours some into his own coffee.

"Hey, Pope. I see you got yourself a shop dog."

Gray looks up at her uncle, who raises his eyebrows as if to say, *I told you so.*

"Careful. That one bites."

"They all bite," Littlejohn says. "Don't they?"

As if noticing him for the first time, her father reaches for the TV remote, points it at him, and pushes repeatedly at a button. Uncle Fenwick laughs out loud.

"What the fuck's he doing?"

"I think he's trying to mute you."

Gray laughs too, and Littlejohn glares at her before leaning in toward her father.

"So this is what you do, now, Yaw? Just sit around the shop like a retard?" Her father shows no reaction. Littlejohn reaches over the table and snaps his hairy fingers in front of his face. "Jesus. What the fuck is wrong with you?"

He knocks on the table, a wooden cable spool that looks just like the spools of colored thread hanging on pegs at the tying station, except enormous, giving the scene the feel of a miniature, as if they've all been shrunken and the shop itself is the size of a dollhouse.

"Earth to Yaw." He leans forward so his face is almost touching her father's. "Come in Yaw." Her father says nothing. Littlejohn straightens up and shakes his head. "Total fucking retard."

"For Christ's sake," Uncle Fenwick says. "You know what he's lost."

"Yeah. His balls."

He walks back around the table so that it's between him and her father, the TV behind him, and takes another wincing sip.

"Your wife dying really fucked you up, huh, Yaw?"

Gray clenches her fists, and the thread she's wrapping snaps under the tension, unraveling the loops she's made around the hook's shank. Uncle Fenwick is watching closely. They both know that if there's anything left of her father in the shell that remains, he'll act. But he looks like he's not even paying attention. He leans calmly forward to retrieve the bottle, fills his mug, and sits back with his feet up on the edge of the table.

"Jesus, Pope," Littlejohn says. "Your shop dog is neutered." He smiles cruelly.

Her father smiles too. Then he kicks the table with both legs, hard, sliding it across the floor into Littlejohn's shins. It sweeps him off his feet and buries him in a landslide of catalogs and magazines. Her father stands up, drains his mug, and puts it down on the table as Littlejohn rises from the floor and rushes at him, swinging a brute of a right. On her feet now, Gray sees that it's all windup, a punch he could not have broadcast more if he'd rented billboards or hired a skywriter. Her father slips it easily and drives his own fist into Littlejohn's stomach, an uppercut that connects with the sound of furniture falling out of a moving van.

Littlejohn doubles over, gasping for breath. Grabbing him by the hood of his camouflage sweatshirt, her father straightens him up and hits him with a duet of jabs that snap his head back like his neck is hinged and follows with a cross that knocks him into a shelf display of wading shoes. As he falls in a tumble of boxes and boots, the rack of shelves teeters, leans for a second at a precarious angle, and then topples across the narrow aisle. As *it* falls, it hits the rack on the other side of the aisle, which is filled with spools of monofilament, plastic bags filled with coiled leaders and tippet material. That rack falls, too, hitting the next one, lined with float indicators, line grease, floatant, and fly boxes.

Gray watches, mesmerized, as most of the Vatican's inventory falls like dominoes. There's a flurry of noise and chaos. A quiet settles over the shop when it ends. The silence only lasts for a moment.

"Oh, for fuck's sake," Uncle Fenwick says.

Littlejohn rises to his feet again, more slowly this time, shedding debris. There's blood on his swollen face, and Gray sees that his expression has changed, the smug anger of his everyday smirk replaced by one distinctly more human, one of pure fear. She looks at her father and understands why—he's pointing a pistol at Littlejohn.

Littlejohn reaches for his holster, but it's empty. He's staring down the barrel of his own gun.

"Jesus Christ, Yaw."

Her stomach closing like a fist, Gray tries to read her father's eyes for his intent, but they're blank. In that moment he's a stranger to her. She sees her uncle making his way slowly across the shop in her peripheral vision, but she's afraid to look, afraid to take her eyes off her father.

"Yaw. Come on, man. We were just fucking around, right?" Littlejohn's voice is shaky.

Her father cocks his head and smiles slowly. "Right," he says. "Just fucking around." He raises the pistol to his head, the barrel against his own temple, and his smile disappears as his black eyes narrow.

"Pop?"

His face still dark, her father points the gun at Littlejohn again.

Then he lowers it, releases the magazine, and pulls the slide to eject the chambered round. The metal-on-metal sound echoes throughout the quiet shop. Dropping the Sig and its magazine on the table, he bends down to pick up the ejected cartridge from the floor, studies it for a few seconds, and throws it at Littlejohn.

"Bang," he says.

Then he turns his back, retrieves the bottle from the table, and refills his mug.

Littlejohn rushes him, faster than Gray would have expected. But she's faster still. Trailing feathers from the tying station behind her like a fox fleeing a henhouse, she grabs her elbows, raising her arms in front of her like the cowcatcher on a locomotive, and cuts him off. They collide hard. She backs him up three feet before he even knows what's happening.

His chest feels like steel plate. The hull of a ship.

She sees the shock on his face and it thrills her. She's his height, maybe taller, and strong, but lean. Just a sliver of his size. But she's also angry and full of unresolved emotion. Stiff-arming him to create a little distance between them, she slides her back leg into a fighting stance, just like her father taught her. Spreads her legs to create balance, in line to minimize the target she presents. Just like her father taught her. Fists up, chin down, acting without thought. Instinct. Muscle memory. Just like he taught her.

Littlejohn stands in front of her, unsure what's happening.

"What's the matter, chickenshit?" Gray says. "Afraid to fight a girl?"

Recovering some of his arrogance, Littlejohn smiles broadly and drops his hands to his sides.

"Is that what you are?" Stretched from ear to ear, like a wound, his mouth exposes teeth like golden raisins. Gray wants to knock every last one of them out. Vicious and dismissive at once, his expression drips condescension, and it infuriates her. *Everything* about him infuriates her. His tree stump neck taut with muscle and vein. His red eyes. The wiry hair growing out of his nostrils and ears.

"Fuck you, Littlejohn."

"You are one manly bitch. Were you raised as a boy? Were your folks disappointed they had a daughter?"

"Were yours?"

He laughs a humorless laugh. Gray has never fought anyone but her father, never fought without gloves or headgear, but no part of her wishes she'd picked someone smaller. Her heart tells her to swing. Her head tells her to wait. That's her training giving her a moment of clarity before the adrenaline drowns her, and it comforts her. Littlejohn's face is as bony as rock, and her balled fists feel the promise of pain. She curses them and wishes they were as big as her father's. She doesn't care. She'll break every goddamned bone in them if she has to.

"You may not have any balls, Yaw, but your daughter does," Littlejohn says, looking past Gray. "If she were a man, I'd kick her ass for her."

"If *you* were a man," she says, "I'd be worried."

"I ain't gonna fight a girl."

"Fine by me," she says, and hits him hard, a right cross to the soft part of his face. She feels his nose yield beneath her knuckles. There's surprise in his eyes. Pain too. And fury. When he hits her back, it's not a great punch, neither well-planned nor well-executed, a punch thrown with more anger and reflex than strategy or technique. She tries to slip it but it catches her on the cheek, a glancing blow hard enough to make her thoughts echo. She hits him again, a three-punch combination, jab, cross, uppercut. The first stuns him. The second twists him. The third snaps his head back with the satisfying sound of a walnut cracking. Her hand feels like it's on fire. She drops back out of reach as Littlejohn puts a thick hand to his face. There's a fall line of blood from his nostrils, a thickening at his lips.

"What the fuck was that?" he says. "What the *fuck* was that?" He brings his fists up again, but her uncle is there between them, pushing Littlejohn away.

"I think we've all had enough fun for one day," Uncle Fenwick says. "Why don't you take your show on the road, Marion?"

His words don't immediately register with Gray, but they do with her father, who is sitting on the couch as if nothing at all has happened.

"Marion? Your name is Marion? Marion Littlejohn?"

Littlejohn looks wounded. "John Wayne's name was Marion too, motherfucker."

"Yeah," her uncle says. "And he changed it. Now get the hell out of my shop."

"Fuck you, Pope. And fuck you, Yaw. And you," he says, pointing at Gray, "we're not done."

"Go. Now. I mean it."

Littlejohn spits blood on the floor. "We're not done." He grabs his gun and magazine from the table. "Neither of you. We're not done."

"Anytime, Marion," Gray says. The strength of her own voice surprises her, how it belies the unsteadiness beginning to grip her. She can't decide if it's fear or anger, or maybe adrenaline. Maybe it's none of those things. Maybe it's all of them. She wants Littlejohn to leave before he sees it.

The reindeer bells ring as he slams the door. They hear his truck start, a diesel dragon spewing clouds of fury. His spinning tires spray gravel against the building.

"Don't be that guy," her father says with a lightness that infuriates her.

Her uncle takes her chin in his hands and examines her cheek. "How you feelin', Hoss?"

"Like someone used me to split wood. How does it look?"

"Like raw chicken."

"Is that good or bad?"

"You'll live. How's the hand?"

She holds it up in front of her and wiggles the fingers. The knuckles are split, bloodied, the hand itself already swollen.

"It ain't broken. Nothing a little ice won't cure." He takes a deep breath and shakes his head. "You're your father's daughter, that's for goddamned sure." The way he says it, it might be a compliment, but it might also be an insult.

"That was a good combo, Gray," her father says, and they both turn to face him. He's slouched on the couch, grinning up at them. "He never saw it coming."

"You need to get your goddamned head out of your ass," her uncle tells him. "I mean it. Get your fucking act together." She's never heard him raise his voice at her father before. The effect is shocking, his anger both hard-earned and genuine. He bends down to pick up a plastic fly box from the floor. "Look at this shit, Lewis. Look at it." He spreads arms to encompass the scope of the damage—the toppled shelves, overturned boxes, and scattered gear—and the mess seems to overwhelm him. He throws the fly box at her father, who doesn't bother to swat it away. "You're a goddamned diaper fire," he says. "You know I love you like a brother. I've always had your six, no matter what. And I always will. But let me tell you, pal, you are testing my goddamned patience."

Her father purses his lips and nods, as if he's in total agreement.

"You can't just sit around sucking bourbon down like a goddamned sump pump and leave your daughter to deal with everything on her own, Lewis," her uncle says, his voice more controlled but no less angry. "Get it together. I mean it. Get it together fast. Your whole . . . *routine* . . . is a shiny pile of shit on a good day, and the shine has worn right the fuck off."

He looks as if he's about to say something more—something he might regret—but catches himself. Instead he pulls out his cigarettes, stabs one into his mouth, and lights it. Eyes closed, he inhales deeply and seethes out a cloud of smoke that encircles his head, swirling around, obscuring him completely. The cloud rises slowly to the ceiling. It spreads out, thinning, revealing his face gradually. Only when it's gone does he speak again.

"You'd better watch your back, Lewis." Gray can tell he's gotten himself under control, his voice laced not with anger, now, but concern. "Littlejohn's gonna be gunning for you."

"There was once a man who liked pictures of dragons," her father says. "He dreamt of dragons, and he spoke only of dragons, until the day a real dragon appeared at his window and he died of fright."

"Fucking Confucius."

Uncle Fenwick takes another drag and sees Gray watching him. He tries to smile but she can tell he's not amused.

"What an asshole," he says. She does not argue.

———

Uncle Fenwick is making shepherd's pie on the Arrow's tiny range while Gray does her homework. The range is two half-sized burners and an oven no bigger than a toaster. A child's toy. He adds rust-colored seasoning from a plastic container the size of a gallon of milk, a vague boost of indiscernible flavors that he uses in everything he cooks—the label on the canister says, simply, SEASONING. Gray is hungry, but she wishes his food smelled more appetizing—or even like food.

"How are your war wounds?" her uncle asks.

She looks at her knuckles. The cuts have scabbed over and the swelling is gone, the lingering bruise on her cheek gone yellow and green.

"Better. I'll be fine."

"Does your face still hurt?"

"Not really."

"I'm surprised." She knows already what he's going to say next. "Because it's killing me."

She gives him the finger to show her displeasure, and he chuckles.

"Where's your old man, Hoss?"

"Haven't seen him all day." Her father's been spending more and more time away. She doesn't know where, and she doesn't like it, but her uncle maintains that it's for the best. Or at least that they have no say in the matter. "Should we worry?"

"What does a five-hundred-pound gorilla do?"

"I don't know. What?"

"Whatever it wants to," he says, stirring the pot. "Wherever your old man is, he's gonna miss this feast. He loves industrial food." That's his umbrella term for everything from his chop suey (elbow macaroni, tomato soup, hamburger: a meal as Chinese as she is) to shit on a shingle (creamed beef on a slice of toast). His shepherd's pie is on heavy rotation, two or three nights a week, and it's not really shepherd's pie. It's a can of creamed corn poured on boiled hamburger crowned with mashed potatoes from a box.

"This is more like prison food."

"What do you know about prison food?"

"I eat at the school cafeteria. This is worse. Way worse."

"The army taught me three major food groups: salty, wet, and hot. If it's good enough for our soldiers, it's good enough for you."

"This is what they fed you in the army? No wonder we lost in Vietnam."

"Who told you we lost in Vietnam?"

"Did we win in Vietnam?"

"It wasn't a contest, Hoss. It was a war. Nobody wins a war."

"It wasn't a war. It was a conflict."

"Your teachers were probably draft dodgers."

"My teachers weren't born yet. I'm not even sure their parents were."

Her uncle points a spatula at her, an unappetizing paste of creamed corn dripping from the blade. "Watch it, Hoss. You're dangerously close to insinuating that I'm old."

Gray looks down at her textbook, flips a few pages. "Did you know that the first televised presidential debate was between Nixon and Kennedy?"

"I watched that debate."

"If you keep telling stories like that, I won't have to *insinuate* that you're old."

Her uncle's phone rings, all tinny treble and no bass. He fishes it out of his pocket and flips it open. Gray can hear the voice yelling on the other end of the line.

"Pope? Get your ass down to the Salt Lick. Now. It's Yaw."

———

Her uncle's normal driving pace is maddeningly slow—if his truck were a bike, her mother used to say, it would fall over—but he stomps the accelerator as they rush to town with an urgency that feeds Gray's own. When they turn onto Main, the Salt Lick comes into view. There's a crowd in the parking lot, a few fistfuls of drinkers, a couple fingers more, standing in the rain with their backs to the street. Gray can hear the shouting and can sense the drunken excitement. She's out the door before the truck has even stopped rolling, forcing her way into the crowd, shoving and elbowing blindly to clear space. On the other side she sees her father and Littlejohn squared off like they're fighting.

But only one of them is. Slumped in front of Littlejohn, her father's arms dangle at his sides. His face is bloodied and misshapen. Blood covers his vest and the neck and chest of his rain-sodden shirt, which is torn in two places. There's blood on his pants, blood on his boots, blood in the puddles of rain at his feet. Littlejohn has his fists up. She can see without knowing how that he's done this before, that he's been trained to fight, but that he's sloppy, his weaknesses glaring, holes in his defenses wide enough to fly an airplane through. She knows that her father sees them, too, but he's ignoring them.

Littlejohn hits him again, a straight right. He doesn't raise his arms to defend himself, doesn't duck or turn away. He just swallows the punch without flinching. She can hear the sickening crunch of flesh and bone. Cheers ring out, chaos given voice. Bodies swarm around her, bumping against her, sweaty and warm despite the December air. Their voices are blood-soaked and frantic, and she can smell the beer and the sweat.

Gray hears her uncle calling for her. Ignoring him, she moves to break them up, but someone grabs her roughly from behind. "Let them fight," he yells. Others cheer in agreement, not quite a chant but something close. Colosseum Romans cheering for the lion. She tries to pull herself away. More hands grab at her, restraining her, the crowd shouting for more. The harder she tries to free herself, the more firmly they hold her, like a steel trap digging into her skin.

Littlejohn swings and connects, two quick jabs. Gray watches her father's head snap back. He grins through the blood and laughs. The whiteness of his teeth are a blinding contrast to the purple skin around them. Littlejohn hits him again as Gray yells for him to stop, yells for her uncle to stop this, for *anyone* to stop this. She yells for her father to hit back, to defend himself. She yells because she can't move, can't fight, can't free herself.

Her father is hurt, his face sinking beneath the swelling, a December jack-o'-lantern. His stubbornness and threshold for pain are the only things keeping him on his feet. When Littlejohn hits him again with a cross to the cheek that might shatter a lesser man, the crowd makes a sound that's half groan and half cheer. For a moment, he looks like he might fall. Swaying on his feet, he stumbles a few steps forward, a few steps back, but stops himself upright, or nearly so. He lifts his head to look at Littlejohn and smiles again, his face bloodied and bruised but for the whites of his teeth and the whites of his eyes. Gray can see his lips move. She can see his breath in the cold air. Some faint word escapes him but she can't make it out.

"What'd you say?" Littlejohn asks. "What the fuck did you say to me? Say it again, Yaw."

He reaches in and grabs her father with both hands. As if by agreement, by referendum, the crowd grows quiet. Her father lifts a single finger and points it at Littlejohn. He turns his hand upside down and wiggles the finger, beckoning him to lean in closer. When he does, her father repeats what he said, a single word drawn out in a mocking tone.

"Marion."

Littlejohn throws a punch with a windup so slow that her father should have time to make a sandwich and still block it, but he just stands there waiting for it. He watches it come and takes it head-on.

Gray's never seen him like this, but through the blood and the pain she recognizes his expression. She's seen *that* before—he's enjoying this. He *wants* this. The realization makes her sick. With each punch that Littlejohn delivers, he seems to enjoy it more. *That's* what's keeping him on his feet, not stubbornness or a high threshold for pain but a longing for it. A desire for it.

"Pop!"

Her uncle breaks through the crowd like a rocket reentering the atmosphere. Just like that, he's between them, separating them, pushing them apart.

"That's enough," he yells. "He's had enough."

But the crowd is not sated. Moving as one, predatory, it envelops Gray, grabbing, fingers and elbows poking her. She feels the heat of the bodies, smells their rankness. Someone grips her by the arm, high up beneath her armpit, the fingers digging painfully in. Someone else grabs her breast, her ass, a shoulder. Someone pulls her hair. It's like being swallowed. It's like drowning. She swears. She thrashes. She kicks. She pulls. The hands gripping her relax, just a bit, but it's enough. Lifting her leg high, she stomps the nearest foot as hard as she can, feeling the bones break beneath her boot. Someone cries out. Twisting free, she swings her own elbows, throws wild punches. Some miss. Others connect. Sipsey appears out of the crowd like a gopher out of a hole, reaching for her. She drills him with a cross that liquefies his nose, and he clutches his face, wide-eyed, as the blood pours out. When he turns to flee, she grabs his rat tail and yanks as hard as she can. Greasy and thin, like corn silk, it separates from the back of his neck with a satisfying jerk, and he runs screaming into the crowd.

Breaking through the mass of bodies, she sees her uncle helping her father away from the crowd, toward the truck, shoulder under his arm, half dragging him. Coming up behind them, her fear and her anger collide with the adrenaline spiking her heart.

"What's wrong with you?"

"Not now, Hoss," her uncle says, without turning.

"What's wrong with you?" she says again, furious now, the anger trampling over her fear and leaving it behind. "You didn't even *try* to fight. You didn't even defend yourself. Why are you doing this? You're not the only one who misses her."

"We need to get him to the hospital, Hoss. We can be pissed at him later." Her uncle's concern is palpable, but she's not having it.

"What's wrong with you?" She's yelling, on the edge of hysteria. "Why didn't you fight? Why did you let him hurt you so bad?"

Her father looks back over his shoulder at her. Though he smiles sadly through missing teeth, his bloody lips swollen like lumps of clay, his eyes show no light, no amusement, no pleasure at all. When he speaks, his voice is weak, but Gray hears the resolve in it.

"I just wanted to feel something else for a change," he says.

V

HISTORY WILL BEGIN WITH US

41

Lewis left Massachusetts with no plans, no route, and no time-line, letting instinct and interest be his only guide. He drove. He camped. He fished. Each night, after stopping for the day, he'd run for miles along dark, deserted roads to burn off pent-up energy from long hours in the driver's seat. He'd cook trout or tins of beans over a campfire and fall asleep in his tent or tucked in his sleeping bag in the open bed of the truck. Looking at road maps, he wondered how much of the country he could reasonably cover in a summer. Looking at the bugs splattered across the grill and windshield of his truck, the dirt caked onto the quarter panels and doors, he wondered, too, how much of the country could reasonably cover *him*. It felt bigger from the road than it looked on paper; big enough to get lost in.

But Lewis didn't want to get lost. He wanted to be found.

He'd seen pictures of the Oregon Coast, how different it looked from the sandy shores where New England met the Atlantic. In the Pacific Northwest, the continent had a broken, ragged edge—just like him. That's where he wanted to be. Away from the life he'd known, away from The Old Man. Already he could feel himself breaking free of his father's gravity, growing lighter with each day, as if he'd been carrying a bag of bricks around his entire life and had only now realized he could put it down.

Driving. Camping. Fishing. Eating by firelight. He could do this forever, live this way forever, disappear from the world and sleep in the grass and piss in the bushes and drink from the rivers and roll in the dirt until one day he didn't wake anymore and the weeds just swallowed him. He could do this forever, and part of him wanted to. If it weren't for Janey, he might. But life with Janey held the promise of something even better—the promise of someone to share it with. Once he reached Oregon he would find them a place and then she would join him.

That was his real destination. Not Oregon. Not away. *Janey*.

But some nights when the coyotes howled too loud or the air hung too heavy and the darkness settled upon him so that he could not sleep, he worried. If *he* could just disappear from the world—if he found the promise so alluring—so might she.

As he drove past the road signs advertising natural and historic landmarks and tourist traps polluting the countryside, lining the interstate like gaudy guardrails, he stopped at nearly every one to look for a postcard he might send her. In less than a month on the road he'd sent her more than a hundred already. Let them be a trail of breadcrumbs leading her to him. Let them guide her to their future. Let them be reminders of their plan not just to disappear, but to disappear *together*.

———

Two months later he met her plane in Portland. Waiting at the gate with a handful of picked flowers he could not identify, Lewis all but convinced himself that she would not be on the flight, that she'd changed her mind and come to her senses. That maybe he'd been victim to some elaborate and extended con. How else to explain that kind and lovely Janey might want to be with him? Some fighters had a glass jaw. Lewis feared he had a glass heart. When a flight attendant in her uniform blue cardigan opened the door to the jetway, a body of passengers crushed out. Bedraggled from the flight, they shuffled past him with bloodshot eyes and thousand-yard stares. Lewis searched among them with growing anxiety, crushing the stems of the flowers in his grip.

Then Janey emerged from the corridor, a flash of red hair and freckled skin. Lightheaded with wonder from her first time in an airplane, she half dragged the scarred fiberglass cello case behind her. They'd bought an extra seat for it, and now the instrument had done something he never had: flown in an airplane.

She looked at him almost without recognition, the sunburned, feral-looking man. He'd grown his hair long and pulled it back into a samurai's high ponytail, let his beard grow thick and matted. Months of living outdoors and away from the gym had chiseled him down to only the essential, tendons and muscles rising like topographical features beneath taut, tan skin. A continent away from the last time they saw each other, he handed her the wilting flowers with the bent stems.

"Lewis," she said.

"J."

"Permission to speak frankly?"

"Granted."

"You look like a wild animal. Like Tarzan."

"That's me. Lewis Yaw, King of the Jungle."

"You look surprised to see me. Were you expecting someone else?"

"I wasn't sure you'd show."

She looked at him oddly, thrown by his words or the idea of them. Then she laughed and threw her arms around him. When she leaned her head against his chest, it filled him with something he wasn't sure he'd ever felt before.

42

The first weeks of winter in the Arrow are excruciating. Despite the tiny propane heater's heroic whine, the air doesn't rise above fifty-five. Gray huddles in her sleeping bag listening to the wind whistle through the thin windows and gaps. When she gets too cold she does push-ups, shaking the RV, her cold muscles rankling at the effort, a soreness in her shoulders and neck that matches the one in her heart.

Reduced by his injuries to something robotic, her father drinks bourbon like it's his job. Like it's his calling. Gray doesn't know where he gets it all, whether her uncle is buying it for him or he's managing his way into town and buying it for himself. Maybe he's summoning it out of nothingness, somehow, a pact with a lesser devil. He walks with a shuffling limp. He spits blood and winces with each breath. The dark pupils of his eyes bathe in the red pools of his sclerae, the flesh around them yellow and green, his scabbed-over cheeks dimpled hamburger. It hurts to look at him. He rarely showers, rarely changes his clothes, just sprawls in the relative roominess of the driver's seat in the Arrow's cockpit wrapped in the bear skin, watching without seeing, his eyes glassy and disengaged. The skin no longer smells like a bear—it smells like him. Like an armpit. Like ass.

The whole RV does. It smells, too, like the cigarettes Uncle Fenwick smokes inside to avoid the weather, filling it with a cloud that never entirely dissipates. Her uncle wears a bright-red winter coat, sleeps in it, even, a puffy down affair that doubles his girth, taking it off only to use the phone booth–sized bathroom, and then only because he can't fit in with it on.

"Living here is starting to feel like a human rights violation," she tells him, pulling on another sweatshirt as she makes her way to the galley for coffee. He squashes his downy bulk into the dining area so she can squeeze by. She doesn't mean to sound ungrateful—she has no idea how she'd be doing any of this alone, how she'd be doing any of this without him—but the dampness cuts right into her bones.

Her uncle studies her. The blower fan shuts off with a clatter, the silence between its breaths a godsend. A brevity of calm.

"You ready to move back home, Hoss?"

"I'm ready."

"OK then. But just so you know, I ain't going to sleep well with you gone. I'll be up all night worrying. Least here we're together, and I can keep an eye on things. Run interference."

"You don't need to worry about me."

"Maybe it ain't you I'm worried about." Her uncle laughs dully.

"Come with us. Let's *all* move back home. There's no point freezing your ass off in this tin can all by yourself."

Her uncle chews his lip, considering it. The space they inhabit is so small she can hear his jaw creak.

"We still need to convince *him*."

"No we don't," she says.

"How do you figure?"

"Just bring the whiskey with us when we go. He'll follow."

———

The next morning Gray stows anything that's not tied down while her uncle pulls the chocks from beneath the wheels, removes the magnetic TV antenna from the roof, and checks the oil. Then he climbs into the captain's seat and closes his eyes like he's saying a prayer. When he turns the key, the engine roars to life with the sound of a planet being born. The thin walls shake and shimmy; bolts and springs rattle deep in the engine's loins. The exhaust belches a cloud of smoke black enough to stain the ground beneath it. But when he steps on the gas, the Arrow lurches forward.

Gray follows in the minivan. Ten minutes later, she waves him into position as he backs up the driveway at Greer Lane. He parks in front of the house and kills the engine, and the whole thing settles with a sigh.

Her father has slept through it all.

"Oh, man." Her uncle high-fives her in the driveway when he steps out of the RV. "Harrison is gonna love this."

"Who cares? We're home."

He lights the pilot and starts the furnace, and slowly the house comes back to life. Gray unpacks their things and loads the fridge. They've already moved everything inside and made breakfast by the time her father wakes up.

They watch from the kitchen window as he limps down the stairs of the Arrow to piss outside. He looks up from his steaming ritual and realizes where he is. Still zipping his pants, he takes in the yard, the garage, and the trailered boat. The rain starts to fall as he turns to look at the house.

For a long time he stands there getting soaked while he considers his situation. Ten minutes pass.

Twenty.

Gray is waiting in the hall when he finally opens the front door.

"It's OK, Pop."

Tentatively he steps inside, dripping rain on the floor. He breathes deeply, unevenly, as if getting accustomed to the atmosphere. When he makes his way to the kitchen to join them, he keeps one hand on the wall for support. Uncle Fenwick puts a mug of hot coffee in the other hand and pulls a chair out for him. Her father stares at it like it's a trap.

They go back to their bacon and eggs while he stands frozen on the precipice of change, of time, of a decision that has all but been made for him.

Then he collapses into the chair.

"Fine," he says. "But nobody sleeps in our bedroom—not even me. It's off-limits."

The look he gives them is a challenge. Gray and her uncle meet it with ease.

———

Late that night, and unable to sleep, she surrenders to her restless mind and gets out of bed to join her uncle in the kitchen. He's reading at the table, her father asleep in another chair, a steady wheeze in his bear skin, head on the table, hands wrapped around a half-empty bottle.

"What are you reading?" she asks, taking a seat.

Her uncle lifts his reading glasses atop his head and looks at the book's cover, as if to double-check. "Bible," he says.

"*The* Bible?"

"The one and only."

"I didn't know you were religious. You've never mentioned it before."

"My mama used to tell me, 'Religion is like your pecker. Don't ever show it to anyone who don't ask to see it first.'"

Gray nods at her father. "Does it say anything in there about what we should do about him?"

"Well, it *is* full of miracles. Seriously, though—religion ain't medicine, Hoss. It can't fix you. It's more like therapy. It can help you fix yourself, but you still got to do all the heavy lifting."

"How about happiness? Does it say anything about being unhappy?"

Her uncle laughs, not unkindly. "Shit. This whole book is full of unhappiness. Wall-to-wall disappointment. People die by the thousands. God smites entire villages. There are more bad fathers in here than in the federal prison system." When he lights a cigarette, the smoke hangs over the table. He waves it away but it has nowhere to go. "Hell. The main character's a boy who loves his daddy so much that he wanders the desert telling everybody how great he is. What does he get for his trouble? His old man heaps punishment and humiliation upon him. Then, to top it off, he lets him die."

"Sounds uplifting."

Her uncle closes the book and leans forward onto his elbows, shoulders hunched. Gray can smell the cigarette on his breath.

"You doing OK, Hoss?"

Maybe it's the lateness of the hour, or the persistence of their circumstances. Maybe it's that she has not once said it aloud. But Gray finds herself on the verge of telling him the truth. No, she's *not* doing OK. The gravity of her sadness pulls at her, bowing her back and neck. It slows her footsteps, it labors her breath.

Her mother is an echo she hears in every word anyone speaks. She feels like she's been denied the opportunity to grieve, and she blames her father for it, and holds it increasingly against him. She misses her father too—even though he's right there, beside her. It's all right there at the surface beneath skin so thin she's afraid it will tear of its own accord. But honesty feels more like another problem than a solution. So she punts the question instead.

"How about you?"

"Me?"

"My mom was your family too. You've had as much change as we have."

Her uncle chuckles quietly and leans back in his chair so his face disappears into the shadows. "I'm doing great, Hoss. What more could a guy ask for out of this life without sounding selfish?"

He flashes a troubled smile to show he's joking, and opens his Bible, looking for something.

"'But now trouble comes to you, and you are discouraged; it strikes you, and you are dismayed.' A reading from the book of Job."

"Between the smoke and the Bible verses, it's like a goddamned AA meeting in here," her father says, startling them.

"Didn't know you were awake."

"Did you ever read the Bible, Pop?"

Noticing the bottle in his own hand, her father takes a long sip. "Never had much use for that particular book," he says. "I've had people tell me that I'm damned if I don't believe. But I don't see how belief is a choice any more than happiness is. I don't think you can just decide something like that. Either you have it, or you don't."

Uncle Fenwick thumbs through the pages. "Faith is

confidence in what we hope for and assurance about what we do not see," he says. "Hebrews 11:1."

Her father stares across the table at him with bloodshot eyes.

"Back when I was fighting, there was this lunkhead from Shamrock, Oklahoma, that everyone was talking about. Some kid with piston forearms, fists like canned hams, a face like a goddamned anvil. Supposed to be the next big thing. But there's always a next big thing, isn't there? So my trainer, Jimmy, who was managing me by then, booked me a fight with this kid way upstate up in Rouses Point, New York. Practically Canada."

He pauses to take a sip of bourbon.

"The venue was this Catholic church. Arched stained glass windows. Exposed beams. A vaulted ceiling with cracks in the plaster. The local athletic club had set up a regulation ring between the pews and the altar, surrounded on two sides by rows of metal folding chairs, and there was this big crucifix looking down on the ring, a massive larger-than-life Jesus nailed to a giant cross. Jimmy called one of the sponsors over, pointed at Jesus, and yelled, 'Throw a goddamned towel over his head. We don't need another referee.'"

Not the kind of man given to emotional confessions or intimate conversation, her father has always held his feelings the way a tree holds sap, leaking them out only when the bark is cut. This is the most he's spoken in months—and he's not done. He takes another sip, wetting his lips.

"There was all this iconography on the walls. Stations of the Cross, statues of the Virgin Mary. Whatever. I told Jimmy I felt like I was breaking some rule just being in that church, never mind fighting there. Jimmy says, 'Listen, Lou'—he called me Lou—'Listen, Lou,' he says, 'Everyone who steps into a church is fighting something. Otherwise this whole religion enterprise would just go right out of business.'"

Her father sits back in his chair and looks at them, as if he's done with his story. They stare at him expectantly as he studies the bourbon remaining in the bottle.

"There was a pretty good crowd that night. I don't think much else happens in Rouses Point, to be honest. During the undercard, all local bruisers looking for some attention, I noticed this one lady down on her knees with her back to the ring, praying. She wasn't there for the fight. She was there because it was still a church. Because it was *her* church. She'd gotten all dressed up, done her hair up, and come to pray. I watched her for a few minutes, how she was just oblivious to the crowd and the bells and all the shouting. Just totally focused, working her rosary beads with her arthritic fingers.

"Sometimes I still think of her, how she looked like she was right where she belonged," he says. "And it kind of makes me wish that I could believe too. Not in God. Not in heaven. Not necessarily. But in something. Sometimes I wish I could believe in *anything* with the same confidence that she believed God was taking care of her."

He looks down at the bottle, which he's nearly emptied.

"I've always had a code. Tried to follow it. Tried to live my life by it. But that's just rules that tell you *how* to act. They don't tell you *why*. So I've always kind of admired people who had faith. People like that woman." He points the bottle at Uncle Fenwick. "People like *you*. I always wondered what it must be like to feel that every decision you make, everything that happens, is part of a bigger plan. How reassuring that must be."

He takes another sip and swallows hard.

"Because let me tell you, it's not an easy life when you don't believe in a goddamned thing." Her father looks at them both in turn. The air feels thickened, like jelly setting in a jar, and for a long minute it seems like none of them can move or even breathe. The fridge kicks on with the whine of worn bearings.

"Anyway, that kid everyone was talking about from Shamrock, Oklahoma? The next big thing? I knocked him out thirty-two seconds into the first round."

"Amen." Her uncle laughs and it feels good to hear laughter in the house again. With it comes what feels like permission for Gray to laugh too. But when she tries, it feels awkward, misplaced, as if it wasn't permission but expectation. As if she's forgotten how.

"Well shit," her father says. "Since we're doing Bible club, I've got one more for you." Pulling the bear skin snug over his shoulders, he gets to his feet, grabs the bottle, and makes the sign of the cross with it. "Spectacles, testicles, wallet, and watch. A reading from the book of Exodus." He walks out the front door and disappears into the cold, dark night.

———

Gray sleeps an uneasy sleep. Her bed is comfortable and warm, a welcome change from the Arrow, but the last time she slept in it her mother was still alive. The house feels both unfamiliar and too familiar. It retains memories of her mother the way someone's scent lingers in a room after they're gone. Though it's been just a couple months, her life is so different now Gray can barely remember what it was like before. Though those are her posters on the walls, her books on the shelves, her clothes in the closet, it's like sleeping in a stranger's room.

Late that night she hears her father come back inside. After that he wanders the house, his shuffling limp in the hallway, his hand dragging along the wall. Once she hears him pause outside her door. The house is full of history for him, too, and haunted

by her mother's presence—not her ghost, but all the things she
left behind. The furniture she picked out and arranged. The
paint she chose for the walls. The sound of her cello filling the
rooms. Gray holds her breath and waits for him to knock at her
door, hoping he wants to talk about it, wants to talk about *her*,
but after a minute she hears him shuffling away.

She wakes the next morning to find Uncle Fenwick tangled
in a blanket on the pullout sofa, a stalactite of drool stretched
across his open mouth, her father wrapped in the bear skin on
the floor at his feet. *For better or worse, this is my family now*, she
thinks, and goes for a run along the river in the cold morning air.

When she returns, her uncle is awake and in the kitchen,
wielding his hair dryer like a sidearm. He uses it solely to render
bread stale for French toast, leaning the slices up against the
backsplash and drying them out with the hot air. The first
time she'd witnessed his method, she'd mocked it—the peri-
winkle-blue blow-dryer looked ridiculous in his meaty hands,
and using it on bread made him look crazy—but she can't argue
with the results.

"My father's recipe," he'd told her. "The only good thing
he ever taught me."

Hungry from her run, she takes a seat at the table. A minute
later her father joins her. He pours a cup of coffee from the
glass carafe, eyes the bread lined up like prisoners before a firing
squad, and sits across from her as if it's the most normal thing in
the world. It's the first time he's joined them for breakfast since
her mother died. Gray trades a stunned look with her uncle but
says nothing, afraid to spook him and drive him away. They're
as still as if a deer has wandered into the yard.

He's there the next morning, too, and then the morning
after that.

"Celebrate every win," he used to say when Gray would

fight what felt like a big fish to the boat only to find a runt on her hook. "Some fish may be too small to keep, but no victory is." That he seems to make an effort to rejoin the human race over the next few weeks—small gains, a "hello" here, a "good night" there, a smile over dinner—feels momentous.

As the weeks pass, his wounds heal, but his face remains misshapen, the nose bent and flattened, one cheek ridged over a fracture that fails to smooth out. When Gray looks at him she sees reminders of all that he's been through, the scars on his skin, the wound in his heart. Her own wounds are scabbing over, too, her skin growing thick and tough over them.

Buoyed by his advances, she even lets herself believe that they've turned a corner. That things will get better from here on out. That their pleas have finally reached him and he's ready to return to being accountable to them and the entire world and not just his own grief. The hope is a breeze. It catches her tired wings and lifts her. It feels good to coast for a change—she's been flapping them for so long.

43

Springtime in Oregon is transcendent. The changing weather helps convince Gray she's right about the better times ahead. April unfolds like origami with colored paper, flowers on the rosebushes, rhododendrons in yards, wildflowers like stage lights. It still rains all the goddamned time. But the rain feels different. Less oppressive. Even the town looks better, as if some janitorial staff has mopped the roads and driveways of winter dirt, taken the leaves from winter storage and put them back on the branches, and turned the lawns back on. Everything goes green overnight.

Each week brings more signs of humanity. Each week brings more hope.

Her uncle starts sleeping in the Arrow again, still parked in the driveway, tethered to the house's electrical system by a long heavy-duty extension cord running in through a window. Her father still won't set foot inside the bedroom, but with Uncle Fenwick gone, he moves off the floor and onto the pullout sofa. One afternoon Gray arrives at the Vatican to find him sweeping the floor. A few days later, he's sitting at the bench, tying flies. He even startles her one morning when he walks through the kitchen on his way to the laundry room holding a basket of dirty clothes. He's not the father she knew, not exactly. But he's becoming someone she's starting to think she might like to get to know.

On a warm April day, she comes home from school to find his truck on the lawn. She parks the minivan and wanders over to where he's dug out a wide circle in the side yard, like a meteor strike, and lined it with giant rock slabs. The circle is incomplete, with a stone missing, giving it the appearance of a mouth. He's sitting on one of the slabs, leaning against the handle of a shovel, panting hard. The dirt on his face is streaked with sweat.

"Fire pit," he says.

"What for?"

"I don't really know. I guess I needed something to do. It just . . . seemed important."

Gray sits beside him. "Where'd you get these?"

"The Terrebonne."

Each of the slabs must each weigh a couple of hundred pounds. He had to haul them up the riverbank and into the bed of the truck, and then wrestle them into place in the yard.

"You moved all these yourself?"

"Lot harder than I expected. Guess I'm not as strong as I thought I was."

"I think you're missing one."

"Yeah. I'm not as good at counting as I thought, either. I'll go back and get one more. Just . . ."

"Just what?"

Her father grins. "Just not today."

———

In May, a week before school lets out for the summer—for good—Gray comes home from an evening run to find her uncle making dinner, steelhead in the oven, potatoes in a pot of salted water. There's even a salad, or what passes for one in his culinary regime: a wedge of iceberg lettuce, a bowl of pickle slices, a bottle of Thousand Island dressing. "It tastes like a Big Mac," he claims. There's music playing on the living room stereo, and the whole scene feels astoundingly normal in a way that stuns her. She practically giggles.

"You're in a good mood," he says as she grabs a bottle of water from the fridge.

"Runner's high."

"I'll take your word for it, Hoss. Before I forget, I made us dinner reservations."

"What about the fish?"

"Not for tonight, genius. For your graduation. Me and your old man are gonna get dressed up and cheer like fools when you walk across the stage and grab that diploma. Then we're taking you out and buying you a steak the size of a Volkswagen. I'm actually looking forward to it. You know how long it's been since I looked forward to something, Hoss?"

The act is transparently fatherly, and she's touched.

"Sounds great. But I'm not going."

"To dinner?"

"To graduation. Genius."

"Why the hell not?"

"Because. It's ridiculous. The whole ceremony is dumb. They make everybody march in those stupid hats and robes like a bunch of penguins."

"It's called *pomp and circumstance*."

"It's pointless."

"Pointless? Hell. We've had a surplus of circumstance

around here, but not nearly enough pomp. This will be good for us."

Gray starts to protest but her uncle cuts her off.

"Trust me on this, Hoss. There are plenty of things in this world you can get a second chance at. Even marriage. But graduation ain't one of them. This is one and done."

"I don't know."

"Do it for me, Hoss. Even *I'm* sick of industrial food. I need that steak dinner. Don't you think we're long overdue for some excuse to celebrate?"

Unable to argue that point, Gray relents.

But all week an unarticulated fear gnaws at her. Though it takes a few days to figure out what it is she's afraid of, exactly, once she does it seems perfectly obvious. She's afraid that seeing the two of them, her father and uncle, at her graduation—the sum total of family she has left in this world—will make her mother's absence too explicit to bear. Isn't that why they ignored the holidays? No empty plate at Thanksgiving dinner, no unopened gifts under a Christmas tree? It's the kind of thing she wishes she could talk to someone about.

It's the kind of thing she wishes she could talk to her father about.

———

All week she looks for an opportunity but never finds one. She's afraid to bring it up, afraid she'll set things back with him and undo the progress they've made by even mentioning it. But when she can't sleep a couple of nights before graduation, she knows she won't be able to until she talks to him. So she pulls on a sweatshirt and wanders out to join him on the back porch.

He's got his feet up on the railing and he's writing in his black notebook, drinking Old Crow. Gray hasn't seen him with the notebook since the Wallowas.

"Are you busy, Pop?" There's no overhead light, just a Coleman lantern on the railing. Its glow is so faint that beyond the steps is only uninterrupted blackness.

"I don't think I've been busy for months."

"What are you doing?"

"There's an old proverb. 'With the first glass, a man drinks wine. With the second glass, the wine drinks the wine. With the third glass, the wine drinks the man.'"

"Fortune Cookie." Her mother called him that, and Gray knows what using it will evoke. "In that little parable, which are you?"

"Drunk," he says, with neither pride nor shame. "Fenwick told me to get cleaned up for dinner this week. Says we're taking you out after commencement."

"He's making a big deal about it."

"It's a big deal, Gray. High school graduation is one of those milestones in your life that you'll always remember."

She's just eighteen but feels like she's already had too many of those, and isn't sure she wants any more. "What was yours like?" she asks.

"I didn't go."

"How come?"

"No one told me I'd regret not going. And I had no one to go with me. Your grandfather . . ." Gray waits for him to finish, but instead he raises the bottle and takes a deliberate sip.

"What about college? Did you go to that graduation?"

"Nope."

"Same reason?"

"No. Your mother would have gone to that one with me if

I'd wanted to go. We'd already been together for a few years by then. We even talked about it."

"So why didn't you go?"

He takes another sip, long and slow, as if the memories exist not in his head or his heart but in the whiskey. "That was the day I left."

"Left what?"

"Home. New England. The East Coast. Your grandfather. Everything, really, except your mother."

It's the most they've spoken of her mother since she died. Gray takes the fact that he mentioned her first as an invitation.

"I'm going to visit her after school tomorrow," Gray says. "I'd like you to come with me."

"What for?"

"So we . . . so we can all be together. For my graduation."

"That's not her."

"It is to me."

"It's not her, Gray. It's just a rock."

"It's her. It has to be." Her own insistence surprises her.

"Why?" His voice holds not challenge but curiosity. Sadness. "Why does it have to be?"

"Because she has to be *somewhere*. I have to think of her somewhere. I have to be able to visit her somewhere."

"Why, Gray?"

"Because," she says, before she even knows how to finish her sentence. "Because . . . I miss her."

There's another long pause in which even the cicadas seem to go quiet. She wants her father to tell her it is OK to miss her mother. She wants him to say that he misses her too. She knows he misses her but for some reason needs to hear him say it.

He holds the silence stubborn and close.

"What does 'History will begin with us' mean?" she asks.

He drops his feet from the railing so he's sitting up straight and looks at her. "Where did you hear that?"

She's been carrying the postcard around since she found it. A totem of better times. She slips it out of her pocket, unfolds it, and hands it to him. As he leans into the light to read it, the words seem to have a physical impact on him, how they leave the card like an archer's arrow and pin him back against his chair. He hands it back to Gray, tosses the notebook on the porch beside him, and turns off the lantern. The darkness swallows them.

"What does it mean?"

"In the early fifteen hundreds, the Spanish explorer Cortés set sail with six hundred men and eleven ships. When they landed on the Yucátan and his men stepped out onto the shores of the New World, Cortés gave them a single order. 'Burn the ships.'"

"Burn the ships? Why?"

"Without those ships, they couldn't go home. Destroying the past was a show of commitment to the future. After that, they had no choice but to survive, no choice but to succeed."

"So?"

"When your mother and I moved out West together, neither of us had ever been to Oregon before. We didn't know anyone here. All we knew was that we couldn't stay *there* anymore, in Massachusetts. That we wanted to build a new life together. That we needed to put the past behind us."

He pauses for a moment, and in the space between words she can hear something moving branches or brush in the woods behind the house, the breeze, maybe, or some nocturnal animal.

"When I met her, I knew I was going to spend the rest of my life with her. I knew it with a certainty I'd never felt before. Nothing before that moment mattered. But since September— since she died—I've been trying to figure out how I could have been so wrong."

"Maybe you weren't wrong. Maybe you'll be together again someday."

Her father makes a sound—disappointment, maybe, or disgust. "Your uncle might believe in that fairy tale, but I don't." He lifts the bottle and takes a long sip.

Gray decides she's not going to let him off the hook. Not this time.

"Come with me tomorrow," she says again. "Please."

She waits.

"Please. For me, Pop? Do it for me?"

As her eyes grow accustomed to the darkness, she sees him relax, sees his posture soften, but still he says nothing, and for nearly a minute he does not even move. Is this what she's been reduced to? Begging her father for simple affection or solidarity still somehow beyond his reach? He's silent for so long that she worries he's fallen asleep.

She's about to give up and go to bed when he reaches out in the darkness and takes her hand. She's almost forgotten how big his hands are, how it feels to have them swallow her own. How when she was younger and smaller, it felt like she could use his hands for shelter. For protection. And how long it's been since she felt that way. She squats beside him, holding his hand.

"I don't want to go there because that's not your mother, Gray. Not to me. It's just a rock in the ground with her name on it."

She starts to stand up, tries to pull her hand away, but he doesn't let go. He squeezes gently, the skin of his palm rough against hers.

"Listen to me, Gray. There are better ways to be reminded of her. Better ways to talk to her. But if it's important to you to visit her there, I'll go with you."

Everything within her had been braced for impact—for a fight—but his words are a spell that undoes her.

"I'll do it for you," he says.

She squeezes his hand.

"Your mother and I didn't come out here to Oregon just to start a new life together, Gray. We came out here to start a family. You're my daughter—I'd do *anything* for you."

Though every muscle in her legs burns from squatting beside him, she stays like that for a long time, staring into the darkness of an Oregon night, listening to the cicadas, and holding her father's hand.

44

Gray wakes to an empty house. Sun is pouring in through the windows, and when she looks outside there's a handful of blackbirds on the lawn. Their heads are nearly purple in the sun, their sides green, and their color changes in the light as they move. She watches them push and pull at the ground, searching for seeds and grubs. Then without warning some invisible signal passes among them and they all take flight in a flutter of wings.

Her father has left a note taped to the coffeemaker, the coffee inside still warm, his handwriting unmistakable and barely legible.

Meet you there after school.

Half-sure he would have forgotten his promise, she'd already begun to make excuses for him in her mind. The note warms her more than the coffee, which she takes outside on the front porch to drink in the sun. His truck is gone. It's unusual for him to be gone so early, or even awake—at least since they got back from the Wallowas to find their world turned inside out. For most of her life before that, he'd been up and gone long before first light. But she's almost done with high school, the coffee is hot and delicious, and the world smells like new grass and pine needles, so she decides it's a good sign that he's up early. The next stage in his healing process. "Fall down seven times, get up eight," he likes to say. Maybe this is number eight. Remembering what he said about happiness being a choice, like religion, she considers that maybe hope is the same way—a choice—and decides to try it. Decides to choose hope. So she sits on the porch sipping coffee and remembering what it feels like to be outside until it's time to get ready for school.

The last day is a formality. A joke. Classes are finished, teachers have turned in grades, and students spend the day cleaning out lockers, throwing away textbooks, and milling the halls. She has only a few dozen senior classmates at her regional high school. Some will go to college in Eugene or Corvallis, Seattle or Boise, maybe Chicago or Denver or somewhere back East. They'll get together over Christmas break and summer vacation. They'll make promises even as their reunions lapse into infrequency and they drift slowly apart. Some will stick around Disappointment, working for their families or wasting their lives away. She's known most of them her entire life. Some of them she calls friends, or at least used to, until they faded away after her mother died. Or until she did. What do any of them know about her life? What do any of them know about what she's been through? She'll see them at graduation, but after that she will not miss any of them and none will miss her. She hugs some of them half-heartedly, nods at others or shakes their hands, signs a few yearbooks, says goodbye to her teachers, the administrators, the lunch ladies, the custodian, and when the last bell rings she steps outside as the school empties like a river spilling into the sea.

Though she's been driving the minivan since September, the detritus of her mother's life still occupies the glove box and the storage bin between the seats: unmailed letters addressed in her handwriting tucked into the visor, awaiting postage; half-emptied water bottles in the cupholders she will never finish; an unopened travel-size bottle of hand sanitizer; pens whose barrels she chewed like a cob of corn. It makes Gray uneasy to be surrounded by so many tiny reminders of her mother's unfinished existence. But to throw any of them out would feel worse. The Previa smells of her too. She finds the scent as familiar and comforting as she finds it sad, and she worries that it fades a little with each day.

The first time she visited her mother's grave she nearly threw up from the pressure in her head and heart. She sat in the wet grass, sobbing, draped over the cold stone until she'd scraped the skin on her cheeks raw. It got a little easier with each visit after that as she learned to talk to her mother, learned to suppress the self-conscious strangeness in the pattern of one-sided conversations, and after a few weeks, she began to look forward to it. She could tell her mother the things she could not tell anyone else. Not just how much she missed her, but how losing her had changed the course of their lives. About the fear she felt for her father, and the anger. And with each visit, Gray began to find a kind of liberation in being able to talk so openly—far more openly, even, than when her mother had been alive. But what surprised her most was the comfort she got from it. How she got the sense that her mother could hear her, somehow. She didn't know if she believed in heaven or God like her uncle— she'd not been raised to—but she didn't *not* believe in it, and the idea of her mother spending an eternity in a better place made her want to believe, if only for her sake. Who wouldn't want to believe in something better than this?

She parks beside a rotten railroad tie outside the gates, grabs a garbage bag from the back seat, and sets out along the path, gathering trash that has been spilled or thrown or blown into the cemetery as she walks, flotsam and jetsam both.

The graveyard itself is just a half dozen acres of fescue-covered hills with a sprawling view of the Terrebonne, a knot tied loosely around Disappointment connecting her life and her town and her family and its history. That she hasn't been on the river since before the Wallowas feels like another loss for her to mourn. In some ways her relationship with the Terrebonne has been the most intimate of her life. She always believed it was mutual, that the river relied upon her as much as she did upon it. But seeing it flow undaunted, unaffected by her absence or her father's, she feels foolish remembering how she used to dream of it, a cloud of *Cinygmula* or *Serratella* hatching, fish rising like surfacing torpedoes, how she would wake with its scent on her breath as if its water ran through her veins. How long since she dreamed of the river?

How long since she dreamed at all? She's had only nightmares, her mother taken, her father out of reach, voices in the growing darkness. They always feel real. But with the sun bright and the grass green and the choice of hope in her heart, darkness doesn't seem possible. Not even in the cemetery.

Gray steps off the paved path and cuts across the grass, weaving between headstones and reading the names aloud. It's her way of honoring the dead, and a reminder that she's not the first person to lose someone.

When she reaches her family plot, she puts down the bag and stands in front of her mother's headstone with her eyes closed, feeling the sun on her face. The warmth feels like her mother's presence. Gray is only there a few minutes when she hears her father come up behind her, and with her eyes still closed, she can feel *his* presence when he stands beside her too.

It's like they're together again, all of them.

She reaches out and finds his arm, finds his hand, and when

she squeezes it, he squeezes back. Maybe he only came because she asked him to, but he came. He's there. In that moment, Gray realizes why this felt so urgent to her, and why she needed so much for him to be there with her—not just to talk to her mother, and not just to visit, but for another reason entirely. When she opens her eyes and looks at her father, she sees that he knows it too. And that maybe that's why he fought it so much. He wipes the tears from his face, and as the warm spring sun beats down upon them, together they say goodbye to her mother.

———

They take their time walking back to the parking lot, meandering through the grounds. Occasionally Gray stops to pick up trash, a food wrapper or cigarette butt she stuffs into the bag. Neither of them says anything, and neither of them has to. She falls behind for a moment, dropping off the path to chase an old napkin blown by the breeze, and watches her father as he walks ahead of her. His limp remains, and some of the purpose is gone from his stride, but he looks more at peace with the world than he has in months. He even smiles at her when she catches up.

When they reach the parking lot, he circles around his truck and leans with his arms resting on the tailgate.

"Got any plans this afternoon?"

"What did you have in mind?"

He looks down the hill at the river.

"I thought we might go fishing," he says, as if it's the most normal thing in the world.

She looks at him across the bed of the truck and smiles.

"Can I bring a friend?"

———

Gray is surprised at how easily the old routines return to her. She checks the trailer tires and hubs while her father hooks up the hitch, and together they stack the rods, stow the fly boxes, and double-check the gear. They tow the boat to the river with the windows down, the warm spring air on their faces. At the put-in she unhooks the transom straps and holds the painter as he slides the boat down the ramp, ties it off while he parks the truck and trailer. Going through the familiar motions feels comfortable in a way she has not felt in some time. It feels like putting down something heavy she's been carrying.

Once they're on the river, she and Exley talk in the bow as her father works the oars near the stern. They laugh easily and often in a way she'd almost forgotten she could. Her father points out wildlife to them, a heron in the shallows, muskrat holes in the bank, an elk chewing moss at the river's edge. The memory of the last elk they saw together seems so distant to her, too faint to even cause alarm. Exley takes it all in wide-eyed. There's a goofiness about him, an innocence that feels genuine and true. Her father studies him with amusement and seems to revel in his simple joy.

"I've never caught a steelhead," Exley says. "I've caught trout and suckers, and a few rotting salmon. But those I snagged, so they don't really count."

"Do you want to catch one today?" her father asks, and the answer comes fast enough to give him whiplash.

He pulls at the oars, positioning them at the head of a long, narrow pool, and Gray watches as he points out the holding fish to Exley, explains how to find them in the river. As he shows Exley the drift he wants the fly to make and where to cast to get it, Gray ties a fly to his tippet for him. It's been months since she fished, more, but her fingers remember the knots. Maybe they always will.

She checks the drag on Exley's reel and hands him the rod. "What if I mess it up?" He looks worried.

Her father just smiles. "Look around you," he says. "You're on a beautiful river on a beautiful day, fishing with a beautiful girl. How could you possibly mess this up?"

As he back-oars the boat into position, Exley drops some line over the gunwale into the water and flicks it forward with a roll cast. Then he lifts it into the air and yanks it over his shoulder. His backcast is jerky—Gray sees that he's over-muscling the line, that he doesn't trust the physics yet—but he shows promise, and her father nods her way when he shoots the line more or less where he needs to.

"Let it sink. Give it a minute." When he tells him to mend it, Exley flicks the line, sending a loop up current. "Good."

They watch the fly approach the fish. Barely visible, the fish moves a few feet beneath the surface, just a shadow flickering, and Gray holds her breath.

In that moment the world seems to stop, as if they're suspended in time. She thinks how moments like this can change the course of your life, sending you in one of two directions— either the fish will take the hook, or not—and how our lives are full of these kinds of moments, some trivial, some meaningful. Sometimes those moments can destroy a life, she knows. They can take everything you love from you and devastate you to the bone.

But not always.

The line goes tight and Exley shouts with joy.

45

They were married a month after he met her at the airport in Portland. The public librarian served as justice of the peace. They invited no one to the wedding, and no one came, the sum total of everyone they knew in their new state. A symbolic gesture, Janey said, about their future together and its relationship to their past in Massachusetts. Even then, fresh on the heels of his summer-long trip across the country, after all the places he'd been, she was the most beautiful thing he'd ever seen.

The ceremony was more officious than romantic. Afterward they went home to their little cabin on the Nehalem River and celebrated with cheap champagne, local oysters from Yaquina Bay, a fire in the woodstove. Rain pelted the mossy roof and dripped down the pilings into the leaves.

"I've never been happier." Janey slurped a big oyster from its shell and tossed the shell into the fireplace. "Admittedly, a low bar."

"We have to start somewhere, J. We both do." He knew what she'd been through in the foster homes where she'd grown up—not the details, not all of them, but the boundaries of it—and she knew it of him, too, had traced the topographical map of his scars with her cellist's fingers, had met The Old Man.

"But what if this is the pinnacle? What if this is as good as it gets?"

Lewis laughed and inhaled an oyster.

"What's so funny?"

"That you think *I'm* the cynic."

"I'm just not used to things going this well, Lewis. A few weeks ago I was living with roommates in Somerville, powdering donuts and slinging hash. Now I'm . . . well, I'm married, living in a cabin in the Oregon woods."

"It suits you." He pried open a shell, severed the hinge muscle, flipped the meaty oyster in its brine, and handed it to her. She slurped it whole.

"I'm afraid it does."

"So what are you afraid of?"

"That it won't last, I guess."

"Wives and fish are best when they're new."

She reached over the candle and punched him on the arm. "Sometimes you sound like a fortune cookie."

Janey looked at him, and Lewis looked at her, and he could see her happiness but he could see, too, a thread of worry stitched into the fabric of her smile.

"Will this last? Will *any* of it?"

"Maybe." He refilled their mason jars with champagne. "Maybe not."

"What if it doesn't?"

Nothing lasts, Lewis knew. Not his mother. Not Quarry. Instinct and experience told him that moments of joy were just that, just moments, fleeting by nature. Impermanent. But he thought, too, of The Old Man, all the beatings, the sleepless nights, the tears, and knew that those hadn't lasted, either. "Maybe whatever comes next is even better."

Janey smiled her crooked smile. In it he could see their lives stretched out, the years to come and all the mysteries they might hold.

"How could I ever have thought you were a cynic?"

"History will begin with us, J."

She looked at him oddly. Affectionately. "You wrote that on one of your postcards. What's it from?"

He told her about the Chinese emperor who built the Great Wall and the army of terracotta soldiers, how he wanted a clean break for the empire—not just from the past, but from every leader who had ruled before him. How he ordered all the historical literature to be burned in enormous fires and all the scholars to be executed in public squares, and issued a declaration that there was no China before that moment. That history would begin with *him*.

"It means our pasts no longer exist," he said. "The slate is wiped clean. Our lives begin now. We can be anything we want."

They didn't own much. She'd arrived in Oregon with her cello and a suitcase and little else, the perils of a nomadic childhood. All he'd brought was fishing gear and guns. Everything else was new to them, bought at department stores and thrift shops. Still, looking around their little cabin, he saw all the tools they would need to build a life together.

"Do we have to burn the books and execute the scholars?"

"Only if we get bored."

They touched glasses and drank to each other, drank to their new life together.

"So. Now that we can be anything we want, what do you want to be?" he asked.

"I just want to be happy. Don't you?"

"I'm not sure I know how. I'm not sure I can *be* happy."

"Of course you can, Lewis. *Everyone* can be happy."

"How do you know?"

Her expression changed as something passed over her, the look she gave him not pitying but not without sympathy, either. "How do I know? Because, Lewis. Because otherwise, why bother?"

"I'm not sure happiness is the point."

"Then what is? What *is* the point?"

In her eyes he saw the sadness his response brought her and knew he was responsible, knew that he'd disappointed her, and knew he would do everything in his power to never do it again.

"I don't know, J. But here's what I *do* know. If you think this is good now, just you wait—from here on out, it's only going to get better. Wait and see how happy you are living off the fame and fortune of a rural fly-fishing guide."

She laughed, her mood and her faith seemingly restored. Without getting up from the floor, she scooted around until she was next to him and put her forehead against his. Her breath on his cheeks came warm and sweet and salty from the oysters, a burst of moisture, like ripping into a piece of bread fresh from the oven.

"Hey Lewis."

"What?"

"I can't wait for the rest of our lives."

Isn't that all he'd ever done, wait for the rest of his life? Maybe this was it. Maybe it had arrived. "I think you're a little drunk, Janey Yaw," he said. The first time he'd spoken her new name.

"Not yet." She reached for the champagne bottle. "But I can't wait for that, either."

When she smiled at him, he felt the hope in his throat and hoped to God it wouldn't strangle him.

46

The next morning Gray catches her uncle on his way out the door. Though he sleeps in the Arrow, he still spends most of his time in the house, joining them for meals and using their shower and laundry. He's got a coffee mug in one hand, a bowl of cereal in the other, and is trying to open the screen door with his elbow.

"You going to eat that in the truck?" she asks, letting him out.

"I'm late opening the shop."

"Don't spill it."

"Don't jinx me."

"Don't tempt me."

"Hey." He pauses at the bottom of the steps. "I called the restaurant and added another seat to our dinner reservation tonight."

"For who?"

"Your friend Exley."

"I didn't ask you to do that."

"No." He flashes her a big, shit-eating grin. "Your father did."

"Exley's just a friend."

"It's good to have friends, Hoss."

She looks into the driveway and sees that her father's truck is gone. So is the boat.

"Did he go fishing again?"

Her uncle nods vigorously. "Can you believe it? Our baby boy is all grown up. I've never been more proud."

Once he's gone, Gray has the place to herself. In fact, she has the whole day to herself until she's due at school for graduation. It feels like a luxury of time and space, and she's not entirely sure what to do with it. She wanders the house aimlessly, content to lounge around, and spends most of the morning snacking with her feet up on the coffee table in front of the TV.

Bored by lunchtime, she makes a leftover meatloaf sandwich and heads out into the yard for a change of scenery. The fire pit her father started is still unfinished, its yawning mouth still open, unfed. Maybe that's something they can do together—find a slab to fit and muscle it into the truck. Bring it home. Light a fire to celebrate.

Maybe her uncle was right about commencement, and about dinner out afterward. It's nice to look forward to something again.

When she hears her phone ringing in the kitchen, she runs inside to answer it. There's a deep male voice on the other end, out of breath and urgent.

"Is this Gray? Gray Yaw?"

"Who's this?"

"It's Kevin."

"Who?"

"Tommy Wheatfall's nephew."

"I'm sorry, I—"

"Fuckface. Everyone calls me Fuckface."

"Oh."

"Can you get down to the river right now? Your uncle gave me your number, told me to call you. Meet him at the put-in."

"Which one?"

"Idaho."

"OK, I—"

"Gray?"

"What?"

"Hurry."

———

Gray drives as fast as she dares along the fire road that parallels the Terrebonne, passing her father's truck and trailer where he's left them at his usual put-in. A few miles downstream the road pulls away from the river for a stretch, winding through the forest where the river narrows and plunges through a wooded canyon. When she enters the forest, the deep canopy of trees blots out the sun so completely that she almost turns on her headlights. But the darkness lasts just a few seconds. When she reemerges, the afternoon sunlight nearly blinds her. The road rejoins the river, and around the next bend she reaches the Idaho ramp.

Uncle Fenwick's truck is parked there alongside several she recognizes as belonging to other guides. She sees Littlejohn's hulking black Dodge. Her stomach sours, and when she swallows, she tastes the anger at the back of her mouth.

She spots her uncle huddled by the river's edge with the other guides and hurries over to join them. Popping up like a prairie dog, Fuckface sees her coming and says something to her uncle, who peels off to intercept her.

"Listen, Hoss," he says, leading Gray away from the others. "Wheatfall found your father's boat."

"Where?"

"In the canyon. There's a blowdown. A widow-maker." It's what they call trees that fall across the river current, creating deadly hazards for unsuspecting boats. "Looks like maybe your father got tangled up in it."

"It wasn't there yesterday."

"No. Wheatfall said it looked like a fresh break."

"Is he OK?"

"We don't know, Hoss. He wasn't in the boat."

"What do you mean?" Gray doesn't understand what her uncle is telling her. She's confused, as if she's suddenly forgotten the words—as if they're just sounds without definitions. "What does that mean?"

"I don't know yet. The boat looked OK. He left some paint on the tree, scuffed up the rails a bit. A guy could maybe survive that."

"Maybe?" she asks, finally understanding. "No. He can swim. He's a strong swimmer."

Her uncle puts a strong hand on her shoulder and leans in close. "It's still spring, Hoss. That water's still cold. Real cold. He'd have to get out of the river pretty fast to beat the hypothermia."

Gray feels the panic explode inside her, feels it rattle everything she's made of.

"What do we do?" she asks, trying to push it aside, to control it.

"There's something else, Hoss. Wheatfall said there was a bottle in the boat."

"A bottle?"

"Old Crow."

"Was it full?"

He shakes his head. "No."

"We have to find him."

"We're all splitting up to look. Cover as much ground as we can. Some in boats, some on the road. You head downstream, past Dancer's Elbow. Look everywhere for him, Hoss. In the river. On the banks. The water's high this time of year, and the current is fast. He could be anywhere."

She tries to say something but words won't come. She nods weakly.

"I'm the central point of contact. Call me if you see him, and I'll let you know if anyone else does." Her uncle leans in close and she can smell the cigarettes on his breath. "Hoss? Are you with me?"

She nods again.

When she turns around to leave, Littlejohn is standing behind her. He looks her in the eyes without hesitation or malice.

"We'll find him, Gray," he says. "We'll find him."

———

The Previa is ancient for a minivan—a few months older than she is—and built for baby seats and beach coolers rather than the ungraded forest road. As she speeds along the rutted dirt, the van's shocks whimper, the struts groan, and the thin-walled cabin shakes like an eggshell ready to splinter. Still she stomps on the accelerator, pushing it to the edges of its capabilities. It pitches and rolls like a boat in whitewater as she rounds corners without slowing. She's traveled this road ten thousand times, maybe more, and knows every put-in and takeout along its length, every sandbar or gravel finger suitable for beaching a boat. As she white-knuckles the steering wheel and shunts a rooster tail of trailing dust, the river itself keeps pace, high with spring rain, the water whiskey colored and cold.

The forest gives way to high desert, trees yielding to rocky cliffs, dirt to clay, as if she's driving fast enough to traverse not just space but time, into the past, before the trees and grasses grew, when the earth was still forming. Decades of truck-and-trailer traffic have packed the dirt into ruts. She takes them at speed, as if her mission is not to find her father but to shatter the Previa to pieces. Let it disintegrate if it will rewind time. Let it fall apart if it will take her back before her mother died, before the Wallowas, before they went into the woods with the dog. Let it undo all that has been done.

Gripping the wheel until her hands cramp, she races downstream, slowing only when she reaches Dancer's Elbow. The fire road runs close to the water along this stretch, with a gravel-and-sand bank and weedy flats. She studies it with one eye on the road, looking for anything unnatural—a flash of color, a glint of metal, an unfamiliar shape—and trying not to think about what might have happened and how this might change things just when they were finding a kind of normal again.

Maybe Wheatfall made a mistake. Maybe they've already found her father upstream somewhere, asleep on a sandbar, unaware that his boat drifted away and caused such a panic. Maybe any minute now her phone will ring and her uncle will wave her off the search. Doubts rise to the surface of her thoughts like bubbles breaking on the river. Then she rounds a bend and time stops as she sees her father's body floating facedown in the current with his arms at his sides, and she knows in her heart that this is one of those moments when the world as she understands it is going to change irreparably yet again.

———

Just downstream, she skids to a stop and leaps out of the van with the engine still running. Stripping down to her T-shirt and jeans as she races down the sloped bank, she slides one-legged through the weeds and dirt like she's sliding into home. Except there is no home. Not anymore. Without hesitating or even slowing she dives into the river.

The water is cold enough to hurt. It pulls at her like gravity, like persuasion, almost too much to withstand, but she fights it and swims into the current at an angle, anticipating the trajectory she'll need to intercept him. She can't afford to miss. Downstream a little farther, just out of sight, the river turns to rocks and falls and rapids. Gray knows she needs to bring him back now or they're both done—there's nothing navigable after this.

The Terrebonne rushes at her, stealing control of her arms and legs. Each time she lifts her head to track his body, and to breathe, she swallows more of the cold water. It's like swallowing glass shards. Sound is both dulled and deafening, a roar of silence; she can't tell if it's the river or if it's inside her own head, every thought she's ever had being screamed aloud.

And then a moment of calm arrives. The noise quiets to a whisper, the murky water grows lighter as the sun penetrates it further. Maybe she's losing consciousness. Maybe she's finding it. Maybe she's becoming inseparable from the river that has run through the lives of her family for longer than she's been alive.

In that moment, it feels as if she's poised at the doorway to another world. The urge to cross over into it is almost too strong to bear. All she has to do is let go.

Give up.

Surrender.

Then her hands brush against something, and with her breath turning to fire in her lungs and her heart exploding in her chest, she grabs her father by the shirt. His body is cold and hard, big and ungainly even in the water, and she struggles to hold onto him as she gasps for breath.

The current carries them downstream. As they gather speed, she fights to hold on to him, fights to keep her own head above water. She does not know how long she can do this for, does not know what to do next other than hope. Already she can hear the falls ahead, the rush of water crashing onto the rocks below. Already the cold is clawing at her, reaching inside and squeezing at her heart.

But she and her father are together now, inseparable, at the mercy of the river. Either it will carry them to an eddy, or to the shore, or it will claim them both.

47

His skin is pale, his body bloated like bread sopped with milk. The brown water has stained his uniform. That's what her mother called it—his uniform: olive drab Carhartts darkened with grease and paint and roofing tar, canvas shirt and vest, bilge boots the color of a cow's tongue. His faded Red Sox cap is gone. Maybe she'll find it washed up somewhere along the banks, or in the boat among those things that he left behind in this world.

Gray lies in the mud beside him, shivering beneath the weight of her own clothes. Too exhausted to move, she could lie there in the sun until she's warm, but she knows she might lie there forever and never feel warm again. She knows, too, that soon she's going to hurt in a way she cannot yet understand.

But not yet. Not now. She's too tired for it now.

Anyway, she'll have the rest of her life for it.

The months have worn her down. They've left her frayed and tattered. The fatigue she's felt since September, the sadness, is still there, but there's something else now too. Something new. An unknowing. A different thing entirely. A complex and difficult knot constricting her heart that she suspects she'll spend the rest of her life trying to untie. Lying in the mud with stones digging into her back, she wonders if she'll ever succeed, wonders if she'll ever understand it.

She wishes she could call her uncle, but her phone is upstream in the van. It's just a matter of time before he finds her, or one of the guides docs, and while she waits she closes her eyes for just a moment.

That's all it takes for her to fall asleep. A kind of self-defense, her body and mind powering down. It's a deep sleep, but she does not dream.

Some time later she wakes to the feeling that she's no longer alone and opens her eyes to see a dog, a stray, its coat matted with mud and burrs. It stands over her father's body licking him fervently with tenderness, or concern.

"Hey there."

The dog turns to stare at her, eyes wide, nostrils flared.

"It's OK," she says. But the dog moves between her and her father, as if to protect him from her. "It's OK."

When Gray gets up onto her elbows, the dog backs away. There are patches of hair missing from its coat. The exposed skin is scarred. Raw. The dog's ribs are visible, and it walks with a limp. This unforgiving world, it doesn't give anybody a pass. For a moment the dog watches her nervously, sniffing tentatively at the air and looking like it might bolt. Then it lifts a skinny leg and pisses onto her father's body. The urine steams when it meets his cold shoulder. Gray makes an involuntary sound, an unwanted chuckle that starts in her chest and rises into her throat, gathering speed and strength until it becomes full-blown laughter—actual laughter—as if a dog pissing on her dead father is the funniest goddamned thing she's ever seen. It feels inappropriate. It feels wrong. But she does not stop. She cannot stop. She's still laughing as the dog trots unevenly away down the sloped bank, laughing so hard she's shaking, heaving as her eyes water until she realizes she's not laughing anymore at all.

"Don't cry," her father told her.

But he's not there and neither is her mother, so she cries anyway, cries until she's hoarse, cries until she's empty, until her throat is as raw as her heart, and then she cries some more and looks at the river, but the river just shrugs.

48

"Is it time yet?" Janey sometimes asked him. Sitting on the porch. Walking along the river. Lying in bed at the end of the day. Lewis looked up from his book to study her expression. Then he marked the page, closed the book he was reading, and turned to face her.

"Not yet."

He didn't explain why. They'd had the conversation a number of times, how they'd agreed to wait to have a child until they found a place to settle. Until they made a home.

Until he was sure.

Before Janey, it had never occurred to him that he might bring a new life into this world—he'd been too busy fighting for his own. But Janey brought things he did not know lived inside him to the surface, Homo erectus discovering fire and trying to wheedle a spark into flames that could sustain life and bring warmth, sustenance, and beauty into the world.

A child. A chance to do right all the things that had been done wrong.

The first time she'd asked, she did so as easily if she'd been asking about the weather or a movie or what he wanted for dinner. "Do you see us having children, Lewis?"

"That's what *you* want?"

When she bit her lip and nodded, he'd realized right then and there how dangerous love could be. How it could pry you open and leave you exposed and make you long for it even as your heart bled and burned. So he nodded too.

"Maybe one."

"Just one?"

"Maybe."

"Just think of all the things we could give a child, Lewis. All the things we never had ourselves."

He considered it, a single child in an unbroken home, a child with two parents who wanted him. Every night they would sweep the corners and open the windows to let any resentment that had found its way into their lives escape. He knew what resentment could do to a man. He knew what a resentful man could do to a child.

"Everything we never had ourselves," he'd said. "That's a long list."

He felt the weight of her head on his shoulder and how different a weight it was than all the others he carried in his life. How had he gone that long without learning that sometimes people touched you to hold you up and not just to knock you down?

Janey's life had been every bit as tough as his. Maybe worse. She'd always have the scar where she'd been removed from her parents, a wound that never healed. If she could still see the world as the kind of place she wanted to share with a child, why couldn't he? But first he would have to learn to be a good man. First he had to be sure he would not screw it up.

"One child," he'd said. "Maybe."

After that, she did not ask *if* anymore, only *when*. And though she began to ask with increasing frequency, her words growing more urgent as time passed, he always gave her the same answer.

"Not yet."

"OK." She nodded. "Not yet."

When she looked at him across the white expanse of pillow, all longing and urges and instinct, desperate to be a mother and waiting only for him, he knew there was a limit to her patience.

"In the meantime I think we should practice every chance we get," he said, reaching for her and pulling her, laughing, to him.

49

Uncle Fenwick rides shotgun. He smokes with his arm out the open window, the cigarette pack on the dashboard white with red racing stripes, like a pair of sneakers. As they drive through town in her father's truck, they follow the tracks he left over a lifetime there, past the dark and silent Vatican, the hardware store, the Salt Lick, the diner, past the bank with its sign of lies, past the hardware store and the donut shop and the taco stand he loved. The trailered boat rattles behind them as they cross the bridge and turn onto the fire road. When they reach his favorite put-in, Gray backs up to the dirt slope and shuts off the engine.

The evening is windless, and the still air holds the promise of something better than the months that have led up to it. The boat is damaged from the accident but it will float. It will do what they ask of it this one last time. As they work silently to ready it, her uncle unstraps the tie-downs and Gray coils the painter and checks that the oars are shipped and locked. He hands her the bear skin, and together they unfold it like a sheet and lay it in the bilge. The hair is soft and dense, and it reeks of her father.

His clothing is still damp from the river when they lift his body from the truck and lower him onto it. She checks his pockets for his flashlight, lighter, and knife, making sure that he will not be without the things he carried in this world if he needs them in the next. There's a picture, too, the entire family together, even her uncle, every single one of them smiling. Gray doesn't remember who took the photo, doesn't even remember the moment, really, but wishes she did, wishes she could better remember a time when they all were together, a time when they all were happy enough to smile. It seems like it's been forever. But it wasn't that long ago. Her uncle retrieved the picture from the house, and now she tucks it into her father's vest for him to bring with him so that he might remember them that way too: happy.

Reaching into the boat, Gray crosses her father's arms and nods. Her uncle has brought a brand-new bottle of Old Crow, and he twists open the cap and raises it.

"To Lewis Fucking Yaw."

"King of the Fucking Jungle."

He takes a healthy swig and passes her the bottle. She does the same. The taste is not exactly pleasant, but not entirely unpleasant either, a conflicting nature that seems suited to their task. He puts the cap back on and places the bottle in her father's hands.

"You'll need this where you're going, old friend."

"Is this even legal?"

"Hell no."

"Are we going to get in trouble?"

"All anyone needs to know is that your old man drowned, Hoss. This river's been swallowing bodies whole as long as it's been here."

"What do you think happened out there?" she says without warning to her uncle or herself, asking the question she's been afraid to ask. "My father knew the river as well as anyone."

"Don't ever assume you know a river. It's a different river every time. That current can move things around. He hadn't been on it in a few months."

"It's just . . . It's not like him."

"No. It's *not* like him. But he hasn't been himself for a while. The thing about accidents is that they can happen to anyone. What was it he used to say? 'Even monkeys fall from trees sometimes.'"

Gray looks at the whiskey bottle, trying to find the words to ask the even harder question.

"What if it wasn't an accident?"

"No," her uncle says sharply. He takes her by the arms, looks her straight in the eyes. "Just no. You don't say that. You don't even *think* it. Whatever happened out there? That's the past. From here on out, you only think about the future."

History will begin with . . . me.

"You read me, Hoss?" He waits for her to nod her assent before letting her go. Then he retrieves the bottle, takes another sip, and returns it to the crook of her father's arm.

"You sure you want to do this?"

"Yes."

"What about the headstone with his name on it? You don't want to bury him beside her?" She answers without thinking, because she's already thought it through. "That's just a rock."

It's still too early in the year for mosquitoes or black flies, but in the dusk she can see insect hatches on the river. Blue-winged olives, *Rhithrogena* and *Ephemerella*. Trout flies. She closes her eyes and keeps them closed for a long moment.

"This is what he'd want. Right?"

"Who the hell knows? Your father was a complicated son of a bitch."

For a long time they look at her father, at Lewis Yaw, the

man they each loved in their own way, the man who did his flawed best to love them back. Then Gray leans against her uncle, both for support and to tell him she's ready.

Burn the ships.

He lifts the gas tank from the bow and empties it into the bilge, shaking the can to douse everything, the wooden seats and planks, the bear skin, even her father, and without another word sets it afire. The flames gather quickly. The heat is sudden and intense. Gray shoves at the boat's transom and sends it skidding down the slope into the Terrebonne one last time. The boat hits the river with a splash and drifts a few feet from the bank, rocking gently until the current finds it and begins to pull it downstream. They watch as flames catch the seats, the ribs, the long wooden oars, the bear skin, and the tears come easily for both of them. They watch as the fire rises high above the rails and into the sky, reflected in the water around the boat. They watch until there is no boat and no body, only flames disappearing around the bend in the river. They watch until there is only river. Only water. Only air.

Her uncle looks at her with tears in her eyes. "Maybe we should have kept the boat and burned the RV instead," he says, and then that air is filled with their laughter.

———

Gray backs the truck up onto the lawn. There's a sparrow in the holly tree, whistling cheerily, and the air is warm with the hint of summer. She can smell the jasmine and honeysuckle on the breeze. The tailgate opens with a groan and the truck sways like a boat when she hops into the bed. Hooking her fingers under the slab of rock, she lifts and flips it over onto the open tailgate. The sound rings out like a gunshot, echoing past the yard into the neighborhood. She hooks and flips it once more, and it drops into the grass with a thud.

She climbs down and stands over the stone, spreads her legs to shoulder-width, and stretches her arms and back. Then she squats down and grabs it by the edges. Its exposed surface is sun-warmed against her arms, but the shaded underside is cooler, still moist from the riverbank. Her forearms are scraped and bloody and her entire body hurts from the effort of loading it into the truck, but she's almost done. Just twenty feet to go.

With a grunt she lifts it from the ground. There's a moment when she's not sure she'll get it past her knees, a moment when she's sure she's going to drop it. But she pushes through it and stands upright, hugging the stone against her, squashing her breasts beneath her T-shirt. Her legs tremble, threatening to betray her as she takes the first step. The muscles in her back fan and pulse, muscles she's trained, muscles she's neglected, muscles she did not know she had. One step at a time, lumbering like she's subject to a different gravity, she walks the stone across the lawn.

She remembers how strong she used to think her father was. It didn't seem possible for anyone to be as strong as him. It didn't seem possible for *her* to be as strong as him. But she doesn't want to be as strong as him anymore.

She wants to be stronger.

Every tendon in her body is taut, the blood in her veins under such pressure she fears they will rupture. Measuring the distance left to go—fifteen feet, ten feet, five—she shuffles across the lawn. When she reaches the fire pit, she lowers the stone into place alongside the others, wiggling it like a loose tooth.

Once she's finished, she collapses onto the grass and lies there with her eyes closed for what feels like a long time, listening to the birds and to her own jackrabbit heartbeat and feeling the sun on her skin. When her heart begins to slow and her breathing returns to normal, she opens them again to see Mrs. Harrison standing on the driveway at the edge of the lawn, looking concerned but maintaining a respectful distance.

"Are you all right, dear?"

"That," Gray says, "is a good question."

Mrs. Harrison nods as if to agree. The gold of her earrings glints in the sun, and Gray puts a hand up to shield her eyes.

"I thought I heard a gunshot, so I looked out my window. Imagine my surprise when I saw you carrying that gigantic boulder across the yard."

"Let me guess. You came over here to find out why? The truth is, I don't know why I did it. Nobody cares that this stupid fire pit was missing a piece. We never even got to use it. It just . . ." Gray pauses, unsure how to explain what sent her back to the Terrebonne to look for a new stone, unsure if she even needs to. "It just seemed important."

Mrs. Harrison tilts her head in a way that reminds Gray of Johnson, which reminds her, too, of how much she's been through and how much she still has left to face.

"Actually, I came over to tell you that watching you do it? Watching you carry that enormous rock all that way? It was remarkable."

———

The empty trailer sits in the driveway with chocks beneath the wheels, parked beside her mother's minivan. Uncle Fenwick will sell them both and deposit the money in Gray's account, just like most of her father's tools and rifles and anything else left in the garage. What he can't sell, he'll haul to the dump. He's going to live in the house until he finds a place of his own, and then sell it, and then he'll send her that money too. She gave him power of attorney that morning when they met with the lawyer who'll settle her parents' estate, such as it is. She'll call in a few months with an address.

If she has one by then.

Everything going with her is already loaded into the bed of her father's truck. *Her* truck. The fly rods and waders, a few boxes of flies. His sun-faded canoe, older than she is, lashed to the ladder racks. She's packed the postcards he sent her mother before she was born too. She read them all, marking the locations on a map and piecing together his route across the country with a bold red line. The route brought him to Disappointment, and the same one will bring her to Massachusetts. Reversing it won't rewind the clock or turn back the calendar, she knows, but maybe by learning more about where her parents came from and what they left behind, she'll learn more about who they were before everything that's happened. Who they were before her. Who they were before they met each other, even. History did not begin with them.

Sorting through her father's things, she found a black-and-white photograph of a young boy and a man. The man's features are mean and sharp-edged, as if honed by the friction of moving through the world in constant opposition to it. The boy is no more than ten or twelve, tall, with a mop of long hair: her father. There's distance between them though they stand side by side, each of them holding a fly rod in one hand and a stringer of long trout in the other, dark blood at the gills. They're not smiling. They're ashamed, uneasy in their proximity, as if the camera captured not something posed but something revealed. Across the white border of photo, written in fading pencil, it says *Parrish and Lewis, Battenkill River Trout, 1983.*

When she took the photo of the sad yellow house from its frame, she found an address on the back in her mother's handwriting. Online tax records show that it belongs to a Parrish Yaw, who still lives there even now. Her grandfather—the one her father told her was dead.

What other surprises might the world hold for her? What else might she find when she gets to where she's going? What will she find along the way?

"You 'bout ready, Hoss?"

Gray nods. She wants to say something, wants to tell him what he means to her, but doesn't know where to start. She tries and fumbles, and he stops her.

"I know, Hoss. Me too."

In the end she says nothing and hugs him instead. He farts loudly.

"See?" he says. "I told you that you were strong enough for this."

She laughs and knows she is going to miss him.

She's ready to leave here. She's ready to be somewhere else, anywhere else. But part of her wants to stay too. Is it possible to exist in two places at once? She's afraid that if she waits too long she might get stuck, afraid that maybe she's stuck already, caught in the orbit of this world and all that it means to stay here. She's afraid that maybe it's too late.

That's not true. All you have to do is leave.

"You say goodbye to your friend? Exley?"

"He got me this. A going-away present." She climbs into the truck, takes a Red Sox cap off the stick shift, and pulls it on tight. "We're going to keep in touch. Maybe I'll see him when I visit you."

"Lucky guy."

"That reminds me." She holds up the car key, which is attached to the faded pink rabbit's foot key chain he gave her for her birthday years ago.

"I guess that wasn't quite as lucky as I'd hoped, Hoss."

"Luck's just something to pin your failures on. That's what *he* used to say."

"Your old man used to say a lot of things. That don't make them all true."

"Speaking of which." Gray hands him her father's black notebook from the seat beside her. Her uncle steps up to the open window to take it.

"His code? Son of a bitch. You read it yet?"

"Take a look." Gray hands it to him and he walks around into the headlights. She watches him turn the pages, one at a time at first and then more quickly, flipping through them with his thumb and discovering, like she had, that whatever her father had written in it over the years, he'd scratched it out, scribbling over every page in black ink until all that remained was a single sentence on an otherwise blank page.

Uncle Fenwick raises a graying eyebrow and looks at her expectantly.

"Turn to the end," she says. "The very last page."

He finds the page and squints to read it. Then he looks up again and laughs. He's still laughing when she pulls out of the driveway, and so is she, remembering the four words written there, the sum total of a father's advice, everything he learned in life boiled down to a single thought as clear and concise as he knew how to make it.

Don't be that guy.

50

After a long, fast run along the river, Lewis stumbled home to his wife, unsteady on his feet, Odysseus returned, still vexed by sea legs. Pausing at the kitchen sink, he filled and drained two glasses of water and waited for his lungs to catch up with his heart. Back when he fought for Jimmy, he'd empty the locker room just before the fight and take a few moments to himself, alone, to consider what he was about to do. To steel himself for it. Alone in the dark, he'd force himself to recall trivia from his mother's book to settle his nerves and clear his mind. Now he found himself doing the same. *Babies have a hundred more bones than adults. They can't taste salt. They're born without kneecaps.* Leaving the glass on the counter, he padded down the hallway, shedding clothes as he went. *More babies are born on Tuesdays than any other day of the week. A baby can recognize its mother's voice at birth, but it can take two weeks to recognize its father's.* When the floorboard squeaked outside the bedroom door, he did not pause, stripping off the last of his clothes as he brushed through the doorway and crawling into bed next to Janey without bothering to shower.

"Lewis?" she asked, sleepy, rolling over to look for his eyes in the dark. "Is everything all right?"

"Yes. I just wanted to tell you something."

"What?"

For such a small woman, she generated a lot of heat, he thought, pulling her body against his. A sun for him to revolve around, a sun to light his way through the darkness.

"It's time."

"Time for what?"

"It's time, Janey. It's time. Let's have a baby together."

ABOUT THE AUTHOR

C. B. Bernard is the author of *Chasing Alaska: A Portrait of the Last Frontier Then and Now* (Lyons Press), a Publishers Weekly and National Geographic top pick and finalist for the Oregon Book Award in nonfiction. His fiction and essays have appeared in *Catapult, Gray's Sporting Journal,* and elsewhere. Though he called Alaska and Oregon home for much of his life, he now lives on the coast of Rhode Island's South County with his wife Kim, a retriever named Nessie, and the ghosts of a couple dogs.

ACKNOWLEDGMENTS

I could write a companion book just naming people who informed, inspired, or championed this one in some way. Consider this an incomplete reckoning of my thanks.

To Kim, for her unrelenting patience and support—this does not happen without her, neither would I want it to.

To my agent, Laura Strachan, for tirelessly knocking on doors; to Naomi Hynes and Rick Bleiweiss at Blackstone for answering; to Michael Signorelli, whose gentle editing improved the manuscript and my confidence in it immensely; to James Burg, for connecting with the story and with me, and for sharing and expanding the vision; and to the entire Blackstone team that not only made this book possible but made it better and beautiful, including Marilyn Kretzer, Josie Woodbridge, Larissa Ezell, Sarah Bonamino, Ember Hood, Ananda Finwall, Megan Bixler, Courtney Vatis, Jim Thomsen, and so many others.

To Chris Crowley, Kurt Mullen, Kate Gray, and Jeanne Nebeker Hilderbrand for their thoughtful reads and critiques, each of which made Small Animals better, and for their friendship, which has made me better. To everyone who talked me off one ledge or another while writing it, including Armin Tolentino, Kate Ristau, Michael Armstrong, Kristin Bair O'Keeffe, Michele Tomlinson, Karen Graham, Katrina Woolford, Mike Harvkey, Nicole Walker, Amadie Hart, Andrew Furman, Suzanne DeWitt Hall, and my sister Shawna Bernard. To Oregon Literary Arts for everything it does for writers and readers, and to Brendan Jones and Amy Butcher for giving this book's first chapter an audience at Bunker Lit.

Bad parents exist in life just as they do in this book, but my own parents, Sarge and Lisa Bernard, are not among them. To the extended family I was born to, the one I married into, and the people who have become family over the years: James Norcott; Jeff Gibson; Picus Pfeiffer; the Morrisseys; Tray Krueger; J. L. Stevens; and, especially, Dan Tuohy, who might know best what this all means to me because we wanted badly together to be writers that cold Vermont winter in our heatless Valhalla so long ago and never stopped. To Chris Lee, for thirty years of unwavering friendship—I can't make sense of the fact that you're gone from this life—and to Dan Murphy, Gavan O'Shea, and John Drake for helping me try. We'll keep his memory alive, boys.

To a lifetime of fishing buddies: Ernie Stone; the Brothers Alsup; Stoney Huffman, Mike Bagley, and Christopher Lehmann-Haupt; Mike Byerly; Chris Maxfield; Ben Stuart; the Rhody Fly Rodders; and especially to Captain Greg Houde and Susan Estabrook, who have kept me laughing on cold fishless mornings and late-night text threads, and whose friendship and generosity transcends the rivers and the seas. A guy could write a book about people like you.

To Shakes, for keeping me company all those early mornings in the writing studio. You left a big, dog-shaped hole, pal—you were a good boy, and we miss you. And to Nessie, for stepping into that hole and smiling back up at us without reserve.

And, finally, to poet Michael Pettit, who gave me a simple and enduring piece of advice nearly thirty years ago that I only now realize is not dissimilar to Lewis Yaw's own code: "Don't fuck up," he said, and to varying degrees of success, I've been trying ever since.